THE TIDES OF LIFE

A Whale of a Tale

Iain Macneil

The characters and events portrayed in this book are fictitious. Any similarity to real persons, living or dead, is coincidental and not intended by the author.

ISBN 9798433210295

For Mum and Dad, Calum, and in memory of Dian

A journey of a thousand miles begins with a single step

Lao Tzu

Prologue

Alan Trout awoke early, as he did every morning, and admired himself enormously. The mirror was his best friend. And although Alan loved his left profile, he thought his right was a smidgen more perfect. His morning routine hadn't changed since boarding school. Even on Christmas and family holidays, Alan would preen himself to perfection before presenting himself to the world. He plucked his eyebrows, though he would never admit it. He clipped his nose hairs twice a day and kept a close eye on any that tried curling out of his ears. He shaved with a straight blade because it seemed a brave thing to do, and he often fancied himself a man-of-action if only he'd been born a century or two previously. He received manicures and pedicures at a secret location, and in the company of his constituents he'd perfected the art of feigning empathy. He'd been coddled and cuddled throughout childhood, steered into privilege in adolescence, and upon leaving the hallowed halls of an elite education knew that the world was his for the taking. More than anything, his pedigree had opened the golden gates of confidence. And that was all Alan Trout needed – you see, for all the tutors, time and money spent on rearing a razor-sharp mind, poor Alan fell woefully short, all things considered. To be sure, he was no idiot, but he was a country mile from the opposite end of the spectrum. Alan left engineering and the sciences to the creators and the curious, and philosophy and the arts to the thinkers and the thoughtful. He graduated with a degree that didn't mean much to him and only played rugby because not being on the team was not an option – his father's words. He could run on the rugby pitch but was afraid of being hit, and so as a youth had perfected the subtlest manoeuvres to wiggle out of any potentially tricky or dangerous situation. A skill that would serve him well in adulthood. You could say that Alan had developed a keen sense of foresight on the pitch all those years ago. From his position along the flank, he would watch the progression of the ball and there his mind would process all the potential scenarios which always, incredibly steered him well clear of the play, and even the slimmest chance of being smashed to smithereens, while never looking like a coward, of course. Alan had the right words and possessed an infinite supply of confidence. He was no scrooge either. Alan knew just how to treat others. His wife's wishes were his command, his girlfriend's desires were always met, and his mistress received beautiful Colombian flowers every single day. He always sent gifts to his constituents and his staff received backhanders fortnightly. Alan had vision, too. He had plans for just about everything. Some thought Alan was a touch delusional, but that mattered not to him and he reminded himself that the greatest visionaries had always been seen as a little mad. So great was Alan Trout's self-belief that not even the reality of how he entered public office tempered it. A lurid scandal involving all of his rivals burst onto the headlines a week before the big election. There were weird leather costumes, doctored videos and hidden cameras. Drugs were found, as were phone numbers for illicit massage parlours. It was a big old mess and no one could make heads or tails of what was fact or fiction. Only Alan knew. But so in shock were the voting constituents that enough hands wavered while casting their ballot, that Alan Trout found himself voted into office by so thin a margin that if you could split people into votes, he sneaked in by one teeny tiny toe.

With one final look in his favourite bedroom mirror, Alan would kiss his wife on the forehead and make his way downstairs. As he strode toward the front door, he would take a little peek, give a little wink, blow a little kiss into every mirror he passed, and ponder his perfection. As he walked into Parliament Alan often glanced at the palace across the road and always the same thought emerged, a thought that he would never share with his parliamentary peers.

This particular day would prove momentous. Alan would be meeting three visitors. But these weren't your everyday visitors; constituents with an ache or a local merchant requesting a tax break. They were: Roger Remington III, a Texas oilman and all-around industrialist. Dr Foo, a Shanghai based investment maestro. And Achmed, a billionaire salesman from Zanzibar who started life as a shoeless nomad wandering the deserts of North Africa. In preparation for the meeting Alan had his one trusted aide perform an analysis of their estimated wealth. When presented with the final figure he was speechless. *Gulp.* 'That much, James? Are you sure?' – 'That much. Alan, they could buy the world.' Well, perhaps not the entire world, Alan reflected privately, but certainly a large chunk of it. So stuffed full of confidence was Alan that he rarely felt nerves. He did on that day. The thought of sitting across from so much wealth gave flight to a butterfly or two. *Settle down there. I'll manage. I'll sell them on progress. And our potential. These are men of action, not words. But – they came calling on me, moi? Well, whatever it is...I'll do my best...I'll...*

Alan Trout would make it happen.

Alan Trout was the perfect politician.

Part One

Ch 1

An Island on the Edge

There are many beautiful islands around the world, of all shapes and sizes. Indeed, our little planet is but a pretty island bopping in the vast sea of the universe, but it is commonly agreed by many that the Isle of Floonay is the most beautiful of them all. Situated near the southern end of the island chain that is the Outer Hebrides, off the west coast of Scotland, Floonay is the jewel amongst jewels of a priceless pendant clinging bravely to the bosom of a very large woman. To the north the islands stretch from Eriskay to Lewis, and to the south from Vatersay to Berneray.

Floonay is a story of contrasts, equally rugged and windswept as it is soft and bountiful. Its hills and glens are carved out of a geologist's dream and blanketed with a florist's most colourful fantasy. From the island's highest point you can see nothing but life-giving ocean in every direction, and along its beautiful wide open beaches you will feel the warmth of the sand on a sunny afternoon. If you want evidence of the island's *wonderfullness* just look to the sky, where innumerable species of birds call Floonay home. All you have to do is peek along a cliff wall or gently pull back a branch and you will find some of nature's most beautiful winged creations chirping away or just eyeing you curiously.

Unspoilt, beautiful, perfect.

But this story isn't about singing birds, pretty flowers or majestic mountains. It is about big business, the machinations of government, one man and his rake, and what happened one lovely, horrible, summer.

As for true?

To some, it might seem improbable, illogical, impossible. If you happen to question the authorities their official stance will be what it always has been: that such a thing could never happen, and they will gladly remind you of their version of the events. But it ought to be remembered that it is accepted government practise the world over to use trickery and deceit and good ol' fashioned spin to distract, twist, and befuddle. They were mostly successful, and instead of this version of the events being recognised as *truth* it was instead catalogued as the stuff of fantasy and tall tales. The thing is, the authorities couldn't contain the story completely and so they pulled from their bag of tricks some of the most tried and tested reality distortion techniques as they played down, hid, and fogged things up where necessary, and sliced, spliced, and diced at will. Governments are good at this sort of thing. And don't be confused here as to what type of government is good at this sort of thing. This is the one area politicians and bureaucrats the world over agree on: whether they are left, right, up or down, democratic, autocratic, plutocratic, whatever – they are all in cahoots.

That lovely, horrible, summer.

That nefarious government decree.

That man.

His name was Norrie MacKinnon, and though he didn't wear a crown his daughters thought he was a king, and to his wife he would always be the knight who had swept her off her feet. Norrie was from a line of shell fishermen, or cockle rakers to be more precise, stretching back to his great times eight grandfather, Archie MacKinnon. Prior to Archie taking up the rake the MacKinnons had been pirates. But a chance discovery along the shores of their fair isle saw Archie's fortunes change and his sword hung up for good, on a peg in the shed. He had thought it fortuitous at the time as the ever-growing sophistication of weaponry was making pirating an increasingly dangerous profession *and* was falling out of fashion. Norrie had a rake in his hands before he could walk and by the time he was three had filled his first bucket. By the age of seven he'd raked the whole beach, and on his fourteenth birthday Norrie quietly promised himself that he would follow in his father's footsteps for the rest of his life, as had his father, and his father, and so on and so on before him.

And, contrary to what some might think, it was not because cockle raking had become a lucrative MacKinnon family business with equity and private holdings and big bank accounts all passed down from generation to generation. The thing is, in the world of cockle raking, there isn't much in terms of capital assets. There's certainly no prized contact list, nor is there any need for complicated debt instruments, credit default swaps, lucrative public offerings, off-shore banking or other such things.

Norrie decided to follow in all those footsteps for one reason.

You see, he came to believe that what appeared to be backbreaking and tediously boring work to some, was actually the greatest job in the world. Whether he was being thrashed by the wet and wild Atlantic winds, or roasted under the midsummer's sun, Norrie understood that there was nothing quite like following the rhythm of the ocean when providing for his family. Every day he followed the tide out as that great blanket of water was gently pulled back to reveal all, and it was like Mother Nature would whisper to him, 'Okay, son, come along and rake up a few of my little gems' Then hours later the tide would come in and inch by inch nudge him away, and Mother Nature would again whisper, 'Okay, son, that's enough for now. You can go home and come back again later.' Norrie MacKinnon was no philosopher, but he knew in his own humble way that there was something special about toiling alongside the tides.

Be warned and don't be fooled. In the following pages you will read of tragedy and triumph, love and hate, despair and discontent, the death of hope and the hope of new life. There's a sea monster that really does exist and the sort of curiosities that go along with island life. But before we continue let us just revisit this last sentence, in the off chance some readers might be thinking, *'Sea monsters? That's just ridiculous. There's no such thing as sea monsters! This is obviously a tall tale!'* Let us be reminded that in spite of what some might think, sea monsters really do exist, and believe it or not, you don't have to look very far to find one. Ask any of the locals on Floonay about sea monsters – they will tell you.

Ch 2

Ancient History to the Great Discovery

Seeing as Floonay has always been the shiniest jewel in the priceless pendant that is the Outer Hebrides, many an eye has caught her glint over the years and many a foot has landed on her shores. With the Nordic countries to the north and east, Iceland, Greenland, and Newfoundland to the west, and Ireland only a few hours' sailing to the south, countless kings, princes, vagabonds and Vikings have waded ashore. Some have brought war and others peace, and it is even said that an enormous canoe from the North American continent a few centuries ago brought some fine tobacco. But not all the world's history has been recorded on camera, finely detailed on parchment, or even chiselled into rock. Simply, it is not all verifiably certain. Sometimes you just have to believe in the stories that are passed on from generation to generation.

A perfect example of this oral tradition is the tale of three exotic princesses who sailed into harbour one calm, sunny day five centuries ago. Wavy manes, dark and shining, cascaded halfway down their backs. Silk and satin clung to tempting curves. Their voices were soft and alluring. Their eyes were full of desire. In the hold of their ship were their choice weapons of war: a thousand cases of the world's finest wines, five hundred head of cattle, thirty chests of silver, and most importantly, a battalion of nymphs. Their plan was to seduce all the men on the island and have them sign over not only themselves as lifetime servants but also, and more importantly to the princesses, their island.

Fortunately for the islanders it was midsummer, and the men had just finished shearing the sheep. The annual shearing was a big deal. As the last pair of shears snips off the last woolly coat a loud cheer goes up that can be heard all around the island. The festivities commence and last three days. Not a soul is left out of the celebration. Every shopkeeper and street-sweeper, blacksmith and tailor, fisherman, stonemason, and everyone in between gets in on the fun. It was a day and a half into the festival when the exotic princesses floated ashore with their battalion of nymphs. The sight of them was the stuff of a lonely sailor's wildest dream. But as luck would have it all the men were preoccupied with the festivities and therefore didn't bat an eye in their direction. The island's womenfolk certainly took notice though and they knew just what to do. Bread rollers, garden rakes, walking sticks, and spatulas were whipped up. Whatever they could get their hands on. And so it would be that no sooner were the princesses swaying their curves and parting hot red lips, that they were chased back onto their ship. They did manage to land one prize though. The local minister was the only sober man on the island, and so under the spell of six nymphs who belly danced around him did he find himself lured aboard, and sadly he was never heard from again.

*

There are several families on Floonay with chequered histories going back a long way, but it was well known that the MacKinnons were the most disreputable of them all. That is until Archie MacKinnon changed things. You see, prior to Archie discovering along the shores of Floonay that which would change the course and reputation of his family, the pirating MacKinnons were a notorious bunch. It wasn't as though they were the only pirates around. To be fair, there were at the time plenty of respectable families – and nations – who made a living out of piracy and did so with pride. It was just the way things were back then. But the problem with the MacKinnons was that they didn't care for any of the commonly accepted piracy 'codes of conduct'. They broke as many deals with other pirates as they made and would even rob from the Vikings. Whenever anyone heard of another MacKinnon raid on a Viking ship, the people of Floonay would shake in their boots because the whole world knew that to incur the wrath of the Vikings was not a wise move. Truth be told, it was amazing that Floonay had survived the retributions that those Nordic warriors used to inflict. In any case, as things go over the course of time, people change. Some faster than others, but it inevitably happens. And it just so happened that Archie MacKinnon was the man who changed first in the MacKinnon clan all those many years ago. It was indeed a fortuitous discovery as he walked along the beach that day, because he was already having misgivings about his family's primary source of income.

So there Archie MacKinnon was, taking a stroll along the beach, smoking his pipe and whistling a tune he'd picked up from a passing Portuguese fisherman. It had been a pleasant day. The tide was receding and Archie was following the same route he had taken thousands of times before. And then he simply stopped in his tracks and looked out to sea. He was at the midway point of the Traigh Mhor (for those whose Gaelic is rusty, the 'Tri Vore' – it translates to the Big Beach), the most expansive beach on the island. He could see his house off in the distance, perched high on rocky ground that overlooked the south-eastern edge of the beach. The sea lapped at his feet, but as every minute passed that great blanket of water gently pulled back and back and back. And for the first time in his life, Archie just stood there and watched. And watched – as the sea kept receding. It kept going...until finally it stopped. But Archie kept watching and it seemed as though the tide was taking a break because it wasn't obvious for a while which way it was going. And then the tide ever so gently started coming back towards him. And what he saw amazed him. How had he never noticed this before? He walked out a few hundred yards and again just stopped and stared. What must be understood is the area where Archie MacKinnon was standing is an extremely shallow bay, and therefore when the pull of the moon does its thing, the tide runs out a very, very long way. Archie was transfixed. Archie was dumbfounded. Butterflies started jumping in his belly and suddenly he started to shake. His pipe fell from his quivering lips but he took no notice. He just stood and stared and couldn't believe what he was seeing. It was like a huge curtain was being drawn back on some enormous secret for the first time. The tide kept coming and coming and because he was standing so far out, Archie soon found the tide lapping at his feet but still he didn't move. The tide passed him by and kept coming in. He just turned around and watched in absolute fascination and soon the tide was a hundred yards past him and he was up to his knees in water. But still he didn't move. 'Archie MacKinnon, what in heaven's name are you doing?!'

His wife had spotted him, and she came running along the beach with infant twins in her arms 'Are you all right, Archie?' one of their neighbours shouted. He was a great big man with a huge shock of white hair, and had joined Mrs MacKinnon at the water's edge, now a hundred and fifty yards from where Archie was standing. 'Get out of the water Archie MacKinnon, right now!' his wife called in desperation. 'So help me God, so help you Archie MacKinnon, if you've gone mad I am going to give you a thrashing! You have nine blessed children to feed!! I'll whip that madness out of you Archie MacKinnon!' A dozen other neighbours had gathered at the water's edge and joined in the chorus trying to coax the young husband and father of nine back to dry land. And then, just like that, Archie blinked and a great smile spread across his face. He was snapped out of the moment, but the smile turned into great laughter and the people along the shoreline all looked to one another with a mixture of curiosity, concern, sympathy, and sadness.

'It's beautiful! It's fantastic! You wouldn't believe it! Wa-hay!' Archie MacKinnon threw his arms up in triumph and ran towards the shore, jumping for as much joy as he could. He managed to trip over himself a couple of times and thus was soaked right through by the time he reached the shore's edge. 'Dear heaven, he's a Cloon.' 'Aye, you're right about that. Poor Archie has turned into a Cloon.' A few comments along these lines were whispered amongst the crowd gathered around Mrs MacKinnon as they watched the spectacle in front of their eyes.

'It's okay, my sweetheart. I'm fine. Really!' Archie was still grinning from ear to ear as water dripped from his soaked clothes. He had two hands on his wife's shoulders, 'You wouldn't believe what I've discovered. It's fantastic! Don't worry, I haven't gone mad. Really! There's a gold mine out there. A veritable goldmine!' Fiona MacKinnon hadn't looked convinced, but deep in her eyes she was searching for any sign of hope. 'Come, I must get out of these clothes, I'm starting to shiver a little...let me share with you what I witnessed...' As they walked the shoreline towards home, with the crowd of neighbours in tow listening intently, Archie MacKinnon started explaining himself. Everyone was dubious at first and many thought he was talking rubbish. But Archie knew once they saw the evidence that they would believe. 'I hope you're right about this Archie MacKinnon, I really do hope you're right,' Fiona said as she blew out the candle that night and slid into bed beside her husband. 'Please, worry not Fiona, the proof will be in the pudding, or more accurately in the sand and then the pot,' Archie replied and promptly fell asleep and dreamt of magical things. And so it would come to be proven that there really was a gold mine right in their very midst.

Well, it wasn't an actual gold mine, but it was close enough and would prove more useful, because in times of need when markets stopped trading or demand plummeted, you could not turn around and eat gold. You can make teeth, necklaces, and earrings out of gold, but you can't feed your children on the shiny stuff.

What Archie MacKinnon discovered was a shellfish unlike any other.

A shellfish so succulent that even after feasting on them tide after tide and season after season, you can still hear the excitement in the seabirds that feverishly peck through the sand searching for them. It's a marvellous sight to behold, and as Archie stood there, he realised for the first time that something special was happening, and it was as though the birds were musical notes, and the rippling tides, as they rhythmically ebbed and flowed, were fluid musical bars that the birds danced along, making beautiful tunes. Some of the birds would hurriedly chase one way, their little legs spinning like the dickens, whilst others would hop around doing circles in another spot, and always they would call to one another and it was like they were singing, 'there's more over here! Come along, these ones are even tastier! Hurry!' And some would just float contentedly along the shore's edge, happy for a moment, then swoop up and come diving down to have a little peck and go back to bopping along the water's edge. And always the rhythm of the tide would continue, moment after moment, day after day, year after year. It was like an unending piece of music, the likes of which no orchestra could duplicate.

Archie could never explain what had made him stop and stare. He just had and that was that. But he could explain what he started thinking as he watched the tide recede and witnessed seabird after seabird chasing along the water's edge. He'd thought, 'My God! There must be something tremendous down there! Something magnificent! If those beautiful creatures are so enraptured, then heaven's to be, so will we! And, by God, there must be an enormous amount of whatever it is, because it looks like those birds burn a lot of energy!'

It's interesting but perhaps not terribly surprising that it took so long for what he would later learn were a shellfish known as *coquille,* or cockle, to be discovered on Floonay. It's simply the way things have been from time immemorial. Some thing: a thought, an idea, is discovered in one place and later somewhere else and somewhere else again. Or knowledge is passed on about that *thing,* whatever that thing might be, to another physical place, another group of people, and 'voila!' – 'good heavens, why didn't we think of that – or see that?!' or other things like this would inevitably float through a few minds. And on and on it goes. The whole spectrum of time over the countless millennia has been one long journey of discovery for humankind.

'Coquilles? That's what they're called? Couldn't they come up with something better?' That's how Archie MacKinnon replied to the local merchant, Murdo MacArthur, who'd sailed to the mainland with a satchel brimming with the newly discovered gems, in search of a potential buyer. 'Aye, Archie. Coquilles is their name and has been for quite some time.'

'Ach, I could have come up with something better.' 'Forget the name Archie...what's important is, on The Continent – well, they just love them. They can't get enough. They've known about them for centuries – millennia even, well, in parts anyway.' 'Is that so?' 'Aye, that's so. They're mad about them. You've made quite a discovery, Archie MacKinnon. Apparently they're quite hard to come by. It's not like every beach is full of 'em.' Then Archie asked, a little perplexed, 'Murdo?' 'Aye, Archie?' 'The mainland is one thing, but The Continent? From what I gather, it's a long way from here? How're we going to get them there before they rot?' Murdo waved a dismissive hand, 'That's taken care of. Holds on a ship – they're filled with seawater and these new-fangled things called pumps keeps the seawater fresh en route. It keeps 'em alive.' 'Is that so?' 'Aye, that's a fact Archie.'

It should be noted that at the time Archie MacKinnon made the magnificent discovery, people lived by candlelight and warmed themselves by peat fires and basically had to struggle mightily just to survive. It wasn't as though there was much time left over to contemplate every single, tiny thing nature had to offer. Of course, after Archie's discovery was made other islanders headed to the beach and marvelled at what they could now see. 'I can't believe I never saw them before.' 'My, my, that Archie...he has quite an eye.' 'Well, I'll be damned. And they're tasty, too.' 'All this time, right under our noses?' 'My goodness, I wonder what else is out there?' 'The Continent? They've had 'em for that long?' 'Better late than never.' These were just a few of the comments made as the locals wandered the beach following Archie's discovery.

The morning after his discovery, while the sun lay below the horizon casting a long red hue to the northeast, Archie was out on the beach. The tide ebbed and not a bird could be heard. It was there in the near darkness that Archie got down on his knees. And he started to scratch the sand. It was cool, hard, and wet, and there was much broken shell mixed in. He ran his fingers back and forth through the sand, but some spots were so dense, a mixture of hard packed sand and sharp broken shell, that his fingers were soon raw. But he kept scratching at the wet surface muttering to himself, 'come on, where are you...whatever you are, I know you're down there, hiding somewhere...if those birds can find you, then so can I.' He crept along on his knees, one hand acting as a support and the other as a rake. It was a calm morning, and as the tide receded it would occasionally surge past him before heading further out. He kept raking with one hand, and though it hurt a little, he kept on going. It surprised him how densely packed certain spots were. It was like rock in areas. His hand was wet and raw, and he was becoming a little frustrated. For a moment his wife's words flashed through his mind, 'Archie MacKinnon, you better not be mad...I'll thrash you...' He forced the words out of his head and kept scratching at the cold, gritty shore, and then, just like that, he felt something solid – it was curved, like a rock. Before he knew it, out it popped.

There in the darkness, as the black sea ebbed towards the thin red glow that preceded the rising sun, Archie MacKinnon held in his cold, raw hand his very first coquille.

He smiled. Excited, and now ignoring the rawness in his hand, he kept raking and raking and raking, and soon more coquilles were popping out of the earth like wonderful gifts, and he didn't stop to take a break until the sun was halfway towards its zenith. He would switch back and forth from hand to hand, and kept moving along on his knees, inch by inch, but eventually he dropped his head in exhaustion, and the pain he had managed to ignore in his bloodied fingers returned. That was all right. He smiled. Perfectly, painfully satisfied.

It wasn't until the sun was high in the sky did the others make their way down to the beach. Word had spread the previous evening after Archie's peculiar behaviour and fantastical talk, and so it was that almost every resident of Floonay had shown up; some curious, some doubtful, some hopeful, and some wondering if Fiona MacKinnon was going to clobber her husband for going mad. By this time Archie had gathered up the result of eight hours' worth of scratching through hard shell-packed sand. And though it was modest, he stood proudly beside a pile of coquilles that probably weighed three or four stone. He enjoyed a cup of tea and a puff of his pipe. He was content. 'By heavens, look at that! He was right after all.' 'Well, I'll be, Archie. That's something else.' 'Aye, I knew he'd find something. That's our Archie.' 'How long've you been at it Archie?' At that question, he shrugged modestly and replied, 'Just a little while.'

And though on that day no one knew what value the pile of shellfish might hold, a little celebration ensued. It was a fine discovery, and as Archie demonstrated, they were edible, and the taste didn't disappoint. A few of the women had carried peat down and a couple of fires were started and all the children hopped and skipped about. Many of the island's dogs approached the pile carefully, sniffing tentatively as though afraid something was going to leap out and pinch their noses. Archie didn't share the thought with anyone at that moment, but he knew that if all those marvellous seabirds were perpetually worked into a frenzy over them, then surely people would be too. When he had cracked the first shell open before the rest of the islanders had arrived, and sucked in the slippery contents, his suspicions were proved right. And sure enough when Murdo MacArthur had arrived back two weeks later from the mainland with the good news of the demand for them on The Continent, well, Archie just looked to the marvellous winged creations in the sky and smiled, and quietly thanked them for showing him the way.

The ceilidh on the Traigh Mhor carried well into the evening on that most distinguished day of discovery, and according to Floonay's official record books it was the island's most productive ceilidh ever. A celebration to be sure, but it wasn't your typical, 'Wa-hay! Let's sing and dance and do nothing else!' Probably obvious to most, as it's a well-known fact that brand new discoveries demand an enormous amount of experimenting. Pots and pans, bottles of wine imported from The Continent, huge wedges of butter, and tin jugs brimming with a dozen different sauces were all carried over the dunes in heavy canvas sacks, and it was all prepared by the peat fires. The coquilles – or cockles – were boiled, fried, and steamed fifty different ways, and everyone chipped in their thoughts as to how each sample tasted. Floonay's musicians began composing cockle tunes on fiddles, accordions and bagpipes, and a few of the island's best dancers locked arms, bowed to the sea and took their first steps in working out a 'cockle dance'. Floonay's two painters had pulled out canvasses, oils and brushes, and their artistic eyes started squinting, sizing up the new shellfish. Of course, all the children played a perpetual game of hide-and-seek among the sand dunes. Many of the men just stood around, smoked their pipes, sipped their whisky and shared in 'the craic' (or gossip and news and entertainment), while chins were scratched and cockle gathering methods were considered. And theories about where the incredible shellfish came from, and how they got there, and came to be, were pondered.

One would not believe how many stories there are from those early cockle-raking days. Things were new and dynamic and for a while it seemed like every single day the island woke up to incredibly exciting – but also sometimes scary – news. Hidden patches of cockles were found, faster and more efficient methods of gathering were developed (the first of which was to start using an actual rake to gather the shellfish), new cooking techniques discovered, and someone even swore they'd figured out how cockles 'got around' (it was thought this might be useful in tracking them). And then there was the dramatic rescue of Murdo MacArthur at sea when one of his ships sank, overloaded with cockles bound for the market. A few pirating swords were hung up for good, but not as many as had been planned, which led to a few clan squabbles. And then, of course, there was the 'great revolt'.

But this story concerns Alan Trout and the machinations of government, the Trinity of Power and their big business plans, and Norrie MacKinnon and Floonay in the almost present day. Therefore, it is time to step into our trusty time-machine and fast-forward several generations.

Ch 3

The Big Meeting

'Harriet, cancel all my appointments, and if anyone calls for me, take a message. Just say I'm not in. Even if it's one of our senior ministers. Even if it's mister big shot. Numero uno, himself. I don't care. Emergencies, too. Emergencies can wait. Please and thank you.'

Alan Trout replaced the receiver, his hand a little shaky. He pulled from various pockets three mobile phones and turned them all off. He needed silence, to be left alone. At a time like this, arriving back at the office just after lunch, he'd normally put his feet up and start daydreaming about women or adventure – or a mix thereof, but not on this day. No way. Well, not yet anyway. He looked down at his hands. They were still shaking, if just a bit. They had good reason to. 'My goodness me,' he muttered to himself. 'This is my chance, my one big chance. How on earth did they find me?' Who cared. It happened. That is all that mattered. *And they want to meet me tomorrow? Get yourself together Alan, you'll be fine. You will make this happen.*

As Alan Trout strolled past the Scottish Parliament in Edinburgh early that morning on his way to work, a shiny black Range Rover had pulled alongside. One of the tinted back windows opened and a serious looking character wearing dark shades said simply, 'Alan Trout, please, do get in. This won't take long.' A man in a dark suit, also wearing sunglasses had stepped out and opened the back door.

Alan had hesitated a moment. *Who, me?* But the vehicle was expensive, the man's appearance was impressive, and the voice had an air of persuasive authority about it. *Indeed, indeed, of course.* In he climbed, a little befuddled. *What could this be all about?* The seats were tanned leather and the vehicle smelled brand spanking new. He loved that smell. In the front was a driver dressed just like the passenger who had climbed back in. Neither said a word. In the rear, the man in the sunglasses, also in a finely tailored dark suit, cracked a smile. He extended a hand, 'Hello Alan, I'm Nigel. Nigel Turner.' Alan shook his hand and as he did so Nigel took his sunglasses off to reveal a pair of bright blue eyes. 'You look a little uncertain, Alan, that's understandable. This will only take a moment of your time. To get straight to the point, I am a senior representative of three individuals, three *very* important individuals. They have a business proposition for you, Alan. If you are interested please meet me at The World's End pub at noon, today. I take it you know the pub – it's just up the road?' Alan simply nodded. *What on earth is this?* 'Good. I will explain in more detail what the proposition is. Have a good morning, sir.' He gestured with a hand. That was it. The meeting was adjourned. He was free to go. The passenger up front had quietly stepped out and was again holding the door open.

It had crossed Alan's mind, ever so briefly, to not show up. But he was full of curiosity. All morning he'd replayed the scene over in his head. And he thought of some of the previous shady dealings he'd had. There was certainly some shadiness all right, and some trickery, but nothing too serious. He sometimes lamented that he wasn't in the pocket of any of the local bigwigs. He (sadly) didn't know anyone in any mafia-style organisation. As far as he knew he didn't have any enemies and so he didn't think there was a reason to suppose there was anything *too* underhanded about the whole thing, or that he was being lured into a trap. Still, you see a fancy Range Rover stop and silent men in dark suits emerge you can't help but be a little cautious, a bit concerned. Was this some sort of police trap? For what? Well, there were a few things – but nothing that serious. Sure, he mostly conned and scammed and tricked his way into office – but the police wouldn't go to that extent – they would just pull up in a squad car and cart him off. And he had, after all, been free to go. They didn't speed off with him bound and gagged in the back. There was nothing to worry about, he'd determined. And so, at precisely 11:45 that morning he'd said 'too-da-loo' to Harriet, walked out of his parliamentary office and on towards a future he could only have invented in his wildest, most inconceivable, imaginations.

Inconceivable it all did seem. But it was all too real. At The World's End pub only Nigel was waiting for him, but it hadn't been the Nigel he was expecting. Gone was the dark suit and serious dark shades. He was dressed like a middle-aged tourist with no fashion sense. He had a large brown bumbag strapped to his waist, and a camera bag was slung over one shoulder. He wore a red ball cap with the name 'Cardinals' printed on it – and – *I don't recall he had a moustache, or had that much hair? Those do look like his eyes though.* 'It's a disguise Alan, come on, let's find a seat. I'll explain everything.' The air of persuasive authority was still there in his voice though. It was Nigel who had spotted Alan. Never in a million years would Alan have recognised Nigel.

Up in Alan's office as he thought about the meeting he'd just had with Nigel, he pulled out the three cards he'd been handed. They were fancily embossed business cards and each bore a name. The names of the Titans he would be meeting the following day. *'Alan, these are for you. Those are their direct lines to their offices, their mobile numbers – look, even their email addresses are there. Trust me Alan, not many people get these cards. It's their way of saying, "We trust you. We have faith in you. Have faith in us,"'* Nigel had explained. The memory of the meeting would be imprinted in Alan's mind forever.

'I know I look a bit ridiculous here Alan, but it's better safe than sorry. We don't want our competitors to know what we are up to and just a few hours ago we got word that a few of their snoops are in the area. It's really to protect you, Alan. They know me. We don't want them making a connection between us and you and risk having them try to muscle their way in.' Alan had asked what this was all about and Nigel went on to explain. 'Alan, this is about an investment these gentlemen would like to make. An enormous investment. An investment that is not seen on this scale very often. In the world of business this is at the top end of things. This isn't your everyday merger or acquisition of a hundred-million-pound company we are talking about. This is in a league of its own. The thing is simply this – we need someone in government to make certain *things* happen, and happen fairly quickly – this cannot, will not, get bogged down in years of bullshit government review – with respect, Alan. If this goes ahead, we cannot have agency after agency, and council after council, all weighing in on things. You know, and we all know, some projects get stuck for years in the quagmire of red tape and public consultations and on and on. We simply can't have that happen. And that is where we hope you will come in.' At this point Alan had been quite worried and it was painted all over his face. Nigel had reassured him. 'Alan, it's all right, it's not like they're needing you to kidnap anyone, or hide some toxic waste. These are good men. Decent men. Google them all you like, you will see for yourself who they are and what they are about...well, partially about. Some things are best kept, not quite secret, but closely guarded by a select few, shall we say. They, we, you, I, heck, the whole world knows the potential for things stalling, for the dreaded delay after delay after delay, and then there will be competing groups, and it will just become a big, old, messy waste of time. We need things to happen with certainty and with expedience.' By this point Alan had relaxed a bit. 'Alan, they are impressed with you,' Nigel smiled wryly. 'They know about you, quite a lot, as a matter of fact, and let me just say, it's not every man who can pull off what you have. You've a wife, a girlfriend, *and* a mistress...there there, not to worry, not to worry, your secrets are safe with us. None of them is any the wiser? You keep them all quite happy and satisfied? It's not your everyday man who can pull off a feat like that. Must get a little tiring at times.' Alan had been at a loss for words. It was all a little overwhelming. And that's when Nigel had slid a small folded piece of paper across the table. 'And that is what is in it for you. You'll get half of that for just agreeing and the other half when the project is underway.' Alan hesitantly took the piece of paper, and slowly opened it. He didn't register the number written. It couldn't be. This must be a mistake. It can't be. 'Alan, there's no misprint there. The zero count is accurate, as is that number at the beginning. You'll have a lot to think about, Alan. Do try and act as normal as you can for the rest of the day – and this evening. You might want to tell Jessica you won't be making it round to her place, and perhaps tell your wife something has come up, whatever, anything you need to do to give yourself time to think about all this as clearly, and cleverly, and as undistractedly as you can. Tomorrow they'll want to fill you in a little more, and then,' Nigel smiled and lifted his pint, 'who knows, perhaps we will be toasting the beginning of something rather special.'

Special. Special indeed.

Alan stared at the three business cards on his desk. He picked one up, and then another. He put them down and picked up the third. Reading and rereading. He picked up the first two again and reread them, as though afraid what he'd read before would no longer be there. But there it was, the same as before:

Remy Industrial Group, Roger Remington III,

Chairman, CEO

Zanzibar Holdings, Achmed, Owner

Shanghai Global, Dr Foo Huang, Chairman, CEO

My my, who are these people? Alan Trout was about to find out.

He hesitated for a few moments, uncertain which one to search for first. He chose the one in the middle and his fingers rattled away on the keyboard of a laptop he'd pulled out of a drawer. It had a wireless connection that bypassed the building's network. Best to be careful. *My God, Nigel wasn't joking.* He rattled away some more and scanned webpage after webpage. Achmed was for real. *My my.* Next: Shanghai Global. *Holy mother of – this is – do I have the name right?* Next: Remy Industrial Group. A few moments later all Alan could do was stare at the screen, in a little disbelief. *Gulp.* For another half an hour he poured through article after article, story after story, and even picture after picture. There they were, giving an interview or posing with one bigwig or another. More articles, more pictures, and more and more any doubt Alan might have harboured, was quickly disappearing. *These guys are for real.* Alan was a confident man. If he were not, he wouldn't be where he was. But though his doubt about who these people were had all but eroded, he nevertheless felt an incredible sense of doubt rising about himself. A feeling he had not experienced since the early days on the rugby pitch at boarding school. That sensation of icy fear, too, crept under his collar and hissed in his ear. *Jesus. Get a hold of yourself.* His mind started to spin. *Alan, relax. You can do this. Whatever 'this' is. What do they want with me?* He unfolded the wee bit of yellow paper and stared at the number written in blue ink: *£90,000,000* – there was no mistaking the number of zeros. After a few moments his mind relaxed and the sensation of fear and doubt abated as his confidence reasserted itself. *Yes, I can do this, whatever 'this' is. But, but...* He could keep this a secret from 99.9999% of everyone he knew without any problem whatsoever, but he had to confide in one person. He had to be able to talk to one individual without the constant 'front'. And that person was his number one aide, the only person in the world he trusted completely. He had, after all, been with him from the beginning. (The man who may or may not have doctored some videos and obtained the phone numbers for certain illicit massage parlours)

Alan stuck his head out the door of his office. He forced a smile and tried to act as cool as he could.

'Harriet, James will be over shortly. He's free to come in,' Alan said before the smile fell away, and he was all serious again. 'But please, no one else – not yet...not even emergencies.'

'No problem, Alan,' Harriet replied as her boss's face disappeared into the shadows, and the door clicked shut.

Ah, okay, Alan felt better now that he had a trusted ally on the way over. For the first time since early that morning Alan found his mind starting to relax. And as it did, he allowed his thoughts to drift just a little...not very far, though. They drifted to his professional assistant, the lovely and sweet Harriet Joyce, with raven hair that was almost always tied up in a bun. *If only...*Ah, alas, he fancied her immensely, but he also fancied her professional side. She was as fine an employee as this wacky spaghetti-bowl of a building deserved, and he did not want to risk losing her. And anyway, he already had three women to satisfy. That kept him busy enough.

*

'Alan, Harriet said you've been acting a little odd this morning, what's up?'

'She really said that? Shit. I'll need to do a better job here. Well, it did all happen quite suddenly. A bit of a shock and all. Here, sit, sit, I'll explain everything.'

James Anderson was as unlikely a co-conspirator to a crooked politician as one could imagine. Or appeared to be, anyway. He was affable, polite, unpretentious, civil to everyone. His looks were a key asset because he looked precisely like your 'everyday' man. Not too tall, nor short. He wasn't big and brawny, nor wee and shrimpy. His features weren't chiselled out of granite, but certainly weren't soft like jelly. He was right there in the middle. And in the grey Marks & Sparks suit he wore that day, looked altogether professional if not a little forgettable. His loyalty to Alan was unwavering. Harriet thought she was confiding in James a harmless little remark about Alan's behaviour, and indeed it was. But James knew the key to their relationship was 100% openness.

Alan explained all, sliding the cards across the table and the little folded bit of paper. 'Go on, take a look.'

James picked it up. 'Holy shit.'

'Holy shit, indeed. Ninety million smackaroos.'

'This business proposition – what is it exactly that they want you to do?'

Alan shrugged. 'I don't know. Guess I'll find out tomorrow. It must have to do with influencing one policy or another.'

James frowned. 'Alan, do they know you don't have any real power in this government. Everyone knows you have no clout. You were put out to pasture at an unusually young age because all your ridiculous schemes and ideas weren't doing this government, or our party, any favours. In fact, they were screwing everything up. I told you so at the time, but you were bitten by that rabid overly ambitious fervour thing…'

Alan mused, *Indeed, indeed.*

James continued, 'Putting aside your constituency responsibilities, they gave you the position you have precisely so you would have as little say as possible in the proper running of this machine, and as a way of trying to shut you up. To be honest, I'm surprised they didn't just find a cupboard to stick you in. I mean – shit, they know you can talk – 'bullshit' is the better word. I suppose that's why they stuck you in the tourism office.' This is, again, why James was Alan's number one confidante. He was brutally honest.

'I know, I know. Don't you think I haven't thought about that?'

James again, glancing at the business cards, resumed, 'But, bastard – I know two of these names well, RIG is the stock symbol for Remy Industrial Group, it's listed on a few markets. They have operations across a lot of industries. And Shanghai Global,' James whistled. 'God's sake, you do not get bigger in the financial world than them.' He paused, frowning. 'Alan, you hadn't heard of them before?' Alan just shook his head in response. 'You really are clueless about some things. Anyway, but this last one, Zanzibar Holdings, can't say I've heard of them. Interesting though, the owner, it's just "Achmed", one name, funny that,' James shrugged. 'He really must be a big shot. Just one word, one name, and everyone knows who you are – like Madonna or Cher.'

'Or Lady Gaga.'

'That's two words, Alan.'

'Aye, aye, I mean like Journey or Foreigner.'

'Those are band names, Alan, not a person's name.'

'Oh, aye, right. Hmm. Like Enya or Tiffany or…'

'Aye, Alan, I get it. It's just interesting for a businessman, that's all.'

'Of course, of course. Sorry. Look, could you do me a favour?'

James sat back. 'Aye, of course Alan, whatever you need.'

'I've gotta go and take a really long walk and think everything through. Could you do whatever additional research you can on them? Maybe a summary of what their businesses actually do? So I – or I should say we – have a halfway understanding of what I am getting myself into.'

'That's not a problem, Alan. I'll put together a nice little report for you.'

'That's great, and thanks, James. And by the way, if this all actually happens tomorrow, and I don't show up at this meeting only to realise it's all been some crazy non-April, April Fool's joke, well, it goes without saying, you will get a slice of the pie.'

'Mucho gracias, Alan.'

Alan wandered the streets of the Old Town that evening. It wasn't yet the summer solstice but already the streets were busy with tourists. Of course, it was nothing like the madness that descended on the place in August, but it was busy enough. In fact, there wasn't really any time of the year that was entirely devoid of tourists knocking about, snapping shots of Walter Scott or Robbie Burns or Edinburgh Castle. The middle of November or January were the low points when the city was perfectly dull and grey, but even the dullness and greyness had an attractive quality to some. But none of that mattered to Alan Trout right then. This was his big chance. Sure, he had his government salary and extremely generous pension scheme (should he get the good ol' bootaroo from office), and thanks to his wife's wealth, had additional income flowing in from other investments. But it was not an enormous amount. A million in today's currency was not what it was a hundred years ago. You could not give up your day job. Not if you enjoyed a certain lifestyle. And add to the relatively lavish life Alan lived with his wife, he also had his mistress *and* a girlfriend to keep happy. Therefore, there was not a chance he could quit his day job – not yet. And so, the money came in, and it all went straight back out again. Round and round it went like a monetary merry-go-round. But – for heaven's sake – with £90,000,000? He could afford a luxurious penthouse in Monaco, a yacht in the south of France, a ski chalet in Switzerland, and...*My my, what on earth am I going to have to do to earn that sort of money?* These were legitimate businessmen, and Nigel had reassured him he wasn't going to be asked to kidnap anyone or do something similarly dodgy. He said they need someone in government to make certain things happen. And quickly. *I can do that. That is just fine. I can make anything happen.* He reminded himself of this, and that made him feel better. Of course, as Nigel had commented, the government is indeed full of rubbish bureaucracy and farcical time-wasting consultations and a labyrinth of legal traps and snares and heaps of incompetence. He concluded that whatever they needed to get done was for the betterment of society. *Roger Remington the Third, whoever you are, and Dr Foo, you too, and Achmed from Zanzibar, you can count on me, I promise. I will make it, whatever it is you want me to do – I will make it happen.*

That evening he booked into a hotel. He needed to be alone, and did not want to risk his amazing wife, or sweet Jessica, or lovely Colette detecting that something was up. Women were far better than men at sussing out these sorts of things, and when they started asking questions it was hard to get them to stop. Nope, not that evening. This was too big a deal. He dined alone, bought some new clothes at the hotel shop, and retired to his suite. He sipped a little Cognac, and then a little more, and eventually fell asleep, dreaming of ocean-going yachts and King Solomon's mines.

Ch 4

No Turning Back

Alan was singing along with Ben E. King's timeless classic 'Stand by Me' playing on the radio, as he worked the knot of his dark blue tie in front of the mirror early the following morning, when a knock at the door interrupted him.

Who could that be? He hadn't ordered any room service.

He opened the door and a hotel porter handed him a letter and bid him good day. *Well, well, what's this all about?* He opened the letter. It read: Alan, place of meeting has changed. I presume you know the pub, The Canons' Gait? That's where we will meet you. 2pm. By the way, please don't be alarmed that we know where you stayed last night. It's for the best. Nigel.

It took him by surprise. He peered surreptitiously out the window at the early morning bustle on the street below. *They followed me last night? My my, what am I getting myself into? Not to worry, Alan, not to worry, you'll be fine. I suppose that is part of the territory with the likes of Nigel and Achmed and company.*

He switched on mobile phone number one and immediately the message light came on. He ignored it. He texted James: 'Do you have the report ready?' Response:

'Aye.' And back to James: 'Great. See u at office'. It had crossed Alan's mind not to go to the office to avoid any chance of being pulled into an impromptu hours-long meeting – it happened a lot in government – but no, he'd make an appearance. It was important to keep up appearances after all, especially on days that were to be anything but normal. *Nothing odd about to happen here. Everything is just fine and dandy and a-okay, completely normal routine today. Zilcho to be suspicious about.*

Alan left the hotel, walked through the Grass Market, up the cobblestone side street and down the High Street towards the wacky Spaghetti Bowl (That was Alan's private nickname for the new Scottish Parliament building that was described architecturally as post-modern). It wasn't especially busy but there were enough people about, a mix of suits and tourists. He found himself looking around suspiciously. *Is one of these people watching me? Following me? Relax, Alan. Shit, of course someone's watching me. They've been watching me for a very long time. They know about Colette and Jessica. It doesn't matter. Think of that number. Okay, that's better. Try to smile and relax. Get a coffee and act normal.* Alan bought a coffee along the way and breezed into the Spaghetti Bowl saying a few quick 'hellos' as he bounded up the stairs.

'Harriet,' Alan said flashing a smile. He leaned over and his voice dropped a bit. *My, my, she smells lovely today.* 'Same as yesterday.' He winked. 'No calls. If anyone shows up on our doorstep, say I'm in a meeting, an important meeting. Even if it's 'you know who' or any of his misfits. Please, please, pleeeease, don't let them by. I know it might be difficult, he, they, can be a bit pushy at times. Use all the charm you have if you must. I have a meeting at 2pm that I can't miss. It's something very important, and you know how things can go around here.'

Harriet smiled. 'Aye, that's fine Alan. I'll do what I can – and here, James left this for you.' She handed him a sealed file.

Brilliant. 'Thank you. Too-da-loo for now.' Alan disappeared into his office, opened the file and started reading. When he was done two hours later he put the file down and just stared at it. *My goodness me.* Later that morning he called for James to pop round to his office. He needed to talk things through.

'I've wracked my brain as to which bill, what policy, what whatever they want me to influence, and I have to say, I can't think of a single one.'

'Aye, I know, Alan. I've been wondering that myself. I mean, we can rule out anything coming through the Energy, Enterprise or Enviro lot. Finance, Employment, Sustainable growth? You know they don't give a toss about what you think. As for the head of Health, Wellbeing and Cities, well, you know she isn't your biggest fan. Learning, Science and Languages? I don't know. What would be worth that much? Certainly all the pending items the Strategic Board is sitting on, well, again, they won't listen to a single thing you have to say. You and I, and everyone, knows that. All you've got left is Tourism, and even that, well, you know our boss isn't really interested in what you have to say or think either.'

'Indeed, indeed, James. This is all rather odd.'

James shrugged. 'It's noon, Alan, I guess you are going to find out soon enough.'

Alan arrived at The Canons' Gait pub half an hour early and ordered a stiff drink. Fifteen minutes later he ordered another stiff drink. *Ah, that's a little better.* At 2pm precisely, a figure he recognised walked through the front door. It was tourist Nigel again, bumbag and all. *What an interesting fellow.* He gave a little wave when he spotted Alan back in a corner booth, ordered a drink, and made his way over.

'Lovely day, eh Alan?' He smiled, sliding into the booth. 'Had to go with the disguise again. Snoops, you know. It's for your own good.'

'Aye, aye. Of course.'

'They'll be along shortly. They're looking forward to meeting you, Alan, I can assure you.' He took a sip of his beer. 'You're not nervous, are you?'

'No, no, everything's all right.'

'That's good, Alan. Don't worry about a thing. And don't forget, my good man, we are on the good side. The right side. This might all seem as though you're being asked to do something, well, let's just say 'naughty', but I assure you, it is not. You are not being asked to sell your country's secrets or dispose of a body. This is just the way things have to work sometimes. And to men like you're about to meet – well, let's just say, that number written on that bit of paper I gave you yesterday – it's their way of saying 'you are worth it' and they appreciate your efforts and all that. And also, it is a fraction of what they earn in a month. You think £90,000,000 is a lot? Alan, you could turn on the taps of all their bank accounts, and they wouldn't run dry in a lifetime.'

Indeed, indeed. Alan's mind went to the report James had prepared for him. The figures were colossal. The breadth of their interests, staggering. There wasn't a part of the world in which they did not have significant operations humming away. Alan looked on with interest at a curious trio of men who had just walked in. They ordered drinks from a bemused bartender.

Nigel looked over his shoulder and gave a little wave. 'Ah, there they are now. Here, let's make a little room for them.'

My goodness, what on earth is this?

'Alan, they're in disguise as well.'

They looked like the Three Wise Men – or like they belonged in a circus.

'They have a lot of competitors constantly snooping around,' Nigel whispered, then rose to greet his bosses. 'Gentlemen, welcome, welcome. Please, please, do sit, do sit. There's plenty of room at the inn.'

My God, what on earth?

A hand reached across the table. It was Moses, who with a wink said, 'I'm Roger. Roger Remington the Third. But you can call me Remy, Alan. Glad to make your acquaintance.'

Another hand was extended across the table. Alan wasn't too familiar with Eastern religions, but for some reason Confucius came to mind. A little bow, the voice polite saying, 'Nice to meet you, Alan. We very impressed. Or should I correctly say, "We *are* very impressed." Sometimes I speak my "in disguise" English and sometimes proper English. It depend how I feel. I am Doctor Foo. Doctor Foo Huang. But also, I am Doctor Foo Sutherland. Huang is made up name. I explain more later. You can call me Foo.'

Alan was looking a little baffled.

Moses said with a chuckle, 'He ain't just Foo, Alan. He's the incredible Doctor Foo. If you could see inside his brain, you'd understand.'

Hand number three stretched across the table. Again, Alan wasn't big on religion but the man offering his hand looked like a prophet – of sorts.

'I, Alan, am a Sufi Mystic,' He winked. 'But really, I am Achmed. Achmed of Zanzibar. It is so very nice to meet you, Alan.'

Moses nudged Achmed of Zanzibar. Another chuckle. 'Alan, this ain't just Achmed of Zanzibar, this is Achmed, the number one salesman on the planet. You mark my word.'

The look plastered on Alan's face said it all. *My God, what have I got myself into?* Nigel the tourist was one thing, but – these three?

It was Nigel's turn. He spoke quietly, 'We thought the disguise was for the best. You would not believe it if we told you, but in their world, the lengths their competitors go to spy on their activities, it's enormous.'

'And a little flattering, but also annoying. Damn this beard is itchy,' Moses said.

'Don't be so alarmed, Alan, this is just a front. A cover. Deep cover,' Achmed commented whilst raising a pint to his lips.

'Alan, we could have had Nigel whisk you to any location to meet us, but our competitors, they watch our every move, as much as they can, anyway, and especially so when they see the three of us together,' Remy said. 'Well, they would know something was up, and if they saw a politician anywhere near us, they'd start putting two and two together, you know what I'm saying? This is for your benefit. Don't let these costumes fool you. We are who we really are, Alan.'

Alan found his voice. 'Of course, aye.'

'You'll get used to this, Alan, just look beyond the facade.'

'Aye, aye. Sorry.'

'I have a special bond with your city, Alan,' Dr Foo was saying, 'a very special bond. A man from here, many years ago, when I was just a young lad – an orphan, he adopted me and taught me much. I am humbly indebted to this place, to your people.'

Alan was a little lost for words.

'He was a banker, Alan, a great banker,' Dr Foo said with a wink, 'who understood the long view.'

'Amidst the chaos of life, not everyone gets the long view, Alan,' Achmed sighed. 'I am sure you understand.'

'Aye, yes, of course, of course,' Alan replied.

Moses leaned forward, his Texas drawl betraying him. 'Alan, let's get to the point. Nigel here has given you the basics. We need someone in government to make something happen and make it happen with as little, shall we say fuss, as possible. We run, as I am sure you are now aware, some pretty big outfits. You could use the word gargantuan to describe our operations – but this is still a big bad world, Alan, and it is a fiercely competitive place, which means to stay ahead, hell, just to stay in the race, you've got to be constantly looking for new markets, new ideas, new everything. Nothing, Alan, in this world remains the same. Can you appreciate what I am saying – what we are saying? This is elementary, of course. Every businessman, businesswoman, any politician, with any sense, that is, gets this. But not all. To use an overused business phrase, a cliché, it's called "continuous improvement". Simply put, I am sure you understand, if you do not improve your product, you will lose. Plain as a Texas waffle, and doggone it, it is as simple as that. You understand that, I am sure?'

'Yes, yes, of course, of course,' Alan said, still a bit bewildered.

'I am sure you are curious as to what we would like you to influence, to do?' Remy paused, waiting.

'Uh – aye.'

'That's good, Alan, real good. Look, we here,' Remy looked around the table before continuing, 'We've been scouring the world for our newest venture. We've been up the Nile, down the Danube, searched the coastlines of every continent, hacked our way through a few mosquito infested jungles and trekked over many a mountain range...'

'Well, we did travel by air-conditioned car and plane quite a bit,' Achmed added.

Remy again, 'You get the point, Alan. We have been searching high and low for where to base our next grand collaborative venture. We've been searching for years Alan, for this one. This capital project is the big one.' Remy sat back. 'Well, one of the biggest in quite a long while, anyway.' He looked around the table, scratched his beard and muttered,

'Shoot this doggone beard sure is itchy.' Then he continued, 'And hey, we ain't getting any younger. We want to get this project off the ground as soon as we can – because, well, it is not your average "let's build a factory and pump out a new product" kind-of-project. This is about as ambitious and enormous as it gets, Alan. And it just so happens that we have found what we believe is the most perfect place in the world for it, and wouldn't you believe it, Foo was right all along. Foo, would you like to do the honours?'

Alan furrowed his brow. Did he miss something? *Foo...was right all along? Right about what?*

'Of course, Remy.' Dr Foo pulled out from under his robe a rolled up laminated map. He slipped the rubber band off and spread the map out across the table. 'This, Alan, is a map of the Western Isles. The Hebrides.' He jabbed a finger at one spot. 'And that, Alan, is the Sound of Floonay. That is where we are proposing to build the future, but there is only one problem.'

Ch 5

The Early Years

The house Norrie MacKinnon grew up in is perched on the same timeless spot as that of his great (x eight) grandfather's thatched stone dwelling, standing high over the south-eastern edge of the enormously sweeping beach that is the Traigh Mhor, near the north tip of the island. Roughly speaking, Floonay is shaped like a decanter of Scotch, with a plump main body, a skinny neck and a head like a stopper. It is on the skinny neck's east side that the Traigh Mhor is located, with the Atlantic a mere two hundred yards to the west. The landscape widens on Floonay's 'stopper' where there is a wonderful hill for climbing and picnicking on, and the view from on top is bested only by Floonay's highest point, Ben Heaval. As one swivels around one is treated to an endless oceanic blanket, a collage of deep-water blues and shallow aqua greens that are constantly caressing vast stretches of sandy white beaches. Sweeping from left to right, or west to east via the north, one can see the mighty Atlantic peering over grassy dunes. Then it is Picnic Hill, with miles of sparkling beach in the foreground. And beyond wee Orosay, South Uist, and Eriskay, the scary island of Stack comes into view. Panning a little east, Gighay, Hellisay, Flodday and Fuay appear and then – looming, sometimes sinister and cruel, sometimes benevolent, always unpredictable – the impossibly mighty Minch.

The beautifully coloured seabirds skimming the ocean's surface, their wings only inches from seesawing swells, rising and swooping, twisting and turning in unison as though attached to some invisible elastic metronome is enough to make any fighter pilot shake his head and wonder, 'Just how do they do it?' It is priceless and it is the view Norrie grew up with every single day.

Only as a young boy, Norrie didn't spend much time admiring the colourful panorama that surrounded him, but he loved running all over it. He'd chase the lambs and sheep up the steep hills and down the deep sandy dunes. He'd run after the seabirds whenever he had the chance as he wanted desperately to capture one to keep as a pet. But alas it was never to be, and sometimes Norrie had the sneaking suspicion that the birds were having a bit of fun with him, letting him get close, but always, just as he pounced, they would take off, leaving Norrie falling to the sand, and he would swear that the chirping noises they made at those moments was bird laughter.

Norrie was the youngest of eight children. In order from oldest to youngest, there was Donald, Duncan, Maggie, Ewan, Rory, Catherine, Morag, and finally Norrie, at the tail end. It was sometimes lonely way down at the end for Norrie because his nearest sibling, Morag, was five years his senior and didn't like chasing sheep or seabirds with him, and his oldest brother, Donald, was twelve years his senior, had smoked a pipe in his father's company for as long as Norrie could remember and only chased sheep when it was time to shear them. But they were all nice to him and it helped a lot in the schoolyard to have so many brothers who were giants, because none of the school bullies ever bothered him.

*

On Norrie's seventh birthday his family and friends had gathered around to watch him blow out the candles that were poked into a big chocolate cake. It had been a wonderfully sunny day with only one minor emergency. Norrie's best friend, Malcolm MacLeary, had broken his nose as they ran over seaweed covered rocks pretending to be commandos. It had been a bloody affair and poor Malcolm had done a lot of bawling, but once the parents evacuated him from the seaside war zone, the rest of the boys promptly got on with their mission. Norrie had won the cockle raking competition (again), and at one point leapt through the air, *just about* snatching a black and white bird with an orange beak that often made a shrilly racket. He had enjoyed himself enormously and thought it was his best birthday to date, but it wasn't until later that evening after all the guests had gone, that it would prove even more fantastic.

This is how the evening unfolded.

Although it was midsummer and the weather grand, a few embers smouldered in the fireplace as they always did. Norrie's father, Michael MacKinnon, was sitting in his favourite leather chair right beside the fire. He pushed a few bits of coal around with an iron poker. Ashes leapt up and the embers glowed with satisfaction.

'Ah, that's more like it,' Michael said and puffed on a hand-carved pipe. He wiggled his wool-covered toes a few inches from the fire and sipped a Scotch.

Young Norrie sat on the stone hearth and put his hands near the heat source.

'Be careful there, son, we wouldn't want you falling in,' his father cautioned with a wink.

'Oh, I won't Papa. I promise.'

Norrie's oldest sister, Maggie, played a slow air on a fiddle as his brother, Ewan, followed her lead on the accordion. Catherine was lost in the pages of a book and twelve-year-old Morag was helping their Mama tidy up in the kitchen. Fourteen-year-old Rory had no musical talents to offer, for which he was mightily grateful. As it was Saturday night there was a dance at Northbay Hall, which meant one thing – lots of *the other kind of* talent. He excused himself as Ewan, two years his senior, eyed him enviously from behind his box. He too liked the idea of lots of dancing girls. Norrie's oldest brothers, Duncan and Donald, had already left for the North End's local, The Heathbank.

After a few more tunes Michael MacKinnon spoke. 'That was some fine playing you two. Go on, you can put those instruments away and skedaddle.'

Oh, thank God! Ewan could barely contain his excitement as he hurried to jam the accordion back into its box. The seventeen-year-old Maggie was just as excited, for she too had a person of interest waiting at the dance, but being much more mature was composed and her neat demeanour did not betray. 'Are you sure, Papa?' she queried without even stopping to put her fiddle away. Not long after, thirteen-year-old Catherine yawned and made her way to bed, and since Morag was already down and Mrs MacKinnon was still in the kitchen making preparations for Sunday morning, so it would be that little Norrie and his father were alone sitting by the fire.

'Here, you're a big boy now Norrie, why don't you put a little splash in this glass for me. But be careful with that bottle.'

Norrie's eyes went wide. 'Are you sure Papa?'

'Aye, of course I'm sure. But let's keep this between us.' His father said.

'I promise, Papa,' Norrie replied, and carefully carried the glass over to where his father's special bottles were kept.

Norrie's father was a hard man. He had skin like gritty leather that stretched tightly over muscle and bone. His back was as strong as a petrol-powered ditch digger, his shoulders were carved from granite, and with the strength in his forearms and hands he could crush both turnips and pineapples – *at the same time.* But he preferred eating them of course. He was also a kind man who thought ill of no one or no thing, and his eyes shone like two North Stars whenever he thought of his family. He also had a large brown moustache from which a smoking pipe almost always dangled.

'Be careful there, Norrie,' Michael called over as his son tipped a bottle as though pouring lemonade from a pitcher on a hot afternoon.

'Am I old enough to try your pipe, Papa?' Norrie asked as he crossed back towards his father. Two hands gripped the glass as though it were a holy chalice.

'My, my – I'm lucky it's a late morning tide tomorrow,' his father commented, accepting the generous measure. 'Dear me.' He took a long sip and put the glass down.

'Can I try your pipe, Papa? Is seven old enough for that, too? It's my favourite smell in the world, apart from chocolate cakes baking in the oven.' Norrie sat on the stone hearth and looked up expectantly.

Michael MacKinnon smiled and struck a match. 'Not quite yet, son. Perhaps in a few years...I'll let you know.'

Norrie's face dropped.

'But here, I think there is something you're ready for – well, a little of it anyway.' And with those words a large leather-bound book appeared on his father's lap, as though part of a magic show.

'What's that, Papa?' Norrie's disappointment disappeared up the chimney like a puff of smoke.

‘This is a special book, son.’ Fingers drummed well-worn leather. Smoke rose from Michael MacKinnon’s pipe and for a moment it looked as though he was having second thoughts.

‘Where did you get that Papa – Papa? It looks so strange. Can I see it? Can I?’ Norrie shuffled along the stone hearth like a hungry crab. His impatient little arms reached upwards. ‘Can I hold it, Papa?’

‘Careful by the fire, son, and calm down.’

‘Is it a comic book, Papa? Is it full of comics?’ Norrie’s little hands were snapping like claws.

‘Norrie, calm down a little, or I can always put it away...’

‘Oh – no Papa!’

‘Maybe I should have waited until your tenth birthday. Dear me, I thought you’d be ready, seeing as you’re now a big boy of seven.’

It took a great deal of effort but Norrie’s little claws stopped snapping and he did his best to sit still.

His father smiled. ‘My, my, son. I didn’t think you’d get so excited.’

Norrie mustered all the willpower his seven-year-old mind contained to ‘stay cool’, as his tenth birthday was far too far away.

‘I’m okay now, Papa. I – promise.’ Norrie was dying with anticipation.

Senior MacKinnon sucked peacefully on his pipe and thought his son looked like a kettle about to boil. Every twitch he made Norrie zoomed in on, like a hawk tracking a field mouse.

‘Papa?’ Norrie looked up at his father with longing in his eyes. ‘Is it a comic book?’

His father smiled. ‘Come on up here...’ Before he could finish the sentence Norrie sprang onto his father’s lap as though he’d been launched from a catapult.

‘Whoa! Easy there, son. Watch that glass.’

Norrie wiggled into a comfy position. He stared at the crusty old leather book like it was a bowl of chocolate ice cream. He couldn't wait to dig in.

'I hope there's lots of pictures, Papa – it looks so old. It looks ancient, Papa. Is it from the olden days? I didn't know they had comics in the olden days, Papa. Papa?...' Norrie was rattling away like an old Bren machine gun.

'Whoa. Steady on there, son, remember what I said. The book's not going to grow legs and run away on us.' He gave it a reassuring pat.

Realising that the book wasn't sprouting legs or wings Norrie settled down. *What a funny looking comic book,* he thought. He ran a hand over its cover. It was rough and leathery and cracked in areas, like his father's skin but a lot older. There were words he couldn't make out and along its edges was rope. Norrie ran a finger over the rope – it was rock hard.

'That rope's been dipped in a special tar – hard as nails, son.'

Norrie was amazed that comic books were made like this – it was all so mysterious, and big – he tried lifting it – and heavy. But there was one thing he recognised well: seashells. His favourite ones! They lined the edges of the rope with a half dozen arranged amongst the strange words.

Norrie looked up at his father. 'Papa, I've never seen a comic book like this before.'

'It's not a comic book, son,' Michael MacKinnon said as he relit his pipe.

Norrie looked down and up and back down at the book. Leathery and ropey and seashells and words he couldn't make out. It was his seventh birthday. He was supposed to receive comic books.

'It's not a comic book?'

'No, son,' his father smiled.

'Well – what is it?'

'It's the Coquilleuous Rakkeronuous Almenikhiaka.'

Norrie gave his father a look of profound confusion far surpassing the normal ability of a seven-year-old. 'Ah...Papa?'

'It's an almanac, son.'

There was a moment's pause as Norrie fell into deep thought.

'An alma – what?'

Michael MacKinnon smiled and tousled the mop on his son's head. 'It's a book of information.'

Norrie wasn't happy. *What about comics!?* 'Information?'

'That's right, son. Information, useful information.'

Norrie looked at the book again and ran his hand over the cover. 'Hmm. But – are there comics, too?'

His father chuckled. 'Well, maybe not comics, but...'

'But! But what, Papa!?' Norrie jumped in his father's lap.

'Whoa there, son.'

'But what – what is it Papa?' Norrie was once again as excited as ever.

'Well, you like pictures don't you?'

'Oh, I love pictures, Papa! Of course I do!'

'Well, I think we can find a few pictures in here you might find interesting.'

And with that Michael MacKinnon creaked open the big book and Norrie was transfixed. The pages were all so different. Some were crinkly, some were smooth. Some had stitches running through them and others yet were bound together with strips of tape. There were different colours and different types of print – and scrawl – and then Norrie caught a glimpse of his first picture – it was a drawing of four of his favourite seashells.

'Papa – those are – cockles?'

'That's right, son.'

'But...' Norrie flipped through the pages. More strange print, more crinkles and tears and colours and stitches – and – another picture. He looked up to his father, curious...

'That's a diagram, Norrie. Of different patterns and techniques.'

Norrie hesitated and his demeanour flip-flopped between curious and frustrated as he turned page after page. 'Aren't there any fun pictures?'

Senior MacKinnon smiled. 'Hold on a sec, son.' He leaned forward and stuck the poker in the fire, bringing a few bits of coal to life. It was near midnight and the light of the fire made shadows flicker across father and son.

'Let's see if I can find you a fun one.'

A moment later they were looking at a colourful picture of people dancing on a beach with smiles pasted on their faces. There were dogs in midstride, and a large fire burned – and it was all frozen in the moment of this picture.

'What is this, Papa?' Norrie wasn't sure to be curious or frustrated. He still hadn't found a comic.

'That's a picture – well, a copy of the original painting – of the celebration the day after the great discovery.'

Norrie was instantly mesmerised. 'Really?' He knew about the great discovery.

After a few moments Norrie spoke. 'Papa?'

'Yes, son.'

'I didn't know they had so much fun way back then.'

'Well, they didn't sing and dance all the time, but that was a reason to celebrate, don't you think?'

Norrie nodded and turned back to the picture, and after a moment heaved the big book shut running a hand over the cover. He still didn't understand the words he was looking at.

His father could read his mind. 'It says Coquilleuous Rakkeronuous' Almenikhiaka. It translates to Cockle Rakers'

Almanac. As I said, son, an Almanac is a book of knowledge – of information and stories.'

Well, Norrie knew a lot about cockle raking, but – 'Papa, why haven't I heard of this book before?'

Michael MacKinnon smiled. 'Because you only just turned seven. You were a little boy before today, but now that you're a big boy of seven, well…' He let his son finish the thought.

Norrie's wheels were turning, and his father could see he was starting to understand. A book about cockle raking? It can only mean one thing! 'Will this book help me find,' he paused, almost not believing it. '…even more?!'

'That's right, Norrie – even more. Not only that…'

'But Papa!' Norrie was as amazed as he'd ever been. 'Where did this book come from?'

'Well, it started with the original cockle-raking MacKin…'

'Great Grandpa Cloon!' Norrie blurted out.

'That's right son, it was Great Grandpa Cloon.' Eight generations was a long time removed, and so instead of referring to the man as 'great, great, great, on and on, grandpa', they simply stuck to 'great grandpa'.

'You see…'

'One second, Papa.' And with that little Norrie hopped off his father's lap and disappeared out of the cosy room, reappearing a few minutes later with a mug of hot chocolate and a plate of chocolate biscuits.

'My, my, son – what's all this?'

'Mama almost made me go to bed, but I told her you were reading a special story to me and I said that since it's my birthday could I please have some chocolate biscuits even though it's really late…' Norrie explained as he climbed up on his father's lap. 'Here, Papa, can you hold this – it's getting hot…'

'Well, well – you are a lucky little boy – I mean big boy now.'

'But Mama said I have to be in bed in half an hour – and said if I'm not, then I can't go cockle raking tomorrow.' Norrie looked solemn for a moment. 'So, Papa – please make sure I'm in bed on time.'

Michael MacKinnon smiled as he struck a match, bringing his pipe back to life.

'Are you sure seven isn't old enough to try your pipe, Papa?'

'What would you want this silly thing for when you have all those tasty biscuits. And anyway, didn't you know that if you want to puff on a pipe then you have to give up biscuits,' he shrugged. 'It's one or the other.'

Norrie sat back against his father and for a moment just looked at the plate on his lap. He took a big bite of a biscuit, and then another and reached for the hot chocolate. 'Okay, Papa, I'm ready for a story about how I can get even more.'

And so, with his son clearly enthralled with the prospect of finding even more cockles, Michael MacKinnon once again creaked open the leathery old book and began to speak.

'It was a few months after the great discovery that Great Grandpa Cloon decided he ought to start jotting bits of information down. At first he did it only for his own sake – he explains everything I'm telling you in here – you know, like what parts of the beach seemed to have more cockles than others, and what the difference in taste was between the various sizes, and how the tides and currents seemed to affect them, and what are the best raking techniques, and how the wind and rain affects your performance, and on and on – but then, as he notes on page 145, he started taking notes for posterity...'

Norrie stopped munching and gave his father a blank look. Michael MacKinnon explained what posterity was. It seemed to satisfy Norrie as he went back to munching.

'Anyway, so naturally at that point, he began elaborating – sorry, explaining things more and more, and adding little accounts of this and stories of that, and warnings about all sorts of things, and not just warnings but there's some scary stories, too, and there are detailed instructions of techniques and on and on and on – and he did it all for us – if you want to be a proper cockle raker, that is.'

Norrie crumpled his brow. 'But – I already am a good cockle raker. I won the competition again.'

His father smiled. 'Of course you're a good cockle raker, son. But there are a few things you can learn...you'll see.'

'Hm.' Norrie munched on a biscuit, took a slurp of hot chocolate and then said, 'Papa, can you find a fun, or – no!' Papa said there are scary stories, too. 'What about a scary story – I don't mind scary stories.'

Michael MacKinnon took a sip of Scotch. 'Well, let me see what I can find here.' He began flipping through the pages and stopped at quite an alarming sight.

It made Norrie shiver and pull in close to his father. 'Papa, what is that?!'

'That, Norrie, is a sea monster.'

Norrie put a hand towards the page but pulled back as though that thing was going to leap off the page and bite his fingers off. It was a black and white photo that took up half the page. There were stormy white capped waves all around and the sky in the background looked angry, and right in the centre of the picture was an enormous creature rising from the water – and there was something sticking out of it.

A moment later Norrie found his voice as his little mind processed the picture. He glanced up at his father. 'Papa, it looks like a whale?'

'That's what it is son – a whale. A big bad and very dangerous whale.'

'But, you said...'

'It might as well be a sea monster – you see that thing there? That's a harpoon sticking out of its eye – and has been for a very long time. It wasn't a happy whale before it acquired that harpoon and became even less happy after doing so. This picture was taken by a seaman of a ship that the whale had rammed – luckily this ship was quite large and didn't sink – anyway, the whale, it's been prowling the seas looking for boats both big and small – it doesn't care – to terrorise and crush, and seamen to munch on, for a very long time.'

Norrie was frightened – and confused. 'I didn't know they had photos way back in Great Grandpa Cloon's day?'

'Oh, no they didn't, son. This picture was taken about sixty years ago. You see, after Great Grandpa Cloon other MacKinnons in our line added bits of information and stories. This was the work of grandpa Chester, three generations back.'

Norrie was lost in thought and seemed caught between his nervous fascination with the picture of the angry whale and this new bit of information.

'But – how did the harpoon get stuck in its eye?' The whale took precedence.

'Don't be afraid there, Norrie. Now let me tell you the story. It was a failed whale hunt. You see son, back in the day, not that long ago, whales were hunted, mostly for all their tons of oily blubber – and when spotted, huge harpoons were fired into them with long ropes attached so the whale couldn't escape. This whale got away. But there's more to it. You see, this whale wasn't being hunted as other whales were, for sustenance. This whale was being hunted for one reason and one reason only – to kill it. This whale has been prowling the seven seas for a very long time, terrorising ships, ramming them, thrashing them to splintered bits. Many a seaman has perished, from all corners of the globe. They say he's exacting revenge for what man has done to his kind. This was before it acquired the harpoon mind you. Things just got worse afterward.'

Norrie shivered with fright.

His father continued. 'It would disappear for long stretches if it didn't want to be seen – or perhaps it was just resting under a giant iceberg – who knows – but then one day he was spotted off the Nova Scotian coast and a message was passed along, and then it was spotted off a large merchant vessel a hundred miles due east of Newfoundland. It was a very large ship, one that even this whale could not cause much damage to. Next stop, Iceland, for the big ol' brute, and it was estimated its trajectory was the northern isles of the Outer Hebrides. The alarms were sounded. The weather wasn't the best, and was expected to get worse, but one brave captain out of Lewis, Capt. George Mackay, well, he and his crew were the only ones up for it. His ship was a 75-foot trawler, and he had two harpoon guns ready to go. If they spotted it, they reckoned they'd have a good a chance as any.' Michael MacKinnon looked to his son, who appeared equal parts fascinated, frightened, and a little uncertain. He tousled Norrie's hair. 'This is a big day, young man. Your seventh birthday and being introduced to this little heirloom of ours. I'm going to leave out a bit of the scarier descriptive bits. Long story short, they engaged that harpoon-less whale in the mother of all whale-versus-man struggles, and though they managed to make a hit, the whole crew, save one, perished. The ship was crushed, and the men were gobbled up. One crewman survived. He was found sprawled out on a bit of wreckage, shivering and half-dead, by a passing ship the following day.'

Norrie could feel butterflies dance in his belly. He looked up at his father and then to the picture and, ever so slowly, carefully, he reached out his hand and gently touched the picture, and then he spoke quietly, not wanting to rouse the big whale from the page. 'But – it's, it's stuck in its eye?'

'Well, you can understand now why it's turned into a monster, or into even more of a monster – it doesn't like us very much. And you see – they, like elephants, have very long memories. There's no telling how many wrecks he's caused. One thing is for certain, since this picture was taken it has not been spotted. He's out there all right, and no doubt he's caused many a mysterious wreck, but no one has lived to tell the tale. It's as though he's become invisible. A horrible, terrible, invisible menace...'

Norrie clung to his father. 'He won't get me, will he?'

Michael MacKinnon broke a little smile. 'No, of course he won't, son. I won't let him.'

'You promise?'

'Of course I promise.'

Ch 6

Young Alan Trout

Meanwhile, if you travelled 160 miles south and east across The Minch, past Tiree, Mull and onto the mainland, wound through Oban, and continued your journey south and east over the rocky braes and green glens, you would finally slip down onto the streets of Auld Reekie, where a lad six years older than Norrie MacKinnon was doing his best to avoid being hit on the rugby pitch.

That young lad was Alan Trout.

And it must be said that Alan had done a brilliant job of honing what had become a most fantastic skill: specifically – avoidance *without* detection. The *without detection* bit was enormously important as he wouldn't have lasted long as a player if his teammates or coaches had started *detecting* that he was purposefully avoiding a situation that would put him in harm's way, because, of all things, *he was afraid of being hit?!* He abhorred it, he hated it, he loathed it to no end. It frightened him to his core. Who could really blame him? He had not wanted to play rugby but, rather, it was forced on him, as, alas, it was a Trout family tradition.

The evening before Alan was shipped off to Ruggers, the most prestigious boarding school north of the border, Mr and

Mrs Trout had sat their frightened son down: 'If you want to get on in life, Alan, if you want to be accepted as part of the team, then you better play rugby.' This wasn't the first time it had come up, but as it was the night before his departure, it was their final chance to make certain he did what was expected of him. 'And don't forget, son, being on the team, succeeding at Ruggers, it will unlock doors for you. That's what it's all about.' His father chuckled reassuringly. 'It's not like you're being asked to play rugby for the rest of your life. You don't even have to play at Uni, son, just Ruggers. *This* is an important period of your life. Do you understand, son?' Poor Alan didn't really understand but he nodded his head a little, trying to be brave, but in his mind big brutes and horrible monsters were crashing into him from every direction. Mr Trout looked to his son and this is what he said. 'Look, son, I know you're scared. But this is the thing; you're the perfect size for a winger. You'll be way out on the flanks, miles and miles from the middle of the scrum where all the banging and smashing and thumping happens. Way out on the edges you will learn to fly, son. Trust me.'

And fly he did.

From the moment he first laced up his little boots that was all Alan Trout did. He ran around the pitch like the devil was right on his heels. At first it was chaos. He was running for his life plain and simple. But amidst the chaos he started learning a few things and eventually he scored his first try, and then his second, and on it went. And the amazing thing was that he actually never had to make a tackle and never was tackled. Ever. If there was a school record kept of such things young Alan held the title. But perhaps even more incredibly was that no one noticed what had transpired. As Alan narrowly wiggled out of a collision or deftly ducked out of the way of some tractor-sized boy, it was always *just so,* that those on the side lines would react with comments such as: 'Oh, did you see that! Just about.' 'Goodness gracious, that speedy little Trout almost got there.' 'Must have slipped on a bit of turf – or a banana peel.' On and on it went. It was incredible really.

And it was what he learned on that pitch, from the ultimate fear of being hit, that would propel Alan Trout into politics, and the rest of his life.

Ch 7

Growing Up

The next seven years plus a day of Norrie's life were simply fantastic.

He grew and grew and grew and with every year that passed the margin of his victories in the annual cockle raking competitions stretched and stretched. And not only that, his victories all came in the age bracket above his own. When Norrie was thirteen, he entered the adult category (18+) for the first time. He won hands down. Every competitor under the age of 18 was enormously relieved to see Norrie move out of their categories, and every competitor in the 18+ category was left in disbelief.

At this time in history there were a dozen or so full-time cockle rakers on Floonay. Aside from the full-timers there were a dozen or so regular part-timers who weren't half bad with the rake, and indeed prided themselves on their seaside productivity. But they had neither the desire nor the stamina to go it full-time. They were quite content with a few bags a week and had other occupations to keep them busy. And of course, beyond the regular part-timers were the remaining islanders who would occasionally stroll down to the Traigh for the odd feed.

It shouldn't come as a surprise that Norrie's father was the one full-timer not left frustrated that his son had won the adult category. But what might come as a surprise is that despite broad public opinion that Michael MacKinnon was the best cockle raker on Floonay at the time, he had never bothered with the competition. There were numerous occasions in his youth when his lack of competitive interest was questioned, and especially so on the evenings before the big competitions. As his pals polished their luckiest rakes and wiped down their favourite wellies and strained their brains about where the best cockle patches might be, they would say things like, 'Michael, why don't you compete?' or 'You're pretty good, you're not a scaredy cat are you?' or other things like this, but he'd just shrug and reply, 'that's okay. You lads go ahead.' As Michael MacKinnon grew and kept raking and raking, it became evident how good he was becoming. But still he had no interest in the annual competitions, and instead focused on raking for purely professional reasons. That his youngest son would take to cockle raking so much was a bit of a surprise. None of Norrie's siblings took any interest in the rake and Michael MacKinnon was not one to prod his children in one direction or the other. Norrie just happened to be the one whose eyes lit up when his three-year-old hands grasped their first bucket and rake. Unlike his father, little Norrie loved the competitions, and it appeared that the competitions loved him, because when he competed he never lost.

Every Saturday night and on every birthday during those seven years plus a day, Michael MacKinnon would share with his son a little part of the Coquilleuous Rakkeronuous Almenikhiaka.

Every Saturday but one, that is.

*

From Norrie's seventh birthday on, he and his father developed a ritual that went unchanged. Senior MacKinnon would wiggle his woolly toes by the fire, stoke the smouldering peat with the iron poker, then light his pipe. For his part, Norrie would carry his father's empty glass to the special bottles' storage area and by the time he was walking back, balancing his amber offering, the big old book would be on his father's lap. Broadly defined, the information contained within the almanac fell into three categories: marvellous adventures, stern warnings, and tips & techniques. Once Norrie was settled in place his father would always ask the same question. 'All right son, which'll it be, an adventure, a warning, or a lesson?' It never mattered, as Norrie was fascinated by everything contained within the creaky old book. And interestingly, the categories would sometimes merge together depending on what story was being told, or lesson taught, which Norrie soon learned when he asked the question, 'Papa, you know the story about the terrible whale, I mean the sea monster. Is that an adventure story or a warning story?'

'It's a bit of both son,' his father had replied.

Over the course of the seven years Michael MacKinnon always managed to keep the most important stories or lessons for Norrie's birthdays. On his ninth birthday Norrie had commented that he'd like to learn something from the 'tips and techniques' category.

His father thought that a fine idea and flipped through the Almenikhiaka to the 'grips, postures, and pattern' subsection of the 'tips and techniques' category. 'If you ever want to be a full-time cockle raker, son, don't rake like this.' His father had turned to a diagram that amounted to long lines contained within a square. 'And especially don't use the 3-point stance, it'll ruin your back.' And he'd pointed to a sketch of a man bent over ninety-degrees at the waist, with legs spread, knees bent, and a rake positioned directly in front. 'For some ridiculous reason all those part-timers do it this way. I'm sure you've seen them down there, son. And not only will it ruin your back, but it's so boring – all those long lines, one after another – you'll never last if you follow in their footsteps.'

On Norrie's eleventh birthday they were reviewing a series of diagrams detailing some of the best patterns and techniques to use. There was 'the circular', 'the sweeping arcs', 'the interconnecting ovals', 'the wave', a funny one called 'the jiggle', and a few others. At one point, Norrie commented that some of the techniques detailed in the Almenikhiaka were similar to how he raked. His father had replied, 'Well, son, we are talking about how to use a simple old rake. There's bound to be similarities, but here, this is the important thing.' And Michael MacKinnon went on to point out the subtle but significant differences in gripping, the length of the sweeping arcs, the depth of the layers, how 'interconnected' to make each oval, how many cockles to expect in a given circle before switching to 'the jiggle', and on and on and on. Norrie began to understand there were enormous differences.

When he thought it time for an extra-important lesson, Michael MacKinnon guided Norrie's gaze to a diagram titled ominously, 'Diagram 9, Beware!'

'What's that, Papa?' Norrie was intrigued.

And if the 'beware!' bit wasn't enough there was a skull and crossbones at the bottom right-hand corner. The diagram was contained within a square that took up a quarter of the page and basically amounted to an innumerable number of squiggly, zigzagging lines going in every direction possible. It was a scribbly mess. Chaos, plain and simple.

'That, son, is *definitely* how not to cockle rake – that is, unless you want to go bananas. Never mind worrying about the boring old raking patterns of the part-timers...'

'Bananas?'

'Yes, you know, berserko, bonkers, crazy...here let me show you something.' His father flipped through the pages and when he stopped, Norrie jumped with fright. They were looking at the picture of a man. A crazy man. His hair was frazzled, his eyes were crooked, his tongue was sticking halfway up a nostril, and there wasn't a symmetrical ounce of being to his two halves. It was like the man had spent his whole life inside a kaleidoscope. 'That is how this man cockle rakes, this crazy man.'

Norrie had never seen such a scary picture in all his life. He didn't even feel safe looking at it. 'Papa, who is that?'

'That, son, is Walter Wellington and he lives in a teeny house over on the west side.'

'He lives *here!*' Butterflies fluttered in Norrie's belly.

'That's right son, but only for part of the year.'

'Who is he Papa?' Norrie was almost afraid to ask.

'He's from down south. He's an artist, son. A crazy artist, that is. My father, your grandpa, added the little bits about him in here. The man has been coming up here to paint for more than thirty years.'

'How come I've never seen him before, Papa?'

'Because he's a recluse, a hermit – that means he doesn't get out much, he doesn't like other people. He comes up here because it helps him paint, supposedly...and he goes cockle raking to calm his crazy brain, or so he thinks.' Michael MacKinnon sipped his Scotch and continued. 'You can see that the pattern he uses when he cockle rakes doesn't help his state of mind.'

'But – I've never seen him on the beach Papa?' Norrie was as equally frightened as he was transfixed by the picture of the macabre unsymmetrical man.

'That's because he only rakes at night, or in terrible storms, or just way way at the north end behind the big rock. He doesn't like to rake around others...but your grandpa spied him a few times – I've seen him scurrying about a time or two myself. I think he's more gremlin than man, to be honest...'

'I hope I never meet that man, Papa.'

'But here, there's more to this little story,' and with that Michael MacKinnon flipped a page and next they were looking at what could best be described as a picture scribbled with crayons by a two-year-old.

'What's this, Papa?'

'That, son, is a picture of one of Walter Wellington's paintings.'

Norrie smiled and suddenly didn't feel as scared of Walter. 'He's not a very good painter, is he?'

Michael MacKinnon smiled a little. 'That's what I thought as well, son. I mean, what in heaven's name is that – some sort of crazy elephant?'

'Or a crazy rhinoceros...'

Both father and son chuckled.

'But you want to know something son...that painting, it's worth millions of pounds. Someone actually paid millions and millions of pounds for that crazy picture.'

'But – why Papa?'

'Why, indeed.' His father flipped a page. 'And this is a picture of the man who paid millions of pounds for it. He's a big shot businessman.'

They were looking at a photo of a well-groomed man in a suit and nice red tie. His face was clean-shaven, and his spectacles were aligned properly, and everything about him was entirely symmetrical, and he looked wholly 'in control'.

Norrie was puzzled.

'Your grandpa decided to add the story of crazy Walter Wellington for more than just a warning about how not to rake – lest you go bananas...but also to remind us that as crazy as Walter and his paintings *appear*, this man might just be the craziest of them all. I mean, who else would pay millions of pounds for crazy Walter's crazy paintings? It's a warning, Norrie. Don't be fooled by looks.'

Ch 8

The Greatest Ever

Norrie's 13th birthday had been more festive than usual as it was the day he took top prize in the adult category for the first time. His brothers, Donald, Duncan, Ewan, and Rory, were especially impressed at what they came to realise was an extraordinary feat. As noted earlier, none of Norrie's brothers took much interest in the rake, and instead achieved professional success in other endeavours. Donald was a sailor in the merchant navy and had already circumnavigated the world a dozen times. Duncan and Ewan owned a fishing boat together. Their passion was shooting creels for lobster and crab, and Rory's labours of love were joinery and sheep shearing. To Rory, there was nothing quite like harnessing his talents as a carpenter to bring a house to life, or shearing the big woolly coats off the appreciative backs of his flock of sheep in the heat of midsummer.

Now, although they had no interest in the rake professionally, they always cheered for Norrie at the annual cockle raking competitions. The thing was, as his victories up to his 13th birthday had all been in the youth categories – and it was *just* an amateur competition – they weren't setting off fireworks as though Norrie had just won the World Cup for

Scotland single-handed. These were men who toiled the sea and land daily. Gruelling work that didn't lack the odd danger, and so they knew how to keep a perspective on life. But as they watched Norrie best all the men of Floonay, well, it must be said that they were looking fairly chuffed. You could see their pride well up and it was as though for the first time they realised that their sprouting brother really had something special. Norrie's sisters, Maggie, Catherine, and Morag, were as delighted as they always had been, and showered him with much attention and affection. But Norrie was a growing boy of 13 now and was finding all his sisters' attention embarrassing and a little annoying. He much preferred his brothers' company, and especially so when Donald gave him the odd shot of his pipe.

There were two chocolate cakes on the kitchen table; one was big and square and had 13 candles sticking out of it, and the other was shaped like an enormous cockle. It was a surprise to everyone. Mrs MacKinnon had secretly worked on it in anticipation that her son would win the competition.

'Well, by heaven's look at that.' Michael MacKinnon puffed impressively on his pipe.

'How did you make this, Mama?' Norrie inspected the enormous chocolate cockle.

'And there's even ice cream inside it. Chocolate, of course.' Mrs MacKinnon spoke proudly, as though announcing the arrival of another child.

'Ice cream!' A few of his siblings blurted out at once.

'But – how did you get ice cream...in *there?!*' Norrie glanced from his mother to the mammoth chocolate cockle.

'Sorry, it's the baker's secret,' his mother replied.

'My my, this is a special day indeed.' Michael MacKinnon slipped his pipe into a pocket and rubbed his hands together in an unusual display of tasty anticipation.

It should be noted that Norrie was at that curious age straddling boyhood and manhood. One moment you're puffing on your older brother's pipe and acting as grown-up as possible and the next you're hopping up and down with all the innocence and excitement of a four-year-old. And it was with boyhood excitement that Norrie waited for his father to creak open the *Coquilleuous Rakkeronuous Almenikhiaka* later that evening. He had learned to contain that excitement finally and looked as cool as he could on the outside, but inside he was bubbling away, just as on his seventh birthday.

'Here you are, Papa.' Norrie held in his hands a generous offering poured from one of his father's favourite bottles.

'Dear me, son, one would think it's my birthday.' Michael MacKinnon placed his pipe aside and accepted the half-full tumbler.

Norrie took a seat on the stone hearth and pulled a plate of chocolate biscuits close to his side, feeling the warmth on his back. He looked up as his father turned the pages of that ancient leathery book, pipe tucked neatly under his large moustache. Well, it was the most wonderful place to be in the world, Norrie was certain.

'Papa?'

'Yes, son?' Senior MacKinnon turned a few pages.

'Um – how many more birthdays are you going to read to me?'

His father looked up and smiled. 'As many as you like.'

'Papa?'

'What is it, son?'

'Are you looking for a good adventure story?'

'Is that what you would like – an adventure story?'

Norrie slowly munched on a biscuit, thinking – and then it dawned on him. 'Oh, I know Papa!'

'Well, well, what will it be for such a special occasion?'

'You decide!'

'You want me to decide – all on my own?'

'Of course, Papa!' Norrie didn't hesitate.

Michael MacKinnon's eyes twinkled like two stars in the night sky. 'Well, well – you mean you don't even want to give me a little hint of which way to turn? A marvellous adventure or another little tip or perhaps another stern warning?'

Norrie took a slurp of hot chocolate then placed the mug down. He was in no doubt. 'Nope. You go ahead Papa. I'm sure it will be good.'

Senior MacKinnon took a sip of Scotch and re-lit his pipe. 'Well, well, what should I choose for a boy of – sorry, a young man, of thirteen – hmmmm – let me see, let me see – you've learned most of the best techniques, and which ones to steer clear of, you've heard some of the best warning stories and about many of the most fantastic adventures – hmmm – hmmm – hmmm...'

'Papa? Has the Almenikhiaka run out – after all these Saturdays and all my birthdays – *Papa?* We haven't run out – have we?'

Senior MacKinnon cracked a small smile. 'No, no – of course not son...I'm just thinking out loud, that's all. And seeing as it's your thirteenth birthday, well – I just want to make sure I choose one that is as special as it can be.'

Norrie relaxed and went back to biscuit nibbling.

'I'm going to tell you the story about the greatest cockle raker who ever lived. His name is Tumsch, Tumsch Galbraith, that is...'

'But Papa – I thought...' Norrie was confused. It had never been discussed before. He just took it for granted – *it had to be one or the other!* 'I thought you were, or, or – Great Grandpa Cloon!' Even though it had turned out that Archie was not a Cloon that miraculous day he discovered cockles, the name Cloon stuck.

'Well, that's nice of you to say – I might be pretty good – but...'

'But Papa! Everyone knows you're the best – even all the other full-timers – I've heard people say so!'

'Well – I might be the best on Floonay right now, but certainly not of all time.'

'But what about Great Grandpa Cloon – he discovered the cockles!' Norrie's voice rose. He wasn't sure whether he was frightened or angry or just terribly confused by what his father was saying.

'My, my – I'm sorry son – I didn't mean to upset you.'

Norrie didn't speak for a moment, and instead looked down, dejected. 'I just thought...' He was slipping into a sullen place.

Michael MacKinnon had to act quickly as he realised he couldn't turn his son's 13th birthday into a miserable occasion. He understood how much cockle raking, and the Coquilleuous Rakkeronuous Almenikhiaka, and all those Saturdays and birthdays over the last six years had meant to him. 'You didn't let me finish – *completely*...' Senior MacKinnon was sure that great-times-eight Grandpa Cloon wouldn't mind him telling a white lie. But truth be told, he didn't even know how much of a lie it would be, because he honestly didn't know who ranked where over all the centuries of cockle rakers. He knew he was pretty good. He'd raised a large family on nothing but cockling, after all. But whether he was 3rd or 7th or 26th or whatever – he had never given it much thought. He'd have to make this good though, to quickly lift the spirits of his youngest son.

'Let me explain – now, when you hear of what Tumsch did, you'll understand why he's the greatest ever, full stop. You know Nugget, who lives up the way on the big hill? Aye, he'll tell you more about him than what is in here. He's his grandson.' For all the little fibbing he was about to do, there was no way he was going to put himself ahead of Tumsch.

'Norrie, he saved *thousands* of lives, thousands and thousands...'

Young Norrie looked up – if not brightening, his interest was at least piqued.

'And then Grandpa Cloon comes in next – but you know what, he was so good, even way back then with those ancient inefficient rakes, that it's not simply *second* greatest cockle raker place that he holds, it's actually "first and a third", or, you know, one point three...' he sat back and lit his pipe. He could see his son was trying to understand what he'd just said. Senior MacKinnon continued, enormously mindful that he could not disappoint his son. 'And I fall in right behind Grandpa Cloon, as the "first and a half" greatest, or, well, one point five...'

Norrie's eyebrows did a peculiar little dance as he tried to process what his Papa was saying.

'We didn't even make it as far down as "second" greatest, it was decided we were so good.' Michael MacKinnon tried sounding as proud as he could.

'Really Papa?'

'That's a fact.'

'They can – *do that?*'

'Of course they can. They can do whatever they want.'

Norrie thought a moment and it appeared to Senior MacKinnon that his son was coming around to understanding.

'Above second greatest – *both* you and Grandpa Cloon?'

'That's right, son – but not quite first – that spot is definitely Tumsch Galbraith. And mark my word, you'll understand why he holds the top spot once you hear this story.'

'But that's pretty good though, right Papa?'

'Well, what do you think?'

Norrie had brightened significantly, and it looked as though he was trying to picture what 'first and a third' and 'first and a half' places looked like. He seemed satisfied eventually and a big smile emerged.

It actually surprised Michael MacKinnon that Norrie hadn't heard the story at some point – in the schoolyard or on the football pitch, somewhere, *anywhere.* Although the Almenikhiaka had stayed in MacKinnon family, some stories had inevitably spread over the years, and especially so the marvellous adventure stories. But, then again, Michael was aware that regardless of their significance some tales simply got lost in the sands of time. He took a sip of Scotch and creaked open the Coquilleuous Rakkeronuous Almenikhiaka...

By the time he closed it an hour later, his son's jaw was on the floor, his eyes were wide and he looked as amazed as his father had ever seen him.

'Papa – he really did – *all that.*' Norrie spoke with a reverence reserved for royalty.

'That's right son.'

'Papa! That's the most amazing story I've ever heard.'

'And although the greatest ever is a Galbraith and not a MacKinnon, you'll be proud to know that he is a distant cousin.'

'Really?'

'Cross my heart.'

'Hold on a sec.' And with that Norrie ran out of the room and reappeared two minutes later with a brand-new plate of biscuits and a mug of hot chocolate. 'I'm thirteen now Papa, I can stay up later,' Norrie said, guessing what his father was thinking.

'Well, well...perhaps I'll just have one more splash – why don't you be a good lad...' Norrie whipped the tumbler out of his father's hand and was already halfway towards his favourite bottle. When the tumbler arrived back Michael MacKinnon mused that it was full enough to tell six more stories.

Norrie settled back down on the hearth. 'Okay, Papa – can you tell me that story again?'

Ch 9

This and That

Fast-forward a year to Norrie's 14th birthday and as you might expect, he again took top prize in the adult category. There were seventeen other contestants, none of whom raked to within 10 kilos of what Norrie had – *and,* he'd even stopped fifteen minutes before the whistle blew.

Norrie had fairly sprouted between his 13th and 14th birthdays. His shoulders had widened, his toes had squeezed through a few shoe sizes, his arms had stretched, and once a fortnight he'd started shaving. His voice, too, had broken, and his oldest brother, Duncan, had even brought him his very own pipe from Santiago, Chile. Norrie was careful to keep it stashed away, and only puffed on it on walks high atop picnic hill, where he had a 360-degree view of any potential tattletales. He had even tried his first beer three months before his 14th birthday. His best buddy, Malcolm, had excitedly explained that he'd 'happened' upon a whole case but was cagey when Norrie pressed him about how he 'happened' upon an entire case. *'I – it was – well – oh, what's the matter with you? Do you want to try one or not?!'* was Malcolm's response. Of course Norrie wanted to try one and so he'd dropped the subject and slurped himself into another rite of passage. But for all the growing up Norrie was doing, he still looked forward to Saturday evenings with his father and the Coquilleuous Rakkeronuous Almenikhiaka.

Later that evening after all the guests had departed and Norrie's siblings had left for a dance at Northbay hall, Norrie was sitting by the fire feeling tipsy and hoping it didn't show. You see, throughout the course of the evening his brothers had sneaked him a couple of beers. It wasn't much, but their contents created a sensation that his young system was still getting a slippery grip on.

He and his father went through their usual routine. Norrie decanted the amber offering into a tumbler, and for his part his father stoked the fire, wiggled his woolly toes, and lit his pipe.

'Well, well, that was some day, eh son?'

'Aye, Papa, of course it was.'

'You went and beat the trousers of all those men again. You're becoming quite a cockle raker.'

Norrie smiled and shrugged. 'Their technique – if they'd only try something else – like the *sweeping arc* or the *interconnecting ovals* – even something as simple as the *circular!* They can see me – it's not like I'm raking behind a big curtain.'

Michael MacKinnon had a chuckle but said nothing.

'Papa?'

'Yes, son.'

'Do you think I could cockle rake forever – I mean, when I grow up, like you?'

'Well, I don't see why not – your mum and I have managed to raise eight children on all my cockling.'

'It's just that some of the boys have been talking more and more about what they want to do when they grow up. Some are even talking about going on in school, to uni – they say that the world is changing and stuff. Some have even said that I'm crazy if I think I'll still be cockle raking in twenty years.'

Senior MacKinnon smiled. 'Well, son – you just keep doing what you're doing and the future will take care of itself – and by the way.' He looked at his son through wise eyes. 'Are you okay?'

'Wh-what?' Norrie stammered. 'What – do you mean?!'

'Oh, it just looked like you were – ach, it's nothing...'

Norrie felt nervous. Was he swaying? Did he sound drunk? He'd only had a couple of cans – *was that a lot?*

'Of course, I'm perfectly fine Papa!'

Senior MacKinnon sucked thoughtfully on his pipe. 'Hmm, hmm, I see, I see. Say, are there no biscuits and hot chocolate for this evening?'

'What? Oh, no. I'm not very hungry.' It was the first time that Norrie had taken his place by the fire without a hot chocolate and his favourite chocolate biscuits. 'But tomorrow night! I definitely will tomorrow...'

'I see, I see.'

Norrie suddenly had a thought. 'Papa?'

'Yes, son.'

'You'll still read from the Almenikhiaka tomorrow night, right, since tomorrow's a regular Saturday?'

'Of course I will,' Michael MacKinnon replied, striking a match.

Norrie watched his father light his pipe and suddenly the thought struck him. 'Papa?'

'Yes, son.'

'Do you think – I mean, is fourteen old enough for that?'

'You mean this?' his father gestured with his pipe.

'Uh – aye.'

Michael MacKinnon shrugged. 'I don't see why not – a little puff can't hurt.' He leaned forward to give his son a puff, but

Norrie jumped, saying he'd be back in a second, and reappeared thirty seconds later.

'Well, well, what do we have here?' his father asked.

Maybe he'd gone too far? Should he have kept it a secret? 'Oh – it's just – I happened to, err, find this...'

His father smiled. 'You better keep that well-hidden, son. If your mother finds out, she'll scold you.'

After a few awkward moments Norrie got the hang of this new ritual and truth be told he thought it was simply fantastic!

'If that door opens, son, you better find a quick hiding place for that thing, and I'll do my best to fill the room with as much smoke as possible.'

Norrie couldn't help but smile. *He and his father were conspiring!* 'Aye, Papa – I promise – I'll slide it right over here.' He glanced just beyond the stone hearth where there was a stack of books and a basket full of all sorts of odds and ends.

'And make sure you don't burn the house down, eh.'

'Oh, I promise – I'll be careful.'

Both father and son fell silent as they savoured the moment, then with the Almenikhiaka closed on his lap, Senior MacKinnon finally spoke. 'You know, son, you'll be noticing some *changes* – now that you're growing quickly into a man.'

His father's comment caught Norrie off-guard. His brow crumpled in thought. *What is Papa talking about?*

'You're almost as tall as I am now, and those feet of yours, well, you could probably fit into my wellies no bother at all. And all that cockle raking you do after school, before school, day after day, year after year – well, I'm sure that back of yours is hard as nails by now, those shoulders, too – and those hands, they don't look like your everyday 14 year-old hands.'

Norrie unconsciously glanced at his hands. He had noticed, over the past year especially, that he was becoming stronger – much stronger. In school he often helped the janitor carry big heavy boxes around. And he often helped the librarian carry tall stacks of books back and forth and twice in the past year he'd given Malcolm a piggyback, each time for well over two miles after he'd sprained his ankles doing the exact same thing both times – playing commando.

'And you know, son, there are probably *other things* happening, if you know what I mean...'

Norrie suddenly felt extremely uncomfortable and embarrassed. *Papa had never talked like this before! This was supposed to be Almenikhiaka time, not THIS sort of talk time?!* Of course, there had been *things* discussed with friends, and some boys even liked comparing and inspecting *things* – and, and then of course there were the girls – they'd started paying more attention, and for some curious reason the girls had started to come across as, well, more – appealing...and there was even one boy that Norrie could swear was looking at other boys as though *they* were becoming more appealing!

But you didn't discuss these *things* with – *your Papa!*

'You know, son...'

Uh oh!

'It's like this, you see...'

Oh man!

'You might or might not know it, but we didn't arrive here on little baby banana boats floating up The Clyde...'

Papa! What the hell!!!

'And if you hadn't noticed the girls in your class, well, *things* are happening to them, as well...'

Arrrggghhhh!

'And, trust me, if I know anything about women, they will be paying a lot of attention to you, especially with your rock-hard cockle raker shoulders and arms – most women, well, they really like that sort of thing...'

'Papa!!' Norrie couldn't take it any longer.

'What is it, son?'

'It's – sorry – nothing, Papa. I just thought, you know, that this was Almenikhiaka time.'

His father smiled and puffed at his pipe. 'Dear me, I'm sorry, son – I should have explained in advance, but this is all covered in the Almenikhiaka.'

'What!!'

'It's all in here,' his father replied, patting the big old book on his lap.

'But...' Norrie was lost for words.

His father spoke. 'What does *that* have to do with the Coquilleuous Rakkeronuous Almenikhiaka? I gather that's what you're thinking?'

Norrie didn't know what to say and was afraid to nod.

'Well, I must tell you, young man, that *it* has a lot to do with *this.*'

Norrie finally found a few words. 'Where?! Under what sections? I don't believe it...'

'As a matter of fact, there's bits under marvellous adventures, stern warnings, *and* even tips and techniques.'

Norrie was horrified. Tips and techniques!? Marvellous adventures!? - - about *THAT!!* No! Not in the Almenikhiaka! This must be some crazy joke. Papa is going to say he was kidding all along and then they can get back to normal adventures and warnings and lessons.

The phone rang in the hallway and Norrie leapt up, seizing the opportunity to escape from the presently horrible *this* and *that* predicament. 'It's all right Mama, I'll get it,' Norrie called down the hall as he beat a hasty retreat from the family room. A moment later he reappeared. 'It's for you Papa...it's Eddie.'

'Well, well, I wonder what he's wanting at this time of night – on second thought, I bet you I know.' Michael MacKinnon put his pipe and Scotch down and made his way out into the hallway.

'Hello there, Eddie, to what do I...' His father pulled the door behind him.

Oh, thank God! What started out as his most memorable birthday, winning the adult competition again and getting to share a smoke with this father, had quickly turned into the most awkward birthday – ever! He was still trying to wrap his 14-year-old head around the fact that *all that* was included in the Coquilleuous Rakkeronuous Almenikhiaka. It just didn't seem right. Norrie took the time alone to try and come to terms with this shocking news. He just couldn't believe that Great x8 Grandpa Cloon would write about those *things*...or any other MacKinnon for that matter!

A minute later his father walked back in. 'Just as I thought. He needs a hand tomorrow. Ronnie's gone missing again.'

Awkward thoughts of *this* and *that* were dropped like a lead weight. Norrie was suddenly excited. 'Papa? Can I go too?'

Eddie was a young fisherman, not more than twenty years of age, who lived half a mile down the way. He was the son of one of Michael's dearest friends, Stuart MacIntosh, who'd died earlier than he should have. It was Stuart who had taught Duncan and Ewan everything they needed to know about fishing and had sold them the boat and many of the creels they now fished with, for as fair a deal as anyone could have wished for. Naturally, Michael had a soft spot for the young man and was willing to lend a hand if he was in a bind. Eddie often worked alone but when he was needing to steam further out and haul more gear it was handy to have a second body on board. Normally that body was his good mate, Ronnie Mcphail, a part time scallop diver who, 95% of the time, was reliable and ready to show up when Eddie would call and 'reserve' him a few days in advance. The 5% of the time was the unfortunate bit – he would inexplicably go missing for days due to a love affair with his beloved *Cutty Sark*. Eddie's younger cousin, Colin, had just moved back from Stirling and was staying with him, and was desperate to take Ronnie's place, but as Eddie explained to Michael, 'Colin isn't even a novice, he's never been out before, period. I'd love to get this gear worked and moved in a bit...I really hate to ask.'

'Eddie, say no more. I'll be there.'

Now, although it wasn't nearly as exciting as cockle raking, Norrie had enjoyed the occasions he'd been out with his brothers and Eddie.

Michael MacKinnon eased back into his favourite chair. He looked thoughtful for a moment casting a glance at the window and the darkening skies beyond. A little wind whistled. 'I'll let you know in the morning.' He reminded himself to pay special attention to the Shipping Forecast on the radio.

'Come on, Papa – I'm pretty good with the creels. Eddie said I've got sea legs! And that if ever I wanted to give up cockling...'

'I'll let you know in the morning,' Michael MacKinnon said evenly.

Norrie could tell when he wouldn't get any further and so he dropped it.

'Now where were we?' Michael MacKinnon smiled.

Oh, God, no! Not this again! Norrie screamed inside his brain.

'Ah, yes, I think we're done with that other stuff...but here, I think you'll enjoy this next marvellous adventure. I think a 14th birthday is the best occasion for it.'

Oh, thank God! 'A proper adventure?' Norrie could barely contain his excitement that they were leaving THAT stuff behind.

'It's probably one of the best ever.'

'Better than Tumsch Galbraith's?'

'Well, not better – different. But most important, it involves one of the greatest secrets known to man, well, to some men. If you were Aristotle you'd probably use a word like esoteric to describe it.'

Not a word was said for a moment, and Norrie watched his father, carefully, for any sign of - anything...

One of the greatest secrets? Norrie didn't have a clue who Aristotle was or what esoteric meant but it all sounded intriguing. 'Papa, are you serious?'

'Of course I'm serious – but here, before we start, why don't you be a good lad,' and with that Norrie had tumbler in hand and was already halfway towards his father's favourite bottle.

Ch 10

It Turned and Turned

Norrie awoke the following morning and bounded down the stairs into the kitchen. He'd had the most fantastic dream of captaining Eddie's boat and unlike some dreams that slip away if you don't think about them quickly enough, he could remember the whole thing. His papa was there shooting creels and Eddie was standing at the stern smoking a pipe and even his brother Donald was there brewing a pot of tea in the wheelhouse! But it was Norrie who had the most important job – he was manning the helm, steering *Odyssey* through enormous ocean swells.

He found his mum and three sisters sitting around the table eating porridge and sipping tea.

'Where's Papa?' Norrie looked around expectantly.

'Your father left an hour ago, Norrie,' his mother replied.

'Papa – he's gone? But....'

'But what?' Morag asked.

Norrie was stunned. He felt like the wind had just been knocked out of him.

'What is it Norrie?'

'I – he said....I was supposed to go...' His voice trailed off and his shoulders slumped and a most horrible look of dejection took hold of him.

'Now Norrie, it's all right, you can go out with them next time,' his mother reassured him.

This was terrible. He was so looking forward to a day on the high seas that he'd actually dreamt of it! *I shouldn't have been dreaming, I should have been up earlier!!* Norrie was so mad at himself. It was going to be a fantastic Saturday, almost like another birthday, he'd thought. His '14th birthday plus a day party', especially because the Saturday was going to end like every other Saturday had for the last seven years; with a reading from the Coquilleuous Rakkeronuous Almenikhiaka. It wasn't often that it occurred *two days in a row!*

'And look at the weather anyway – as your father said before he left, this is no day for a novice to be out there.'

Norrie's eyes were drawn to the window. Sure enough, it was a dreich morning. The skies were wet, grey and unsettled, and the wind rattled against the windows, sneaking in with a whistle where it could.

'It's supposed to pick up as well. Moving in faster than they'd predicted,' Maggie commented.

Norrie's disappointment flew out of him as a chill ran down his spine. He gripped the counter and stared out, transfixed. It was a view he knew inside out, looking northeast across the Sound of Floonay, beyond the islands of Gighay, Hellisay, and the supposedly haunted Black Stack. The wind was howling in from the northeast turning The Minch and the Sound into a sea of white caps. It wasn't an altogether unusual scene, but something made a sickly scrunch in Norrie's belly.

'Donald's out, too...'

'He is?' The sickly scrunch scrunched a little more.

'Norrie, are you all right?' Catherine asked.

'What? Yes, no...'

'Don't you worry Norrie, your father assured me they'd be in not long after noon, well before it's supposed to really turn...and Eddie knows what he's doing – they all do.'

Norrie looked out the window again. The sea was a vast wet blanket of perpetual motion, capable of swallowing mountains when it so desired, and at that moment something tremendous and restless moved underneath it.

He turned and spoke quietly, not wanting an answer. 'Are Duncan and Ewan...'

'Now, you know they'll be okay. They do this for a living. They'll be just fine,' his mother said with a brave face.

Norrie looked around the table. They were all wearing brave faces. This was an island used to taking the best of what Mother Nature dealt. It had forged in its people over millennia a quality of character rarely matched anywhere. It was an island one hundred percent accustomed to getting hammered.

But, yet...

Norrie looked back out the window. He didn't like what he saw.

'Norrie, you know they'll be careful...' The brave, if wavering, voice trailed behind him as he bolted from the kitchen.

Norrie pulled on his oilskins and wellies, grabbed his favourite rake from the Nissen hut and set off at a trot for the Traigh Mhor. The wind and rain lashed him but he took no notice. He descended the rocky landscape and struck out across the big sweeping beach. *I don't care how horrible it gets. I'll stay out here until I see their boats coming in.* And Norrie started to rake. First he raked with his back to the howling wind, but had to keep looking over his shoulder for any sign of the boats. And so he turned into the storm, not caring how much it punished him. Every few strokes he would peek up, expecting any moment to see either boat rounding the north tip of the island. Nothing but a wild and wicked scene, and it was like that tremendous restless thing that writhed under the ocean's surface would go into wild unexpected spasms, which was accompanied by gusts that buffeted and blew Norrie around as though he was seaweed barely clinging to a bit of driftwood. *Where the hell did this weather come from?! They weren't forecasting it to be this bad!!* Norrie held fast his rake and although it wasn't easy, he kept raking and raking and raking, keeping a faithful eye out for the two boats that carried his father and three brothers. Nothing but a wild and wicked monster. *They should have known! They should have known! How could they not have known! What the hell were the Shipping Forecasters forecasting!?* A time or two he thought he caught a glimpse of a bow – a surge of hope! But the glimpses just turned into froth, and hope would disappear in the giant swells. It was becoming harder and harder to stand his ground, and his muscles were weakening and he tried hard not to let doubt creep into him, but the more he looked around it was like doubt was everywhere, slithering towards him like a thousand vicious sand snakes. The tide was now well on its way in, forcing Norrie to retreat west, but still he stayed, moving a little only when the tide forced him to do so. The storm was unrelenting and more than once the thought conjured in Norrie's soaked head, *how could such a violent squall have gone undetected?* He simply could not believe it. But there had been stories....

And it wasn't done.

That restless and spastic monster turned The Sound of Eriskay into a frenzy of froth and wave the likes of which Norrie had never seen before. The weather turned and turned and turned and if it had turned anymore it would have turned inside out. Norrie became afraid now of looking up, for it was as if every time he did it was drawing him closer to something horrible and dark and inevitable – something he didn't want to know...didn't want to believe. No! He refused! *They'll be okay! They are okay! They're probably tied up together somewhere. Maybe they're even having a cup of tea and telling jokes...and – Papa's probably even thinking about what story to tell me tonight, and maybe there will even be another incredible secret!*

Norrie raked on and on and the tide kept rising and it was like all the ferocity of the Seven Seas were being funnelled up into the North Atlantic and straight into the Sound of Floonay. Norrie was now well west of where any cockles could be found, but still he raked. Norrie teetered between dread and hope. Dread, that as every second washed away into the tide it brought something closer that no person should have to face. But still there was a glimmer of hope. Hope, that at any minute he might catch a glimpse of a bow struggling through the storm.

Norrie tried to be as brave as he could, but even so a little tear welled. *Tonight, Papa is going to read to me from the Coquilleuous Rakkeronuous Almenikhiaka! I just know he will! Like he has for every Saturday and every birthday for the last seven years! I just know he will.* He tried not to let any other thought register – and he raked and raked and raked and was becoming more afraid of looking up. The tide was now well up, and though it was summer, and the days were long, a terrible darkness enveloped the place. *And maybe Duncan and Ewan and Donald will want to sit in with Papa and me for a little story.*

He tried to stay brave.

The sudden contact, a hand on his shoulder, took Norrie by surprise. Norrie looked up. It was his neighbour who was a giant of a man, Dougie Campbell. He was dressed in yellow oilskins and a big hood half covered his face. His lips were moving, but the racket of the gale was whipping the words away the moment they left his mouth. He gestured, *come on in Norrie!*

Well, poor Norrie didn't want to leave the beach. He pulled away from the giant man and kept on raking. He felt the hand again, firm on his shoulder.

'Come on Norrie! Come inside!' Dougie Campbell leaned in close, shouting against the wind.

Norrie didn't want to. To leave was to give up. To leave was to lose hope. To leave was to turn your back.

'Norrie!! Come in! ---------------------------- Norrie! Come on, son!! We're going to get blown all the way to Iceland!!'

Then so be it!

The tide was now at its highest point. Seawater and horizontal rain lashed the two figures, as the freak gale threatened to pick them straight out of their wellington boots. Norrie tried to will the big man away, tried to will the storm away, the whole day away – so he could tell his father not to go, to tell his brothers to stay in. *Why did they go!?* Norrie continued raking, then bravely looked up. His eyes burned and were squint almost shut. He could barely see for the torrent coming straight at him. *Where were they?! Why? Why?!* Well, poor Norrie wanted to stay and wait for his father and brothers....poor Norrie didn't want to give up on them....poor Norrie, exhausted, didn't want to turn away...but the inevitable approached, and although the gale made a tremendous racket, it was like the *inevitable* silenced it, dwarfed it, and Norrie could see *IT* perfectly, could hear it whisper, cold and cruel and wicked...

Why...why did you go....Why???!!!

And so it would be that Norrie buckled, and had it not been for the strong hands of his neighbour Norrie would have been blown straight over the dunes and probably wouldn't have stopped until making landfall in Newfoundland.

Ch 11

North Stars

Despair took root in the MacKinnon household that day. As the hours passed a growing anxiety made its intolerable rounds. But hope had not been abandoned completely, and instead clung, fluttering. Nothing had been heard one way or the other. There had been no distress calls made which seemed unusual considering two boats were missing. If something had happened surely one of them would have sent a message. It was this hope that Norrie bravely clung to. As time passed the strength of the gale diminished, but it was still a considerable force. As the evening turned into night with still no word, even the most courageous souls found they could not escape the strengthening grip of a wretched darkness. A composed Mrs MacKinnon had shed a few tears as the evening wore on, but as midnight was left behind and early morning approached, her defences crumbled and she broke into sobs. Her daughters comforted her and a few friends stayed faithfully close by. Rory sat, numb and red-eyed, a whisky in hand.

The first Saturday in seven years that Norrie's father had not read to him from the *Coquilleuous Rakkeronuous Almenikhiaka* was now three hours gone – and it would never return. And though despair clung to Norrie like gravity, he did all he could to feel that tiny speck of hope. Norrie made his way to his room but had no intention of sleeping. He just wanted some time alone. He fumbled in a drawer for the pipe Donald had brought him from Santiago, sat by the window and looked up into the night sky, still dominated by dark and foreboding clouds. Norrie thought of Duncan, Ewan, Donald and his Papa – and as he did so, he looked up and through a break in the clouds, he glimpsed the clear dark sky. It was there that Norrie saw four stars burning brightly. They twinkled like North Stars. And it seemed to Norrie that they shone down just on him and they looked awfully kind.

Ch 12

Space and Time

Hope shone like a blazing Arabian sun the following morning. Someone had been found washed up on a beach in Eriskay, barely clinging to life. It was Eddie. 'If Eddie has made it then perhaps Michael and his boys are out there somewhere, too!' Search parties doubled and trebled and quadrupled in size and barely a soul was left indoors. Every beach up and down the southern Outer Hebrides was searched, every dune scrutinised, along with the surrounding land. A temporary command post (of sorts) was set up at Am Politician, Eriskay's main watering hole. Binoculars were whipped up from every window ledge, and the seas were scanned for any sign of life. Three RNLI lifeboats and every fishing vessel that didn't have a hole in its hull searched the Minch and the back of beyond. The hours ticked along that Sunday morning. Noon soon gave way to afternoon, which in turn relinquished its grasp on time to evening sooner than anyone thought fair. But, still, hope was strong. And nowhere was it stronger than in young Norrie MacKinnon. His father was the strongest man he knew. And Duncan, Ewan, and Donald weren't far behind, and they all knew how to swim like fish. Norrie was the only one who never learned how to swim, as he was always too busy cockle raking. Norrie was in a search party that included his brother, Rory, Floonay's top cop, Constable Callie Currie, and their giant white-haired neighbour, Dougie. But the way Norrie was moving he was in actuality a one-man search party.

As the islanders searched for the lost MacKinnons, the medical staff at the hospital were busy tending to Eddie. He had come in hypothermic and had a few broken bones. For a day he drifted in and out of consciousness. His eyes finally opened and for a moment he wondered if he was in heaven or hell. Or somewhere in between. He recognised a few faces. They certainly looked like angels. It was either heaven or Floonay, Eddie concluded. After a period of adjustment, he spoke of their ordeal. The tale he told would strike fear into the heart of every man, woman, and child in the Outer Hebrides.

'We were a mile northeast of Stack, just the back of Eriskay. We could see *Zephyr,* about a mile north of us. The sea wasn't being kind, but it wasn't unlike many other days. But then we looked up and saw an enormous dark mass bearing down on us – I knew then it was THE squall of all squalls. It stretched across the horizon and moved at a merciless pace and there was a wickedness about it, and we knew we better head for shore. I called *Zephyr* but the boys had seen that beast, too, and were already swinging round to port. And though we were being thrashed *Odyssey* was holding true. The boys weren't far behind. The teeth of that beast caught us up as we neared the turn between Stack and Eriskay. I knew the south side of Eriskay would give us shelter. I remember looking astern and seeing *Zephyr* rounding the corner. We were relieved at that moment because as that greatest of all squalls passed over us, we did indeed have shelter! And I remember thinking we would take cover there until it passed. Then there was this tremendous smash, and I thought we'd hit a reef. I gave her full throttle and swung to port and was terribly confused. You see, I know that channel. I was nowhere near a reef. And then there was another great smash that sent us crashing to the deck of the wheelhouse. I recall looking to *Zephyr* and it was as though she was being lifted up out of the water and then she came down with a crash. I swear I saw something. A – a massive body...strike her. In my life, I'll tell you, I've known a few shades of fear, but what I witnessed – that fear went to a dark and forbidding place. I was reaching for the radio and my heart was pounding and I looked to Michael and then Donald, and though I saw great courage, steel, in their eyes, I knew they, too had seen, had felt, something beyond...and it was then that the hull was split in two. The last thing I remember seeing as I glanced astern was an enormous glistening mass passing through the shattered hull. It moved with such ease – right through us! And just as we disappeared under the swells, I swear to you, I never knew that bastard was real, but I swear to you there was something sticking out of it, well out of it. And then there was what happened after – the thrashing. That bastard wasn't satisfied. I swear on my heart that is what I saw, what I heard...and I will never forgive myself for taking them out...we didn't have to go, we didn't need to...' *That's how it happened...I am sure of it.*

But still, hope remained – sort of. Eddie had made it. And though he spoke of that great monster thrashing about, and of the cries of anguish that pierced the storm, not a person thought twice about giving up the search. For days the searches continued. Every dune, beach and rocky enclave along the shoreline was combed, again and again. Every uninhabited island and reef within a three-mile radius was landed on and searched, and every set of binoculars in the southern Outer Hebrides kept a vigilant watch on the seas. But as days stretched past a week the number of searchers decreased – people had to work and shops needed opening.

And though creels needed working, at least the fishermen could keep an eye out for the lost MacKinnons as they went about their business.

The inevitable arrived ten days after that stormy Saturday.

No one wanted to admit it. But truth be told many had felt it all along – a gnawing feeling of dread, a sickly, horrible sensation of fear. During those days, the combined strength of the island kept something enormous from crashing down, as though a giant invisible boulder hovered above the place, being held up by all their quivering arms.

The inevitable: hope fluttered and faltered.

Hope finally faded and it was like trying to stand on the side of a steep mountain gushing dark crude oil from its peak with the heavens raining thick buckets of the slippery darkness, and though you try madly, feverishly, to grab onto something, anything, your grip slips, and you descend...

Hope didn't so much crash – it was swallowed by a black abyss.

The search was called off.

Mrs MacKinnon was a wreck, as were Norrie's sisters. Rory kept himself brain deep in whisky in an effort to dull the pain. But it wasn't just the MacKinnon household that felt the loss of Michael and his three sons. There was a whole island of grief, and it seemed precisely because it was an island that it lingered, not wanting to leave Floonay's shores.

For Norrie the worst part of the ten days since his father's and brothers' disappearance was getting through the second Saturday evening of the last seven years without his father reading to him from the Coquilleuous Rakkeronuous Almenikhiaka. It pained him profoundly but he got through it, sitting up in his room, staring out the window and clutching the pipe that Donald had brought him from Santiago. And though he had shed many a tear in the last ten days and felt a great heaviness and discomfort in his young heart he was the only person who had not given up hope. That evening, as his Mama and brother and sisters regrettably turned their attention to official 'arrangements' Norrie sat up in his room and wrote his first letter:

Dear God,

I read that you are in control of the seas and the skies and everything in between and probably everything even in outer space. So could you please send my father and three brothers back up? I really miss them and am confused as to why you would let the ocean gobble them up in the first place.

Thank you,

Norrie MacKinnon

p.s: I'm not sure where to post this letter to but I heard someone at school saying something about 'space' and 'time' and that you've existed all throughout these things. So I will address it to 'space time'. I hope it finds you.

Now, as Norrie penned his first letter to God, the problem being discussed in the kitchen below was what sort of funeral arrangements or memorial service to organise for four souls who are missing their bodies. Do they warrant a gravestone and coffins in a proper cemetery, or a memorial plaque up on a hill? The question was answered the following morning by a particularly macabre discovery. An arm and half a leg with a yellow welly still fitted on was found washed ashore. The news couldn't be contained or massaged in any way, and when Mrs MacKinnon and her three girls heard they all fainted in shock. Rory screamed in agony and drank a lot of Scotch. Norrie, after vomiting, ran up to his room to write his second letter to the nebulous entity who had obviously fallen asleep at the wheel.

The arm, it was a right arm, was identified as Donald's, as it had a long tattoo of Chile stretching all the way down it, with a star representing Santiago – Chile was one of his favourite places in the world. The half-left leg and foot were unidentifiable and so it was decided that both body parts would be placed in one coffin and there would be one gravestone for all four men.

Dear God,

I don't know what you're up to, but if you're as powerful as I hear you supposedly are then could you please piece my father and brothers back together? Thank you.

I don't know what you're thinking! You're obviously not paying a hell of a lot of attention. Perhaps you've tripped on a crack and have fallen in a hole or something.

I would appreciate it if you could send them back as soon as possible. Look what you've let happen to my Mama and sisters and Rory. I'll be waiting.

Thank you,

Norrie MacKinnon

Right after writing that letter Norrie wrote one more.

Dear God,

I don't know why you would create that terrible whale! Even though Papa had told me the story of it a long time ago and I'd seen that old photograph I always thought that maybe it wasn't real and was just a scary story. Now I know it's real and I don't know why you would give life to such a monster.

I swear to you on the souls of my father and three brothers, if you don't send them back to us, that I will hunt it down and kill it, if it takes me a thousand years.

Thank you again,

Norrie MacKinnon

The following morning was a Thursday and it was announced that the funeral service would take place on the Saturday. Norrie wrote two more letters to God that day asking him to please hurry up with piecing his father and brothers back together. Nothing happened. Late afternoon on Friday Norrie took a good look around the house and outside and in the Nissen hut and everywhere he could think of that God might have put them. Again, nothing. So he wrote two more letters to God asking him with a little more urgency to please hurry up. Nothing. Saturday morning while everyone was getting ready for the service, Norrie blurted out that it should be postponed. He was greeted with much sympathy but he didn't relent and instead became more forceful with his request. *'Now, Norrie, you know we can't do that. I know this is hard...' 'But Mama! They might come back!' 'Oh, Norrie, please...' 'But they might! I, I...'* He hadn't told anyone of the letters he'd been writing to God and was about to, but hesitated. His sisters tried to comfort him but he shrugged them off and ran out of the house and down onto the beach where his father had first taught him how to cockle rake.

Ch 13

Another Surprise

Norrie didn't attend the funeral. His brother, Rory, their neighbour, Dougie, along with Constable Currie and a dozen other men had tried to bring him in, but when he spied them coming across the beach towards him, spread out in one long line he ran north, up and over the dunes and across the machair and over Picnic Hill. The men gave chase but Norrie just turned south and ran right past them, up steep hills and down slippery glens. He flew over rocky shores without missing a beat. He wiggled in and out of every nook and cranny he encountered. The men gave chase as best they could. They huffed and puffed after him, but there was no catching Norrie MacKinnon. If he didn't want to be caught, he wouldn't get caught. The service and funeral were not going to be cancelled. Exhausted and defeated, Rory, Dougie, Constable Currie and the rest of the men, wiped sweat from their brows, adjusted their ties and caps, and headed for the church.

Untimely and sudden deaths are always tragic, and Floonay has known its fair share over the centuries, but there was something particularly cruel about what had happened on that fateful Saturday. Three sons and their father were laid to rest (or, in this particularly grizzly affair, what was left of them). They were eulogised, memorialised, honoured, remembered. They were given first class tickets to what lies next. They would never be forgotten. Their spirits would remain hovering over the island, always. The wake lasted three days. Not a shop opened, nor or a creel shot, nor a scallop scooped up in that time. Constable Currie didn't even bat an eye when Eddie punched Ronnie in the nose, screaming, 'It should have been you and me, you bastard!' he'd seethed, and lifted Ronnie from the floor by his collar as the man cried in agony. Eddie was about to strike again when Dougie held fast his wrist and spoke firmly, 'Duncan and Ewan were already out. It could have been anyone, Eddie, anyone.' Eddie glared at the big man, then relented. He knew. Everyone knew. One never knows when that immensely powerful *force* is going to roll its shoulder and claim another victim. The bloody thing was, they had escaped the sea, or so they had thought, but it was one of her inhabitants who had struck the final blow. 'I'm sorry Ronnie. Let me get you a dram.' Eddie apologised and handed two handkerchiefs to Ronnie who was grimacing in pain, clutching his bloodied nose.

Norrie hadn't attended the wake either. As a matter of fact, Norrie didn't return home for six weeks. Search parties hunted high and low for him but the truth was that when Norrie didn't want to be found he wouldn't be found. Rory had put a stop to the searches three days after the wake. 'He just wants to be alone. Leave him be. He's fourteen for God's sake! Men have gone to sea and war younger than that!' More than a few people also reminded Mrs MacKinnon that Floonay was a small island and a safe place, and not some crime-ridden big city. Constable Currie was no stickler to whatever the laws were as he himself had faked his age when he'd gone to sea. 'Don't you worry, Mrs MacKinnon, I'll keep an eye out for him,' he'd reassured the grieving widow and mother.

Norrie finally returned but did so to an empty house. He looked everywhere but no one was home, so instead he just left this note on the kitchen table and went back out.

Hello Mama, Rory, Maggie, Catherine, and Morag,

I just arrived back and there's no one here. Sorry for being gone so long. I kept searching thinking that maybe Papa and Donald and Duncan and Ewan would show up somewhere, but maybe I was wrong.

I'm off to the Traigh to rake a few cockles. See you for dinner.

Norrie

Norrie was facing east, following the tide as it gently pulled back and back and back. It was a pleasant, calm day, and the sun was out with wispy bits of cloud here and there. Lots of little seabirds scurried about searching for a feed. It had felt reassuring to get his hands back on his favourite rake. Six weeks was a long time to go without cockle raking. And by heaven he'd hit a good spot. Within an hour he'd already filled his bucket three times.

A few specks far along the shoreline to the south caught Norrie's eye. There were four bodies. Four running bodies. As they drew closer he could see hands in the air and they looked like they were celebrating some wonderful thing. He knew who they were. Norrie stayed where he was, an elbow propped up on his rake. There was no reason for them to be so damned excited, he thought. They ought to have known I wasn't going far. Their pace slowed as it was quite a long way from where he was working, and it seemed from their body language that they were confused as to why he wasn't running towards them. They finally arrived all out of breath, his mother and three sisters.

'Norrie, where in God's name have you been?!' his mother asked between breaths as she threw her arms around him.

'Not very far.'

'Oh Norrie! We were so worried!' His sisters all took turns giving him hugs.

'You'd no reason to worry. I was around.'

'Norrie, you weren't there for the service, the funeral, the wake. We missed you. We needed you.'

'There's no reason to get all in a fuss.'

His mother spoke, 'Now Norrie, you really shouldn't have...it was hard on us all. It still is.' They were standing around him looking both joyful and annoyed.

He glanced towards Stack. 'I hadn't given up. I had to look for them.'

'Oh Norrie, you knew what they found. Oh, I'm sorry, it was awful.' Maggie shivered at the thought.

Norrie decided it was best not to mention that he was trying to convince God to piece them back together and send them back.

'Well, never mind. The important thing is you're back. Let's go and get you a nice hot meal. You look famished,' Mrs MacKinnon said, trying not to think about the body parts that washed ashore.

Norrie insisted on raking for a little longer. They insisted he come home with them, but his mind was made up; he was staying out for another little while. They eventually relented and left him to finish up.

Half an hour later Norrie finished up, poked all the cockles into the last net bag and turned for home. Walking alongside the tide he thought about two of the more interesting and unusual methods of gathering cockles that Papa had taught him. You had to take your wellies off for one, and it was called the 'toe wiggle'. It was actually his great x five Grandpa Calum who had come up with this one, and had added it to the Coquilleuous Rakkeronuous Almenikhiaka. He was apparently a bit of a funny man. You walk along in bare feet and every now and again you just give your toes a little wiggle in the sand and see what they find. This method is enormously unproductive but is a lot of fun with children. That was what basically inspired Grandpa Calum to come up with it, because he had had twelve children to entertain as a father. There is one giant warning concerning the 'toe wiggle': if you have really fast toes you must watch out for the razor fish. (Ask anyone who has harvested razor fish – it can be a painful experience if your toe meets one, unaware and at speed) The second method was the more interesting of the two and, amazingly enough, could be hugely productive. It is called the 'walkabout': leave your rake at home and take only your bucket and a few net bags. When you arrive at the beach just start strolling, looking down and all around. You will be amazed at what has been left on the surface. If you wander about long enough, you can easily gather enough for a few meals. And remember that stormy weather always leaves more in its wake.

Norrie recalled Papa telling him that if there are times when you don't feel like picking up your rake, go out anyway and take a little peek around. You'll simply be amazed at what you might find.

*

Norrie got a huge surprise when he arrived home and asked where Rory was.

'He what!!'

'He joined the Army – and he's gone a long way from here.' Mrs MacKinnon was holding a sealed letter and trying to sound brave. 'Here, this is for you. He said he'd be back.'

Norrie took the letter and went straight to his bedroom and shut the door. He tore open the letter and sat at the corner of his bed and read:

Dear Norrie,

I'm sorry I'm not getting a chance to see you before I leave. But you haven't been around. Maybe you'll come home today before I board the ferry.

I can't take this place anymore. Every direction I go I see the sea and I think of Dad and Donald and Ewan and Duncan. I hate it. I don't want to see the sea ever again and that's what I told the recruiter and he promised me I would be posted to a unit hundreds of miles from any ocean.

My joinery work has gone to hell and I can't hold a pair of shears because my hands shake so much Norrie because the only thing I've done for the last five weeks is drink whisky to make the terrible thoughts go away, but it seems to make things even trickier.

I remember my history teacher, Mr MacIntyre, saying that our people helped create some fine places around the world, that in turn grew and grew, and that they gave the world much and that what they did was good, even though sometimes dodgy things took place, but that is bound to happen he said, and even though the empire has changed shape there is still much work to do. I remember he said our mark is everywhere. Perhaps in the Army I can go and help people somewhere else. Can you take care of my sheep while I'm gone Norrie? Thanks. See you later. I hope you're safe.

Rory

Norrie stared at the letter not wanting to believe it was true. That Rory was now gone. But he'd be back, Norrie reminded himself, trying to suppress the bit of guilt that surfaced for being away so long. Norrie read the letter a few more times and prayed that his brother would be okay. He then tucked it back in the envelope and placed it in his secret drawer, pulling out his pipe from Santiago. He cracked the window and at that moment didn't care if anyone walked in and caught him. He poked a little tobacco in, struck a match and sat propped up by the window. He looked out over the Traigh Mhor, the most beautiful beach in the world. Beyond it were the sweeping dunes and the machair and then Picnic Hill. He wondered, not for the first time, how and why such horrible things could come to so beautiful a place?

Ch 14

Wales

Although Norrie was a fourteen-year-old Hebridean boy, he didn't know much about taking care of sheep, which was unusual. Most island boys his age knew exactly what to do – how to control their sheepdog in rounding them up, how to grab the woolly beasts and flip them over, how to whip a line around three legs, and most importantly of all, how to use a pair of shears properly. Apart from that there was the marking of them, the tarring of any cuts, and how to stretch a rubber band around their testicles to castrate the unlucky ones.

A lot of families on Floonay have sheep, not to mention cows and chickens and ducks and pigs. There are a dozen or so ponies to carry the peat over the hills, if need be, or just to feed carrots and apples to. (That's what the ponies prefer) And there are even a few horses for the more well-to-do. Dogs are a-plenty and there's enough cats to keep the rats and the mice on their tiny toes, and if you ever need an instant feed look no further for there are more rabbits than anyone knows what to do with. But Rory was the only MacKinnon boy who'd had sheep. Donald had been a merchant seaman and was gone for long stretches and thus it would have been impractical for him. Duncan and Ewan, although they'd been local fishermen, chose to focus on raising cattle when on dry land. The three of them were, however, decent hands when it came time to help out. It was only Norrie who wasn't the greatest at handling sheep. He'd had a few tries over the years at grabbing them by their woolly coats and shearing them before slapping the MacKinnon mark on their sides, but he'd never castrated one and he didn't have a clue how to control Rory's sheepdog. The thing was, during the annual shearing when all the men were gathered at the pen doing their bit, and if the tide was on its way out, Norrie would nudge his father and say quietly, 'Papa, look, the tide's slipping away, do you mind if I cockle rake instead? I promise I'll try and shear a sheep next time.' Well, his father would cast a squinty eye over to the Traigh Mhor, take a thoughtful puff on his pipe, and say, 'You go ahead son.' And at that Norrie would run like the wind, as excited as a child on the last day of school, to fetch his rake and bucket from the Nissen hut and then fly off down to the big beach. This happened year after year, and that's why three weeks after arriving home from his six-week search, Norrie found himself trying to figure out how to control Bonzo, Rory's half-mad sheepdog, and how he was going to shear 200 sheep all on his own. Well, as it happened, he wasn't on his own. His neighbour, Dougie, was at hand along with other men from the village. But it was still hellish for Norrie, as he had to put in all the effort possible to shear as many sheep as he could, even though the sheep were looking like they wanted anyone else instead. Those shears were sharp, and the sheep had to live with the trimming they got until the following summer. It was a trial by fire, and though there was a little blood spilled and a lot of *'meheheheing'* that didn't sound like happy *'meheheheing'*, Norrie managed all right.

Two months later Norrie received a letter from Rory. It was the happiest day Norrie could remember in a long long time.

Dear Norrie,

I hope you're doing fine. And I hope you managed okay with Bonzo and the sheep during the shearing. I forgot to tell you, but there's a whistle in an old copper tin in the Nissen hut, just to the right of the spanners. Give that a blow and he'll pay attention to you. If you don't have the whistle he'll just run off and hump the first bitch he comes across. I hope he wasn't too much trouble to rein in.

Well, I'm officially a soldier. They said I can try out for one of the more elite units. I'm not sure right now. I have a little time to decide.

I've got some leave coming up so I'll be able to come home for a few days. I should be able to make the ferry crossing okay, even though I still don't like the sea anymore. I'll have a few beers in Oban to relax before I climb aboard, and maybe it will be a nice gentle crossing. And when I get home you can check out my new uniform.

See you soon,
Rory

Well, Norrie couldn't believe it. He was as happy as could be. But then two days later he received another letter.

Dear Norrie,

I'm sorry I won't be able to make it home so soon. They said I had to decide on going on another training course that is starting shortly. I could wait for the next course to begin but that won't be until after Christmas and so I figure since I'll be sleeping outside a lot, I'd rather do it this time of year than in the dead of winter. I'll see you at Christmas.

Rory

Norrie was disappointed and felt a big lump in his belly, but he understood, sort of. The new school year was in session and life for the MacKinnon household moved along. The girls were busy and Mrs MacKinnon went about her business and Norrie did his best to focus at school, but it was hard. He cockle raked whenever he could because that was the only time he really felt any touch of joy or satisfaction. The truth was, there was still an enormously dark cloud over the MacKinnon household. This was understandable, as it had only been a matter of months since Michael and his boys were laid to rest, and, of course, it hadn't helped that Rory had become afraid of the sea and left. But there was plenty of support. Others were always at hand to have a chat and help bake a cake or cook a roast. The whole island was basically one big family, even if there was the odd squabble or rivalry. But the thing was, when the sun set and lights dimmed and bodies slipped under cold blankets with hot water bottles or already toasty warm electric blankets, the truth of the matter was that Mrs MacKinnon, Maggie, Catherine, Morag, and Norrie were left alone with their own thoughts. And in those thoughts darkness lurked. The pain remained, the loss, the sorrow. Broken hearts don't mend that easily.

But there were also better places. Dreams of happier days, of a caring husband, a tender touch, of a father's smile, of endless love, of reading by the fire with Papa and his smoky pipe, of three fantastic brothers, three wonderful sons. These, perhaps, were actually the worst dreams, because at least from the darkest dreams you awoke to something better.

*

Christmas with Rory never came. He died in a helicopter training accident over the Irish Sea. The cause of the crash was never determined. There was no distress call. One eyewitness strolling down a beach along the coast of Wales that day said she saw a bright flash far away on the horizon, but it would never be known if that explosion belonged to Rory's helicopter or not. It probably did. What happened the authorities could never figure out. What was for certain – wreckage was strewn over two square miles. Of the eight souls onboard three bodies were recovered. Rory's was not. It was mid-November of that sad, devastating year, and when news reached Floonay the island doctor and psychiatric nurse had to sedate Mrs MacKinnon and keep her sedated for quite some time. Maggie, Catherine, and Morag didn't need sedation. Something in their brains did it for them. They were in shock and stayed in shock for a very long time. When Norrie got the news, it was the messenger who felt the impact first. He'd been summoned to the fearsome headmistress's office where Constable Currie was waiting. As the words came out Norrie yelled and swung his right arm, cracking the constable on the nose. He ran out of the office and out of the school and didn't stop running until he reached Floonay's highest point. An anger he had never known before burned inside him. He punched the big stone pillar marking the top of Ben Heaval, cracking a bone in the process, then ran off through the middle of the island and didn't stop until he reached the Traigh Mhor. He reached the shoreline and just stood there, dumbstruck. He looked northeast to Eriskay and Stack where the first terrible tragedy occurred. He swivelled all around and looked south, towards the Irish Sea. He muttered, 'They told him he wouldn't have to see the sea.' Then he shouted at the top of his lungs, 'They told him he wouldn't have to see the sea!'

Norrie didn't move from where he stood.

The tide was on its way in. At first, he was only toe deep and then ankle deep, but as the tide flowed in, he was soon calf deep and then knee deep and up and up it crept. He didn't move. A few villagers called to him from the shoreline, but he'd shut his ears off and was oblivious to everything in the physical world. His hand throbbed and stabs of pain pulsed up his arm, but it was nothing compared to his loss, his family's loss. The almost invisible pale moon continued to pull that great blanket of life up the beach. Eventually the MacKinnon's giant neighbour, Dougie, waded out and brought Norrie in.

Ch 15

Godzilla

The MacKinnons made it through that horrible winter, tough as it was. The three girls, aged 20, 21, and 24, all could have left for the mainland, either to continue their education or for a job, but they chose to stay on Floonay. With their father and four of their five brothers now gone it was highly unlikely they would ever leave. The youngest, Morag, helped out in The Butcher's, Catherine assisted in the primary school, and Maggie made the rounds providing assisted care for the elderly. Of course, their attendance records over the previous nine months had, from time to time, seen a few shelves needing stocked, the primary teacher desperate for a hand, and a few pensioners wondering when their dinner was arriving. They did eventually make it through the winter, and slowly ever so slowly things improved. Mrs MacKinnon regained a touch of her old self, and was able, by Easter, to function effectively on her own and without medication. They were able to smile every now and again, and that in itself was an accomplishment.

Norrie had, for the most part, stopped talking. When his teachers asked him a question, he'd just shrug. When his best friend, Malcolm, asked if he wanted to play he'd say no and walk away, and one time when he pestered Norrie, desperate to play Commando, Norrie punched him on the nose. 'Ahhh! Norrie! Why d'you hit me!! I just wanted to play!!' Norrie replied, 'There are no games anymore! And I don't ever want to play Commando again! Rory played Commando and look what happened to him, the Irish Sea swallowed him!' 'Ahh, my nose...it hurts!' Norrie ended with, 'Life is a bastard, Malcolm...there are no games anymore!' And then he turned and strode off leaving his best friend hopping in agony. Norrie's mother and sisters would attempt to converse with him but he'd say he was too tired to talk and would go to his room. He kept cockle raking, of course, but even that had lost most of its joy. It did help, though. Every day when he pulled on his wellies it felt as though they were full of lead, and when he grabbed what used to be his favourite rake it felt like someone had switched it for another – it didn't feel quite right. But he kept on. He'd trudge, no longer fly, down to the beach. He'd pick a spot and start. It had become drudgery, but it was an escape and it kept him occupied. It helped him, if just a little, to feel the tiniest speck of, if not joy – but satisfaction. Just the tiniest speck. He tried his best not to look towards Stack or Eriskay, although he inevitably would. He hated thinking, because to think was to question, and to question was to seek an answer, and what sort of worthwhile answer was there for cruelty and death and loss?

A handful of Floonay's fishermen would still stop by for a chat, but Norrie kept the conversations as brief as possible. No, he wasn't interested in heading out fishing. No, he wouldn't be going to the dance. No – no – no. He was closing up.

And although he kept the *Coquilleuous Rakkeronuous Almenikhiaka* tucked away under his bed, reading from it every Saturday evening – a little adventure story, a few tips and techniques, the odd warning – he had stopped thinking about the story with the greatest secret ever, that his father had shared with him, because it wasn't real. What sort of place contains that sort of secret and also lets such terrible things happen? It was pure rubbish. Tosh!

He didn't stop writing his letters to that character he was beginning to doubt had any powers whatsoever, because he never received a response and his Papa and brothers had not been delivered back to him. One day at school a girl in his class had what the teacher explained afterwards was an epileptic fit, a seizure. It had been a particularly severe case and she was flown to the mainland for evaluation and some sort of surgery. After cockle raking later that evening, Norrie sat at his little desk and penned another letter.

Dear God,

There is a girl in my class and today she had a terrible accident, an epileptic fit the teacher said. It was a frightening scene. She was banging on the desk and on the floor and she even smashed her head a few times against the ground. Her legs were kicking and she looked to be in terrible pain.

It took three teachers to get a hold of her.

Why would you let such a thing happen?

I heard someone say that you made us in your image. I guess that means you also get epileptic fits. Does that mean I will, too? Will everyone?

You know, a long time ago, after I heard you were so powerful and were in command of so much and that you had only one son, and I thought to myself, 'how could such a thing be? He must have lots of sons, hundreds or even thousands or millions, and daughters, too?'

But now I realise after all these tragedies and terrible things that I hear about, that perhaps you don't even have one son, and if you do, he must be locked up in a dungeon somewhere not being able anymore to do what he's supposed to be doing.

Perhaps something has sapped your power? I don't know, because you don't even have the power or energy to reply to one of my letters. Maybe you're being kept locked up in a dungeon as well.

Well, perhaps I'll keep an eye out for you, too, and if I do find that you've been tricked and locked up somewhere I'll try and help you escape so you can do whatever it is you're supposed to be doing.

Thank you,

Norrie MacKinnon

Norrie received no response to this letter and he still hadn't stumbled across his father and four brothers anywhere. And nor did he find God wedged under a boulder looking for a helping hand. News arrived from the mainland that there was a complication with his classmate's surgery and that she would be in hospital longer, and Norrie overheard a few teachers whispering that if she did pull through, she might never be quite the same again.

One thing didn't change that year, or the next, and it was much to the dismay of more than just a few islanders. Norrie kept taking top prize in the cockle raking competitions. But it wasn't just that he took the prizes, it's how he did it. When he stepped onto the Traigh Mhor that first summer after the tragedies, it was like a year of frustration and anger was released all at once. Although his day-to-day raking had provided him with just the barest amount of satisfaction, and his daily walks to the beach felt like death marches, it somehow fuelled his performance on the day that mattered. He didn't let up for one tiny second and expected no quarter in return. When the whistles blew, the results were so lopsided you'd have thought he was raking with twelve arms and six rakes.

Now the thing was, and this was what really had a vocal group up in arms, he not only beat the trousers off the adults, but he re-entered the 14 – 17-year-old group. 'You can't do that Norrie!' one father had protested. And soon after, other grumpy voices joined in. They mobbed around the competition committee who were seated around their desk, along the western edge of the beach. Well, the rule books were reviewed and checked and nowhere was it stated that this could not happen. Their decision had been final: Norrie MacKinnon could compete in his own age category as well as the adult category. There were cries of protest and it was quite a riotous scene for a few moments, but tempers subsided when people caught sight of Mrs MacKinnon and her three daughters sitting by the dunes. Then they looked over at Norrie standing with his rake, and everyone remembered the previous summer. The grumbling diminished and everyone eventually took their seats. Some parents could only peek through fingers and some didn't watch at all. A few of the boys Norrie was competing against quivered in their wellies. One was so frightened he peed his pants, and another threw down his rake and quit before the start whistle sounded. Norrie annihilated the competition, but life went on for everyone except for Norrie's epileptic classmate – she died from surgical complications.

*

One uneventful day during Norrie's last year of school he was called to the headmistress's office. It was a blustery grey October day. A low-pressure system had parked itself right off the western coast of the Hebrides and was reminding everyone why there were so few trees around – they had all been blown away. And why every building was made of stone – because if they weren't, they would be blown away as well.

Norrie didn't have a clue why he was being summoned. He hadn't been in any fights recently, his attendance record was pretty good and he hadn't been giving the teachers any grief. Mostly he would stare off into space and keep himself to himself.

The headmistress's secretary showed him in, all the while giving him a most curious look. Her nose was scrunched up as though she'd just smelled something repulsive, her mouth was tight lipped and all wriggly as though she was chewing on some foul thing she couldn't spit out, and through her ancient spectacles her eyes were wide, casting a look that was both fearful and furious.

What's wrong with her?

'Norrie MacKinnon here to see you, Mizz Fizzlezwit.' And with that the secretary retreated as though backing away from an infectious virus.

The door was shut and Norrie looked around. 'Mama?'

And Mama wasn't the only one. Norrie looked around some more. What a strange collection of people, he'd thought. There was Constable Currie, the island doctor, the local psychiatric nurse, the parish priest and local reverend, *and* – the head postwoman?

'Oh Norrie,' Mrs MacKinnon wailed. 'What have you done?' She dabbed an eye trying her best to stay composed.

'What – Mama?' Norrie was confused. If it had just been the creepy headmistress and Constable Currie he would have simply expected more tragic news, but – *this* collection of people?

Constable Currie cast him a look of sympathy. Norrie translated it to, 'Don't worry, son, you'll be all right – *maybe*.' Norrie liked Constable Currie. He had broken the policeman's nose and could have been in a fair bit of trouble for doing so, but nothing had ever come of it. Constable Currie had come knocking and Norrie had thought that he was done for, but instead they'd just had a quiet chat. Amongst a number of items discussed Constable Currie had informed Norrie his punch had resulted in the fifth time that the ex-sailor had his nose broken.

The island doctor, Dr Samuel Bartlett, was studying him carefully through a set of thick black glasses perched on a long straight nose. He sniffed at the air and Norrie wondered if that's how he diagnosed patients. The priest and the reverend were standing side by side, Father John and Reverend Cullen. They each had a firm grip on a bible. The priest was tall and thin with jet black hair combed straight back. The reverend was on the shorter side, corpulent and with bushy, sandy hair. They both wore glasses and their looks hovered somewhere between the secretary's mixed state of fear and fury and the doctor's careful scientific eye. They all appeared puzzled. Norrie's gaze next landed on Floonay's head postwoman, Mrs McCracken. Mrs McCracken had shoulder length auburn curls with which she couldn't stop fidgeting and her right foot ground an imaginary cigarette into the carpet. She was clearly uncomfortable. And then there was the headmistress, Mizz Fizzlezwit. Well, she had sharp, wary, battle tested eyes that were magnified by horn-rimmed spectacles. Her hair was wound all around and fashioned up like a nest for a giant bird – a giant scary bird. Her features were taut, with bone and sinew writhing under the surface. She was a force to be reckoned with and could strike fear into the heart of many an adolescent. But there was also something else that she couldn't quite conceal behind her considerable armour, though she fought hard to suppress it – a touch of uncertainty as to the strength of this new adversary. Norrie glanced to his Mama, who wasn't doing a good job of staying composed, and then he looked to the last person in the room. It was one of the local nurses, Ms Campbell. Her eyes were bright blue and happy. She didn't look angry or afraid or worried or furious, and instead was just as calm and peaceful as could be.

'Ohh, Norrie,' his mama sniffled. 'Why – why couldn't you grieve like a normal human being.'

'What Mama?'

'And I thought all those evenings you were just reading your comics.' More sniffles.

What? What were all these people doing in Mizz Fizzlezwit's office? He hadn't done anything wrong.

'Ohhhh Norrie, why couldn't you have just stuck to your Commando comics?' Mrs MacKinnon sniffled and dabbed her eyes with a tissue.

That's when Norrie realised there was a cardboard box situated right in the middle of Mizz Fizzlezwit's desk. It had no top on it and inside there was a little mountain of...envelopes? Some of them were open and you could see the unfolded letters. He suddenly recognised those envelopes and letters. *Those are my letters?!* And then he noticed that *everyone* had one in hand.

He'd posted them to God. *How did they end up here!?* He looked to Mrs McCracken, who mouthed the words, 'I'm sorry.' *What had she done with my letters?!* Norrie had the terrible sensation that he had been betrayed.

*

Earlier in the day the well-intentioned and gentle Mrs McCracken had approached the formidable headmistress with her concern, along with the big box of letters. You see, for the previous two years she had been putting the letters that were addressed to God in Space Time in the special box for undeliverable mail and although she considered them a bit strange she gave them little thought. But recently a return address had appeared: N. MacKinnon, 10 Steagh, Isle of Floonay, Outer Hebrides. And it appeared again, and again, and of course she knew who lived there, and obviously was aware of the great tragedies and thus her concern lay with Norrie's wellbeing. Well, there was Mrs McCracken and Mizz Fizzlezwit and the big box of letters in her office. At first Mizz Fizzlezwit just observed the box with a curious squint in her eye, as though waiting for it to start creeping like a turtle. And then, carefully, she waded her hand in turning over one sealed envelope and then another and yet another. *My, my, what in heaven's name is this?* Her curiosity blossomed. *My God, what sort of boy does this? There are hundreds! Addressed to God? In Space Time?!* This flustered Mizz Fizzlezwit, though she hid it well. *What in heaven's name is Space Time?! How dare he!* She did not like the fact that this had her flustered. *How dare that little MacKinnon!* She was not a happy headmistress, and it was then that she broke the seal on the first envelope. 'But Mizz Fizzlezwit...' Mrs McCracken started. 'But what?' Mizz Fizzlezwit glared hard at the gentle soul. 'I'm sorry. Nothing, Mizz Fizzlezwit...' She skimmed one letter and then another and another yet. *Dear God! What – is this?! Who, who in their right mind writes this?!* Mizz Fizzlezwit was aghast – never in her life had she read such blasphemy, such heresy, such strange and inappropriate things! *And right here on Floonay!*

This needs dealing with immediately and with extreme prejudice!

It was then that she'd hatched her plot, and it was as if it simply materialised right before her mind's eye. Like a miracle, a *vision!* It was a message from God. It must be God's will, she'd concluded: Mrs McCracken would attend to testify, Mrs MacKinnon would attend to be shamed, Father John and Reverend Cullen would attend to offer any final prayers for the unredeemable, Dr Bartlett and Floonay's psychiatric nurse, Ms Campbell would attend to sign the necessary paperwork and sedate the patient in preparation for transport to the finest (by that she meant cruellest) asylum the mainland had to offer, and finally Constable Currie would attend to restrain the wicked little devil if he did not willingly comply.

That was her secret plan.

A few emergency calls later the stage was set for the inquisition, and within fifteen minutes everyone was assembled in her office. Now, fifteen minutes was not a long time and so Mizz Fizzlezwit had to think lightning fast. She had not the time to review every single letter, barely scanning a dozen of them. But there was one unshakable objective. And it was with that in mind she realised that the evidence might just need a little altering, a little spicing up, to ensure everyone was in agreement. *I'll hand one out for each of them to feast on, but the others will be staying right here under my control.*

In the hastily arranged meeting:

'He's been writing letters to God. Hundreds and hundreds of them *and* putting them in the post and addressing them to Space Time. He thinks our Lord lives in Space Time! Here, look at this...and this...' She started shoving a few letters into the hands of the attendees.

'Ohh, my Norrie, what's happened to him?'

'Your Norrie indeed, Mrs MacKinnon. I'm afraid he has a serious problem.'

'Ohh, noooo, not another tragedy.'

'Now, now, Mizz Fizzlezwit, Norrie and the MacKinnons have been through a lot...'

Everyone was in agreement that there was reason for concern. Certainly plenty of children post letters to Santa Claus during the run up to Christmas, and to the Easter Bunny as March hops along, and many people do write little blurbs to God thanking him for love and pretty flowers and nice sunsets and such like, and stick them all under fridge magnets or in diaries or whatever. But when they learned that young Norrie MacKinnon was *actually* posting letters, *hundreds* of letters, to God, with stamps and all, well, this could definitely be the symptom of a serious underlying issue.

'And you wouldn't believe the things he's written! Vile! Swear words even! Plenty...'

Of the dozen letters she had read she had not come across one swear word, but was certain they were there somewhere. And then the formidable headmistress's eyes narrowed. Of course! I bet you it's in there, too...probably...most certainly...the ends justifies the means...God understands what I must do to get this wretch to an asylum...Mizz Fizzlezwit needed everyone shocked, disgusted and onboard. Her grip tightened on the box. 'And, do you want to know what else he's written, Mrs MacKinnon, in these – *these* terrible letters?'

Mrs MacKinnon looked meek, shook her head and didn't know what to say.

What followed was a moment of dramatic silence as Mizz Fizzlezwit looked slowly around the room and then her gaze settled heavily on Norrie's Mama.

'Vile, vile, terrible things, Mrs MacKinnon.'

'Wh - what, not my Nu - Norrie?'

'Yes, your Norrie, Mrs MacKinnon.' Forgive me this teeny-weeny little fib, Lord, but you understand sometimes these measures are necessary, and besides, I've only read a few of the hundreds of these things – it's probably in there somewhere.

'Ohh, my, ohhhh no, not my Norrie....'

'I'm afraid so Mrs MacKinnon. Terrible, terrible, wicked stuff.'

The others in the room took second glances at the letters they'd been handed. There was a mixture of curiosity and fear. Father John, Reverend Cullen, and Mrs McCracken were petrified of stumbling across some word or phrase they'd missed, whereas Dr Bartlett and Ms Campbell re-read the letters they were handed through a clinical lens. *Poor fellow seemed in despair and questioning things...but?* Mrs MacKinnon couldn't bear to re-read hers and Constable Currie couldn't be bothered.

'I didn't want to poison your minds, ladies and gentlemen. The X-rated letters are in here. Safely tucked away so they can't do any damage.' Mizz Fizzlezwit's cold, bony grip tightened on the cardboard box. And at that she'd buzzed her secretary to send for the condemned little wretch. She had to make sure to keep things rushed and a little off-balance, so that with any luck the little monster would be strapped in on the 4pm flight bound for the mainland.

*

Norrie was front and centre. Mizz Fizzlezwit looked around the room with the fierce eyes of a skilled predator, and the letters rustled in her claw so violently that it made the postwoman jump again. She revelled in tension and successfully raised it to a more pleasing level.

‘*Weeeee’ve* just been reading through a few of your letters, young man. My, oh my, haven’t you been a busy little bee. Busy indeed. Busy doing *the devil’s* work!’ Mizz Fizzlezwit rustled the letters because it made her feel powerful. ‘Do you know, young man, that there was a day that *THIS!* would have seen you charged *with HERESY! BLASPHEMY!* do you know what they used to do with *HERETICS!?!* with *BLASPHEMERS!?!* You think God lives in *Space Time?*’

While Mrs MacKinnon sobbed a little, the others in the room shared a strange look: *errr, what was that again?*

Mizz Fizzlezwit was such a frightful and powerful oddity that no one really knew half the time how to act, or react, in her company. It was a bit like tiptoeing around a landmine. And she was the headmistress after all. She had power and influence, and it always came back to this – she could be a terrifying force for young and old alike.

Precious few ever tried to steer her thoughts, let alone interrupt her. But Father John was one. He had to be brave and try, for one of his flock was clearly not well. ‘Norrie, my boy, God lives in…’

‘I think that’s quite enough from the good Father!’ Mizz Fizzlezwit shoved her voice back into the conversation. She indulged herself and read from the damning evidence. *This should convince a few of them - and I don’t even have to alter anything – yet.* ‘Dear God, I read in Papa’s book, the Coquilleuous Rakkeronuous Almenikhiaka, that you have a light side and a dark side…’ she peeled off her horn-rimmed spectacles. And though she wanted to damn Norrie and shame his mother for even proposing such a heretical thing such as God having both a light and a dark side, she couldn’t stifle her curiosity and this is what came out instead, ‘What – in God’s good, heavenly, and holy name, Norrie MacKinnon, is the *Coquilleuous Rakkeronuous Almenikhiaka?*’

Norrie looked at his upset Mama. She was shaking her head.

'WE-E-E-LLLLLLLL?'

'It's – it's my Papa's special book.'

'Your Papa's *special book?* Your Papa's special book thinks God has a – *dark side?'* Her gaze fell hard on Mrs MacKinnon, where it stayed, burning, for quite some time.

'But it's not just that! It's mostly about cockle raking!' Norrie piped up.

'A book about cockle raking? Interesting, very interesting. Please, tell me about this book.' Dr Bartlett suggested and tried to steer the conversation to a more reasonable place.

Norrie could tell that the doctor was interested and this excited him and for a moment he forgot all about the fiery Mizz Fizzlezwit. 'Well, it's a book on all things to do with cockle raking. How to rake and where to rake and what techniques to employ...'

'Really?'

'Oh, yes, really. And there's also lots of stern warnings and adventure stories.'

'Adventure stories? Is that so?' Dr Bartlett was jotting little notes on a small pad and everyone in the room, except for Mizz Fizzlezwit, was relieved that the mood had lightened.

'Oh yes! Stories like what Tumsch Galbraith did.'

'Tumsch Galbraith?'

'Oh – he was the greatest cockle raker ever! And he saved thousands of people, too – it was at the end of the Boer War and he'd decided to stay in South Africa for a little while longer because he heard of some people who needed help, but he had to sneak away from his regiment because they were getting ready to sail home. It's an amazing story. But my Papa wasn't far behind in terms of being the greatest cockle raker ever. He wasn't even as far back as second best! He was first and a half – almost the same as great times eight Grandpa Cloon, who was first and a third.'

'Great times eight Grandpa Cloon?' Dr Bartlett was thoroughly interested, and wasn't the only one who was wondering how in heaven's name you come in first and a third or first and a half?

'Oh yes! You've never heard of Great Grandpa Cloon? He was the first person to discover cockles on Floonay. Well, I think someone from France found them first because they used to be known as *coquilles*. But Great Grandpa Cloon was definitely the first person to on Floonay. He even put a little note in the Coquilleuous Rakkeronuous Almenikhiaka that he thought the name sounded silly and that he could come up with a better name, but since they'd already been named he had to stick with it. '

'Well, young man, I can honestly say I never knew that.' Dr Bartlett looked around the room. 'Did anyone else know that?'

'Well, I knew it was a MacKinnon. Didn't know who or when. It was a long, long time ago,' Constable Currie said, relieved that Dr Bartlett had taken control of the conversation.

'Yes, yes, indeed, Constable.' Dr Bartlett nodded his agreement. 'Great times eight Grandpa is a long time ago, Norrie.'

Norrie was excited to be talking about his favourite book and he'd forgotten all about Mizz Fizzlezwit's anger, even though he could see her out of his peripheral vision, and it appeared as though she was mightily discontented. Like an angry volcano, she clearly wanted to spit out more fire.

'Well, well, that is interesting.'

'Oh yes! And then he started taking notes about lots of different things, so any future MacKinnons who wanted to cockle rake could learn a few things and wouldn't have to start from scratch again and get all bloodied like he did in the beginning, and then subsequent cockle raking MacKinnons all began contributing little bits of information here and there, and the Coquilleuous Rakkeronuous Almenikhiaka grew and grew and grew.'

'Like a volume of encyclopaedias, eh son?' Constable Currie said encouragingly. This was turning into quite a pleasant conversation.

'Oh yes, except it's a lot more exciting and interesting and some of the stories are even scary – but a good scary!'

'Like a scary ghost story,' Nurse Campbell smiled.

The pretty nurse's smile made Norrie smile. 'That's right. Except the stories from the Coquilleuous Rakkeronuous Almenikhiaka are real!' He paused and reflected. 'Well, most of the stories are real, and the tips and techniques and the stern warnings are, too – but some of the stuff isn't exactly true.'

'Well, well, perhaps this just about wraps things up...' Constable Currie started.

The conversation was not going the way the headmistress had planned! *THIS WRAPS NOTHING UP!!! Didn't you all hear what I said he'd written!! He's a devious little monster!! He's posting letters to God!! Isn't that enough? Ahhh!!* If you could have peeked inside Mizz Fizzlezwit's brain you would have seen a frightening sight.

'That's quite enough about his crazy damned *COCKLES!!*' Mizz Fizzlezwit pierced the newly pleasant atmosphere and detonated a grenade of hostility and tension. *Much better!* Mizz Fizzlezwit flipped a page and prepared to read more damning evidence, *I better find some good stuff...I better make this brilliantly revolting....Aha! Perhaps this will help convince these non-believers, especially that damned atheist Dr Bartlett!* (The fact that Dr Samuel Bartlett was actually a man of considerable faith, who could be found in church always on time, was irrelevant to Mizz Fizzlezwit. If she decided that you were an atheist, then that is what you were.

She would have had a great career during the Spanish Inquisition.) As she scanned the letter she became momentarily confused – *what on earth does this mean?! who writes these things! He's just a boy – ah, a boy maybe, but he's a wicked little spawn of the Devil!* With the Will of God undoubtedly fuelling her, Mizz Fizzlezwit prepared to make her first edit but changed tack instantly and instead said this. 'Mrs MacKinnon, in this letter in my hand, your son and that cursed book of his blames all of our earthly ills on God. Can you believe it? All of them!'

Norrie's memory scrolled through the hundreds of letters he'd sent over the years. *What? That's not right...*This was the contents of the letter:

'Dear God, I read that you gave the power of free will to man and therefore all that he does is his responsibility. Well, where was my Papa's and brothers' will allowed to exercise itself against that horrible storm and that terrible monster? And what about my classmate who smashed her head and died? Where was her free will to stop her head smashing against the floor? And I read in the paper the other day about a baby born with no arms? And then I overheard two of our teachers talking about a friend of theirs who had lived with some mental disorder her whole life that made her flip out and overreact all the time and then she killed herself because her life was so screwed up and she simply couldn't cope? Where did you put their free will? Maybe you accidentally dropped it in a bush or something? Maybe you're not what people think you are. I read in the *Coquilleuous Rakkeronuous Almenikhiaka* that free will might just be your alibi. Why do you give such great strengths to some and not to others? Is this some sort of tricky game that you like to play? And why, oh, why, do you let such terrible things happen? I am really and truly confused...'

Back to Mizz Fizzlezwit burning her fiery gaze into poor Mrs MacKinnon:

'Your husband had a book, your son *has* a book, that blames God for our earthly ills??!! Your son thinks that God dropped free will in a big bush!? I don't know what sort of man your husband was!'

At those words Norrie froze. Mrs MacKinnon had started sobbing again and tried muttering an apology. As for the rest of the room, well – everyone had known Michael MacKinnon and his boys. The headmistress had crossed a line that only she thought was okay...not that she cared one tiny bit.

How dare she! Norrie was fuming. 'Why!! You – *that's not right!'*

Father John raised a calming hand, 'Please, please, let's just settle down. Now, Norrie, we know you've been through a lot these past few years and it must hurt terribly, but if you want to 'talk to God' well, you should come and see one of us.' He gestured to Reverend Cullen who nodded his sincere assent. 'It's much safer. We have plenty of pre-written letters, prayers, Norrie, for you to recite. Our prayers come in quite handy, and it will save you from just rambling on with all these thoughts and questions.' He wagged a finger. 'Too many questions can get a little dangerous, young man. You're best to stop writing letters and do remember that God wants the best for you and is looking out for you, and...'

'He didn't look out for my Papa!' Norrie cried out. 'Or Donald or Rory or Ewan or Duncan or...or, or *anyone!'*

'Now, now, calm down...uh, Norrie,' Constable Currie said, keeping a wary eye on the headmistress.

Now, if Norrie wasn't so fuming from what Mizz Fizzlezwit had said about his Papa, perhaps he would have focused more on the pack of lies that had just come out of her mouth, but he didn't, and instead he focused on his Papa. He might have been physically standing in that office but in his mind he went somewhere else: there was his Papa, with his big moustache and his smoky pipe and kind eyes. And then he came back to the physical world and there in front of him was his horrible headmistress. Her words sailed through his mind like a black ship of death.

Mrs MacKinnon sobbed and shook her head – she didn't want her son to say anything else, or if he did to *please, please, please!* make something up or say it was all just one big joke.

'If I drew a picture of the smelliest fart in the world, it would be better looking than you.' Norrie said these words so quietly and so in control, (they were also so unexpected) that all everyone else could do was just stare.

Well, Mizz Fizzlezwit shuddered, and her fingernails sank into the desk. Her love for anger was real, but she always managed to top it off with just the right amount of conjured disgust. In this case, however, there was no need to pretend anything. At that moment steam not only whistled from her ears, it rose from her skull, seeping through her giant bird nest – like smoke that wafts from a smouldering bush just before it bursts into flames. Mrs McCracken fidgeted nervously, and Father John's and Reverend Cullen's brows had crumpled into perplexed messes. Mrs MacKinnon was sobbing away, and though Constable Currie remained alert he rolled his eyes at the whole charade. Dr Bartlett found this young man very, very interesting, and though Ms Campbell had serious misgivings about the state of the headmistress's mind, she looked as pleasant as ever.

My verdict is assured! Is this not enough? Mizz Fizzlezwit's mouth burst open and along with all the steam that whistled out she bellowed, 'Norrie MacKinnon! Who the devil do you think you are?!!'

'Go to hell! *YOU HORRIBLE WITCH!'*

Ch 16

The Aftermath

Norrie's words scorched the headmistress's ears something awful. She leapt from behind her desk like Godzilla from the deep blue sea as a harpoon is fired up his backside. It was an impressive sight.

'WITCH?! WITCH!! Why you devil, Norrie MacKinnon!!'

'YOU'RE WORSE THAN A WITCH!'

'In all my years I've never known such a wicked little MONSTER!!'

'You're a, you're a...' Norrie tried desperately to fend off the headmistresses' fiery assault, but it was hard for she was amazingly skilled in the art of anger.

'You BLASPHEMER Norrie MacKinnon!'

'You're a...you're a...' Norrie was trying hard

'...We should be tying you to a stake and burning you to redemption!!' Volleying hate was no problem for Mizz Fizzlezwit.

'You're worse than a witch!' he just managed to sneak through the headmistress's assault.

'HERESY AND BLASPHEMY – Norrie MacKinnon!' Mizz Fizzlezwit swatted Norrie's words away as though they were flies and hers were giant cannon balls.

And then Norrie managed to hold off the headmistress's verbal barrage long enough to get this out, 'You're a wart! A wart too horrible for even a witch's nose!'

'A – A?' Mizz Fizzlezwit came to a jerky astonished halt.

'Too horrible for even a WITCH'S NOSE!! Or a frog's! Or anything!!'

The room fell silent. Even Mrs MacKinnon stopped sobbing for a moment, as all eyes swivelled from the headmistress and then to young Norrie.

It didn't take long for Mizz Fizzlezwit to locate her detonation button. *'A WHAT DID YOOOUUUUU SAY!!??!!!'*

Well, *HOLY MAMA*, that harpoon was just rammed in another yard and it was like a dozen firecrackers were snapping, crackling, and popping under the headmistress's incredibly impaled backside. And so it would be that with all the righteous steam whistling out of Mizz Fizzlezwit's head and with Norrie daring to take a stand, things got enormously crazy in the headmistress's office. Classes from one end of the school to the other felt the tremor. Mizz Fizzlezwit thundered on something awful and as she did Norrie's poor Mama started wailing like never before, and at the sight of all the wailing and anger Mrs McCracken had a severe panic attack and God's two earthly representatives shook with fright as though they'd been thrown into an exorcism ritual that they weren't qualified to perform. Dr Bartlett sniffed the chaos and quietly observed the whole spectacle, like a scientist who studies the curious habits of things in the wild.

It took Constable Currie to finally settle things down, 'Oh for *GODSSAKE!* Mizz Fizzlezwit! Would you *PLEASE* shut up!! And Norrie, *TAKE IT EASY!* Ms Campbell, take care of her!' He looked from the nurse and then over to the poor postwoman, who was reaching the zenith of her anxiety. 'And you two, heaven's to be gentlemen, pull yourselves together!' He put a gentle hand on Mrs MacKinnon's shoulder. 'Now, let's just calm down here people.'

Well, as you can probably imagine this was a tall order. But with a bit of effort the chaos subsided. Father John found some inner strength and did what he could to get the headmistress calmed down, as Reverend Cullen dipped into a previously hidden reservoir of courage and approached Norrie with body language that signalled he was coming in peace. Although a little surprised by the headmistress's behaviour Dr Bartlett remained mostly unaffected throughout the whole ordeal. He jotted down indecipherable notes, all the while keeping a careful eye out for a flying shoe, or textbook, or paperweight. Ms Campbell soothed the frayed nerves of Mrs McCracken out in the hallway. Constable Currie consoled Mrs MacKinnon, whose tears had finally started drying up, and Norrie and Mizz Fizzlezwit retreated reluctantly to their corners like a pair of boxers who didn't want the round to end.

What came next could be best described as an awkward moment. With a certain measure of calm descending, a look was shared – where does this little meeting go from here? Well, Norrie wasn't interested. Without punching anyone on the nose he walked out of the office and down the hall and out of the school. He vowed to never step one foot back inside.

*

And so it was that Norrie never would.

On that blustery October day after leaving Castlebay school for the very last time he did the only thing he loved to do: with his yellow wellies slipped on and his favourite rake in hand, he trotted off to the Traigh Mhor. Of course, things were far from rosy in the MacKinnon household. Mrs MacKinnon had left Mizz Fizzlezwit's office in a great state of distress and uncertainty, and though she wasn't quite broken, she was close it. The headmistress had not succeeded in having Norrie sent to an asylum, but her mission of shaming his Mama had worked better than she could have ever imagined. Mrs MacKinnon would end up back on her meds to help her cope, and it would appear that all the healing of the previous winter was gone forever. Norrie's sisters weren't sure how to deal with this new twist in the family's cruel fate. They loved their little brother but – *what he'd been doing? What he'd been writing? The things they'd heard?* It was a difficult thing to discuss and made just about everyone feel uncomfortable.

<u>Regarding The Letters</u>

Dr Bartlett and Constable Currie had approached the headmistress and asked for them to be returned to their rightful owner. Mizz Fizzlezwit being Mizz Fizzlezwit did not attempt to intimidate individuals of similar stature, but she was able to maintain her granite solid stance of ultimate moral superiority and declared that the burning of the letters was the appropriate thing to do. 'Just imagine, gentlemen, had those letters ended up in the hands of some innocent child? The damage they would have done? The chaos they would create? I did what God wanted me to do – I burned them.' 'Did you know, Mizz Fizzlezwit, that those letters didn't belong to you, they were not yours to burn.' What shock! 'Well, Constable, and who do they belong to? Norrie MacKinnon voluntarily relinquished them, and how was that fragile wreck Mrs McCracken going to post them to heaven!? She can barely walk out her front door in the morning without frightening herself to bits! But I'll give you this, gentlemen, since they were addressed to God, perhaps, just perhaps Father John or Reverend Cullen had the rights to them? Which one? I was doing God's will, now if you excuse me gentlemen, I have a generation of children to influence!' And that was that.

The interesting thing was that when Mizz Fizzlezwit first read the letters they had actually gone beyond repulsing her in the same way that she regularly got repulsed by lowlifes, dimwits, beggars, the indolent, the physically and *especially* the mentally weak and, of course, the poor. It was as though a few of those lines Norrie had written had opened up just the tiniest crack in her mind and for the briefest moment she peered into something that confused and frightened her to the core. She, of course, managed to fill in that crack lightning-fast and realised the matter needed dealing with immediately and with extreme prejudice. It was the only way.

News of the incident had spread around the island faster than flatulence in a small stuffy room. And though more than a few raised an eyebrow at the headmistress's reported behaviour, the majority of the gossip focused squarely on Norrie MacKinnon and the hundreds of letters he'd posted to God. It was a difficult thing for most to understand or forget. And the supposed content of those letters?! Mizz Fizzlezwit did her best to ensure, in the manner only skilled manipulators are capable, that her accounting of things didn't die – whilst queuing at the Butcher's, the Post Office, or the Top Shop, on her way in to and out of church every Sunday, anywhere and everywhere she could think of she kept the flame alive, as it were. This went a considerable way to ostracising the whole MacKinnon family. Even the most polite and kind folk couldn't help but feel uncomfortable around Mrs MacKinnon or her three daughters. No one was openly hostile to them – things were just awkward. Mrs MacKinnon found she wasn't being invited to as many social gatherings and her girls were often left scraping the bottom of the barrel for a suitable dance partner at the local ceilidhs. This had led to a great deal of frustration, and as much as they loved their weird little brother, the three girls couldn't help but vent all that frustration in his direction.

Whenever Constable Currie found himself drawn into what had become the 'inevitable conversation' for quite some time, he did his level best to keep thoughts and opinions and assumptions from getting out of hand. The damage, you could say, was done to the MacKinnon household, and Norrie found little reason to spend much time anywhere but on the Traigh Mhor. When he wasn't on the big beach he'd tinker in the Nissen hut and for a long long time ate all his meals out there only venturing into the house to sleep. He eventually started sleeping in the Nissen hut as well as he was becoming more upset with what had become a terribly discontented household. He had given up trying to convince anyone of what he had and had not written. He just stopped caring what anyone thought. His father and brothers had been taken away. He no longer believed that there was any God whatsoever and as far as he was concerned the world was a cruel and terrible place. He thought *it* might as well be dead. And that is the way things would stay for quite some time.

Ch 17

Serendipity?

Despair, frustration, anxiety, dread, ultimate misery, anger, and unrest all festered in the MacKinnon household like a virus. Not entirely unexpected considering what the family had been through. Tragedy was stacked upon tragedy, upon tragedy, like a pile of rotting corpses. And the discovery of Norrie's letters ensured it was all smeared with a heavy grimy layer of shame and embarrassment. Mrs MacKinnon was on her meds and washed them down with a lot of vodka and gin. Morag ended up leaving her job at the Butcher's because the pressure of working in the public eye became too much to bear. It wasn't as though that many people were openly hostile in her company, although there always were a few who couldn't help but express their contempt for her brother. A snide remark here or a comment dropped there. It was a constant drip, drip, drip that she couldn't ignore, because it dripped like a corrosive acid into her brain. Worse, actually, were those who didn't mean any offence. It was the awkwardness people felt in her company, in any of the MacKinnons' company. Conversations were stilted, strange affairs. It was taking its toll. Finally, one drizzly afternoon as Mizz Fizzlezwit reached for a packet of mince pies just within earshot of Morag (who was stacking loaves on a shelf), she quietly reminded her of Norrie's weird and devilish ways, did Morag throw her apron down in a huff and storm out. She followed in her mother's footsteps with the vodka and gin but managed without the meds. Maggie kept up her rounds of caring for the elderly for longer, but eventually quit as well. Some of those in her care were getting a little senile, and thus in place of clever and carefully dropped remarks were blunt statements and questions about her brother's strange ways. It was the same thing round after round after round. Seeing as Catherine worked at the primary school, she went the quickest, as children can be quite merciless once they spot a weakness and something to laugh about. Maggie and Catherine didn't follow their sister and mother quite as far down the alcohol soaked path but did find themselves in quite a dark, discontented, and frustrated place.

Norrie was living full time in the Nissen hut, along with his brother's half-mad sheep dog, Bonzo, only venturing out to cockle rake. The walk to the big beach had reverted back to the death march he'd felt all the previous year, but as before, once he planted his rake in the sand things got a bit better, if only for a while. When he was done his shifts on the beach he would take the long way back, roaming through the hills, and avoided everyone he possibly could. The Witch's curse had turned his family home into a dysfunctional wreck but there was nothing he could do about it. He did his thing, and his Mama and sisters did theirs. There were still a few loyal souls who would call round with cakes and roasts and scones and pots of soup, and did what they could for Mrs MacKinnon and her three daughters. And, truth be told, it was probably because of these acts of kindness that they eventually 'came around'. Norrie refused to talk to just about everyone. Constable Currie would stop in every now and again and managed the odd chat. Not that it did any good. He was barely seventeen. Constable Currie would talk and Norrie wouldn't listen.

Of course, a few of the local fishermen tried to drag him out of the 'state' he was in, especially Eddie, who had a particularly close connection with the family. He even offered Norrie the opportunity to join his crew, but Norrie turned it down...and no, thanks, he wouldn't be going to the dance, or The Heathbank or anywhere else for that matter. Again and again, this happened, and thus the boys were dropping round less and less.

That was how things went, well into the following year.

Spring, as it does, helped brighten things. As every day passed, the sun would rise a little earlier and set a little later. The fields and hills blossomed with colour as petal after petal gently opened. Birds sang and lambs were born, and everywhere pollen was being whisked around under the power of ten million tiny, transparent, wings. Mrs MacKinnon and her three daughters, in their own time, were coaxed out of the abyss they'd stumbled into. The soup, the cakes, the scones, had all done their bit, as did *time,* and in time they were able to walk down main street without feeling overwhelmed by shame or embarrassment, or distraught at the sight of Mizz Fizzlezwit. And, naturally, with the passage of time, more and more people forgot about Norrie's letters and the things he had or had not written, and thus more people came around to interacting with the MacKinnons in a more natural way. Mrs MacKinnon was again receiving more social calls, and the three girls were being asked to dance again with more desirable stock. Things were, indeed, brightening for the four female MacKinnons.

Things had not changed one tiny bit for Norrie.

The world was a cruel and twisted place and he wondered why spring even bothered showing up. To their credit, his Mama and three sisters tried to coax him out of the Nissen hut and thought that perhaps he should see Dr Bartlett or Ms Campbell. True to his form he would have none of it. *'But Norrie, you have to do something. Things can't go on like this forever. Those stupid letters don't even matter anymore! It's all right!'*

The middle of the summer arrived and with it was the regular surge of visitors. They came from the mainland, the continent, and across oceans. And it was from the continent and across the seas four individuals would arrive that would change the MacKinnons' lives forever. Call it coincidence, fate, destiny, or just dumb luck. One was a businessman by the name of Hank Stetson, who had decided to drop in on a recommendation by a man named Hamish. Hank had been travelling home to Idaho from Lithuania, where he'd been attending the annual conference for the International Association of Potato Growers. But the connection between Vilnius and London changed everything. The other three gentlemen, entirely unrelated to Hank, were missionaries from Kenya, who also happened to be brothers. Their names were Mwaka, Akili, and Darweshi, and though they were men of God, they were strapping gentlemen, with wide shoulders, long strong legs, and mouths full of pearly white teeth – and the moment Maggie, Morag, and Catherine met them walking along the beach behind the sandy little airport, they nearly melted.

*

The three sisters had been picnicking amongst the big dunes. The day was sunny and a little breezy. They were content, and the conversation was casual. Their little brother inevitably surfaced in their conversation and they pondered what to do about him. But he did seem to be managing okay, for someone who lived in a Nissen hut with a half-mad sheep dog, and spent his days raking cockles. *He'll come around,* Maggie had said, running a hand through her wavy auburn hair. They'd all managed to make it through the last two years and they were certain Norrie would, too. He was no weakling, of that they were certain. He had grown up in the image of their father, after all. During the darkest days of the past winter, and though they all had been in their own messy states, it was their mother they'd been most concerned about. But even she had managed through. So if anyone could – eventually – it would be their sort of strange little brother. They never spoke of 'the incident' anymore, but every now and again they did wonder, *what on earth was he thinking?* In any regards, as they nibbled at sandwiches and scones and tasty biscuits, their conversation turned to where any conversation among three healthy young ladies eventually turns – to boys. Although their prospects were looking better, none of them had met that extra-special one, just yet...

It was a few minutes after packing up their picnic. Instead of turning east and back towards home, Catherine suddenly felt compelled to change direction. 'Let's take a walk along Traigh Eais. It's so lovely on the west side!' The others thought it a grand idea as it was a fine day and they had nothing pressing waiting for them at home. And so it would be that they climbed one big grassy dune, and tumbled down the other side laughing like school girls and then scrambled up, crested another and out in front of them was one of the most beautiful beaches in the world; a mile long, soft white sparkling sand, and at either end great outcrops of ancient rock – like ramparts that have stood defending the shores for millions of years. The surge of the great Atlantic broke into waves and it licked the shore, again and again and again. It was then that they looked north along the shoreline. The wind was blowing their hair into their faces so at first they thought they were seeing things, a mirage perhaps – as though their imaginations were teasing them. But after a few moments they realised – no – it was no mirage and they weren't figments of their imaginations though they might as well have been.

For his part, Hank Stetson was no mirage or figment of anyone's imagination, either, nor was he exactly the stuff of most women's wildest fantasy, but he was a millionaire (not that it was known at the time) – and, anyway, as owners of giant potato farms go, he wasn't half bad looking. He had a toupee fit for a top-flight anchorman, and cowboy boots made from crocodile skin. His moustache was real and well cared for and there was a twinkle in his deep brown eyes. He spoke with an accent straight out of the Idaho backcountry and when Mrs MacKinnon first heard, 'Xcuse me Ma'am, but can you tell me what in heaven's name this here Stornoway Black Pudding is?' she fell in love.

Ch 18

Stornoway Black Pudding

'Is that so, Ma'am?'

'Oh, yes.'

'Well, that sounds as tasty as can be.'

'Oh, you wouldn't believe how tasty it is. Incredibly – scrumptious.'

Hank Stetson had a 12-inch long, thick, black sausage gripped firmly in his right hand. It was some weight and stiff, almost like a big old dinosaur bone that had fossilised in a tar pit.

'Well, well, I'm gonna have to try me some of this.'

They were standing at the back of the Butcher's by the cooler units. Mrs MacKinnon had been reaching for a carton of eggs when Providence walked into her life and asked for her help.

There was a moment's hesitation. Mr Stetson was evaluating the long, black sausage, but seemed to be evaluating something else as well. Mrs MacKinnon was staring starry eyed at the strange man with the amazing hair and deep brown eyes. They twinkled and he half smiled and Mrs MacKinnon's heart fluttered.

'My name's Hank, Hank Stetson, Ma'am.'

Mrs MacKinnon drew a sharp breath and for a moment found herself dizzy and unable to think.

'Are you alright, Ma'am?'

'Oh, sorry – yes. Yes, I'm okay. Just a – thank you, I'm fine. I'm Margaret, Margaret MacKinnon.'

'Well, Margaret, Margaret MacKinnon, it's a great pleasure to meet you, Ma'am.'

They were like two teenagers standing in the middle of a bustling shopping centre about to embrace, oblivious and uninterested in the world around them.

'Margaret?'

'Yes, Hank?'

'I'd like to carry your basket for you, if you don't mind, that is.'

Mrs MacKinnon caught her breath and almost fell back into the shelving that was stacked full of bread. Hank caught her by the elbow.

'Oh, my – I'm sorry...'

'That's all right Margaret, are you all right?'

Mrs MacKinnon took a moment. 'Yes, yes, sorry.'

Hank smiled. 'That's quite all right, Ma'am.'

Mrs MacKinnon looked at the stranger who had just walked into her life. The incredible hair, the moustache, the twinkle in his eyes, the gentlemanly touch, the kind touch. Who was this man who had just been sent to her? She hesitated, but not out of doubt. She just hesitated, taking it all in.

'Hank?'

'Yes, Margaret?'

'You can carry my basket anytime you like.'

*

Norrie was sitting on a stool by the Nissen hut entrance working the rust off his favourite rake with Bonzo curled up at his feet in a slumber, when a curious sight unfolded at the end of the driveway. There wasn't much in the world that piqued Norrie's interest at that time in his life but the circus at the end of the driveway did just that. Even Bonzo awoke and crooked his head at the odd scene. There was a tall man in a tan cowboy hat – and, three – black men? Norrie had never seen a real live black man in his life before. He'd seen them on TV and on film but never in real life. And, oddly, they each were holding a hand of one of his – *sisters?* And that man with the cowboy hat was holding hands with his – *Mama!* – and she was cradling a picnic basket? Maggie was carrying a picnic basket, too! Bonzo and Norrie frowned.

The Idaho potato-man and three Kenyan missionaries shared a queer look. As did Mrs MacKinnon and her three daughters.

You must understand, the two separate parties – *literally* – had bumped into each other at the bottom of the driveway, creating bewilderment. Love and excitement were in the air, so a barely decipherable verbal carousel turned.

'Mama, this is Mwaka – Mama?'

'Name's Hank, errrr, Hank Stetson, how do...'

'...were down on the beach when...'

'...here visiting Father John and...'

'...in the Butcher's...'

'We are missionaries...'

'Oh my goodness, Mama?!'

'And I am Darweshi...'

'...was just reaching for some eggs...'

'...appeared from the dunes on high...'

'Well, hot diggedy dog, this is some kinda' island...'

And so the verbal carousel turned some more. Everyone was talking at the same time and each and every person was completely lost as to what the other was saying. But that didn't matter one teeny bit, for they were all happy and ecstatic and over the moon with joy, and for a moment it seemed as though the carousel was going to turn, and turn, and keep on turning.

Bonzo made them all pause. In their excitement they had not seen him approach. He sniffed at one leg and then another. It was then that the men looked down, and just like that, Bonzo raised a hind leg and unceremoniously peed on one of Hank's crocodile-skin cowboy boots, then turned and trotted back up the driveway. Mrs MacKinnon and her girls were momentarily horrified. After a brief moment Mwaka, Akili, and Darweshi started to laugh. Their laughter was deep and hearty.

Even Hank cracked a smile, 'Dang it all.'

That's when they looked towards the Nissen hut and for the first time noticed Norrie. Bonzo had disappeared behind the big door and Norrie did the same, closing it behind him. Mwaka, Akili, Darweshi, and Hank Stetson shared a look and their laughter died away. At that moment the four MacKinnon women knew the inevitable had appeared, just like that – before they even had a chance...

Hank Stetson being Hank Stetson, was not one to beat around the bush. 'That young man – is he all right?' His words were thoughtful.

The MacKinnon women were at a loss for words. They'd all just fallen in love over the past 6 hours. They'd talked about much but hadn't quite got around to everything.

'There's – ah, few things you don't know about – us...that's, err, our brother, Norrie,' Maggie explained bravely.

'Hmm?' Akili pondered, feeling the gravity of Maggie's words. 'I see, I see.'

'Well, shoot, ladies, I sure could use a nice hot cup of coffee, if you don't mind that is,' Hank said, keen to rid these nice young ladies and the woman he'd just fallen in love with, of their moment of uncertainty. He flashed a big smile and the three missionaries followed suit and they, too, chipped in, reminding the three sisters of their offers of cups of tea and lovely fresh scones.

The MacKinnon women shared such a look of relief that you would have thought the air in their lungs had flown out of them but had decided to do a U-turn right back in.

'By golly, that is quite a view,' Hank said, admiring the open expanse of sea laid out to the north, bordered by the small craggy islands to the north and east, and the enormous beach sweeping west and north, and wrapping east and then north again, underneath the watchful eye of Picnic hill. 'I'll tell you, when I was flyin' in two days ago I thought I was just coming to sample a few of what I heard were some of the finest tayters a man can buy.' He smiled broadly and winked at the woman at his side. 'Man oh man – I owe that Hamish fella' somethin' fierce.'

As the story went, Hank was on his way from Vilnius back to Idaho, via a connection in London and Chicago. He was sitting in his usual seat, 1A, and struck up a conversation with the gentleman beside him. To cut not such a long story a little short, the gentleman turned out to be quite a potato-man himself, but not on the scale of the Idahoan he'd just met. Just a bit of an amateur garden-nut who lived on the mainland. He did, though, have quite a potato patch – enough to keep himself and a few others in tatties for the winter. He also entered all the produce competitions he could, both on the mainland and the Inner Hebrides. He was explaining all this to Hank when – almost reluctantly, as though he'd be committing some sort of sin for not sharing with a fellow potato-man this little nugget of news – he turned his attention to the finest potato he'd ever had. 'Without a word of a lie, Hank, I was staying at a friend's on the Isle of Skye, and after I took a nice steaming mouthful of what was on offer, I says to Seamus, "I don't remember yer tatties tasting quite like this before." It took a few minutes of probing and Seamus finally relented, "Aye, you're right, Hamish, they're not mine. They're from Floonay," Seamus had sighed. "You know Hamish, I've had tatties from every island in the Hebrides, Inner and Outer – and Floonay's are the best I've ever tasted. Vatersay's aren't far behind, mind you, but," he'd shrugged, looking defeated. "It's the mix of the soil and the sand and the sea air. It's perfect. What can I say. But Skye's are definitely the best between the Inner Hebrides and the mainland, and don't you forget that Hamish." Well, when Hank Stetson heard this story – he had his mind made up. As soon as the flight landed in London, he called his office outside of Boise and told them he'd be a few days late, and made a straight connection north to Glasgow and waited impatiently for what he then found out was one of the most incredible flights anyone could ever take. 'And by golly,' Hank's words – it was.

Well, if the MacKinnon women had even the tiniest doubts left concerning anything, as they walked into the kitchen they were put to rest. Hank, Mwaka, Akili, and Darweshi were gentlemen of the highest order. They were thoughtful and kind and did not lack in the humour department either. The conversation flowed and flowed, as the three brothers spoke of their homeland: the beautiful countryside, the lush green rolling hills, the spectacular Mount Kilimanjaro and the race they once had to the top. And then there was the wildlife...

'Ah, ha ha! Mwaka, tell them about the time you climbed that tree and fed a giraffe that head of lettuce! It was soooo funny...I'll tell them...the giraffe almost took his thumb off – and Mwaka, well, he didn't know how fast giraffes can eat – they're all relaxed and cool, but that giraffe ate it so fast and it didn't look happy when Mwaka started climbing down with no more lettuce on offer – ah ha ha!'

'Dang it all Mwaka, that is some fu-nnee stuff!'

They laughed and laughed, but the laughter died when they started talking about the hippos and the rhinos. The conversation became intense and enthralling, and downright frightening, when Darweshi spoke about watching a hippo catch a zebra crossing a shallow river.

'That poor zebra. He didn't stand a chance. There were other hippos in the area, and I swear to you one spied me, and I don't know what it did next because I turned and ran as fast as I could not daring to look back! They've been known to eat people, you know. You must be careful of hippos. That was the scariest day of my life.'

'It all sounds so fascinating, so incredible,' Catherine said.

'Hmm, fascinating, fascinating indeed,' Darweshi replied and the look they shared spoke volumes.

*

As Mrs MacKinnon started clearing up she said, 'The photo, in case you were wondering – that's my husband, Michael, and my sons, our sons. Norrie is the only one left...' She caught herself. '...Sorry.' You couldn't not notice it. It was hanging on the kitchen wall.

A great and heavy silence hung in the air and the four men felt the gravity of the moment. They didn't budge. A look of great pain spread across the faces of the four women, and the four men knew it was a pain, a deep sorrow, that no person should ever know.

Mrs MacKinnon continued, 'They died at sea. Rory in the Irish Sea, a training accident in the Army. The others, Donald, Duncan, Ewan – and – Michael,' Margaret gestured. 'Out there, just across the Sound.'

Mwaka spoke gently, 'That is a terrible thing. I am sorry for your loss.'

The girls nodded, keeping their emotions in check.

'I didn't think it would be so hard,' Mrs MacKinnon said quietly, 'to talk about it. It's been a few years now – it's,' she let out a sniffly little laughless-laugh. 'It's the first time we've ever talked to strangers about it,' she instinctively looked to Hank. 'Not that you're, you know – sorry...'

Hank nodded. He understood.

It took a few moments but the heaviness of the moment lifted, and ever so gently, they spoke of the accidents. The men were sombre and sympathetic and let the women just share what they were comfortable with, and after a little while it was Hank who spoke.

'I know how you feel, well, perhaps just a little – sorry...I shouldn't say.' His voice dropped a chord.

'No, no – it's okay, it's...'

'Of course you can speak,' Akili said, as though speaking to a friend he'd known for 20 years.

'Ah, dang it all – I shouldn't ah said a word.' Suddenly Hank's eyes filled up with tears. He uttered a mirthless chuckle. 'Lost my wife to cancer five years ago. Spread all throughout. Couldn't do a thing. And then...' and this time he paused and shook his head. He smiled bravely and a few tears rolled down his Idaho sun-baked cheeks. 'A year later – my two boys. Killed in a wreck. Ah, goddamn it all! That damned sports car they were in – hit by a runaway dump truck. I knew I shouldn't have listened to 'em – that damned puny thing – I wanted to get 'em a big strong pick-up, you know – but they wanted that teeny little thing...and in Idaho no less...'

Darweshi put a hand on Hank's shoulder. 'I am so very sorry, Hank. So sorry.'

Hank took a moment and wiped his eyes with a personally embroidered red, white, and blue handkerchief. 'Thanks there, Darweshi, shit – I haven't cried in maybe, what, like over two dang years – was barefoot in the kitchen and picked up this big ol' bag of tayters and wouldn't you know it, the bottom came out and *whacko* right on the toes – son of a gun – you wouldn't believe what damage fifty pounds of tayters can do. All the nails on all my toes went blacker than you wouldn't believe.'

It was Catherine and Morag first. They couldn't help it. Little snorty laughs. Then Maggie. And next it was Mwaka, Akili, and Darweshi and just like that, everyone was laughing. And probably nobody more so than Mrs MacKinnon herself.

Ch 19

A New Beginning

It was close to dinner time on that most miraculous day, and it just so happened that all four MacKinnon ladies were thinking the same thing, *perhaps they'll stay for dinner?* But it was the four men who, being the gentlemen that they were, and mindful of the young man who lived in the Nissen hut, were thinking it was probably time for them to leave. They would love to stay, but – perhaps another time...

Hank shifted first, creaking up from the chair. 'Margaret, I had a most wonderful day. And it was lovely to meet your daughters.' He could see a flicker of worry in her deep blue eyes. *When will I see you?* '...I was hoping perhaps – tomorrow...' Mrs MacKinnon was already saying yes.

Mwaka, Akili, and Darweshi started shifting as well.

'Father John and the good Reverend will be wondering where we got to. I promised them a fine Kenyan dish for tonight,' Darweshi said and grinned widely, '...I, too, hope to meet you again, Maggie?' His two brothers followed suit and everyone made their way outside.

The sun was still well up. It was lovely and warm, and as they said their goodbyes, a lone figure caught Hank's eye, way out in the middle of the big beach. It was like a little toy soldier bent over, and had a hold of some sort of stick. And there was a smaller figure doing circles and figures of eights around him.

'That's Norrie – and Bonzo.' Mrs MacKinnon spoke with a fondness.

Everyone watched for a moment, not saying a word.

'You know, Margaret, I was thinking – well, maybe tomorrow, that is...'

Mrs MacKinnon could read his mind. 'You can try...I'll talk to him tonight – or try to anyway. He can be a bit difficult sometimes.' She paused and thought what effect this was going to have on him.

'He hasn't talked to anyone in a very long time. There's just a few he'll even let near him,' Catherine said.

It was *all* in the past, and Norrie's Mama and sisters wished he'd let it go, but it was what it was. The tragedies had been a tough road to travel down, and the four gentlemen assumed that that was the sole, or primary reason, why the young man and his dog lived in a shed.

Goodbyes were exchanged and the three missionaries promised to see the three sisters again very soon. All six were quite grateful that though they were missionaries, their faith did not preclude them from engaging in romantic relationships. The girls were over the moon to hear that they would be on the island for another week – mostly assisting Reverend Cullen, but Reverend Cullen, being the good Reverend that he was, had offered to share them with Father John, and everyone was more than happy with this arrangement. As far as Mrs MacKinnon knew, Hank was in town only for another two days. What he hadn't told her – yet – it would be a surprise for the following day – was that he would be calling his office to inform them that he wouldn't be back for another 10 days. Maybe even longer. He was a potato millionaire after all. So long as his potatoes were well cared for he could afford to stay away for as long as he wanted.

Dealing with Norrie later that evening proved more difficult than Mrs MacKinnon had hoped. Norrie wouldn't grant access to the Nissen hut when she asked to speak with him earlier, and thus when she arrived with a big plate of mince and tatties, she did what she had done many times before, and left it at the door. She gave a little knock to announce dinner had arrived. He only ever asked for the plate to be left outside the door when he was in a particularly 'distant' place. This frustrated his mother greatly, but she was not going to push things.

When Norrie heard the knock at the door, he said to Bonzo, 'fetch'. At that command Bonzo knew just what to do. Norrie was well back in the Nissen hut at the work bench whittling the end of a new pole that he was going to attach to a rusty old rake head he had found deep in a wooden box, discovered under a pile of other wooden boxes.

The sight of his Mama holding hands with a man who was not his father had been unusual. Surreal. Unsettling. He didn't understand what his Mama was doing. Why would she be holding hands with another man? It was strange indeed. And his sisters? Well, Norrie's day had become quite unusual. Norrie wondered what his father would think? It was all a little overwhelming.

It wasn't until his Mama had come knocking at the Nissen hut door did he suddenly feel angry. She'd knocked and asked to speak to him about something important, and that was when a feeling of betrayal swept through Norrie. He had said he'd nothing to talk about but his Mama persisted, and he continued to refuse. His Mama persisted some more and said, 'I'd like to talk to you about Hank, the man I met today. He's a nice man, Norrie.' Well, when Norrie heard that, the feeling of betrayal transformed into something much worse – it was an ugly feeling, and he couldn't help but think that his Mama had done something very wrong. But he kept himself mostly in check and crossly replied that he didn't want to talk about a man named Hank. His Mama wouldn't relent and Norrie became quite angry and he shouted through the door, 'That's not right, Mama! That's not right what you've done – what you've done to Papa!' There was silence for a while, and on one side of the door Norrie stood with Bonzo at his heel, and on the other side his Mama stood, alone. And then she said, 'Norrie, Hank lost his wife a few years ago, to cancer. And then he lost his two sons – they were run over, Norrie.' There was a pause and Norrie did not respond and then his Mama said simply, 'Norrie, he's a good man, a kind man, and I'd like to have him over for dinner tomorrow night. Oh, and the three men your sisters met. They're missionaries from Kenya. They'd been gifted a trip for some cricket tournament down south, to see their home team play. Someone they'd worked with in Kenya always spoke of the Hebrides and they took the opportunity to come up and visit and do a little work with the local churches, and they met your sisters walking along the beach. They'd been planning on heading to Vatersay for the day to see the beaches there but someone recommended they check out the 'Tri' and so they did, and your sisters emerged from the dunes, and well – I don't know Norrie, it's been one of those incredible days, miraculous even...' Mrs MacKinnon stopped herself, and perhaps wished she hadn't said that. As she turned back towards the house, she heard her son speak. 'Please just leave it at the door.'

Bonzo might have been half mad, as sheep dogs go, and had a single-minded impulse to hump the first bitch he came across if not kept in check, but he was also one of the smartest canines on all of Floonay. Norrie was grateful for what he assumed was his brother's solid groundwork in training Bonzo, because when it came time to teaching Bonzo a few new tricks it came relatively easily. When Norrie said 'fetch' Bonzo knew just what to do, and – amazingly – knew just how much was his share. His ability to restrain himself when it came to eating, would, most likely, leave most other dogs feeling pretty embarrassed.

About halfway up the inside of the big double doors of the Nissen hut, there is a simple latch. Pull upward on the little metal knob, then slide it back two inches and voila, the door can be opened. Well, with his front paws up on the door, Bonzo knew just how to release the latch, and the next bit – pulling the door open – was easy. Next, he would bite the side of the piping hot plate of whatever was on offer, and pull it into the Nissen hut, all the way along to where the work bench was. Next, he'd trot back over, nudge the door shut, pull the latch back closed, trot back and would wait for the next command, which Norrie would faithfully give. *'Eat, Bonzo.'* And then Bonzo would slobber and munch his way through half the plate, and then stop. He'd look up at Norrie, with all the loyalty in his eyes one could imagine, panting, his tongue hanging out. And that's when Norrie would take over. He, of course, would use a knife and fork and lift the plate up to the workbench. It was all quite remarkable.

When Norrie was finished, he put the plate back down, giving Bonzo the extra treat of licking the plate clean, tail wagging and loving every second of it – that was his dessert. When the plate was licked clean there was no need for any extra command, as he automatically went through the process of removing the plate, nudging it back out the door and securing it shut.

After Norrie heard about the fate of the wife and sons of the man he now knew of as Hank, the anger and feeling of betrayal that had welled up slipped away. It was all still greatly confusing, though. There was so much he didn't know and too many questions and no answers anywhere.

Ch 20

Miracles

The day had ended better than what Mrs MacKinnon or her daughters could have ever hoped for. The most wonderful men imaginable had walked into their lives and because of that they were glowing with those special feelings that accompany such events, but it was what transpired after dinner that had them pinching themselves. *This can't be? But – it is. What an incredible day! I just knew he'd come around!*

Norrie walked in and before his sisters or Mama had a chance to say a word, simply said, 'You know, it's okay, I don't mind if a man named Hank comes for dinner tomorrow. That is a terrible thing that happened to his family. If you say he's a nice man then I'm sure he is. Anyway, I can't talk too much right now because I'm busy with stuff in the Nissen hut.' The women were left staring dumbly at one another. What on earth had happened to him? Mrs MacKinnon was not very religious. She'd been born into her faith and went through the motions without giving it much thought, and – especially because of the tragedies that had blighted her family, she had serious misgivings about it all, and particularly in her dark alcohol-soaked days had asked *why* more times than was probably healthy. But hearing her son's words, really hearing them, well, she was inclined to believe that perhaps miracles really do happen.

Norrie was out the door before his Mama or sisters had a chance to say anything. Upon arriving back in the Nissen hut he did not lock the door behind him, and thus a few minutes later his Mama and sisters tiptoed into his domain. They knew not to push and prod too much, but they had to see for themselves whether it really was true. Whether the young man they saw and heard a few moments ago wasn't some apparition. Norrie was by the workbench and had the big book flopped open. He was busy flipping pages and Bonzo had his front paws up on the bench and was watching his master intently. When Mrs MacKinnon saw *that book* she frowned.

'Norrie?' Mrs MacKinnon said quietly. Catherine, Morag, and Maggie were just behind her, each peeking over a shoulder of the other.

Norrie was flipping page after page and at first didn't notice he had visitors.

'Norrie, what are you – doing?'

'Oh, hi Mama.' He spoke distractedly.

'Norrie?' Mrs MacKinnon hesitated and bit her lip. 'You really don't mind if Hank comes for dinner?'

'No Mama – that's all right.'

The four women looked to one another – it was not an apparition.

Then Maggie asked, 'Well – maybe Darweshi could come, too?'

'And Akili?' said Morag.

'And Mwaka?' added Catherine.

Mrs MacKinnon hesitated – *everyone?* She had had a romantic dinner in mind – just the two of them, but no, *this* would be much better she realised. There would be plenty of time later for romance. 'Norrie, would you – you know, would you like to join us for dinner, too? I think Hank would like to meet you.'

'And Darweshi,' Maggie quickly added. 'I know he would like to meet you, I promise.

'Akili, too,' Morag hastened to add.

'And Mwaka,' Catherine was right on her heels.

Norrie shrugged and thought *why not.* He was especially curious about Hank's cowboy hat, as he'd never seen one in real life before. And, of course, he'd never had dinner with three black men before, or even one. *This should all be very interesting.* 'Aye. That sounds fine.'

Well, the four MacKinnon women were overjoyed and couldn't help but get a little giddy, and the fuss they were making had Norrie and Bonzo wondering why women got excited about such silly little things.

'Oh, we're going to have just a wonderful evening!'

'Wonderful and fantastic!'

'We'll have to make something special!'

'Hmm. I wonder what Mwaka's guilty pleasure is?'

'Catherine!'

They went on and on and it wasn't until Bonzo barked did they snap out of their moment of excitement.

'Oh, well, perhaps we should just leave you – uh, both – alone.' Mrs MacKinnon spoke delicately, as though afraid Norrie would change his mind. Catherine, Morag, and Maggie clumsily agreed as they attempted to stifle their excitement. They awkwardly bid their farewells and tiptoed out of the Nissen hut.

The next day went better than any of the MacKinnon women could have ever imagined. The four men were delighted with the invitations to dinner and to hear they would be meeting Norrie. Hank was going to wait until the following day to surprise Margaret with the news that he'd decided to stick around Floonay for another 10 days, if not longer. But when she'd rang him up at his B&B and he could hear the joy in her voice, well, he had to tell her right then and there. And for her part, although the reality of the fact that Hank was just visiting had flittered through her mind, it didn't dampen the strange and wonderful feelings of love – I suppose it goes without saying that when *love* is involved everyone knows not to worry too much – the details would work themselves out. Most of the time anyway.

The day of the big dinner the tide was at its lowest point in the late afternoon, and thus Norrie had spent the afternoon raking away, following the ebb. Hank, unbeknown to the three missionaries, had decided earlier in the day to head to the big beach and bond a little with the young man. And the three missionaries, had likewise, decided to do the same. The timing of their arrival wasn't quite as remarkable as the previous day, but by mid-afternoon the four men and Norrie and Bonzo were all out there in the middle of the big beach. The MacKinnon women looked out from their perch and the sight made them happy. Hank had bought a brand new rake from the island's Top Shop, and the three missionaries had borrowed a few rakes from Reverend Cullen, and three pairs of yellow wellies from a few fishermen that Father John knew. Hank had no need for wellies, (he had explained first to Norrie, and then to Akili, Darweshi, and Mwaka) as his boots were made of crocodile skin and thus were as tough and as impenetrable as anything you could ever imagine. Norrie had never seen a pair of cowboy boots on the beach before, and thought it a little peculiar, and the three missionaries couldn't help but find their new Idahoan friend oddly entertaining. *'Crocodiles live in salt water, boys – least I think they do. These here boots are gonna be just fine.'*

The four men were rookies at cockle raking so there was much explaining for Norrie to do – but he didn't want to overwhelm them with too much information, and thus tried to keep things simple. For their part, the men were quite impressed with Norrie's productivity, and they quickly came to realise how backbreaking the work was, and how getting the *knack* wasn't quite so easy.

'Dang, my back is gonna hurt tomorrow. What on earth?' Hank glanced over to where Norrie had planted his rake, and though he'd spent a considerable amount of time coaching the four men, he'd pop back and forth to rake a little. Well, the amount of cockles he'd gathered was more than double his pupils' – *combined!*

To his surprise, Norrie found he was having quite a good time, as was Bonzo, who kept trying to pee on everyone's legs. He explained that Bonzo did that to everybody. After a time Bonzo gave up trying to pee on them all and instead just ran around chasing birds, and what could only be described as his invisible friends. Norrie found the three missionaries very amusing, and especially because they laughed so much and so readily – it seemed that they found humour all around, even in the teeniest and tiniest things – and Hank and his crocodile boots, not to mention his cowboy hat, kept Norrie intrigued.

The day was a remarkable success and eventually Norrie and his new friends made for home. Dinner was a wonderful medley fresh from the sea – crab and lobster and scallops, and of course cockles. The men couldn't get over how tasty everything was. Potato salad was on offer and Hank had to admit – not for the first time on his visit – that Floonay tayters were without doubt the finest he had ever tasted. 'PEI tayters – that's Prince Edward Island – they're pretty good, too. Have to admit, a little better than my own beloved Idaho tayters – Idaho are the next best, mind you, on the North American continent that is. It's a soil thing, you see. You can replicate a lot of things, but in all my years in the business, well, soil is the one thing that can't be reproduced completely, like exactly-completely. Heck, even trucking it in is a 'no can do' – it's got to do with the air as well, and temperature and all that. How it all mixes together.' He paused, musing, as he nibbled on a crab claw. 'Shoot, if I could just figure out a way to replicate your lovely little island, well, I'd probably put the rest of the tayter industry out of business. Ah, but that ain't gonna happen. Impossible.'

Hank regaled them with potato stories large and small, and that evening over dinner was the first time that Mrs MacKinnon, and the rest of them, started to realise that Hank Stetson wasn't just your average travelling potato businessman. For all his show, Hank was a humble man. The fact that he owned his own company and dealt in tayters in quantities exceeding tens, if not hundreds, of millions, was revealed without him realising it. By accident! He hadn't planned on telling *his* story but some stories just have a way of surfacing...

How he had started, poor, practically homeless, and living in a shack with holes in the roof in the Idaho backcountry. He'd been an orphan, and when he was a teenager his adoptive parents were wooed into joining some crazy cult and moved to Central America, never to be heard from again. They'd left him $500, and the rest, the proceeds from the sale of the house and his family's modest assets, all went to the 'crazy ass cult leader – sorry, pardon my tongue. It makes me so mad sometimes to think of...' The story had everyone mesmerised and even Bonzo, who was allowed into the house for the special occasion, wore a certain look – he understood a great tragedy was being spoken of. Hank talked about how he'd stumbled through his teen years working at car washes and cleaning toilets in a strip bar (actually, he left out the bit that it was a 'strip' bar, as it was unnecessary information, and besides, the only time he was there was in the morning, cleaning up after the shenanigans from the night before). Anyway, after a series of bad turns (he shortened all this, too, as it was too much to go into) he wound up living in a shack in the woods halfway up a mountainside. 'Dang, there was mountain lions and cougars and bears and all I had were two bullets to go with the rusty old rifle I had…' But then one day, as he was scavenging behind a truck stop for scraps to take back up to his shack where he was busy distilling moonshine – or at least that's what he thought it was – he found a box of mostly mushy 'teeny tiny tayters with shoots stickin' out of 'em.' The label on the box was from one of the conglomerate potato companies in his state. He knew well that Idaho was known for its potatoes. Anyway, the box was full of hundreds of potatoes and he got a strong whiff of a few of the mushier ones and the first thing that popped into his mind was that he'd try and figure out how to make vodka, as he knew potatoes were the base ingredient for some vodkas, and it appeared as though the fermentation process had already started. So, off he scurried back up to his wreck of a shack. The table was silent and everyone was riveted to this most remarkable story, none more so than Mrs MacKinnon. 'But something happened up there. It was a few days later, and without going into it all or we'd be here till next week, but it started to dawn on me that something wasn't right, you know what I mean? Like really not right. I was wasting away up there with no prospects and not a lot of hope, and then I just looked at that box of mushy tayters, and, well, I ended up planting the ones that looked like they weren't completely rotten, and, there's a lot more to this story. But one thing led to another, and it took a long, long time, but slowly, ever so slowly, my little operation grew and grew and at first I was just selling tayters at truck stops and gas stations and on the side of the road – anywhere really, and then I had saved enough to buy a bit of decent land – and, well, as they say "the rest is history" and Stetson Tayters, Inc. is now an industry leader. Sorry, not meanin' on braggin' or nothin'.'

After dinner the girls pulled out their instruments and quite a Ceilidh ensued. In between dances the three brothers told more stories of their native land and much of their telling was colourful and exotic. It was the first time that the MacKinnon girls had a chance to get their hands on the men, and when they danced they could feel the strength in their firm limbs, and so it was inevitable that between the exotic tales and the physical contact and their wonderful smiles the girls became all hot and bothered and each, quite spontaneously, started plotting how they were going to find a moment to escape into the night with their knights.

All good things do eventually come to an end, at least for a while, and so it would be that the evening did start drawing to a close. It was nearing midnight when Norrie announced he'd be hitting the sack. Low tides were at 5am and 5pm the following day, and so he wanted to be up early to catch the morning, as well as the late afternoon tide. He said his goodnights and made for the kitchen door, and it was then that his Mama spoke. 'Norrie, you're not going to sleep in the Nissen hut – I mean, you've got a bedroom.' 'Oh, that's okay, Mama, I'm used to it.' He'd come around, mostly, but he was quite used to sleeping out there and didn't feel like moving back into his bedroom. Not yet anyway. 'Of course, sorry.' 'That's fine, Mama.' 'You sure you don't want to stay, son?' Hank chipped in, a little out of breath from the dance they'd just been twirling to. 'That's all right, it's comfy out there and it is the summer – it's like camping, really.' 'Hm?' Hank was thinking. It was a lovely evening and the Nissen hut was on a prime spot overlooking a spectacular beach – and, well, his B&B was on the other side of the island, and he hadn't ordered a taxi and...he had enjoyed the young man's company and he thought it might be fun. Chat a bit like around the campfire. He piped up, 'Norrie, would you mind if I crash in the Nissen hut? Only if you don't mind, of course – just that it's a long way back to my B&B and, well, only if it's all right with you?' He paused and cracked a smile. 'It'll be like mano-e-mano time.' Norrie replied, 'Aye, if you like.' It didn't take but a moment for the three brothers to chime in and ask if there might be enough blankets for them also (they were going to have to leave early as they had visits to make with Father John and Reverend Cullen in the morning), and so they should probably get a decent night's rest and they'd leave at the crack of dawn. *Well, why not?* Norrie said they were all welcome and thought that there ought to be enough old blankets poked away in some box or another. And so, pretty swiftly, the Ceilidh was over and the four MacKinnon women were left to say their goodbyes, and though they knew they'd be seeing the men again soon, it wasn't soon enough to tame their desires.

Ch 21

Just the Boys

Arriving back in the Nissen hut, Norrie went about foraging for blankets as Hank and the brothers inspected his dwelling under the illumination of two hanging light bulbs. 'Not a bad little set-up you got here, Norrie,' Hank remarked. 'Like a cross between my barn and ga-rage back home. Hell, come to think of it, this was the sort of deal we slept in back in 'Nam.' It was a man's paradise: a workbench and tools and lots of old dusty crates, tins full of nuts and bolts, and long deep shelves packed full of rusted bits and pieces that had seen better days. There was a little gas stove and an old shotgun shoved between a few boxes. An ancient transistor radio sat perched on the far-right side of the workbench and a dozen creels were stacked along one side with coils of rope tucked inside them. Norrie dragged a big tarpaulin down for a few of them to sleep on and dusty wool blankets were distributed. There was one spare fold out camping cot, apart from Norrie's, which the brothers insisted Hank should use. They would sleep on the heavy tarpaulin. Norrie brewed a kettle on the little stove for tea for himself and the brothers – they had to rise early and needed to be fresh. To Hank's surprise, Norrie produced a half-bottle of Scotch and handed it to him. 'Thought you might like a sip. It's been there a while. It was my brother's, Rory's.' Well, Hank was left almost speechless. He tried to refuse the offer (he suspected that Norrie was keeping it for something special), but Norrie insisted. It had been an instinctive gesture. Hank was a nice fellow. Next, Norrie pulled out his pipe, poked some tobacco in and struck a match. Cups of tea were distributed and a little Scotch poured in an old tin cup. Everyone settled in for one last yarn of the night, and what happened next took Norrie and the brothers a little by surprise.

Hank, sitting on the side of the cot, pulled off his left boot then pulled off his right. Next, a few straps were unbuckled – a moment of confusion for the four observers – and just like that – half of Hank's right leg was separated from his body.

'Hank, it would seem as though you are a magic man. You were just dancing,' Mwaka exclaimed.

Hank smiled and took a sip of Scotch. 'Years of practice, Mwaka.'

'What – happened?' Norrie was entranced. He'd never seen a false leg before. Hank had a full leg just a minute ago. He was cockle raking a few hours ago. Mwaka's right – he was just dancing!

'Got her blown off in Nam in '69. There we were in that hot ass son of a bitch jungle, full of mountains and scary critters, and we had our foe on the run – or so we thought. Big range of mountains runs up and down the middle of this one area. Our force had to separate. One half went one way round, and the other half, the other way round. I was on the eastern side, 3rd infantry. You could say we were divided and conquered,' he shrugged. 'Maybe they'd a got us anyway? Maybe it was the dang heat, the fact that we didn't belong there, ah, who knows? Maybe it was just the way things were meant to work out. But they came down from the mountains and chased our tails all the way outta there...funny thing is, this here,' he patted his prosthetic leg, 'this happened when we were almost all the way back. Dang friendly fire. I'll never forget that clumsy son of a gun, couldn't shoot worth a hoot either. Private Jeffrey "Jimmy" MacDonald. Stumbled over a rock, safety wasn't on. And voila, shredded my leg with his machine gun.' Hank took a comforting gulp of Scotch. 'Had to give the bastard credit though. He got that tourniquet on pretty dang fast. Else I'd a probably bled to death. Then he asked if I was all right. Phew, I was in so much pain at that moment and everythin' was goin' blurry, but ol' MacDonald looked sadder and afraider than a lost puppy in a cold dark alley and in more pain than I was in, and well, how could I be too mad, you know? I could see he cared and was real sorry, so I said, "I'm fine, Big Mac" – he was a big bastard – "now get me on that dang stretcher and let's get back to base before the Reds get us." I'll tell you boys, that was somethin' else, that march back...and not just for me, you know. You could reach out and touch the misery. It was like a sticky dang molasses, and it was stuck all over everyone. The medic had run out of morphine and so my leg had me in all sorts of agony. I drifted in and out of consciousness.' Hank paused and patted his prosthetic leg. 'But we made it and I got me this little marvel to help me around – and that's all that matters.'

'You are a very brave man, Hank, brave indeed.' Akili spoke with a distinct reverence.

'I'll tell you what, Akili, I wasn't feelin' very brave. I just wanted to get home, get back to Idaho and my budding tayter business and leave the fightin' of the world to someone else.'

As things turned out they stayed up half the night talking. They might as well have been five eager boys on their first night around a campfire, telling story after story. East Africa came to life in Norrie's mind like some marvellous magic land, full of the most colourful and majestic creations in the world. And the way Hank described Idaho, a place Norrie had never heard of before – it simply sounded enormous, and it wasn't even its own country, but could easily fit his own country within it with tons of room to spare. Norrie mostly listened and the others spoke. He was content with the arrangement, an arrangement Hank and the brothers understood. Even Bonzo appeared satisfied, lying at his master's feet. The wee hours of the night ticked along and eventually the men started to drift off to sleep. There would be plenty of time for more stories and for the first time since the tragedies, as Norrie slipped into the land of nod, he, curiously, felt the presence of his father. And thus, he drifted off into a peaceful sleep.

*

Hank extended his stay indefinitely. For the time being he was comfortable managing his business from a distance. He'd make calls to Idaho a few times a week to check on things, but for the most part he trusted his team of managers to run Stetson Inc. in his absence. The three brothers, too, extended their stay, for which Father John and Reverend Cullen were thankful. The extra help was always welcome. The four relationships entered a particularly blissful and intense period. The MacKinnon women were grateful for the prolonged spell of fine weather as they all became one-on-one tour guides to the remotest parts of the island they could find. They didn't necessarily plan it – it just happened something like this: If Maggie nonchalantly said, 'Oh, I think I'm going to take Darweshi on a walk north of Traigh Eais tomorrow,' one of the others would choose another corner of the island, and on it went. There were four of them and they basically did a rotation, always announcing where they were going so as not to surprise the other high on a hilltop or deep between two steep dunes. Their little system worked like clockwork. Norrie and Bonzo were glad to see them gone for such long stretches of the day for they had become quite a frustrated and agitated lot for a little while. But after their escapades started, upon arriving home it was like they were floating through a dream world, looks of divine satisfaction lighting up their faces.

It didn't take long for word to spread around the island. Once started, the speed of sound travelled at the speed of light. And it became the most exciting bit of gossip Floonay had known in a long time. The local islanders were used to the regular passage of 'normal' travellers: people in campervans, on bikes, cars with boots full of beach gear, hikers with big packs, that sort of thing, and most blended together. But the three missionaries and the tall man in the cowboy hat did stand out. And it was because the gossip included these four fellows that an extra layer of intrigue and excitement was added to the whole affair. The three brothers, for their part, had turned the heads of most of the island's women – and men, for one reason or another. They were strapping gentlemen and of the exotic sort not usually seen in the North Atlantic. For Hank's part, beyond the hat and the boots, the finely groomed moustache, first class head of hair that everyone thought was real, and the Idaho accent – it was the manner in which he carried himself that left the greatest impression. Everyone he met was left thinking the same thing: 'What a nice – curious, fellow.'

Norrie got quite used to the four men coming and going and enjoyed their company. When they could, they'd join Norrie down on the big beach and try and improve their skills at cockle raking. They didn't improve very much and were continuously amazed at Norrie's ability. Not only was it back-breaking work, but they all swore that wherever it was that Norrie planted his rake there were always more cockles waiting for him to discover. At least once on every occasion one of them would look to Norrie's spot and see how many he had, and then they'd glance at their own pathetic piles, and they'd get Norrie to switch spots with them – for they swore Norrie was sneakily steering them to rubbishy spots – but it never worked. Norrie would start raking and the cockles would be popping out of the sand and the four grown men would, again, be scratching around in vain wondering where they all went. Akili even wondered out loud more than once that maybe the cockles followed Norrie around under the sand, that perhaps he had them trained – or something. But anyway, despite the lack of improving their cockle raking skills, and despite the toll it took on their bodies, they all had a lot fun.

One particular evening, whilst the women were in the kitchen making preparations, and the men and Norrie were out by the Nissen hut drinking beer and getting the barbecue ready, Hank asked Norrie if he'd ever heard of baseball.

'Aye, of course.'

'You ever play?'

'No.'

'You ever see a game?'

'No. Just heard about it.'

'Well, I'll tell you Norrie, I bet you'd make a dang good player.'

'How's that?'

'Cause all that strength you got in those arms of yours – and that back. All that cockle raking. You must be made of steel.'

'He *is* made of steel,' Mwaka noted. 'My back and my shoulders, they hurt so much after raking – and look.' He flexed a muscular arm, then lamented, 'These arms are not puny – but they hurt after all that raking.'

Hank sipped his beer. 'I hear you Mwaka. Hell, I've lifted many a sack of tayters over the years, but when I come off that beach I feel like I ain't never lifted a finger in my life,' then he squinted, sizing Norrie up. 'But it ain't just the strength, boys.'

He looked between his Kenyan compadres. 'It's the grip that's his secret, I think. And that's why he'd be a dang good ball player. You need more than strength. Some sorta' mixture of strength and, like a feathery touch, you know. Controlling that bat and seeing that ball coming at you at a hundred miles an hour and knowing when and where to swing – it takes some skill.'

'Ah, yes, I think you are right, just like cricket,' Darweshi added, suddenly feeling illuminated. 'And also, that is why he doesn't tire like us. He must flit between the two, very quickly. Between feathers and strength, you know – so fast that we can't tell. We are straining so much and he is only using half the energy – is that your secret Norrie?'

'I think there must be a little magic, too – to know all the spots,' Akili conjectured. 'We are tired and sore and can't find any – I think he must have some spell that makes them come closer to the surface when he's wiggling his rake. Will you share with us your magic spell, Norrie?'

Norrie laughed. 'There's no magic involved, but here, I've something to show you.' He disappeared into the Nissen hut and reappeared moments later carrying the Coquillueous Rakkeronuous Almenikhiaka. 'I've never shown this to anyone before. This is the only secret I have, or magical thing, if you like – but it's not really magic.'

Hank, Akili, Mwaka, and Darweshi gathered round Norrie and stared in awe.

Mwaka finally spoke. 'Norrie, what is – *this?*'

'This is the Coquillueous Rakkeronuous Almenikhiaka.'

'The Coquill-ee-racker-what's that you said, Norrie?' Hank was terribly mystified.

'The Coquillueous Rakkeronuous Almenikhiaka. It's a book of knowledge. It first started with my great times eight Grandpa Cloon...'

'Great times – come again, Norrie?'

'Great times eight Grandpa Cloon – he was the first cockle raker on Floonay.'

Hank and the three brothers shared a curious look. *Very interesting.*

'Before that my people were pirates but Grandpa Cloon made the great discovery and soon after, realising what a marvellous discovery it was, he started taking little notes of this and that. It's all about cockle raking – and some other stuff, too. There're tips and techniques and stern warnings and even some scary adventure stories. And the thing is, after Grandpa Cloon, all my other MacKinnon Grandpas would contribute little bits and pieces over the centuries and the Coquillueous Rakkeronuous Almenikhiaka grew and grew and grew, and...' he paused, reflecting.

'And – what is it Norrie?'

'My Papa used to read to me every Saturday night.' His voice trailed off.

Hank, Akili, Mwaka, and Darweshi understood the gravity of the moment.

Darweshi finally spoke. 'It *is* a very special book.'

'Aye.'

'May I?' Mwaka gestured with his hands.

'Aye, of course.' Norrie handed Mwaka the big old book.

Mwaka held it with a special reverence. He ran a hand over the rough leathery surface and the cockles embedded in it. He then creaked it open, and Hank, Akili, and Darweshi gathered round. Carefully, one crackly page after another was turned and the men were thoroughly intrigued. There were grainy pictures and drawings of wide ranging quality and all different types of writing: some neat and legible and other bits a little scribbly and hard to make out. Mwaka was turning the pages and they were all very curious when suddenly he stopped turning. 'Norrie, what is – *that?*'

Norrie paused before answering, and when he did speak his voice was grim. 'That's what killed three of my brothers and my Papa.'

The four men were silent as they all just stared at the old black and white photograph.

Akili finally spoke. 'What a terrible – *creature.*'

'It's a sea monster. But not a proper sea monster.' He gestured to the harpoon sticking out of its right eye. 'I'd like to put a harpoon in its other eye – and push it all the way in.'

'It's still – out there?' Darweshi asked nervously.

'Aye. Been roaming the seas for decades. No one's been able to catch it, never mind kill it.'

'Dang. That's one mean ol' whale.'

The three brothers felt deeply for Norrie, and his sisters and mother, but they were also thinking something else at that moment: they had accepted an offer to go on a little day cruise the following week with one of the fishermen, to visit some of the uninhabited islands that surround Floonay. They'd be cancelling that kind offer with much regret and gratitude.

Norrie explained how it was never one hundred percent verified if it was the harpoon that turned it angry, or simply angrier. 'At the time, the thinking was simply this – the hunt was to get rid of what was already a growing menace in the seas.'

Hank responded. 'Well, let me tell you boys somethin', those big ol' things might look all cuddly an' blubbery an' all but I reckon there's a good chance – well, you gotta be careful of these dang things in the wild. Had a friend of mine over yonder in Montana – got one of his shoulders bitten off by a big hungry bear. He's lucky to be alive. Just managed to reach his revolver – big ol' Colt bear-stopping .50 Cal. Put three rounds into it just as its jaw was closin' in on his head.'

'My goodness. Your friend was lucky indeed.' Akili agreed. 'You know, in our homeland, and all over East Africa, there are so many dangerous animals. Lions, rhinos, those horrible hippos, and poisonous creepy-crawlies and slithery snakes.' He shivered. 'They can be so scary.'

'Even a zebra can give you a good kicking if you're not careful,' Darweshi added. 'I knew a gamekeeper who lost all his front teeth to the flying hoof of one. Broke his nose, too – it was half hanging off. It was a horrible mess.'

All five winced at the thought. Ouch.

Norrie, suddenly remembering, 'Oh, here, turn to – where is it?' Mwaka still had a hold of the big book but Norrie was turning the pages. He eventually found what he was looking for. It was a picture of a big woolly sheep lying on its side. There was a man with a rifle standing beside it, posing, grinning from ear to ear. The sheep was clearly dead. 'It had rabies. Was bitten by some mad dog that had swum – or doggie-paddled, to be more precise – over from Eriskay. The dog was found and shot but the sheep evaded its hunters for months. Rabies normally kills within weeks, but this sheep just kept going and going. It truly was a *wild-sheep.* Terrorised the island during that time.'

'Is this truly true?' Mwaka asked, astonished. 'What did it do?'

'It killed half a dozen dogs and feasted on its own kind. Didn't kill any humans, but did bite this one poor shepherd who tracked it down once – over on the west side, had it cornered up by these giant dunes, went to fire his shotgun and the gun jammed and that's when the sheep charged and bit him – well, you know where – a big proper crunchy chomp...'

The four men winced and felt the poor shepherd's pain. Ouch and eek.

'...then it ran off into the hills and wasn't seen for another few weeks. The shepherd was flown to the mainland for emergency treatment. Never did quite walk the same again. The frothing, rabid sheep was finally tracked down and shot a few weeks later.'

'Astonishing.'

'Astonishing indeed.'

Ch 22

Amazing

The inevitable eventually arrived.

It was bound to happen.

Things could not stay as they were forever. The summer was drawing to a close, and the brothers' missionary HQ in Nairobi had called Father John and Reverend Cullen a few times politely asking when they might be willing to relieve them of their duties and send them home. And Hank's management team – as competent as they were, were keen on seeing their boss back on Idahoan soil. Stetson Industries wasn't the same place without Hank Stetson around.

There was never any doubt as to the love the four couples had for one another. Hank and Margaret, Darweshi and Maggie, Akili and Morag, Mwaka and Catherine – they were matches made in Heaven. But these were summer romances and they happen all the time all over the world. People meet. Seem perfect for each other. *Are* perfect for each other. Sparks fly and everything is wonderful. The *inevitable* isn't talked about. Not right away anyway. You just go with the flow, and live and love in the moment, and let things unfold as they may. And more often than not the inevitable is one or both have to go separate ways. Welcome to the real world.

There's heartache and tears and promises to meet again – perhaps – and a few letters go back and forth, and the sick, horrible, gut-wrenching sadness, of being apart, is very real – for a while....and, eventually, people just drift. Drift in different directions. Separated geographically, life moves on, the tears dry, and memories, fond, beautiful memories, are stored away in a special place. Forever. Untainted, unspoilt, perfect summer love.

Each couple, in their own time, spoke privately about their circumstances – about the inevitable. It was tough, especially tough at first. A slightly awkward start to the conversations. Quivering lips bit, hands held, hugs, lots of hugs, a few misty eyes. Considering how the previous few years had treated the MacKinnons, the girls and Mrs MacKinnon could not believe how fortunate, how blessed, how lucky – how in love they were. And as a bonus – an enormous bonus, Norrie had crept out of his Nissen hut and had smiled for the first time in forever. Mrs MacKinnon had even a quietly restored faith that there just might be some sort of higher power, that maybe *something* does occasionally shine down on you. This was a difficult one for her to reconcile but she had managed back into church a few times and she had felt that what happened that wonderful summer had been quite a miracle.

But – but...

The unavoidable had arrived for all four couples. Hank couldn't stay and manage his company from the Outer Hebrides, and Mwaka, Akili, and Darweshi could not stay either. There were so many people across East Africa who needed their help.

The inevitable. The unavoidable.

Hank was going back to Idaho, and Mwaka, Akili, and Darweshi were due to leave for Nairobi the following week.

But it so happened that the *more often than not* inevitable thing did not happen. On Floonay, that wonderful summer, the inevitable instead would be that Margaret would move to Idaho to be with Hank, and Catherine, Morag, and Maggie jumped at the marriage proposals by Mwaka, Akili, and Darweshi, and move to be with them in Kenya.

*

When word spread, there was no end to the fizzy excitement of it all. The reactions were a mix of curiosity and joy and intrigue. All four of them? All leaving? With the crocodile boot man? With the three *missionaries?!* The island wouldn't be settled by humans if this didn't cause a little bit of shock. And it wouldn't be human if there wasn't a little scandalous talk as well. This was mostly stoked by the fearsome Mizz Fizzlezwit and a few of her followers. But for the most part it was simply a bewildered sort of excitement. As it settled in, many people congratulated the MacKinnon ladies and wished them much happiness and success. The turnaround in their fortunes truly was astonishing, as there had been times over the last few years when more than a few had wondered, *gravely*, what would become of Mrs MacKinnon and her girls. Not to mention Norrie.

It had certainly all taken Norrie by surprise, too. He liked Hank and the three brothers, and without ever saying so, he was grateful for their friendship – their company. He hadn't dwelt on it much, just accepted it for what it was. He definitely hadn't given much, if any, thought as to what would come of his Mama's and sisters' relationships. It was the summer, they were having fun, he was enjoying life for the first time in a long time, and that was just the way of it. What was to come next? Who knew? Who cared?

'Norrie, why don't you come to Idaho? You'll love it. I promise.'

Hank and Norrie and the three brothers were having a beer out by the Nissen hut one pleasant sunny evening.

'Your Mama and I've talked about it and, well, we think it's a great idea, you know. I gather you left school a bit early, but if you wanted to go to college, well, don't worry about a thing – I know people, I'll get you into a good school – or, or, as it seems you might be more the hands on type, a man after my own heart, you can just skip all that classroom nonsense and come and work for me, for Stetson Industries.' He gave Norrie a wink and took a long pull on his can of beer.

Norrie didn't say anything at first and seemed to be thinking things over.

'Hey, I know it'd be a big move, a dang big move. But let me tell you, Norrie, hell, things would be good. If you start a career with Stetson Industries, well, you'd start, you know, plantin' and a pickin' and basic sort of stuff around the fields, but if you work hard – and let me tell you, I've seen you out there on that big ol' beach with that rake, I don't think there's a problem in that department, you know what I'm sayin'? Well, you could, no, you *would* work your way up, managing your own tayter pickin' team and your own few acres. You could do a stint in the tayter tastin' laboratory, the tayter research facility, wherever. On and on it would go. We've got thousands of acres that we manage. Logistical operations span the continent. There'd be no limit to what you could do, no limit all.'

Norrie was still silent.

'And, hey, we'd get you a bat and a glove and a few balls, and we'd get you up to speed real quick. Get you playin' a little ball with one of the local teams and you never know where things might go. You mightn't never played ball before, but as I told you already, it seems like you got that right touch, that knowing how to flick between feathers and strength deal, you know? You got instinct, I can tell. And that's what you need more than anything.'

'Hank speaks the truth, Norrie,' Akili chipped in. 'But, let me add, you can also come, you are more than welcome, to come to Kenya with us. And there you can play cricket. It's more exciting than baseball.' He smiled at Hank.

'Well, hell boys, I don't know much about cricket, but – well, Kenya's an awful long way from Idaho.' He paused and looked thoughtful. 'I'd a miss you Norrie if you didn't come – and your Mama...' he checked himself. 'Sorry, hey, it's your choice, my friend.' He toasted Norrie and the three brothers. 'You just think on it a little bit. There ain't no reason to rush the decision, no reason at all.'

Norrie looked extraordinarily thoughtful for a moment. 'Hank?'

'You gotta question – fire away Norrie.'

'Does everyone in Idaho sound like you?'

Hank chuckled. 'Well, not *exactly* like me, but sorta I guess. Depends on where you are, of course. Might take a bit gettin' used to for ya, 'specially some of the crazier accents once you step outta Idaho and head south – if you go way south and east they get even crazier. You try understandin' what a good ol' boy from the hills of Tennessee is sayin', 'specially after he's drunka bottle of Jack. Not sure anyone can understand 'em. I don't think they even understand themselves.' He chuckled again. 'But I'll tell you somethin'. It's pretty hard understandin' you all over here. Well, not you all out here in the islands, of course. Nice, gentle lilt and all – but, dang, over there on that mainland – it's like my ears and brain are getting tossed and spun all around, gets me all confused. Can't hardly understand a word.'

Norrie was looking thoughtful again but remained silent.

'What is it Norrie?' Hank enquired.

'Do they have beaches with cockles in Idaho?'

'Afraid not, Norrie. Well, not that I know of anyhow.'

'Hmm...are there any beaches?'

'Oh, there're beaches all right. There's a few lakes around but they're freshwater, you know. If you're lookin' for the ocean you gotta' scoot on over there to Washington or Oregon, or up there to Vancouver – I got a good pal who lives up there and they got big mountains, too – huge mountains. You got ocean and mountains. Double the dealio, and hey, they might have cockles there, we'd have to investigate and find out. You could potato farm during the week and if we can find any cockles somewhere on the west coast, well, you can shoot on over there and cockle rake on the weekends.' Hank was looking extremely hopeful. 'Not a bad deal, huh? And, hell, you can even bring Bonzo with you. We'll get some sheep for him to chase.'

Hmm? Norrie was lost in deep thought.

Ch 23

Big Plans

Norrie had never even been to the mainland never mind some faraway land across the ocean. He hadn't even been all around the Hebrides. He'd visited Vatersay a few times when he was younger. It had a nice big beach, but it wasn't as nice as *his* beach, and didn't have nearly as many cockles and so he hadn't felt compelled to make the long trek too often. He'd taken the little ferry to South Uist a few times with his Papa years ago, and once sailed to Eriskay with Eddie, and they'd stopped by the once inhabited Isle of Hellisay to check on Eddie's sheep on the way back across the Sound of Floonay. And that was it.

He, of course, knew there was a big, wide world out there, but it had never dawned on him that he'd have a need to journey to any of these other places. Along Castlebay's main street The Butcher's was there for food, milk, chocolate cakes and whatever else. The Top Shop was there if he needed new rake handles or wellies or oil skins or woolly socks or other bits and pieces. The Post Office was there, of course, but he'd given up posting letters some time back. And then there was the bank – not that he'd ever used it, as he kept all the money he made from cockle raking in a tin box under his bed. But if he ever did need to put any money in the bank it was there for him. You couldn't forget, of course, about the local pubs, but at that point in Norrie's life, he wasn't a frequenter of these establishments. And that was it. He didn't need anything else.

So why bother going anywhere else?

It had never occurred to him that his Mama or sisters would ever leave Floonay. It was all a bit overwhelming. He took a walk across the big beach one evening and it was one of the few times he'd ever stepped on to the beach without his rake and bucket in hand. He just had to get away and think, and also try and not think, at the same time. Checking to make sure he had the pipe his brother, Duncan, had brought him from Santiago, he set off. Bonzo, as always, wasn't far behind. It was a pleasant enough evening, with a little breeze coming from the southwest. The tide was about halfway out, which meant he could strike an almost straight line towards the lonely white cottage a mile north on the other side. He looked all around: the giant windswept dunes off to the west and then to Picnic Hill to the northwest. The teeny island of Orosay lay a mile out in front of him, which could be reached by foot when the tide was out. Beyond Orosay – Eriskay, Fuay and South Uist were visible, stoically set in the sea. To the northeast was Stack, with its forbidding, taunting cliff face. And sweeping further east, Gighay and Hellisay. Everywhere he looked was the sea. She was settled that evening, and as he stopped to light his pipe he spied two Gannets circling high above the surface, their long, graceful wings moving as though in slow motion. They locked on to their targets, turned on tails and dove straight down, plummeting, disappearing beneath the surface, emerging moments later with their prizes. There were other birds about too, some snapping up cockles and dropping them from a height, as they would do over and over, until the shells cracked open and revealed their treasures. And still others, little legs scurrying, following the tide back and forth, pecking at unseen riches. The beach and sea were alive – *teeming with...everything.* This was his home. How could he leave all of this? *I'm sure Idaho is nice and it certainly sounds enormous, and, well, Kenya sounds quite exciting and colourful and exotic, but – this is my home...I can't leave.* Bonzo seemed to read his master's mind because he suddenly started running around more madly and excitedly than usual. He didn't want to leave Floonay either. Norrie had made his decision. The tide was creeping further out and so he was able to walk to Orosay and he took a seat on the grass, resting against a big rock, facing south. He looked to his family home, the spot on which his line of MacKinnons had had one dwelling or another for countless generations. And now that he'd made up his mind his thoughts shifted to what it was going to be like not having his Mama and sisters around.

*

'Oh Norrie, are you sure you won't come?'

'I'm sorry, Mama. I've thought about it. This is home.'

Mrs MacKinnon nibbled her lip nervously and looked from her son and then to Hank. They were seated in the kitchen along with his sisters, and Mwaka, Akili, and Darweshi. Perhaps it had been a false hope, but Hank had spoken encouragingly with Margaret that Norrie might just decide to accompany them. Beyond the new-found love in their lives there was one grave concern the MacKinnon women had, and it was simply this: If they left Norrie alone what would become of him? Would he slip back into that awful dark place that he'd been lost in for so long? This was a matter that produced not an insignificant measure of guilt in all of them, and thus they had talked about this at length. They had all been in relatively dark places, and each in her own way had managed through. But things were a bit different with Norrie – there had been the letters. But he hadn't spoken of them in ages and although they would have preferred that the letters had never happened it surely wasn't the worst or oddest thing an adolescent had ever done – especially in a period of trauma. Some people swear they've seen ghosts and goblins, own talking dolls, and have make-believe friends. All he did was write a few letters. But still, the concern was there. What would happen to him? Would he be okay? They reminded themselves that he was seventeen after all, not far from turning eighteen. People went to sea, joined armies, went off to school in faraway places, moved for work, did all sorts of things, at Norrie's age and even younger.

'I'll be just fine, Mama. I'm almost all grown up. I've got Bonzo here.' He gave his four-legged friend an encouraging pat on the head. 'And I've got my beach.'

True love only comes around once in a while. Mrs MacKinnon had had that love with Norrie's father. Still had that love for him. It would never leave. And she never thought she'd know that kind of love again. She never thought she'd want to know that kind of love again – to share that love with another person. But providence had brought her Hank and she couldn't have felt more blessed, more grateful, more fortunate for a second chance to know that kind of love. To deny it, to try and suppress it, would not just be impossible, it would be a dishonour to what love is. Hank was downcast. 'Dang, Norrie, I'm sorry. I don't know, I wish I could change your mind.'

Mwaka put a hand on Norrie's shoulder and spoke in soft melodic tones. 'Norrie, you are like a brother to us. I understand your decision. This island is beautiful. I don't think, if I were from here, that I would want to leave either. If I weren't Kenyan, I would like to be Floonish.'

Hank sighed. 'You got that right Mwaka. If I weren't Idahoan, hell, I'd be dang proud to call myself Floonish.' He looked around. 'Hell, I already feel a part of me is Floonish.'

'Indeed, Hank, indeed,' Akili commented. 'You cannot come to a place as special as Floonay and not have it influence your spirit. I, too, feel a strong connection to this place. I feel a presence here, a special presence.' He didn't want to turn it into a religious conversation, but he was thinking *I feel the presence of God's work here and it is unusually strong.*

'Well, shoot, it ain't like we're movin' to Mars or anythin',' Hank said encouragingly. 'We'll visit when we can, and Norrie, anytime you want to visit, you just say so and I'll send you a ticket.'

'You must come and visit Kenya too. You will be our guest of honour – anytime you like. We will take you on safari and you will see the giraffes and the lions and you will be amazed at everything,' Darweshi assured him.

That all sounded wonderful and, as who was going where sank in with Norrie, he felt a certain contentment that he hadn't known before. His sisters and Mama were very lucky to have met such nice men, such decent gentlemen. And though seeing his Mama with someone who wasn't his Papa had taken a bit of getting used to, he had come to accept it and understand it. He was happy for them.

With that settled, Mrs MacKinnon (with her three daughters eyeing her intently and urging her on) added, 'Uh, Norrie, there's one other thing.'

'What is it Mama?'

Hank, Darweshi, Akili, and Mwaka looked at one another and shared a knowing smile.

Norrie could see something was up. Curious, he asked, 'What is it?'

'Well, we decided, you know...since we we're, um,' she fidgeted nervously with a teaspoon, 'going to – anyway...'

'What Mama?'

'We're going to get married – here, before we leave.'

Norrie blinked. Stunned. More bewildered really. He looked around the table and everyone was smiling. 'What? All of you? Before you leave?'

They all nodded.

'That's right, Norrie. Together. Well, we were gonna' get married sometime anyway – I was real keen on makin' an honest woman out of your Mama, and so the other night the idea came up and wouldn't you know it.' He shrugged. *Voila.*

'Father John and Reverend Cullen are going to officiate at the wedding on Saturday,' Akili added. 'They are very happy for us. It is rather short notice, only three days to go. But three days can be a very long time as well. I hope it is anyway, as we have a "four weddings in one" wedding to plan. We hope it is not too much different than a "one in one" wedding.'

*

As that extraordinary summer drew to a close on the Isle of Floonay, Alan Trout was contemplating his future. With three years of university and two gap years under his belt, Alan knew now, more than ever, what it was he was going to do with himself.

He had known years ago what his limitations were. He had attended one of the best boarding schools in the land, and his family's resources had provided the best tutors money could buy. It had been their job to put the finishing touches on what should have been a razor sharp and wholly comprehensive set of mental tools, a set of tools that would strengthen and sharpen in university. After that the world would be his for the taking.

Well, the world would still be his for the taking – that much he knew – but he struggled mightily in many areas. Maths, sciences, engineering, history, the arts, philosophy, and economics, to name a few subjects. He tried. He really had. It just wasn't for him and he knew that. Just like the sport he loathed. Rugby. But he had been forced to play for all those years. It initially frightened him to his core, but, slowly, curiously, he learned to control his fear – mostly. Thankfully, the Trout family tradition of playing rugby didn't extend into the university years. But, in spite of all the fear and sleepless nights before a match, he discovered one of the two skills he had, and it was this – that he was so slippery and wriggly that he never actually got hit on the pitch. Incredible. Always far out on the flank, always ducking and avoiding and hopping over charging bodies. Baffling really. Perhaps more baffling than the fact that he was so wriggly was the realisation that no one ever noticed. An idea started to germinate at some point over the years deep in his mind that this skill – *avoidance without detection* – might just come in handy one day. The other skill he eventually realised he had was simply this: he could talk. He might not have had a clue about any number of subjects but, crazily, he could speak about them all – as though he was a maestro of everything! *I know it all! Least it seems to sound like I do, hmm, interesting, interesting indeed!* And the fantastic thing was whenever he found himself on the spot, to answer an extraordinarily direct question on a subject about which he knew absolutely nothing, skill number one, 'slippery and wriggly' came to aid skill number two, and he was able, always, to extricate himself from the predicament, with the questioner being none the wiser.

Alan Trout decided that his passion would be just to talk. Add slipperiness and wriggliness to a passion for talking and you had a lethal concoction.

Politics!

That summer Alan finally realised where his destiny lay.

Upon further reflection, he realised there was *no* choice, no decision for him to make. Passion was involved after all. *It chose him!*

Alan Trout was going to become a politician. *I am going to shape the world with what I have to say,* he reflected, not knowing, really, what he was going to say. But he knew it was going to be good. And was certain that people would believe him.

Ch 24

Four (Weddings) in One

'I do'

'I do'

'I do'

'And so do I!'

Father John and Reverend Cullen both smiled and spoke in unison. 'Hank, Mwaka, Akili, Darweshi, you may kiss your brides.'

A huge cheer went up on that most remarkable Saturday as the four couples turned to face the congregation. Their smiles were beaming, and what a sight it was to behold. Seeing as there had been only three days to plan the wedding it had proved impossible to find three MacKinnon tartan kilts to properly fit the three strapping missionaries. It was a shame, but at least appropriately fitted kilts were eventually located. Hank had wanted to wear his favourite cowboy boots, but Mrs MacKinnon had put her foot down at that request – it would look utterly ridiculous. Margaret and Hank proudly walked from the altar first, followed by Catherine and Mwaka, then Morag and Akili, with Maggie and Darweshi bringing up the rear. The pews were teeming with clapping guests and the new brides and grooms waved and smiled and were the happiest people on the planet that day. Two pipers were playing outside and would continue to do so until all the guests had spilled out and congratulated the newlyweds. They would then march everyone down the steep hill outside of the church and all the way to the main hall in Castlebay. Bonzo had watched the whole thing from a window, front paws up on the stone ledge, tongue hanging out and tail wagging furiously. It was a marvellous sunny day, and the evening reception – the ceilidh – turned out to be one for the record books. Everyone danced until the sun was coming up. And some even danced a little while longer. Even Father John and Reverend Cullen stayed till the sun was rising – something they would regret doing as they had sermons to deliver a few short hours later. Consequently, the sermons on that Sunday lasted maybe ten minutes, if one were generous, which had led many to agree they were the shortest sermons ever.

The celebration for some continued until the following Thursday, the day the newlyweds departed Floonay by aeroplane. Those four days were wonderful, but they were also quite frenzied, as the ladies fretted about what to pack and where things should go and on and on. Hank, the three brothers and Norrie just let them get on with it. Best not to get in a woman's way in these matters. For their part, though Hank, Mwaka, Akili, and Darweshi were newlyweds (and would normally be spending the nights with their new wives) they instead continued their little sleepovers in Norrie's Nissen hut. They only had a few nights left and thoroughly enjoyed the male bonding, having a dram and sharing a few last tales, some tall, some not so tall. The women didn't mind, as it would be the last visit with Norrie for quite some time, and anyway, it was only when they were retiring did they venture out to the Nissen hut. The couples were together during the day, when the new brides weren't busy packing and organising, and in the evenings for dinner and a ceilidh. Those two nights that the men spent in the Nissen hut were a memorable and special time. Hank regaled them with more stories of his time in the Far East and of the trials and tribulations during the early days of Stetson Industries, and the brothers, in turn, spoke of the endless wonders of East Africa, and even Norrie told a few stories from the Coquilleuous Rakkeronuous Almenikhiaka. The men marvelled at the incredible book and all lamented that they didn't have great-times-eight-grandpas who had had the foresight to start such a magnificent thing. It was one of those precious periods – moments in time – that one wished would linger for longer, if not go on forever.

But, alas, time marched on and Thursday soon arrived and, just perhaps, one precious period would pass into another. Family and friends of the MacKinnons gathered by the edge of the beach to bid their farewells. A light breeze brought the grassy dunes to life and wispy clouds high above moved gently from west to east. Far out on the Traigh Mhor, beyond the airport markers, a few of Floonay's part time cockle rakers paused to watch, rakes held high in salute.

Mrs MacKinnon gave Norrie a huge hug for the umpteenth time and kissed him on the cheek.

'Mama, I'm going to be just fine,' Norrie said, slightly embarrassed at all the attention. He hadn't thought his sisters would stop, and even now looked as though they wanted to give him one more hug. *Enough already, go on, scram! Everything's okay!*

Hank, Mwaka, Akili, and Darweshi said their goodbyes and reminded Norrie to come and visit anytime. It was such a huge moment for them all. This was it. They were actually leaving Floonay. Catherine, Morag, Maggie, and their Mama – they were so in love with their new husbands and knew the decision to leave was the right one, but standing there as the door to the plane opened and the steps folded out, well, it all made them so nervous as well. Bonzo was doing circles just a few yards away, saying goodbye in his own half-mad way.

One more hug from them all and they were being beckoned aboard.

'Take care of yourself Norrie...'

'We'll write often...'

'...Call when I can...'

The women were reduced to what seemed like inconsolable tears, but managed to wrench themselves away from Norrie and clamber aboard the plane.

As the brothers climbed aboard, they all said the same thing as they glanced back. 'You are our brother Norrie, don't forget that.'

Hank was the last one to board. He put a hand on Norrie's shoulder. 'You ever change your mind, you come right on over to Idaho, you hear me?' He took one last look around. The sweeping dunes, the woolly sheep, the grazing cows, Picnic Hill, the islands to the north and east, the solitary white cottage at the point, a lonely potato patch a hundred yards away. He stole one final glance at Norrie before climbing aboard, smiled, and said, 'Floonay definitely has the best dang tayters in the world.'

And with that, the door shut. There was a pause before the engines made a whining noise, then they coughed, spluttered, and roared to life. Faces in the windows, with a few last teary waves. The plane taxied directly east a few hundred yards. Turned to face the wind. A pause as the pilot did his pre-flight check. The engines whined, the props screamed, and a cloud of sand kicked up behind the plane as it started to move. Eighty yards later the nose of the plane was lifting off the beach and shortly after that was rising, passing over the tiny terminal and the waving crowd below. It climbed some more, banked north, and then east, and continued climbing and soon was just a dot disappearing into the clouds. Then, it was gone.

Ch 25

The Trinity of Power

As Norrie MacKinnon settled into his routine of cockle raking and adjusting to life without his Mama or sisters around, Alan Trout was daydreaming in his economics class. Economics bored him to his core, but it was mandatory reading as part of his course. The other two subjects required to study, Politics and Philosophy, were no less boring but he knew that if he was going to find any success in the world of politics he needed this degree. It should be made clear here that Alan somehow understood that the study of politics was different from the act of politicking. Yes, he found the study of it horrendously boring, but he also knew once in office, things would be much different. *Leave the studying to the academics, let me get out there and make a difference in this world.*

As the bearded, bespectacled and highly esteemed doctor spoke of Keynesian economics, Adam Smith, David Hume and some fellow called Schumpeter, Alan sighed and his mind, once again, drifted into space and out over the world. He'd just finished reading The Prisoner of Zenda for the fifth time. Ruritania was most exciting. The adventure, the intrigue, the subplots, the King's betrothed...*if only, if only - if only it had been me who'd been travelling there.* Next, he was drifting over King Solomon's Mines and could practically smell the action, and then he was submerged beneath Jules Verne's waves and was heading down 20,000 leagues. Stevenson's *Kidnapped* and Doyle's *Lost World* were never far from his imagination, and, seeing as he was an aspiring political *mover and shaker*, Buchan's *39 Steps* was never far from his heart. Alan loved all these classic stories of adventure and intrigue, excitement and high drama, conspiracies and hidden treasure. Stories of real-life explorers, such as Shackleton and Livingstone, were quite remarkable, too, and he was especially fascinated with the story of the man who had had a country named after him. *What an incredible feat...hmm? Troutesia? Alanerica? Troutland? Alanany?* Choices, choices. As usual, as he read all these tales of fact and fiction – it didn't matter which – he unfailingly slipped himself right into the main character's skin. Whether running across rain sodden braes being pursued by malevolent forces, scrambling through a steamy jungle with a tribe of headhunters hot on his tail, or passing top secret negatives to a pretty young spy in a dark alcove of a smoky bar – always – unfailingly, it was Alan Trout. Alan was saving the day and defeating the enemy, liberating the enslaved and discovering the treasures. And, of course, he was always getting the girl – or girls. That went without saying. And if he happened to be reading a story that he'd, once again hijacked as his own, and there was no glamorous princess or sultry spy falling head over heels for him – well, he would just add them. Alan was certain he had been born a century too late, perhaps a century and a half. *If only, if only – I would have been out there – adventuring, discovering, inventing, creating. What would I have been? A Captain? Perhaps Major? Admiral even? Viceroy – with my very own harem? The possibilities were endless. If only...*

'Alan – did you hear me? Alan?'

Suddenly Alan was yanked out of his adventure kit and pulled out of the frozen cockpit of the bullet riddled biplane he was flying across the snow peaked Carpathian Mountains. 'Sorry, pardon me professor?'

'The Walrasian Equilibrium, Alan? Your thoughts?'

Alan frowned, shifted in his chair, and summoned all his will power not to roll his eyes. He didn't care too much about economics and this was one of the reasons why. It was the haven of ridiculously named theories that contradict one another, and of abstractions that often make no sense to anyone but the creator. It is a social science – a pseudo-science more like it. And Alan knew (in his sort of knowing way) it was the softest of all the sciences that man had ever conceived. It was soft and ambiguous and made to look hard with all sorts of concocted formulas and statistics. *Alchemy's got more traction than this strange brew.* It was the King of Subjectivity. And no matter how much any one person tried to understand it, wholly, to explain an event, a shock, a cycle, a dip, a dive, a recession, a depression, a whatever, it was, mostly, unexplainable. Mostly. Not completely. Little windows of clarity appeared here and there, but they were snap shots, a series of snap shots, a short narrative, into an enormous infinite abyss, with an equally infinite number of moving parts. In summary and if he was being entirely truthful, young Alan found it all quite confusing and – and – he didn't have a clue about the Walrasian Equilibrium.

Think Alan, think.

The good doctor was waiting patiently and the other students in the class were all turned in their chairs. He knew he was supposed to have read about it but the Prisoner of Zenda and Ruritania had proven much more exciting. *Come on, Alan, you better come up with something!* He coughed, making a show of clearing his throat. Now, although he found economics both boring and confusing the one amazing thing he realised about it was simply this – it was like some incredible revelation dawned on him one day, illuminated inside him, and it was a real *aha* moment – *this is perfect – perfectly boring, perfectly confusing, but also there is...perfectly – no right or wrong, there were just variations, shades, depending on circumstances, interactions, intent, desire, there might be a slightly different angle, leading to – who knew where?* It was perfect for him!

'Well, I do find it all very interesting. Interesting indeed. If you take the key bit – the equilibrating forces, and give them a good knock – that natural "state of things" will shift, perhaps, but then again, that can't be for certain – what, after all, *is* the natural state of things here or – say, there – values rise and fall.' He shrugged. 'I can see both sides of the argument – of the conundrum. Do we start from here?' He made a show of pointing to an imaginary place just to his left, 'and go there?' He made a further show of pointing to some invisible place a foot to his right. He wiggled his fingers a bit as though massaging or testing something only he could see. 'Or vice versa. And for what purpose do we make that, quote unquote, *journey?* Difficult call, difficult indeed.'

He sat back, satisfied. A few of his classmates looked sufficiently perplexed and the good doctor frowned, adjusted his spectacles, turned to the blackboard and picked up a bit of chalk. 'Interesting Alan, interesting indeed. Well, let's consider Keynes' position, shall we?'

*

As the future politician's mind drifted upwards, following the air currents east and back to the craggy and frozen summits of the Carpathian Mountain Range, piloting the bullet riddled biplane through icy winds swirling over the highest peak, three individuals who would become known as the Trinity of Power to Alan were experiencing life in their own ways.

A Texas gentleman by the name of Roger Remington III, or simply, Remy, was expanding his business. The heart of Remy Industrial Group *(RIG)* was Remy Oil, and it was going gangbusters amidst an industry that, at the time, was quite volatile. Every morning when Remy awoke he didn't do anything before first saying a prayer, counting his blessings and reminding himself how fortunate he was. He'd been given a second chance, an enormous second chance. Remy saw it as the *gift of life* after the light of life had all but extinguished. In the budding years of Remy Oil there was no oil. Only a vision, a promise, and a few square miles of dusty Texas land. The land had been a gift from one whom the rest of his family called 'crazy drunk Uncle Fred'. Crazy drunk Uncle Fred had been on his deathbed when he bequeathed the arid plot to his favourite nephew. Fred lived in a dusty old shack that couldn't have been in starker contrast to the abodes of the rest of his family. You see, the Remingtons in Texas were a well-known family of artists that stretched back generations. Remington art graced the walls of judges' chambers and the halls of power, the offices of politicians, generals, high flying lawyers and CEOs, millionaire mansions and luxury hotels. Name a place of wealth and influence and a Remington creation was there, boldly staring out at the world.

Fred was the black sheep – or the white sheep amongst the black – colour him however you want, perhaps purple – he was the outcast, the forgotten, the down and out, the one they mocked and scorned. He was a drunk and a loser (their words) and gave up on everything to chase a fanciful dream. And for a long time after he died the rest of the Remingtons despised him even more for how he had influenced young Remy. Coughing and wheezing, with only Remy at his bedside, old, defeated, Fred, had pressed the crumpled will into his nephew's uncertain hands. Fred Remington's face was sunken and his eyes sad, but not hopeless. Deep in those eyes, amidst the rubble of a million memories, there was certainty of *something.* He took a sip of brandy from a dirty old mug that young Remy had to hold for him – Remy hadn't wanted to give it to him, but could not turn down what he knew was one of the last wishes of a dying man. A little brandy dribbled down his chin, that Remy wiped away with the sleeve of his shirt. He whispered hoarsely, 'Remy, it's there...I know it is. Find it, I know you can. You're not like – them.' He glanced involuntarily to a 'them' who were not present in the dingy old shack. He gripped his nephew's right hand with a strength that surprised young Remy. 'Remy – it's there – I searched and searched...I tried, I failed.' He released his grip, settled back, and one last time looked to his favourite nephew. His voice was but a whisper, 'Remy, it is calling you, you know it is, like it called to me. P-put those damned paint brushes away and start paying attention... but, but, please, Remy, don't make the same mistakes I did - promise me that,' And then he closed his eyes and was gone. 'I promise, Uncle Fred...'

The big incident that almost cost Remy his life occurred five years later. For five years after turning his back on what could have been a mildly successful but intolerably frustrating career as another Remington artist, Remy had searched "crazy drunk Uncle Fred's" barren and dusty land for the elusive black gold until one fated day he fell into an old disused mineshaft. He'd landed awkwardly in a dark rotten heap of who knew what after bouncing off countless bits of timber on the way down. There was the most horrific crunch and his world faded to black. After coming to and groping blindly, Remy realised, with a horror he'd never known – that there was jagged bone sticking out of his right leg – a leg that was splayed out and twisted in a most unnatural way. After some time of agony and misery, with his strength diminishing, as he felt life seeping slowly out of him, Remy closed his eyes and amidst the infinite pain managed to turn his thoughts to the Prince of Peace (his family of artists were atheists and didn't believe in anything but money and art, but Remy understood things differently), and asked for His help. Remy vowed that if he managed to get out of this most unfortunate situation, he would do His work.

It was a few minutes later that something quite remarkable happened – and by God, it would turn out that crazy drunk Uncle Fred was right all along.

*

At the same time that a young and nearly dead Remy heard a voice deep down in that revolting rat infested mineshaft, a fellow known simply as Achmed was well on his way to making his second million, and also, he loved the view of the Indian Ocean he had from the balcony of his offices in Zanzibar. 'Achmed, my my, what a lovely day this is. And look at that water, sparkling and shimmering just so' – his thoughts, as they often did, went to the parents that he'd never known and to the brothers and sisters he didn't know if he had...*I know you did not abandon me*...and, quite naturally, his thoughts often wandered back to the desert, and to his adopted family, the nomads, who cared not a thing for possessions beyond the barest essentials. He was young but already had an impressive reputation as quite the wily dealmaker. Achmed was known in practically every souk, bazaar, and marketplace across the Middle East and North Africa. Even the odd car boot sale. Wherever and whenever goods were being bought and sold and deals were being made Achmed was there. And one way or another Achmed always, eventually, got the better end of every transaction. You see, he had an eye for spotting hidden gems amongst the rubble, and, perhaps more importantly, he had that innate talent of convincing someone of a great bargain. He was the perfect salesman, and everyone knew that the Arabs were the best salesmen glued to the planet. So, this made Achmed numero uno in the world.

This came in handy when he was trying to shift, say, some rubble that had no hidden gems. The transaction had to be made, the product needed shifting, and money in one form or another, as since time immemorial, needed to change hands. It was the way the world had always worked, and more than likely, always would.

Achmed had adopted Zanzibar as his home but started life as a child with no country and no name. He did not remember the moment, as he was too young, but knew the story well.

He was found wandering the desert, alone, by a group of nomads at a position roughly straddling the spot where Egypt, Libya and Sudan meet. He was in rags, barefoot, and little salty tears had been running down his sun-baked skin for a long time. The nomads went to his aid immediately. They'd set up camp to gain shelter from the scorching sun, and fed and watered the poor little boy. The women of the tribe cleaned him up and dressed him in fresh nomad rags (still rags, but an upgrade from what he had been wearing). After a time, he fell asleep in the arms of a young woman he would later learn was called Fatima. The men of the tribe sent out riders on horseback in all directions to search for the family of this poor boy. Where could they be? They could not be that far away? Was he abandoned? Who would abandon a child? The riders didn't find anyone who knew the child. How long had he been walking? This caused much consternation amongst the tribe. The emotions were a mixture of frustration, infuriation, and perplexity. But also of joy and gratefulness that he had been found. The only possession the young boy had was of an old black and white photograph, tucked inside his rags. It was a photo of three white men dressed in desert khakis, two of whom were sitting in a jeep and one was casually leaning up against its side. A machine gun was mounted on the back on the jeep. Three names were scribbled on the back but the nomads could not read them. Where had this come from? Who were these people? Why did this little boy have this? Further confusion. The young woman known as Fatima put it away for safekeeping. After a few days at camp, with no news of anyone searching for a missing child the tribe decided to adopt him as their own and called him Achmed. He grew up with that tribe, wandering far and wide across North Africa. He loved them greatly and held them in his heart as his family. As Achmed grew up, he heard the story many times of how he had been found so he knew he had another family, somewhere out there. And then there was that *something* that tugged at him, pulled him, called to him. It was to venture out, alone, into the wider, if uncertain, world, and find his gift. And so it would be that at the age of fifteen, and with the tribe's consent, Achmed struck out on his own.

*

The final man to form the Trinity of Power that would eventually cross paths with Alan Trout, was the incredible Dr Foo. He had a different upbringing entirely. He had never been in the dire straits that Remy and Achmed had found themselves, except for the fact that his immediate family had all perished in an avalanche when he was too young to remember. It was Foo, as a streetwise boy of twelve, who had saved the life of a man he had observed was walking directly into a situation that had dire straits written all over it. The man was a foreigner in Shanghai, sticking out like a sore thumb in the bustling marketplace, and had naively wandered into a part of the market where only illicit things happened. He, Tom Sutherland, would never know how close he was to being bundled into the decrepit old van – most likely never to be heard from again, after being separated from his fancy watch, wallet and fine leather shoes. But judging by the way the young lad had reacted, yanking him this way and that amongst the stalls, he assumed it had been perilously close. As a way of thanking young Foo, and especially upon hearing that Foo was an orphan who spent his days kicking around the streets pickpocketing as a means of survival, Sutherland, in broken Mandarin, offered to raise him as his own. ('There's a lot of good in you, laddie, a shame to see it wasted.') But because of the rules and regulations in Shanghai at the time, Tom Sutherland had to keep the impromptu adoption of his young saviour *on the down low,* as they say in some places.

Ch 26

The Great Unravelling

Things were fine that autumn on Floonay. Norrie maintained a steady routine of cockle raking, tide after tide, day after day, week after week. Bonzo was always there at this side and the two of them were perfectly content. The only surprise came when his best pal from his school days dropped by to tell him he was leaving for the merchant navy and didn't know when he'd be back. Norrie hadn't seen very much of Malcolm over the years. It was a friendship that hadn't ended but simply drifted apart. Norrie felt a little bad that he had not made more of an effort – but that's the way these things go sometimes. Malcolm hadn't either, but of course he'd been the one on the sore end of a fist to the nose. Malcolm promised to keep in touch, and Norrie wished him luck, and that was it. Eddie, Colin, Ronnie and a few of the other boys would stop by on occasion. Norrie appreciated their company. It had taken some effort by Eddie to convince Ronnie that Norrie didn't blame him and to join them. Ronnie had felt exceedingly guilty, and still did, as it should have been him out there and not Norrie's father. Eddie had spoken to Norrie about it beforehand, uncertain as to how things would go but

Norrie had said simply, 'I don't blame Ronnie. It's not his fault. It's that bastard of a monster out there that is to blame.'

Others, too, would stop by with bags of scones, cakes, piping hot plates of mince and tatties, or for just a wee blether.

As it had been his Mama and sisters who used to do all the cooking, that was one area he was still getting used to. Meat pies were easy, as were boiling potatoes, and making fry-ups. But he wasn't straying too far into the culinary world. After a few attempts he got the proportion right for the Bisto in the mince and that made him happy. There wasn't much else he needed to know. And he received an invite for a Sunday dinner at least once a fortnight, which was usually a nice big roast.

He'd spoken to his Mama a few times and she'd even sent a few letters, as had his sisters. They were all settling in nicely and had plenty of exciting and wonderful stories to share with him. He had already heard some of it from the men themselves but it was good to hear that they were all adjusting well and still excited about their new lives. Of course, he'd promised he would go and visit sometime but they had only been gone a few months. The days were getting shorter quickly, affecting which tides he could work in the daylight. He'd raked in the dark before when the tide was out, but it was much more efficient during daylight hours.

One thing that didn't change from the summer, and indeed from the previous year, was Norrie's living arrangement. He chose not to move back into the house and instead maintained his sleeping digs out in the Nissen hut – this seemed to please Bonzo immensely. He would use the kitchen and the bathroom in the house but had become quite used to sleeping out in the big metal shed. It was still an adventure. In the evenings he would read from the Coquilleuous Rakkeronuous Almenikhiaka, under the light of an old Tilly lamp. One Saturday night in October, the idea surfaced that perhaps he would take the big book into the family room, light a nice warm fire and sit in his Papa's old chair. The days were shortening and the nights were getting colder after all. He did just that. With a nice warm fire blazing and his pipe full he settled in for a few hours of reading before heading for bed.

Sitting there, alone for the first time where his father used to sit, the memories started to surface; of Papa reading, smiling, smoking his pipe, having a dram, and tousling his youngest son's hair. He could smell his presence, and – it just didn't feel right. *Was it too soon? Should I have waited longer?* He tried to ignore the anxiety of the moment but could not. No. He wasn't going to force it, and swiftly decided to abandon the effort. The past summer with Hank, the brothers, his Mama and sisters having ceilidhs in the room had been good. But no, sitting there, on his own – with the memories and the big book. Forget it.

It was back to the Nissen hut where all was well. After rummaging around he found a wee iron stove – *perfect – that will do nicely.* He cut a hole in the roof to poke the skinny chimney through, stuffed a few bits of crumpled newspaper with handfuls of coal in and lit the fire. It wasn't long before the Nissen hut warmed up. Norrie smiled contentedly that Saturday evening, and Bonzo was looking like the happiest dog in the Western Isles.

The third day in December was a bit of a tough day as it marked the third anniversary of his brother, Rory, plunging to his death into the Irish Sea. The day was pleasant; sunny with just a light breeze, and the air was crispy. It was as though the atmosphere around the Traigh Mhor was doing its best to keep the day as bright as possible for young Norrie. And he did his part to keep the day a positive one, occupying his time by raking as much and as fast as he could in an attempt to suppress the memories. He focused and raked, using a half dozen different techniques, but inevitably, his brother kept waltzing right on into his head. Rory had loved tending to his sheep as much as he loved his work as a joiner. And he'd loved Bonzo deeply, even though he wasn't a very good sheepdog. Norrie would occasionally glance over to Bonzo, who was never far away. Usually, Bonzo would dart off and chase the seagulls, or if he spied people in the distance he'd run after them, tail wagging and tongue flapping in the breeze. He'd startled many an unsuspecting passer-by, raising a hind leg to pee on a boot. He always returned, only to run circles around Norrie, and even occasionally paw for cockles. But Bonzo seemed to sense there was something special about that day. And thus, he spent more time than usual sitting still, just staring up at Norrie with great affection in his eyes. Bonzo rarely sat still during the excitement of the day.

It had been the same the previous two anniversaries. Norrie had thought about that dark day so often. The one place Rory feared most was destined to become his grave. Thinking of the terror his brother must have felt as he and the rest of the helicopter's crew plunged towards the sea filled Norrie with such gut wrenching sorrow that it made him so afraid for Rory, even though he had been gone for three years. There had been an explosion before the helicopter went down and Norrie had hoped countless times that perhaps Rory had mercifully met a quick end thereby avoiding the terror of falling to his death. As dreadful as his father's, Duncan's, Donald's, and Ewan's deaths were, there was some smidgen of comfort that it had happened close to home. Not all their remains had been found, but at least what did wash ashore was buried there, on Floonay. Rory had been alone. And because of that, in Norrie's mind, there was something extra cruel about it.

That evening in the Nissen hut, with Bonzo nestled at his feet by the warmth of the stove, Norrie didn't do anything but sit in the silence, with his pipe from Santiago and a bottle of

Rory's favourite whisky. The time passed and as he drank he shed a few tears for Rory, and also for Duncan, Donald, Ewan, and his Papa, too...*Why do these things have to happen? It's not fair. It's not right...I miss them, so...*

Norrie woke laying at the foot of the fire, with Bonzo curled in beside him. After a moment he creaked himself to an upright position, dusted himself off and headed for the kitchen. He cooked himself a fry-up; plenty of black pudding, bacon, eggs and toast. And as he did, he uncharacteristically took a few swigs of whisky – *that will do just nicely*...and then he slipped on his wellies, picked up his bucket, rake, and a few net bags and headed for the big beach. The day went well. Being youthful, strong and out of doors, working hard to earn a few quid, he quickly recovered from the murkiness of the night before.

Norrie mostly forgot about the evening of 3 December, notching it up as a 'one off'. These things happen. You remember, you mourn, and you move on. His Mama and Hank had tried to persuade him to join them for Christmas in Idaho. He'd seriously thought about it that first year but decided against it. His Mama and Hank were disappointed, and considered travelling back to Floonay for the holidays, but Hank had many dear friends who were tripping over themselves to welcome his new wife, so they decided to stay in Idaho. His sisters were busy being whisked around Kenya and would not be travelling home either, but that was fine. Norrie was quite content with Bonzo at his side, and he had more than enough choices regarding where to spend Christmas Eve, Christmas Day, Boxing Day, any day for that matter. There were many doors open to him, but strangely, Norrie was finding, more and more, that there was nothing he preferred more than being on his own with Bonzo faithfully at his side. His routine was a comfort to him: cockle raking, tinkering in the Nissen hut, and sitting by the old stove reading the Coquilleuous Rakkeronuous Almenikhiaka. He spent Christmas in the Nissen hut.

*

That year transitioned into the next and it would mark the beginning of 'the great unravelling'.

If you ignore the first six words of Dicken's classic, *A Tale of Two Cities*, and focus instead on the following six words – that, essentially, summed up the darkest stretch of Norrie MacKinnon's life. *It was the best of times, it was the worst of times.*

Life can and does go on through highs and lows, some extreme, some not so extreme. For Norrie's, things really started to unravel – and quickly – when he literally jumped into the Minch. It was an alarming sight for the passengers on the ferry who witnessed it. *What in heaven's name is he doing?!* Alarm bells sounded. The crew went into emergency mode. The lifeboat from Castlebay was despatched and one was swung out and lowered from the ferry's deck.

It was mid-April of that following year and Norrie had finally given in to his Mama's wish for him to come and visit Idaho. And so, with a small travel bag, and ferry, train, and plane tickets tucked in a pocket, he boarded the big ferry bound for the imposing mainland. Norrie had never been to the mainland before, and approached the trip with a mixture of curiosity and trepidation. The wind was fresh from the southwest that day and there was a fair chop in the water, but it was certainly not what one would call stormy, not by Hebridean standards anyway. With everyone aboard and the gangplank raised, the ferry heaved around. It glided past Kisimul Castle in the middle of the bay, navigated through the narrow Sound of Vatersay, and it was just as they were steaming past the big lump of rock known as Muldonach, that two frantic passengers barrelled into the ship's mess deck yelling that someone had just jumped overboard.

Ch 27

A Strange Strange Thing

If the passengers who witnessed Norrie jump got a shock, it paled in comparison to the strange overwhelming sensation that drove him over the edge. *What a bizarre and curious thing.* But it was all too real and he felt much better upon hitting the water – even though he couldn't swim, because for a moment he had escaped whatever 'that' was. It had overwhelmed him so forcefully and completely. It astonished him. He'd known anger, frustration, and fury before. Sadness and profound sorrow, too – but he'd never known *that*?! *What the hell is happening to me?* Well, he didn't wait around for a response but assumed it had something to do with the ferry, and so over he went. Within a moment he realised the terror of being unable to stay afloat. Thankfully, three lifebelts splashed down in his vicinity, and he just managed to grab a hold of one. Within a few minutes he was being plucked out of the water by the lifeboat crew. There was no way he could explain why he did what he did, so he started making things up. His subconscious took over. There was no stopping it. He felt an extreme level of shame, not for what he had done, but for what he had *felt,* and thus as a way to manage that shame, the make-believe took over.

The lifeboat crew were perplexed by Norrie's version of what had happened, as it varied significantly from what they'd heard. 'I was leaning over to see the dolphins and then, and then, I just fell over, I don't know – sorry,' and, later, when Constable Currie paid him a visit he altered his story upon realising the policeman wasn't buying the whole 'falling in' bit, and insisted that it was Bonzo he was really concerned about. That he wasn't going to be fed properly. 'Norrie, you can't go jumping off ferries because of a dog! And as far as I know, you can't even swim. For God's sake, Norrie.' Constable Currie had eyed Norrie suspiciously. 'You sure there's nothing else?' Norrie was adamant and certainly also sorry, professing that he didn't know you weren't allowed to jump off ferries, especially when it was still so close to land. 'I didn't have that far to, er, try and swim, Constable, Floonay was just right there – I thought it would come naturally...sorry, I won't do it again, promise!' And it was a promise he would most certainly keep, because he knew he would never again step foot on a boat – and though that relieved him, it also bothered him greatly.

Constable Currie remembered the letters from a few years back and it crossed his mind that perhaps anyone capable of penning and posting hundreds of letters to God, was also capable of pulling off a mad stunt like jumping off a ferry to make sure his dog was properly fed. He let the matter drop and told Norrie that if he needed anything not to hesitate to ring him. The whole island had heard of the incident within hours and you could fairly say that Norrie's ears were burning. Mizz Fizzlezwit was particularly gleeful at hearing the news. 'Excellent. You're going mad. That's what you get you little monster!'

That evening, back in the Nissen hut, Norrie sat by the old stove, with his pipe from Santiago, a comforting bottle of whisky, and one happy half-mad sheep dog to keep him company. His thoughts meandered through the day and the years; from Rory's fear of the sea – *at least he made it across the Minch* – to the story he overheard between the two teachers, of their friend who had killed herself because she was always anxious and couldn't cope. He hadn't understood, really, what they were saying until now, and his thoughts wound back to that very morning and what forced him to jump. And the thoughts just looped, but by no means in a frantic state. If anything, he was relaxed, quietly thinking, contemplating, considering things. *What a curious thing. What a ridiculously curious thing. I loved going on Eddie's boat. Why has this happened?* He hadn't been on a boat in a few years, since before the tragedies. It was Eddie's old boat, *Odyssey*, that he was last on, the one that ended up smashed to smithereens between Stack and Eriskay. Smashed to smithereens with his Papa and Donald aboard. *Perhaps it has something to do with that? It has left a bigger mark on me than I realised.* Well, whatever, he had made his decision and it was final. He had to protect himself against *that.* He looked down at his four-legged friend who was curled up at his feet, by the warmth of the stove. 'Bonzo?' Bonzo's ears tweaked and he looked up expectantly. 'I am never, ever, in my whole life, going to get on another boat. Ever again.' Bonzo wagged his tail and was happy for his master.

Dealing with his Mama and sisters when they called was easy. When protecting oneself against *that* and seeking to mask the shame, it was amazing how agile and inventive one could become. Not that the excuses sounded any less ridiculous – 'the ferry was turning hard, and I was leaning over to see the dolphins and then I just fell over'. 'Will you be taking another ferry soon, or perhaps you can take the aeroplane?' If the ferry made him feel that, there was no way he was going to hop on an aeroplane. 'Well, I just received a big order of cockles – it's huge, biggest ever. From Nelson, the new shellfish buyer. I've committed to it. I'll reschedule for later...sorry Mama.' Norrie knew full well that later would never come. In the following days he wasn't short of visitors stopping in to check on him. Of course he was fine, just lost his balance, that's all. No, he wouldn't be heading to Idaho anytime soon. Too busy with cockle orders. No, those people must have been seeing things. That's not what really happened. Within a few days it was mostly forgotten and people stopped asking questions.

For Norrie, what wasn't mostly forgotten was the memory and his own questions. He had a good handle on things though. He stuck to his routine of cockle raking, tinkering in the Nissen hut and reading the Coquilleuous Rakkeronuous Almenikhiaka. And, of course, he thought of *it. What a strange, strange thing.* One evening the thought surfaced, *I wonder if there's anything about 'that' in the Big Book?* And so he continued, flipping crusty page after dusty page after rusty page. There certainly were plenty of stern warnings about what not to do, and perilous stories, and pages with skulls and crossbones. The Book was so enormous he still hadn't been through the whole thing, even after all those years of his Papa reading to him and in the subsequent years of reading it himself. He flipped around from here to there. There were plenty of stories with frightful little bits. And the picture of the crazy artist who lived in the lonely shack on the west side, Walter Wellington, was a bit scary, but Norrie didn't happen upon a story or even a scribble or an explanation of how *that* happens and why it would make someone jump off a boat. Frustrated, he closed the Big Book and turned his attention to refilling and lighting his pipe. 'Well, Bonzo, maybe it will just go away, and I won't have to worry about it anymore.' Bonzo looked up expectantly at Norrie, his tongue hanging out, his tail wagging enthusiastically. 'I know you do, Bonzo, I know you do.'

The months ticked along and Norrie stuck to his routine of raking, reading, tinkering – and thinking. For no particular reason he was seeing less and less of other people. He still received invites here and there for Sunday dinners or special occasions, but he was turning down more than he was accepting, and thus he was eventually receiving less invites. He simply found he was preferring his own and Bonzo's company. By no means had he retreated to the gloomy place he was in before, when he spoke to virtually no one – he spoke with whomever he happened to bump into – it was just that he felt more comfortable *doing his own thing*. Nothing wrong with that. Good news arrived from Idaho in September of that year – his Mama was pregnant, and not only that, she was expecting twins! Incredible. His Mama was just into her forties after all. So not a complete surprise. It does happen.

*

The day of ultimate cruelty started like all the others. It was mid-October. Norrie awoke in his folding bed, stretched, yawned and swung his legs over the side. Another stretch, another yawn. He shivered and made his way to the kitchen for a bit of breakfast before heading to the Traigh. It was that time of the month that the tide was 'biggest', which meant at its lowest point it stretched a long way out. This in turn meant Norrie could spend longer raking in parts of the beach that, at other times of the month were completely submerged. There was a light breeze from the west and the sun broke through scattered clouds to the east and shimmered across the Sound of Floonay as he and Bonzo clambered over the rocks and struck out across the big beach, as that great blanket of life was ever so gently pulled back.

By the time the tide was lapping at his wellies, nudging him back up the Traigh six hours later, Norrie was satisfied. And because Norrie was satisfied, Bonzo was as well. He showed it in his usual manner, running excitedly in circles and figure-eights. Five net bags brimming with cockles, about a hundred kilos worth he estimated. A better than average day. He left his take out in the tide as he usually did, to be collected later in the week on landing day. The pair followed the shoreline home where Norrie made a couple of tasty rolls laden with cheese and ham and tomatoes. He put some scraps out for Bonzo which were gobbled up in seconds flat (Norrie had stopped splitting his meals with Bonzo a few years previously). The day was only half over and it remained pleasant with light winds and a mostly clear blue sky. Norrie thought they ought to take advantage of the good weather and go for a walk in the hills to the west, up along the southern side of the Traigh, and venture to the west side and circle back around the north side, across Picnic Hill, and just enjoy the day out while it was still light. He filled a flask with tea, grabbed a few chocolate biscuits, and off they adventured up into the heathery hills.

Bonzo being Bonzo, he darted this way and that, up and down and all around and it was as though he had an infinite supply of chaotic energy. No wonder he wasn't a very good sheep dog, Norrie often thought. He's far too bonkers. A good sheep dog needs energy – but it also needs to be controllable. Even with the whistle Rory had struggled to keep him in line. Norrie wasn't keeping sheep so had given up using the whistle a long time ago. Bonzo would run around wildly, disappearing for hours – and God only knew how many poor unsuspecting bitches he'd snuck up on to hump – but he always, eventually, circled back around, and at the end of the day he was there faithfully at Norrie's side, bedding down in the Nissen hut. Up on the highest prominence of the hills that stretch along the southern side of the Big Beach, Norrie took a seat, poured a steamy cup of tea, and nibbled on a biscuit. When he cared to contemplate it, he realised that the view really was amazing.

He'd grown up with it, and as such was used to it. The tide by that point was well in and formed a temporary bay on the east side, and not far across the grassy dunes the Atlantic gently lapped.

With the tea warming his belly Norrie struck off again and Bonzo dutifully followed, in his usual zigzagging, roundabout way. Walking the shoreline of Traigh Eais, and north towards Picnic Hill, Norrie thought of his sisters and the three brothers. It was there that their lives had come together. Along the shoreline were countless grass topped dunes that wove in and out like a labyrinth. One could get lost very easily amongst them, and it was the perfect place for a romantic couple seeking a little discretion. And further north, along the western shoreline that wrapped the base of Picnic Hill, were plenty of other coves and caves and hidden seams if one wanted a little privacy or were looking to hide a treasure. And the rest of the island was no different. If the old tales were to be believed, there was many a treasure still tucked away in dark corners or buried under layers of peat – waiting to be discovered or to lie untouched forever. The pair ascended Picnic Hill, where Norrie once again took a seat and had another cup of tea. By that time Bonzo was ready for a little rest, and for a few minutes sat by his master, tongue hanging out, panting and content. A few minutes was long enough for Bonzo to rest and he was again eager to move. His eyes darted this way and that, his ears tweaked and turned, looking for any reason to get up and run. Usually that reason was no reason at all and he would just get up and run for the hell of it, but, as it happened, out of the corner of an eye he spied a rabbit that had hopped out of its burrow, unaware of the two-armed-two-legged creature and four-legged canine downwind from it. Norrie watched Bonzo, the four-legged rocket: legs pumping, tail flailing and tongue flapping in the breeze, disappearing over the back side of Picnic Hill. It would be the last time Norrie would ever see his faithful companion run.

Ch 28

Bonzo!

Norrie descended the back side of Picnic Hill expecting to see Bonzo zinging one way or zanging another, or if the rabbit was quick enough, Bonzo would be furiously sniffing the ground wondering where on earth the little thumper had disappeared to. But on that afternoon there was no sign of him. No tell-tale sighting of a tail, an ear, a flash of something, anything. Norrie continued on and soon the ground levelled out, and all that lay ahead of him was the last flat stretch of land before the most northern shores of Floonay that looked across to South Uist.

He didn't understand at first.

But he knew what he was looking at.

Norrie neared, still keeping an eye out for Bonzo. The thought emerged, *they must have had a flat tyre or broke down*. It was a big vehicle: a holiday campervan. You would see plenty of them in the summer, but during the rest of the year they were quite scarce. There was a couple out in front of the vehicle, but the bonnet wasn't up and none of the wheels looked jacked up. The man was bent over by the side of the road and the woman had a frantic and worried look about her. They caught sight of Norrie approaching and the man called to him.

'Excuse me, son, we're terribly sorry. Would you be able to help us...'

That is all Norrie heard.

At first, he didn't believe it. He couldn't. *This isn't real.*

His body was limp, and there was a sloppy, bloody mess squeezing out of his side. Norrie dropped to his knees and held Bonzo's head in his lap. He was panting, a struggled panting, as though the breaths weren't going where they were supposed to. Bonzo looked up at Norrie and there was desperation in his eyes. They pleaded with Norrie and Norrie just held him, glanced at his broken, bloody body and he didn't know what to do. 'It's okay, it'll be okay,' he managed – and Bonzo just panted and held Norrie's stare, and in those eyes Norrie could see his friend's desperation grow. 'It's okay, Bonzo...' it was as though some flicker of hope shone in Bonzo's eyes, that his master would make things okay. Norrie's tears dripped onto Bonzo's face and he said he was sorry for that and asked his best friend to hold on, but he didn't have a clue what to do, and the sight of what was hanging out of his side was the most ghastly thing Norrie had ever seen. He leaned in closer and held Bonzo to his face and begged him to hold on and not go anywhere. Bonzo weakened considerably and Norrie looked into his eyes begging Bonzo not to leave him.

And then poor Bonzo was gone.

Norrie held his best friend close to him and sobbed quietly. The couple standing nearby felt dreadful and miserable. They weren't sure what to do. The man tried to form a few words – to explain what had happened, that one minute it was a clear road in front of them and out of nowhere came this blurry streak of black and white, and that there was nothing they could do. But he couldn't quite get it right, then offered a quiet apology before his voice trailed off. They stood there, uncertain, a little awkward. Norrie didn't register what the man had said, nor even that they were still standing there. Norrie wiped his eyes and realised what he had to do. 'Sorry, little buddy,' he whispered, pushing Bonzo's guts back through the tear in his lifeless body. He stood up with Bonzo in his arms and walked quietly towards the Traigh without looking back.

It wasn't just Bonzo that died in his arms that afternoon. His brother, Rory, had as well. As had Duncan, Donald, Ewan, and his Papa. They had all died for a second time, in Norrie's arms. Every step he took across the big beach was heavier than the last, and it was as though the combined weight of his four brothers and Papa were being added step by step. Bonzo had been an enormous link to them – he had not realised the magnitude, the importance, of that link. But now he did, and in one cruel, lightening flash, it was gone.

Arriving home Norrie wrapped Bonzo snugly in a blanket to keep his guts from slipping any further out. He dug a hole beside the Nissen hut and was about to bury him when he paused. Blood and other slippery fluids covered Norrie's hands and clothes. He caught sight of a few slimy slugs doing their slimy thing, and instinctively he knew exactly what they were in search of, along with the rest of the creepy creatures of the earth. They were not going to feast on Bonzo. Instead, he gathered a large pile of wood and placed Bonzo's wrapped body carefully in the middle. He doused the lot with petrol from a can. He didn't say a prayer because he didn't believe in prayers. 'Goodbye Bonzo, I'll miss you,' he said quietly, and then he lit the fire.

And it suddenly dawned on him – *No!! Bonzo!!!*

He lunged into the roaring fire and yanked him out in an instant. Norrie singed his arms and eyebrows and the blanket was on fire, but Norrie rolled it about and within a few seconds the flames were snuffed out. The large pile of petrol-soaked wood was starting to burn intensely and Norrie realised if he'd waited even a few seconds longer it would have been too late.

I know what I'm going to do with you my little friend.

And with that he carried Bonzo into the Nissen hut making sure he had him wrapped extra well – and then as he thought even further, decided what was best to do for the time being, *it might be a few days before I can get him to Oban.* He took Bonzo into the house and placed him in the large freezer. The decision had not altered Norrie's extreme despair and feeling of utter emptiness, but he knew it was the right thing to do. He exited the house, nipped into the Nissen hut, retrieved the essentials and then went back outside and sat near the fire to watch it burn. With his pipe and a bottle of Rory's favourite whisky, Norrie sat there in silence watching the mesmerising flames, with only his thoughts for company, and proceeded to get as drunk as possible. He passed out lying by the fire and awoke in the early morning darkness, chilled to the bone. There was a breathing body beside him and for the briefest of moments in his groggy, semi-conscious state Norrie thought it was Bonzo. He stretched out a hand, but instead of the familiar feel of Bonzo's coat, he felt wool. The sheep woke with a fright and bolted into the darkness.

Norrie wobbled through the dark to the Nissen hut, groped around and found a Tilly Lamp to light. But instead of dusting himself off, having a feed and prepping for a productive day of cockle raking, he reached for a bottle of whisky and took a mighty long pull. By the time the sun was casting its glow across the horizon half the bottle was empty. *That's a little better.* Though he had no desire to lift his rake and head to the Traigh he did find small comfort in tinkering about the Nissen hut. And throughout all the useless tinkering he'd sip a little whisky and smoke his pipe. The tinkering and the whisky kept his thoughts as subdued as possible.

The following day started much the same as the previous one, except there was no sheep lying beside him and he did sleep in the Nissen hut with the door shut. Norrie took the frozen remains of Bonzo and walked the seven miles to Castlebay, his mind focused on one thing. He knew that Barry MacLean, owner of the Butcher's, would be making a run to Oban on the ferry the following day. What Norrie asked of Barry took him a little by surprise. 'Are you sure, Norrie?' 'Aye, Barry, I'm sure. That's what taxidermists do, isn't it?' 'Aye, Norrie, I suppose it is.' And with that Barry took the frozen canine into his possession and placed him in a cool box. Before Norrie left, Barry asked, 'Norrie, is there – well, do you want him sitting or standing or lying on all fours?' Norrie thought for a moment, 'Sitting on his hind legs will do, Barry.' With Bonzo now in safe hands, Norrie headed north. Two miles from home he stopped into the north end's main watering hole, The Heathbank. He ordered a few pints and double drams from Joe, the barman, and then a few more. Before leaving he ordered a carry out laden with bottles and then struck a course for home. *Much much better.*

The path Norrie had stumbled upon was dark, twisted, and strewn with debris. In the world's history of descents, Norrie's ranked somewhere between top and bottom. He gave up reading the Coquilleuous Rakkeronuous Almenikhiaka in the evenings, and instead just let the bottle keep him company. That, and his pipe, and tinkering. He found no joy in anything and essentially gave up on life, without giving up on it completely. These things have a way of happening. As far as cockle raking went he lost all his passion, and when he finally did start raking again, he raked only enough to put a little grub on the table, poke a little tobacco into his pipe, and fill his belly and cloud his mind with whisky. There was no spring in his step when heading to the beach, and doing a full shift was out of the question. There was no routine, no order, no regularity to his actions. He stopped paying attention to the tides, and because of that the tides stopped paying attention to him. All of this resulted in Norrie losing his rhythm. He fell out of sync with the body of life. But Norrie didn't care one tiny bit. For a while, others would stop by to see how he was doing – word had been getting around after all, that Norrie was not doing so well – but he began turning away more and more, cut conversations short, and eventually stopped responding to the knocks at the Nissen hut door. The only two things Norrie did one hundred percent successfully was drink far too much and retreat into his shell. Not even Eddie or any of the other fishermen were welcome anymore. How could he explain why – it wasn't that he blamed anyone for the tragedies or for his own grief, it was the level of discomfort he felt every single day. It was the shame. It was all a vicious cycle and the only thing he could rely on was the effects of the whisky to keep everything subdued.

The newly stuffed Bonzo arrived back six weeks after his journey to Oban. It was three weeks before Christmas. Norrie placed him by the stove in the Nissen hut and the first night sitting there staring at him, he was torn. Had he done the right thing? It brought back a flood of emotions and for a while it just made things worse, but Norrie didn't dare get rid of him. It just took a little getting used to.

Since he rarely crept into the house anymore, he didn't have to concern himself with receiving calls from anyone, but he received regular letters from his sisters and Mama. It was inevitable that word trickled through the international grapevine and thus their letters began to show their concern. He eventually found the effort to pen a few lines back stating that everything was okay and that in memory of Bonzo he'd had him stuffed, and whoever they were hearing whatever from were most certainly exaggerating. He missed Bonzo, of course, but he was getting along just fine. His Mama expressed her feelings of guilt in one letter and openly questioned whether she should have left and asked the question: did he blame her for anything? And now she was married again, had infant twins, and was living half a world away in a giant home. He replied, explaining that everything was okay and that he didn't blame her for anything. Even Hank decided to write a few lines on the back of a large postcard shaped like the State of Idaho wrote, 'Dear Norrie, I hope you're doing real good. It's turkey day here soon. Sorry to hear about good ol' Bonzo. I'm sure you're missing him pretty bad. I liked the little fella even though he peed on my fav boots. You gotta come on over for Christmas Norrie! I'll send you a ticket. I'll even make it first class. No probs there my friend. All my tayters are sellin' like crazy! We'll watch some college bowl games and have a good ol' time. Boise State's doin' pretty good this year....' He had run out of room on that postcard and had to nip out to the shop to buy another one. It was shaped like a giant cowboy hat. It had stood out and made Hank smile. He hurried home and continued his message. 'Hope you like this card, Norrie. College football is the best sport ever! Well, besides baseball that is. You ever seen a game? It ain't like your football. It's a little like if you squish rugby and, well, hmm? Oh yeah! – rugby and playing catch together. There's tons of games over the holidays. I'll take you all around. We can even go on up to Edmonton or their archrivals, Calgary, and see a good ol' hockey game. Them Canucks are crazy as ever about hockey. Hey, and don't forget to bring some of that Stornoway black pudding! Some of my buddies here don't believe anything could be as scrumptious as I've told them it is....dang....running out of room here – take care Norrie! See u soon I hope. Hank.'

Well, Norrie had never seen a college football or a hockey game before and he wasn't about to start that year. He wasn't going anywhere for Christmas. Not to Idaho, or Kenya, or

Calgary, or Edmonton. And not to any house on Floonay. It was easy to come up with excuses. He was staying right where he was in the Nissen hut with his whisky and tobacco, and that was just fine with him.

Mwaka, Akili, and Darweshi were busy travelling all over East Africa, with Norrie's three sisters in tow, doing the Lord's work. They, too, had sent a few postcards to Norrie, writing little notes of encouragement without being too obvious. From what they knew of Norrie personally and via the stories they had heard from their wives – well, there were different ways of dealing with different people – they understood that subtlety was the only way with Norrie. For some reason he couldn't explain (or rather never questioned why he did it) Norrie would tack the postcards up in the Nissen hut, along the wood framing around the big workbench. As the weeks passed the line of postcards grew.

Norrie negotiated Christmas and the holidays without having to speak to a soul, except Joe, the barman at The Heathbank, Barry at the Butcher's (he needed whisky, tobacco and a little grub to keep limping along in life), and Nelson, the main buyer of his cockles (he needed a little cash for his whisky, tobacco, and grub). In one of his Mama's letters that arrived just before Christmas she reminded him to try to make sure that he calls, as every time she'd tried he'd been out. A few parcels and cards arrived in time for the 25th. He opened the cards but didn't bother with the parcels. Those he just put aside. He managed to scribble a few lines on two cards and posted one to Idaho and the other to Kenya.

The following year brought news from Kenya that his three sisters were all pregnant, and incredibly, his Mama was pregnant again. This news temporarily shifted, or 'bumped' Norrie's outlook on life. Not for very long though, because his routine was erratic and the whisky was in full control (it had long ceased to be a relaxing, pleasure to drink. It had become his only defence against his mind, from which he found it hard to run away).

Later that year he came out of his dark shell a little, not much, but a little. It was when the anger started again. Like the anger he felt when he broke Constable Currie's nose upon hearing of Rory's death. And the fury he felt when punching the stone marker at the top of Heaval. A tempestuous wrath of someone whose heart is so heavy with loss and sorrow and grief, it lashes out like a whip. And in order to vent that anger he needed to start hitting more than the concrete blocks in the Nissen hut. He began spending time, a lot more time, at The Heathbank, and without having to give it much thought found lots of excuses to get into arguments, which more often than not led to some good old honest punch-ups. And that was just fine with Norrie. He started breaking the noses of men who were once his friends, and friends of his Papa and brothers. Everyone was left shaking their head. It didn't matter. And because of this he found himself more than a few times locked up at Constable Currie's pleasure. He even managed to break his nose another time. He was barred from entering The Heathbank (but Joe being Joe, had whispered sympathetically once, 'If you need a carryout come around the back.') Word spread through the global grapevine and his Mama's and sisters' letters again began expressing more concern. Norrie's responses were quite standard: not quite true, a little exaggerating going on, you know how island gossip can get all twisted around and magnified, etc. Regarding his run-ins with the law, well, 'boys will be boys', etc. One of Hank's postcards, that was shaped like a giant Smith & Wesson six-shooter, had the following written on the back: Dang Norrie, I hear you're gettin' in a little trouble, and that you're still living in the Nissen hut? That true? You got that whole house to use? You got another half-bro on the way, and you ain't met your other half-bros yet, and you got 3 coming along in Kenya! You gotta come out and visit, Norrie! Hell, I'll even charter a plane for you. Runnin outta room here, words gettin all squishy. Hank.

He received a surprise postcard that year from his old pal, Malcolm, who had, as far as he knew, jumped ship the minute it had docked in Hobart, Tasmania. As he began reading it became clear he had left Australia behind. This is what it read: Dear Norrie, I love it here. I made it from Oz to New Zealand. The weather is great and there are so many sheep to shear. I'm gonna make a mint. Also, I'm getting into horse doping and bootlegging a bit. Not the most legal venture. Probably shouldn't be writing this on a postcard. Ah, whatever, there's no return address for the authorities to trace. They'll never find me. Fill you in some other time. Hope things are good on Floonay. Take care, MM.

For some reason just the simple act of reading his words did 'something' to Norrie. It wasn't much, but it moved him a teeny bit. It was something.

That was Norrie's second most ruinous year. There was nothing but a trail of rubble behind him and what lay ahead was a forbidding unknown. This was a gruesome time. Norrie would drag himself to the beach, his rake trailing behind him, and would think of only one thing amidst the darkness that veiled the light of the day around him: the next bottle. His mind, he still could not escape, however much he tried. It was shackled to him and weighed him down more and more, tormented him, tricked him. He stumbled from that year and fell face down into the next. The year that would prove the most ruinous of all. That most ruinous year would be the year that he decided to give up on life altogether. It was only a matter of how.

After waking in a heap by the old stove one cold, dark, February morning, Norrie stumbled in the darkness groping for the Tilley lamp. He lit it and took a look around the sorry state of his life. The wind buffeted against the aluminium siding and the patter of rain echoed through the big, empty space. Spying the remains of the previous night's bottle he grabbed it and took a long pull. And then another. An invisible pulse washed through him. He put a hand on the workbench to steady himself. He looked at Bonzo, frozen in time. The lump in Norrie's belly hadn't gone away, and so he took another swig and slumped back in an old chair. He had only just woken up, but a disorientated exhaustion enveloped him. And that's when he spied it stuffed among a few boxes and, inexplicably, a thought surfaced. He reached up and slid it out. His Papa's old shotgun. And through the murkiness of his mind thoughts formed, and from some dark corner a cold whisper blew. There lay his answer. He turned the muzzle first to his chest, and then peeked down the barrel. There, a few inches from him, was his release from everything. There was oblivion. A pure, perfect, nothingness. He placed the gun down and rummaged for the boxes of shells he knew were somewhere, and while he did so he opened another bottle of whisky. With the shells found, he slid one into the chamber. He sat back, and for a time, whilst sipping the whisky, just stared at the loaded gun. Then, without another thought, he held the gun up. It was a stretch to reach the trigger as the barrel was so long, but he just managed. He held it there. And then he glanced at the timeless Bonzo and spoke, 'Goodbye Bonzo. I don't suppose I'll be seeing you again.' He knew that because he didn't believe in Heaven or God or all the things Father John and Reverend Cullen spoke about. In his hands lay the answer to his suffering. He would disappear and he would never know it. Poof. Gone. Vanish into thin air.

As he stared down the barrel of the gun he glanced over and a line of 'somethings' caught his eye. His eyes focused. They were the postcards from Idaho and Kenya. And they were all different shapes. The gun wavered in his hand. The distraction annoyed him but he eventually lowered the gun, reached for the bottle and took a drink. Then he poked some tobacco into his pipe and lit it. *Maybe tomorrow,* Norrie whispered and slid the gun away. This went on every day for the next month. He would say goodbye to Bonzo, and then after lowering the gun, annoyed, he would whisper, 'maybe tomorrow,' and turn bleakly into the day.

It was the rope from the creels that next caught his attention, and in the grogginess of his mind option two presented itself. He lashed one end over a metal beam and tied a noose at the other. Between sips of whisky he prepared himself and stood on the chair. He would always glance over and say goodbye to Bonzo and then the odd shaped postcards would catch his eye and he would frustratingly climb down muttering to himself, 'maybe tomorrow.'

After a month of failed attempts option three materialised and instantly he knew it was the best one of them all. It would mean going into the house and doing a bit of rummaging around, but he was sure he would find them. Back when his Mama was in a bad way after all the tragedies, Dr Bartlett had prescribed for her several different medications. Norrie had no clue what they were, but they seemed to have some effect. There must be some left over, he thought, because he also knew that she didn't like taking them. *I'll mix them all together, along with whatever else I can find. I'll swallow it all with a mug of whisky and that will be it.* It was the perfect plan. A short time later he emerged from the house and made his way back to the Nissen hut, the mission a success. Stored away in cupboards here and there, he found a dozen bottles of one prescription or another. He poured out the contents into a little pile on the workbench, and for good measure added the contents of what he knew were some sort of medicinal pills for which a prescription was not needed. *Perfect. This ought to do the trick.* He went through the same preparatory steps. Goodbye Bonzo. Gulps of whisky. And the misshapen postcards would come into view. Frustration. Hesitation. He couldn't touch the pills. *Maybe tomorrow.* This, again, went on for weeks until one day in a fit of extreme frustration with himself, he lashed the rope up and slid out the gun and laid it on the table beside the pile of pills. *One of you is going to release me! Perhaps all three at once!* Of course, none did, as day after day ended the same way: *maybe tomorrow.* A few frustrating weeks later, in a moment of sublime inspiration, Norrie realised what he had to do. *Definitely tomorrow.*

Ch 29

See You Later, Alligator

The following day, with Bonzo stuffed away and out of view and the postcards gathered up and tossed behind the workbench, Norrie turned to the task at hand. On the workbench was a neat pile of pills and beside it a mug full of whisky. Beside it lay the shotgun with a single cartridge in the chamber. And strung up just to his right was the rope with a noose at the end. He sat back for a moment and took a big, sloppy gulp from a bottle. 'All right, which one of you will it be?' He looked between the three objects and contemplated the three paths to serenity, to the peace that lay within his grasp. There was no rush, as this time Norrie knew it would be final. He took his time pondering each pathway. Generous gulps of whisky helped soothe his mind of any annoying discomfort and in a state of increasing numbness, a sort of contentment, he drew closer to his final choice. It was quiet in the Nissen hut and with the objects that had made him hesitate for weeks and weeks hidden, Norrie finally decided. *It would be the easiest, cleanest,* the thought surfaced in the foggy debris of his mind. The pile of pills was considerable, and he had to make sure he shovelled enough down his throat as quickly as possible to ensure success, and so he prepared himself. He took a few big swallows from the bottle. Then made his way towards the workbench where a full mug of whisky awaited him alongside the pile of pills. It crossed his mind to say goodbye to something, anything, maybe just even the world, but it wasn't worth it. None of it mattered anymore. The world, life, was a cruel tragedy, full of pain and suffering and despair...all sorts of wretchedness....

As a murky afterthought Norrie decided to mumble one goodbye. Well, he not so much mumbled it as the thought just wobbled through his misty consciousness. It was more a statement to the entity, the God, that he no longer believed in: 'I don't believe in you, God, but if you did happen to exist why would you make a place with such destruction. If you do exist you are a fraud...the Coquilleuous Rakkeronuous Almenikhiaka is right....the free will of man is your alibi for not taking any action, but since you don't exist it doesn't matter....it's all lies....so many have been left with nothing to look forward to but despair and pain....nothing matters....but death....'

Death must be the only purpose to life. Death is the only answer to life. Only death triumphs over life. *Ah whatever!* It didn't deserve one last thought. Norrie drained what was left in the bottle in his hand, let it drop to the deck and he put his hands out and scooped up as many pills as he possibly could. This would be perfect. With one eye on the mug of whisky that awaited to wash the medicine down he raised his hands to his mouth. Without thinking, he spoke quietly, 'Goodbye Bonzo, I'll miss you, maybe I'll see you...' and what came next was a perfect nothingness. Silence. Bliss.

Norrie MacKinnon's body couldn't have collapsed to the deck in a more lifeless fashion. Like a body whose bones had just vanished.

After a time of perfect nothingness Norrie was flying through space over the Atlantic. Whitecaps crashed along the rocky shores of the Outer Hebrides and there were large, puffy clouds all around. Up ahead was what looked like some sort of cloud city and he got the sense everything was a little different, a little off, a little squiggly. This confused him and he had a terrible sense of unease regarding where he was, and then inexplicably Bonzo was flying alongside him and he looked over and barked and then flew off ahead and shot off up into a cloud. He was wearing a blue cape. A suffocating sense of being trapped, of not being able to do 'something', anything, swept through him. *Where am I?* And then he saw a face he recognised and simultaneously felt an enormous jolt, a spasm, as though he'd just fallen off a cliff and – *smackaroo!* – hit the ground.

*

It took a long, confused moment for Norrie to realise where he was. It took another long and confused moment to comprehend the face he recognised – and the object propped up on a dusty old table.

'Hank?'

'Dang right, my good buddy. One hundred percent Hank Stetson. Well, maybe ninety percent Hank, ten percent prosthetic leg.'

Norrie was in his old bedroom, under the covers of his old bed. He hadn't slept in the room in years. He pushed himself up. 'What am I – what are you...' He glanced between Hank and the object he recognised. It was Hank's prosthetic leg.

'Gets a little itchy sometimes. Gotta take her off and give a good scratch, you know.'

'But – what...'

'Don't go talking too much there.' He gestured to the side table. 'You should take a few sips of that there and just take 'r easy. You gotta mend that body of yours – and that brain, I reckon.'

Norrie's memory started piecing together the last few moments he could recall. It was a bit of a hazy, foggy mess, and it was like a pitiful, wretched jigsaw puzzle: The Nissen hut, the gun, the rope, the pills, the whisky, the decision, his hands full of pills...the end of life. Then nothing.

'But...'

'You dang near gave me a heart attack. Just as I poked ma head in – thank God you'da forgot to lock yourself in – you had a mountain of pills gathered up in your hands and looked as though you were gonna shovel 'em down your gullet – and then just like that, you dropped to the deck like an empty tayter sack...I saw the gun, too, Norrie, and the rope.' Hank paused. 'And I seen that pile of empties over there in the back corner. Like you'd been a havin' a party for a hundred people. I bet there weren't no hundred people though.'

Norrie finally managed to string a few words into a whole sentence. 'But, what are you doing here?'

'Well, you go on and take a sip of that drink there and I'll a tell ya.'

Norrie looked to the side table. There was a big mug, the contents of which were steaming. 'What is it?'

'Don't you worry about that – it's a Hank Stetson special. It'll help you get better, Norrie – now go on there.'

All jumbled up in the head and feeling pretty rough, Norrie had no strength, nor will, to protest. He picked up the mug and took a sip. And then another, and another.

'Not bad, huh?'

'Uh, aye, it's all right.'

'Dang right it's all right. Got the recipe from this good ol' boy, a cowboy, 'bout as old as the earth, hardest man I've ever known. Lives deep in the back country with his horses and dogs. He got the recipe from his father, and he, from his father before him. Tried and tested it most definitely is. I got a big pot of soup simmering downstairs, too. We're gonna have to fix you up real good.'

Norrie just sat there propped against a few pillows and sipped the steaming concoction. This remarkable turn of events had him in a state of shock.

Hank sipped his coffee and paused, gathering his thoughts. He knew he had to be enormously careful. This was a delicate, serious, situation. 'I was back over there in Vilnius, Norrie, annual industry get-together, you know. Rubbing shoulders and all that. Then I was on my way back, and, well, for a while I've been a gettin' this sense that things weren't goin' too good with you, you know. Like really not good...'

Norrie instinctively gave Hank a *'what? Who me?'* look

'Norrie, for starters, no one's even seen you in what seems like forever...and all the excuses. We've heard the stories, Norrie. And so I thought I better drop on in asap, a little sneak attack, you know.' He winked and thought perhaps he shouldn't have been too flippant, knowing Norrie was going to eventually rouse from his stupor and perhaps become defensive and close up. 'Norrie, when I poked ma head round that door, well, for a moment you put one hell of a fright in me. Thank the heavens though, you passed out when you did. Anyway, I hurried on over to ya and tried bringin' you to, you know. Even gave you a slap or two. Nothin'. But, well, at least you seemed to be breathing all right. So, I carried you in here and you ain't stirred in about 10 hours.'

Hank paused. He sipped his coffee, giving Norrie a moment to process his thoughts. There was a lot going on behind those bleary, blue eyes, that much was obvious. It appeared to Hank that Norrie wanted to say something but didn't know what to say, or how to say it, or where to start.

'Norrie – look man – now just hear me out, all right? Let me tell you a little story. Two actually. Remember me tellin' you all about before I got my tayter business goin' and I was living up in that ol' shack distillin' moonshine and things weren't too good and then I happened upon that mushy ol' box of tayters – remember the story?'

'Aye.' Norrie said quietly.

'Well, I sort of glazed over the whole deal, you know. Skimmed the surface. But Norrie, I'll tell you somethin', I was in a bad, bad place. Was about your age, too. A serious dang funk. My parents were gone. Tricked by that no-good preacher down in Central America. Course, I ain't got no siblings. My prospects were bleak. I was drinking too much and things were just gettin' bleaker and bleaker. Was gettin tremors – never did see no pink elephants or any crazy shit like that but man, I was in a bad enough way. I tell you what, if I hadn't of happened upon that box of stinky ol' tayters...well – hey, Norrie.' He caught his eye. 'I'm a bein' totally honest with you here - you know, I had a rifle in that shed, too, just a couple a bullets.' Hank took a deep breath. 'I can't say the thought didn't cross my mind.' He let the words settle. 'That mushy rotten box of tayters no doubt saved my life.' There was a long pause. He took a deep breath before continuing, 'And then after Susie died, and David and Gary, I was in as dark a place as ever, once again – even worse in a way. I took to the bottle to help things along – it's a tricky business that, mixing booze and pain and lookin' for an out.' He had a little tear in his eye. 'By then though, I had a business goin'. It was a couple of guys that work for me – with me – they pulled me aside one day – they could see, hell, everybody could probably see, that I was in a bad place. At first I protested – but, hell, I'm sort of a man's man you know, but I ain't that proud. They recommended I go and get a little, well – help, you know. And that's what I did. It took a little time, but I eventually came around.'

Again, Hank just let the words sink in. Though a torpor clung to Norrie, Hank could see he'd surprised the young man. He was thinking deeply.

After a moment of silence Hank spoke, 'I tell you what, young man, you get a little rest. I'm gonna go give the soup a stir and do a little more dusting. You come on down when you like, all right?'

A pause.

'Aye,' Norrie said quietly.

Hank reached for his prosthetic leg, strapped it on, and slipped his cowboy boot back in place. He creaked off the old wooden chair. 'All right, my man, we'll see you in a bit then.' He paused at the door and turned to Norrie. 'I feel real bad, Norrie. If I'da known, or paid more attention earlier. Well, I hope you understand. You'll be okay.'

Ch 30

Routine

Hank was on his knees giving the stinky, mould infested fridge a good scrubbing when he heard Norrie coming down the stairs. It was sooner than he was expecting the young man and thought it a good sign.

Norrie walked into the kitchen and had the empty mug in hand. He hesitated then spoke quietly, 'Do you have any more of this stuff?'

Well, good ol' Hank grinned and took the mug from Norrie, 'Course I do. I gotta warn you though – this ain't no regular vitamin health drink, you know what I'ma sayin'? This is a special concoction – can't have too much of it. Just somethin' to get ya goin' again, you know. Give you a little boost.'

'Aye, a boost – that's fine.' A moment later Norrie had another steamy mug in hand. He took a sip, sat, and looked around.

Hank creaked down onto a chair across from Norrie. 'Been a while, huh?'

Norrie blinked, 'Aye. A while.'

Hank sipped his coffee. 'Hell, I can't believe you been livin' in the ol' Nissen hut all this time. And you got such a nice pad here.' He paused, reminding himself to be careful. He had

Norrie in the kitchen and that was a start. 'Well, I suppose the ol' Nissen hut's a better place to live than that shitty old shack I was a livin' in up in them mountains – you shoulda seen it Norrie – a shittier place than ever. Come to think of it – the good ol' Nissen hut's like a ho-tel compared to my dirty old digs, you know. I tell you what – that was some time I had in there, some time indeed. As rotten a deal as you can get, you know.' He shrugged. 'Ah, but hell, it gave me a little shelter – and that's about all I could have asked for, you know what ah'ma sayin'?'

'Aye.'

'Aye is dang right, Norrie.'

Hank could see that Norrie was wanting to say something, or perhaps more so – was wanting to understand what had happened, was happening, to him. Confusion was plastered all over his face.

'I tell you what, Norrie. You and me, we gotta few things to sort out, you know. I'm gonna make you a deal.' He didn't wait for Norrie to reply. 'I'm gonna hang here for a bit – no need to get back to Idaho any time soon – Stetson Industries is in good hands, and your Mama's got plenty of help at the house. I'll tell her you an' I are just having a little man-o-eh-mano time.' He winked. 'No reason to get her all worried 'bout somethin' that didn't happen – or anyone else for that matter...'

Norrie shot him a surprised look.

'But you're gonna have to promise me one thing.'

Norrie took a sip of the steaming concoction and Hank's voice floated through his mind – *you're gonna have to promise me one thing.* What also emerged from the recesses of that very same mind was what had become Norrie's naturally defiant side. *Hold on just a second...*

Dang. Hank could see it register as plain as day. It was like a placid sea's initial reaction to the arrival of a squall. Hank had to divert its course asap. 'Then again, Norrie, you don't gotta promise me nothin', my man, nothin' at all.' And he instinctively put his hands up – he was no threat. 'I was just a hopin' you'd a hear me out, that's all.'

Well, to Hank's pleasure it seemed to work. With Norrie disarmed Hank turned their attention to the simmering pot of soup, and freshly baked loaf he'd picked up from the Butcher's.

'Soup's got tayters and carrots and onions. Good stock of ham, too. Lentils galore. Hope it's not too thick, you know. What'd you say we give it a try and then maybe we'll take a walk. I got a little somethin' I'da like to share with you. And maybe after that we'll just hang out and have a barbeque and a brew. That's not a bad deal, eh?'

After a moment that hung for longer than Hank was hoping, Norrie replied, 'Aye, all right. Not a bad deal Hank.'

Hank had to stop himself from exclaiming, *Dang right it's not a bad deal, Norrie!* and instead just nodded, then rose to see to their meal.

Two things managed to penetrate Norrie's defences. Number one was Hank's remarkably affable nature. And two was the effect that the story of Hank and his rifle in the shitty old mountainside shack had on Norrie. Hank was someone Norrie realised he could relate to. Naturally though, Norrie being Norrie, he would stay somewhat guarded.

That afternoon they walked and talked, and that evening they pulled out the barbeque, had a few brews and talked a little more. Hank, quite naturally, did most of the talking but that was quite all right. Hank had no carefully crafted plan of action, he was just going to take it one moment at a time. He recounted in more detail the dark days in the shitty old shack and the even darker days after Susie and his two sons died, and of the sessions on the couch of the head doctor afterward. 'Hell, Norrie, I tell you what, one thing I learned there on that couch was I was not alone in that whole department, you know. There's a lot of people that know how I felt, know how you feel, Norrie.'

The next day they headed for the big beach to do a little cockle raking. Hank recalled how the routine of cockle raking daily had helped Norrie out of his dark place that first wonderful summer he had on Floonay. Also, Hank was keen on improving his skills and he implored Norrie to share some of his secrets. 'There's no real secret Hank, you've just got to keep at it, and well, as I told you before, there's a few tips in the Coquilleuous Rakkeronuous Almenikhiaka.' The following day they did the same, and the day after, the same again. They developed a routine and that's when Hank, as carefully as he possibly could, tried to remind Norrie what he needed to do – get back into his routine. 'It can be hard some days. Real hard, you know. But you gotta try. It's a slog sometimes, and some days you'll feel a little bummed out, but, man, I'll tell you, you stick with a little routine, it'll help see you through. You have to try and persevere. Even if it's just, well, little things. The minute you let things go, get all out of kilter, well, you are leaving yourself open to an even greater assault, mark my words, Norrie. Well, I probably don't have to, you know, tell you that.' To Hank's great pleasure, Norrie seemed to be getting a bit of his old form back.

Hank and Norrie were out by the barbecue again flipping burgers and having a few beers on the fifth evening, after a long productive day of cockle raking. Well, it had been productive for Norrie, but good ol' Hank was struggling mightily and his back and shoulders were as sore as they'd ever been. That was all right with him though, for as much as he'd have loved to improve his cockle raking skills, that was second place to his first priority, and that was simply getting Norrie back to a better place and to ensure he stayed there.

Hank told a joke that Norrie didn't get, about what the Idaho tayter said to the Prince Edward Island tayter when they met at the boiling pot. Hank thought it as funny as anything and couldn't stop laughing. Norrie assumed it must be a North American thing.

Norrie was curious about something and interrupted Hank's laughter. 'Hank?'

'What's on your mind, Norrie, fire away?'

'You haven't mentioned what it is, you know, that you wanted me to promise you. That one thing?'

Hank grinned and took a sip of his beer. He put a hand on Norrie's right shoulder. 'I'll let you know in three days, if that's all right with you.'

Norrie hesitated. 'Aye, that's fine.'

Hank squinted as the sun caught his eyes. 'I gotta question for you, if you don't mind me asking that is.'

'Aye, fire on.'

'You ever, you know, had a girlfriend, Norrie?'

The question threw Norrie and for a moment felt a bit embarrassed. He paused, then shook his head.

'Dang. Hey I'm sorry...didn't mean to, you know, pry or nothin' like that.'

'Ach, no – that's all right. No, it's just, you know...'

Hank, you're such a dumb son of a bitch. No shit Sherlock. It's been a hell of a run for ol' Norr-meister these past few years. Good job moron. 'Hey, my man, I get it.' He gave him a wink. 'I get it. Hey, that's cool. You know, between you and me – women, well they can be a bit of a pain in the backside sometimes – not your Mama of course! She's as wonderful as anythin'...'

Norrie smiled.

Hank continued, 'Yeah, and a guess, well, cockle rakin's pretty much a lonely pursuit. Hey, I get it, man, I get it. But you know, sometimes it can get a little extra lonely. Nice to have someone else around sometimes.'

Norrie felt a little uncomfortable with the subject and it showed.

Hank chuckled. 'Hey, sorry Norrie. Maybe I'll just shut my big trap, you know. But mark my words, my good buddy.' He looked around conspiratorially – good, no one was listening in. He dropped his voice. 'When you are ready, well, I'll tell ya', you'll have your pick, Norrie. All that dang cockle raking you been doin'. Them shoulders of yours – they're like rocks. And those arms, I tell you what, they might not all admit it, but women, Norrie, you know, they like that sort of thing. A lot.' He winked and it caused Norrie to laugh.

Norrie didn't say anything for a moment and Hank could see he was staring into some far-off place – some distant memory.

'What is it Norrie?'

Norrie hesitated before speaking. 'My Papa. It was the last time he read to me – before that, that...day.' His voice trailed off a bit, but he gathered himself. 'He said the same thing – well, mostly the same. He was reading from the Coquilleuous Rakkeronuous Almenikhiaka – he said there were 'things' about girls and 'stuff' in there – I couldn't believe it......but then the phone rang. It was Eddie....' Norrie's voice was quiet but full of emotion. Hank focused and understood. 'When Papa came back into the room – well, he changed the subject – I was so grateful...God...'

Hank smiled just a little.

'I just couldn't believe all that "stuff" was included in my favourite book – and, and in all three sections no less...marvellous adventures, and stern warnings, and – even – tips and techniques...I could not believe it.' Norrie shook his head and Hank thought it all right to smile a little more.

'Well, well...'

Norrie continued, lost again in the memory. 'But then, instead, he told me a different story – from the 'marvellous adventures' section. It has to do, had to do, with one of the greatest secrets in the world and I remember him saying – I remember this well – he was smiling a little when he said it...that if you were Aristotle you would call it 'esoteric'...I didn't know who Aristotle was, or what esoteric meant. It was some story though – and the secret was some secret. But I don't believe in it anymore – because of what happened,' and Norrie's voice trailed away into the sands of time.

The following evening after another productive day of raking cockles, good ol' Hank and young Norrie MacKinnon were out by the Nissen hut prepping the barbecue once again and enjoying their evening routine. Hank was enormously pleased and relieved that Norrie had come around so quickly. Maybe, just maybe, he would actually be able to keep his promise before leaving and not tell a soul about what he happened upon. If something were to happen later and he had not, at the very least, involved one or two more people, well, Hank wasn't sure if he'd ever forgive himself. *But the young whipper snapper,* Hank thought, *was doin' all right.* As he's been reminding Norrie, you just need to keep the routine going, even if some days aren't as productive as others, or you might feel a bit bummed out or whatever, well, you gotta do a little something – anything.

Whilst moulding and slapping a pound of minced meat into a few burger patties Hank spoke (it was as good a time as any). 'You know, Norrie, your Mama, she told me 'bout them letters you sent way back.' He tried to sound as nonchalant, 'no big deal at all', as he possibly could. 'Them letters, you know – to God.'

Norrie said nothing. Hank thought it safe to continue.

'That you even stuck 'em in the post with stamps an' all...hundreds of 'em.' Hank raised an eyebrow, and after placing the patties on the sizzling grill, wiped his hands and had a sip of his beer. Norrie still wasn't saying anything. 'I'll be honest with you, I ain't never heard of anyone doin' that before – not that I know too much 'bout that sort of thing, mind you.'

Still nothing from Norrie, but he wasn't reacting negatively. To Hank he seemed to be reflecting and so he went on, 'Said there was one after another, after another – your Mama told me 'bout the whole scene with the Headmistress.' He waved a dismissive hand. 'But never mind all that, you know – I'm a sure everyone knows that old cow was full of lies. But it got me thinkin', you know – maybe, with all them words that you seem to be able to conjure up, well, perhaps you oughta've been like a scribe, a wordsmith of some sort, you know. Matter of fact, if I ain't mistaken, the advertising department at Stetson Industries is looking for a body or two – and hey, there's always the company rag – The Tayter Times – only comes out once a month, but it's always jammed full a' tayter tips and tales. You got my word, I'll get you in there if you like, you just say the word, Norrie.'

For a moment it looked like he wasn't going to get a word out of Norrie, but then to Hank's delight Norrie finally responded, though it wasn't the response he was hoping for.

Norrie shook his head. 'I wrote those letters for one reason and one reason only – and my Papa or my brothers never reappeared. I'm not interested in writing for any other reason. Haven't written a word since, apart from the few words sent to Mama and to Kenya. That was a stupid thing to do...should have known better.'

Hank hadn't told Norrie, but he was planning on leaving Floonay in three days' time. He was going to wait until the day before leaving to get Norrie to promise him something. But as they were close enough to the subject, he thought right then was a better time than any.

Hank sipped his beer as he flipped a burger, and as cool and casual as possible, he spoke. 'Hey, I just remembered, Norrie, 'bout the whole thing I'da like you to promise me – since we're talkin' about writin' an' all.'

Norrie looked dubious.

'Now, don't worry, it's not a big deal. If you don't want to write for Tayter Times or whatever, no problemo – but, hey, check this out. You remember all them postcards I sent you? You still got 'em.'

'Aye. Yeah. Somewhere,' Norrie said suspiciously.

'Well, I tell you what I'd like you to do. Now you gotta promise me this Norrie – like a right proper promise, you know what I'ma sayin'?'

'Aye – go on.'

'Well,' Hank bit his lip and secretly implored Norrie to agree to his terMs He was as anxious as he'd been in a long time. *Please Norrie! come on.* 'My promise to you Norrie is I won't tell a soul about, well, you know – but you gotta promise me that you'll send me and your Mama one postcard a week, you know, just to say your doin' good and all that. Don't have to be all long and crammed full a words. Just a line or two. Hell, even just, "Dear Mama, Hi Hank. All is good on Floonay, All the best, Norrie." Anything. Just to say, well as I just said, to let us know you're doin' all right.'

Norrie didn't say a word and just stared off across the Traigh Mhor. It was a pleasant evening and the tide was well on its way in. Norrie reflected on the last few days with Hank around, and he realised it had been a terribly long time since he'd felt the relative amount of contentment, of satisfaction, that he had the last few days. It was quite a remarkable turnaround, and though he felt miles better than he did a few short days ago, Norrie sensed that where he stood in relation to that dark forbidding place was much closer than one might guess. One, two, three wrong moves, and voila you were right back in the black, tripping amongst the rubble and fumbling for rope, pills, or staring down the barrel of a gun. How horrible a place to find oneself. *I don't want to be there again...I don't think I do anyway...how did I trick myself so easily?*

Norrie turned to Hank. 'I swore I wouldn't write another word – ever ever again...'

Dang! Hank wasn't feeling too good about things. *Come on, please Norrie!*

And then Norrie said, quite simply, 'Aye.'

Hank blinked, confused. 'What's that you said, Norrie?'

'Aye, all right Hank.'

Hank, for one of the few times in his life, was at a loss for words. He stammered, 'You – you, really, you mean it?'

'Aye, I'll send the postcards – once a week.'

There had been, up to that point, seven occasions in Hank Stetson's life that had made him the happiest man on the planet: his two marriages, and the birth of his five children (the death of his first wife and first two sons had also made him the saddest man on the planet but that had not taken away from the joy they shared in life). Hearing Norrie say, 'Aye' also ranked up there in the happiest moments of Hank's life and he had to try hard to show a little restraint.

'Well, Norrie, I promise that you won't regret it. Hell, you might even end up havin' a bit o' fun with the whole thing, you know. Maybe we can even try and out-do one another. I promise I'm gonna send you a postcard once a week, too – try and get the funniest or strangest ones I can – maybe you can do the same? What do you think ol' Norr-meister – sorry, I mean Norrie.' Hank had trouble with restraint. But Hank also had this sense that the whole postcard thing would help Norrie more than either of them could imagine. Norrie needed to keep a good routine going, and just as importantly he needed to keep his focus on the world outside his head. What worried Hank greatly was that someone in Norrie's position, or one similar to it – that of a cockle raker – was not used to interacting with too many others on a regular basis. It was a lonely profession and lent itself to thinking too much without the benefit of bouncing those thoughts off someone else. It was just you, your rake, and the elements out there. Without Norrie realising it, the postcards would be a form of therapy – if just a little.

'What is it Norrie, you're looking, well, thoughtful or somethin'?'

'I'm just thinking that those burgers look like they're getting a little burnt.'

'Aw, dang it all!'

*

It was T-minus three days before Hank's trip back to Idaho when he bumped into Eddie and took up the offer to head out for a day on the high seas. Hank mentioned to Norrie that he ought to come along, but Norrie declined. He had plenty of cockle raking to keep him busy. 'The experience of a lifetime!' Hank commented more than a few times afterwards. Eddie took him on a tour of the smaller islands to the north and east of Floonay. There was work to do, too, and Hank was keen to get in on the action. The unhappy residents of all the creels had the born and bred Idahoan as equally fascinated as he was frightened – but it was a good sort of frightened, he'd explained. He didn't want to lose his fingers. There were green, velvet and brown crabs! And lobsters, a few sea urchins, and some other crazy looking things that Hank swore came from outer space. There were even a few octopuses, one which made Hank jump with fright when Eddie tossed it over to him. He'd almost fallen overboard at that point. They had as grand a day as Hank could ever remember. They rendezvoused with a few of the other boats when it was time for lunch, and as they enjoyed a few cups of tea and meat pies

Hank was told many a tale, some true and some a little stretched. They steamed north close to Eriskay and passed through the narrow sound that separates that island from the treacherous cliffs of the Isle of Stack – the scene of the 'terrible tragedy'. For a bit the mood was sombre and Hank asked Eddie how it had felt to head back out. It was an honest question.

Eddie stated plainly that it had taken some time, but eventually he managed. Hank continued, 'That dang whale. I seen a picture of it. Norrie showed me. It's still...out there?' For a while Hank felt a little unsteady and looked at the sea a little differently. Eddie took a moment before replying as they steamed back south. His voice was haunted. 'Aye, she's out there all right. Somewhere. God only knows where, doing god only knows what damage.'

Hank's inaugural day on the high seas was capped off with a grand barbecue once again. It turned out to be quite a party with the other fishermen bringing their families along, but that was just the beginning. Word travelled through the grapevine and a whole host of people showed up at one time or another. Constable Currie arrived and told everyone not to worry as he'd declared himself off-duty for the rest of the day. Hank regaled everyone he met with his adventures on the high seas, but also lamented the fact that there was no sea in Idaho.

The evening passed into the wee hours, and the following day Hank and Norrie were not the only people on Floonay with serious hangovers....but that was no excuse, and so...

After filling their bellies, the two injured souls trudged down to the beach, although it was the last thing either really wanted to do – especially Hank! At least Norrie was a good cockle raker. Frustratingly for Hank, he had not improved his skills one bit. He had blisters on his hands and his back wasn't getting any better and to top it all off he felt uncharacteristically wobbly on account of the previous night. Mercifully, the weather that day was tame by Hebridean standards. After a little while both got used to the routine, and though their productivity was not what it usually was (Hank's was virtually nil, but at least he was moving his rake, albeit hopelessly, back and forth) something was better than nothing – and *that* was what Hank was desperate for Norrie to remember. Slowly, but steadily, the hours ticked along and eventually to Hank's immense pleasure (he kept this mostly to himself), the tide had turned and was nudging them back up the beach. *Thought for a bit there that the moon had gone on strike or somethin'. Whew. Guess it's time to head home soon!*

*

'You are gonna love this sauce. It's a secret recipe got from this fella in Kansas City,' Hank was saying as he lathered bbq sauce onto a grill full of ribeye steaks. It was his last evening on the island and they were doing what they had done every other evening of Hank's trip – have a barbecue out by the Nissen hut. A few of the fishermen stopped by to say goodbye but no one stayed too long as it was evident everyone was in recovery mode of some sort. Hank assured everyone that he would be back and wished he could take a bit of Floonay away with him. That did give him an idea though.

'You know what I'm a gonna do when I get back to Boise, Norrie?' Hank said, full of the eagerness of a child.

'What's that Hank?' Norrie sipped his beer, curious.

'I'm gonna build me a Nissen hut. I just love this thing. I'll tell ya, Norrie. I like my barn an' all and my ga-rage is a pretty cool man-cave, you know. Got tools and a few old cars and all sorts of junk in there – you'd a like it, Norrie. But, man, this here thing. This is like the best of both, you know. And it'll be like I've got a little slice of Floonay with me all the way across the pond. Maybe I'll even get it set up a little like yours. Get a few creels to stick in a corner an' everythin'. What'd ya think, Norrie, not a bad deal, huh?'

Norrie smiled. 'Aye, that sounds good, Hank.'

'Dang right it does.'

Later in the evening a most important moment arrived (as far as Hank was concerned). He pulled from a pocket a folded sheet of paper.

'Hey, check this out Norrie, I got a little something for you – and for me.'

The list was titled 'Hank & Norrie's Survival Tips', and the seven bullet points were as follows:

1 – Tell a joke every day, even if it ain't too good

2 – Keep your routine going no matter what, even if you ain't making much progress

3 – Don't take anything too dang seriously

4 – Don't overreact

5 – Give thanks even for little things

6 – Remember the good old times and think of the good times to come

7 – Don't quit – don't give up

'This is just a little somethin' I came up with. I got a copy for me, too. Gonna stick it up in my new Nissen hut – somewhere I can see it, you know. Maybe by the workbench. Maybe, you know, maybe you can, too.' Hank handed Norrie the list and tried to affect an 'ah, it's nothing too much' manner. 'As I said, Norrie, just a little somethin' to glance at every now and again, in times of, well, if you're ever feelin' a little down – or hell, even take a look every day – that's what I'm a gonna do.' Hank then took a long drink of his brew. 'Dang, this is good beer.'

Norrie carefully studied the list Hank handed him.

'And, and, before I forget,' Hank began. He fished out a leather-bound documents' holder. 'I know you're liking the cockle raking and all right now, but if you ever do decide to get in on the fishing game and get your own boat.' He opened a cheque book and started scribbling.

'Hank. What are you doing? You don't have to!' Norrie started. He was never going to step foot on a boat again.

'No, no, I insist. This is just in case. I've heard from the boys that you got it in you, you know...we'll just pin it up over here.' Hank made his way to the workbench. 'Up in this corner, out of the way. It's made out to you, it's signed. Left it blank,' he said, winking. 'I trust you Norrie. And make sure to get yourself some good gear. Don't forget that! Ain't no good having a boat with shitty gear.'

Norrie continued to protest but Hank insisted more, and Norrie finally relented.

'I'm not sure what to say, Hank. I'm grateful for your offer, your generosity. Truly, but – I'm certain I am never ever going out there. Ever again.'

Hank got a sense of something he hadn't quite *got* earlier – but he let it pass.

'No probs, my good buddy. Well, let's just leave it where it is anyway – a teeny tiny remote "just in case" deal, you know.'

Norrie wasn't going to make an issue out of it and just let it be. 'Aye, Hank, that's fine. We'll just leave it there. Just in case.'

'That's good, Norrie, real good, but hey,' Hank turned his attention to the piece of paper Norrie had in his hand. 'It might seem a little silly to some. But hey, I just thought it ain't a half bad idea to keep it around. I've told you before, Norrie, I know what it feels like – what it felt like an' all – you find yourself in a dark place and it ain't no good. Dark and dull and devoid of anythin' good and, well, it can be real hard, man. I get it, and so do a lot of people – and hell, I know, and probably you know, can seem a bit embarrassin' once you've managed out of that dark hole, and sometimes you mighta try and quantify it or evaluate it and sometimes you're just like you don't know what to think of it – did I over emphasise, over analyse, make too much of it, I don't know, you know what I'm a sort of sayin'? But, Norrie, don't forget man, what you, well, thought of doin' – what crossed my mind back up in that shitty ol' shack – well, it becomes all too real for hundreds of thousands every year and then there's those that attempt and make a big ol' wreck of things, you know – and then there's all the others affected. It's a bad deal, my man, a bad deal indeed.' He tried to lighten the mood. 'Ah, hey, it's my last night, let's not worry too much about this stuff...just thought, you know, as I said, it'd help you a little – and me, too. I sometimes get a little down, even nowadays.'

Norrie couldn't imagine Hank ever being anywhere but in what certainly appeared as Hank's perpetually happy place, but he seemed genuine enough.

'I'll stick it up here, beside the cheque.' Norrie grabbed a hammer and a small nail and stuck it up above the workbench.

Well, that made Hank smile, and the proudest feeling he had ever known welled up inside him. He had to fight hard not to shed a little tear. Instead he made a show of reaching down into the little fridge to grab a few new brews.

The next day, after a big breakfast that included Hank's favourite Stornoway Black Pudding, it was...to borrow a line from a well-known song... 'time to say goodbye.'

Hank drained the last of his coffee and stated plainly, 'That was dang good! Guess I better get a move on.' They were men, after all, they weren't going to make a big fuss about his departure.

And it was with those words that Norrie MacKinnon and Hank Stetson made their way along the south side of the big beach and followed the path that eight generations of cockle raking MacKinnons had walked, and many others besides. At the airport terminal a small group of well-wishers were there to say goodbye. It naturally got a bit emotional for good ol' Hank Stetson but he mostly kept it together. He was of half a mind to stay a few more days but the pilot was waiting, and the hatch of the little plane beckoned. The last thing he said to Norrie before he boarded was, 'Don't forget about them postcards.' He gave Norrie a big hug and winked. 'Take care of yourself, Norrie.' And with that, he turned, made his way up the little steps, and disappeared into the belly of the plane.

*

Norrie kept true to his promise to Hank, and week after week would pop a postcard in the red mailbox at the end of the road. There wasn't too much of a variety on Floonay, between the selection at the Top Shop, the Butcher's, and the Post Office, and so many of the postcards were duplicates. Pictures of Castlebay, pictures of the Traigh Mhor and the airport, pictures of frightened sheep standing in the middle of the road relieving themselves, pictures of cows eating grass, that sort of thing. As for his cockle raking, he kept a decent routine going. The tides welcomed him and were glad to see him back in rhythm with them. He, too, was glad to be back and felt a deep satisfaction when down on the beach – though the pesky seabirds seemed a little annoyed that they had to make room for him on a regular basis once again. But Norrie being Norrie, when away from the beach he still managed to stumble more than he meant to. Although he was in a much better 'place' he still struggled mightily, from time to time, with the loss of his Papa and brothers. And there was the other little matter – the ferry experience – that kept him from ever considering taking Eddie up on the occasional offers to crew with him. There were times when a few of the other fishermen would ask if he could temporarily fill in, a day here or there – he was forced to make excuses as to why he couldn't go. It was just something he had to deal with. He locked it away somewhere deep in his subconscious – but truth be told it bothered him. It affected him though he tried hard not to think about it. It didn't help that every day, in the Nissen hut, he would see Hank's blank cheque pinned up above the workbench. *Would I have? If things had been different? No! It was always going to be cockle raking. I wouldn't have anyway. It doesn't make a difference. It doesn't matter!* But things were not a disaster. This did, however, mean that he could, would, never leave the island. That was out of the question.

The years passed, the cockle raking continued, as did the sending and receiving of postcards to and from Hank. He'd tack them up in the Nissen hut and soon the line of pictures and scenes from all over Idaho, and beyond, grew and grew. As he was sending them regularly to Idaho, he started sending some to Kenya, to which his Kenyan relations reciprocated. He received a visit or two a year from either Kenya or Idaho. And though they would insist and practically beg him to visit them, he would find a reason why it wasn't the right time. That was not an option.

The cockle raking continued, the postcards continued, and life moved along. There was, though, one area of Norrie's life that was blank, had always been blank, and that was the presence of any love interest. It had simply never happened. He hadn't crossed paths with that special someone – with that *anyone*. That was until one evening close to Easter of Norrie's thirtieth year. He'd been at The Heathbank in the company of Eddie, Ronnie, and a few of the other fishermen. As usual, the pints had flowed and the drams doubled. The following morning the tide would be high, which meant Norrie wouldn't be cockle raking until early afternoon and so he had used that as a good excuse as any to have a few extra, until he eventually wobbled off into the darkness for the one mile walk home. He almost made it. To just past the junction where the road splits on the way to the airport. But that is where the journey would end as he unceremoniously dropped straight into the ditch. Fortunately for him it was a dry, calm night and so when he opened his eyes to the light of the next morning it was just the cold that greeted him, and a little hangover – and – and – oddly, there was the presence of – a silhouette. It took a moment for Norrie to focus. The silhouette was blocking the rising run. Another moment....

A shape.

Hair, as golden as the rays breaking all around, flowed over two shoulders. The arms were crossed and *the shape* struck a pose that seemed familiar to Norrie. But as he focused some more, pushing himself off the ground, he couldn't say he recognised anything else about the shape. It was a woman, a girl, somewhere in between. Her skin was fair and her eyes as green as emeralds. She wore a modest skirt that fluttered in a light breeze and a big cream-coloured jumper that left everything to the imagination.

'Well well, Norrie MacKinnon, just look at yourself,' came a voice from between two lovely lips.

Now, you have to remember, although Norrie had never had a girlfriend before, it didn't mean he was not unlike any other red-blooded Floon. Things had just not worked out over the years, that's all. Wrong place, wrong time, right place, wrong time, wrong, right, whatever. It had not happened. But standing there, over him, was the most beautiful creature he had ever laid his eyes on. And though her words were ones of reproach, her voice was as beautiful as she was.

'You're a wreck, and you're extremely lucky, Norrie. You could have died, you know – such foolishness...' She was bending down to give him a hand up and as she did the tone of her voice transitioned from reproach to concern. 'You should really learn to take better care of yourself, Norrie. You could have broken an arm, a leg, fallen on something sharp and bled to death in the darkness. And then what?' By this moment Norrie was out of the ditch and on his feet. She had a steadying hand on Norrie's right elbow and as he looked into the beautiful emerald eyes of this still unknown person, he saw a great affection, a worry...

He finally found his voice. 'I'm sorry, I'm not sure – do I know you?'

That brought a smile to her face, as though he had said something that pleased her.

'I didn't think you would remember me.'

Norrie was trying hard to put a name to the face, and to the place he was supposed to maybe remember her from.

'Sorry, I'm not sure...'

'Well, you are a few years older than me. I wouldn't have expected you to notice – pay any attention...'

It clicked, sort of. 'From school?'

'Aye, that's right.' She ran a hand through her hair.

School. Especially the last year of it, did not stir the fondest of memories for Norrie.

'I was in S1 when you were S4.'

Ah, S4, the end of Norrie's academic pursuits. What a year that was.

'You look confused, and a little cold, come.' She gestured to his place which was just 200 yards up the road. 'Let's put the kettle on and get you warmed up.' She was moving before Norrie had a chance to decide. He obeyed.

'What's your name, then?'

'Samantha.' She glanced over. A smile. 'Samantha MacKenzie.'

Samantha. Samantha MacKenzie. He was trying to place her. Floonay was a small island and almost everyone at least knew *of* most other families. Maybe not every single member, but at least had an idea of roughly who belonged where. Norrie's intelligence, however, was lacking in this department as he'd lived a little like a troglodyte for a good few years. It was early morning, there was no car or bike to be seen, so she couldn't be from Castlebay or way over on the west side. Maybe somewhere down along the eastern shores, or from north of the airport. She certainly wasn't from his own little village. He knew every house and family there.

'Just past Picnic Hill. Third croft past the cemetery. That's my father's place. My mum's side is Lewis.'

Just past Picnic Hill? Of course he knows the spot. Couldn't say he knew the family though. But Picnic Hill and beyond he knew well. It was along that road that Bonzo was run over by the camper van. It held a tragically special place in his heart.

'Samantha – that's a pretty name.'

'You think so?'

'Aye, of course, it's a lovely name.'

'I think there's lots of lovely names.'

Norrie paused. 'Aye, I reckon there are – but Samantha, well, I think it's well up there.'

Some part of Norrie's brain could not believe he was saying what he was saying. It was like something else was in control. Not only had he never even had a girlfriend before he had barely spoken in all his years to any girl who wasn't related to him. A few at school, but not many – he'd had no interest in girls before he'd stormed out of the headmistress's office. He felt at that moment, apart from hungover, a little ridiculous, a little nervous, a little shy.

'That's nice of you to say.' Samantha reached over and touched Norrie's hand. It was the gentlest of squeezes. It was just a moment, but in that moment something electric, magical, mystical happened - something beyond the realm of *complete* human understanding.

Ch 31

Falling in Love

Norrie MacKinnon realised he'd fallen in love whilst sipping a cup of tea.

With the small fireplace in the kitchen giving off warmth, Norrie listened. Samantha was a woman of the world. He gave answers when asked a question but Samantha did most of the talking, and it was apparent that she knew much more about Norrie than he knew about her. She had arrived home just a few weeks previously, after travelling and working abroad for years.

'As soon as I'd finished high school, I was gone, I was desperate to leave. There was so much I'd heard about the world. So many places to see. Things to experience.'

Well, Norrie wasn't much of a traveller but he was mightily intrigued by Samantha's stories. She'd travelled across continents and been to places Norrie had never heard of. He'd heard of Paris, though, Amsterdam too, and even Istanbul. But no, he didn't know it was once known as Constantinople. Samantha had worked in all these places. Travelling wasn't cheap, she'd explained. She had to work when and where she could. She'd work and work and save diligently, and then when she thought she'd saved enough for a few months, off she'd go. She'd seen the pyramids in Egypt and the Victoria Falls along the Zambezi River. She'd trekked across Indonesia and even bungee jumped from a bridge in New Zealand. South America, North America, and a few places in between had seen the treads of her boots, the soles of her feet. The list went on.

After a while, she shrugged and said, 'But, I don't know. This place – home, it just seemed to call to me. I can't really explain it. I loved every minute of my travels. I met so many people. Most wonderful, some not so wonderful. The experiences were just that – experiences. And all experiences are good experiences – even the not so good ones, in their own way. I guess what I'm just saying is, it was all, taken as a whole, wonderful...I've never regretted the decision. But I knew that it was time to come home.' She let out a short laugh. 'Oh, my mother, my poor, dear, mother. She was over the moon.'

Well, Norrie wasn't sure what to say. It was all quite incredible and a little overwhelming. A lot to take in. But at the centre of all those travels, experiences, places, was Samantha. And with her Norrie had fallen in love.

She half-smiled as though she could read his mind. 'And, you know. I never – forgot about you.' The words hung in the air.

Uh oh. Norrie was experiencing emotions he'd never known before.

Samantha insisted on making him some breakfast as he washed up. He protested, wanting to make her something, but realised he was a bit dishevelled (and probably stank), and for the first time in his life became aware that he wanted to make a good impression. Off he went, reappearing a while later scrubbed clean and wearing his Sunday best, which still wasn't that impressive. They spent the day together, and Samantha admitted as they walked along the big beach that she'd seen him down there over the last few weeks, raking away. She'd wondered what had come of him – as she knew of *'all that other stuff',* and without holding much back, said she was glad to see him out and about. This all had Norrie's mind racing. She asked him to show her how to cockle rake. He hesitated but soon came to realise what a good idea that was. He was in his element with the rake in hand and toiling along the shore. He explained what areas were better than others and showed her a few special techniques, and even shared with her a few tips that he hadn't shared with anyone else. Well, Samantha was impressed and amazed and seemed more in awe of what it took to toil away along the shore than Norrie had been with the stories of her years abroad.

While showing her how to properly position her hands on the shaft of the rake and the best way to get the most out of the 'sweeping oval', Norrie smelled the alluring, flowery scent of Samantha's hair. Their bodies touched, for brief moments, and hands lightly brushed over hands, and suddenly, an electric charge connected them. They became keenly aware of something powerful. Something overwhelming and unstoppable. Something beautiful. And it would happen to be, that down there along the shore of the Traigh Mhor, as two rakes dropped to the wet, sandy earth, was where Norrie kissed the first and only girl that he ever would. The passion was making the wet sand start to steam and Norrie was as clumsy as a new born giraffe. It was Samantha who took the lead and before Norrie knew where he was, they were behind a big rock out on the wee Isle of Orosay. It was closer than heading in the other direction to home. What happened next was best kept out of view from anyone strolling along the beach.

*

And what happened next was a bit unusual but not wholly so. In the millennia long history of people falling in love it was certainly not the first time. Far from it.

It was about fifteen hours after they had met.

Inexplicably, but not a surprise to him – somehow, he knew he would – Norrie turned to Samantha. They were out by the Nissen hut watching the sun set, as it arced down and away beyond the big dunes, just behind the wee airport a mile to the west. He said, 'I know this might sound a bit...well...do you...'

Samantha put a hand to his lips, silencing him, and for a moment Norrie felt a wave of unease. Holding her golden locks away from her face in the light evening breeze, she smiled, and her emerald eyes looked deep into his soul. 'You beat me to it, Norrie. I was just about to ask you the same question. I think that's a grand idea. So, yes Norrie! Yes...I would love to marry you.'

They embraced, and it was the most wonderful sight to behold on the Traigh Mhor that evening. Even a few sheep stopped their perpetual grazing nearby and looked on and 'bahaha'd' their approval.

*

Well, wouldn't you believe it, but when Hank Stetson heard the news he flung his cowboy hat with such force as he hollered a giant *'whoopee!'* that it smashed a window at Stetson Industries HQ. Norrie's Mama was up in Calgary, Alberta on a short visit to old family friends, originally from, of all places, Calgary on the Isle of Mull (not far from Floonay), when she got the news. Margaret MacKinnon smiled warmly, looked to the sky, and thought of Michael, Donald, Duncan, Ewan and Rory. When Norrie's Kenyan brothers-in-law heard the news they were in a small, dusty village 200 miles west of

Nairobi helping care for some dirt poor children. They just smiled and nodded to one another and their hearts were full of joy. Norrie's sisters couldn't contain their excitement, and when they heard the wedding would be held as soon as everyone could make it back, they immediately booked their flights: Nairobi direct to London, up to Glasgow and then on to the trusty Twin Otter out to their native island. For Hank's part, he was due to head to Argentina for a big conference with his South American compadres. He called them up and explained in terribly broken Spanish that his plans had changed, and why they had, and said he was real sorry but he had to go. They, of course, understood and told him in not-nearly-as-terribly-broken English that they hoped the celebration would be a wonderful one and to make sure he had a good time. *Dang right Hank Stetson would be having a good time!*

Stetson Industries was doing better than Hank had ever dreamed possible from its meagre beginnings: a few seeds in a box of mostly mushy tayters carried up to that shitty old mountainside shack. As Hank would say to anyone who asked though, ‘Shoot, it ain't been too straight or flat a road, you know.' Life had both cursed him (his adoptive parents were tricked into leaving for Central America) and blessed him (he somehow struggled along) and cursed him again (half a leg was shredded by machine gun fire) and blessed him (his non-shooting brother in arms fixed that tourniquet pronto) and blessed him some more (his tayter business started a growin') and blessed him even more (he met his first wife and had two wonderful sons) and then it kicked him in the teeth with a force that could smash granite (his wife and sons died tragically young) and then it blessed him again (somehow, with the help of a few friends and a pretty head doctor, he made it) and, again (he met Mrs MacKinnon in the Butcher's *and* was introduced to the most scrumptious food ever:

Stornoway Black Pudding) and, once again! (he had three more wonderful children) and it kept blessing him (his tayter business grew and grew and grew). And because Stetson Industries was doing so well Hank had purchased a corporate jet, and on the side of that shiny bird was emblazoned the name *Flyin' Tayters!* (He'd initially wanted to go with the name 'Totally Tayters' but one of his Idahoan rivals had beaten him to it. Now, there was no law barring him from also using the same name, but Hank knew it didn't do to copy. Too unoriginal. And anyway, as his El Capitano explained, 'Hank, it's a plane. I think Flyin' Tayters! suits something that flies more than Totally Tayters.' 'Yeah, you know, John, maybe you're right!') It was Hank's pride and joy and though the passenger cabin was as plush a ride as one could ask for Hank mostly liked to sit beside the pilot in the co-pilot's seat. 'I hope you don't mind, Rick,' he would often say to the co-pilot, who had indeed started to mind. Hank would continue, 'You can go on back there and put your feet up. Bar is fully stocked, pour yourself a drink and relax.'

And it was aboard *Flyin' Tayters!* that they were going to travel to Floonay. Upon hearing that they were landing on a beach, his El Capitano questioned the wisdom of doing so. Hank assured him it was no normal beach. There was at least two square miles of open space and most of the surface was as hard as a regular runway. And besides, a little twin-engine Otter already makes the scheduled roundtrip from Glasgow. 'Teeny bit smaller than our little baby here, but trust me, you could land a 747 on that beach.' Hank was a bit disappointed that they weren't going to make it in one leg. 'We're going to have to stop in Newfoundland to refuel.' (*Dang, shoulda gone with the bigger model,* Hank had privately thought), and was disappointed again when hearing they'd have to make a second stop, 'Hank, we have to clear customs going into the UK. Sorry. And it's normally protocol to file a flight plan before departing. We've got to say where we're landing.' An image of the Western Isles formed in his mind, and then further to the east, the mainland, and south of the Western Isles was Northern Ireland and its friendly neighbour. Hank fell into deep thought and then said, 'But you can change your mind on the way, change course or destination?' 'Of course. Just have to let air traffic control know.' Hank was thinking deeply once again. He was desperate to get to Floonay ASAP and continued, 'Well, let's try to make sure we don't have to head too far past Floonay. Don't want to waste too much time just a' flyin' all around, you know. For now, we'll go with Glasgow as our destination, but, hell, who knows – maybe they got a passport office up in Benbecula or Stornoway.' 'I'll make sure to call, Hank, once we enter UK airspace and see what changes we can make en route. In the meantime Hank, I've gotta get this bird fuelled and ready. Let your wife know we're leaving in 30 minutes. There's a storm front coming in. Would like to get ahead of it. Make for a smoother ride for your youngins', you know.' 'You got it John!' Hank slapped the shoulder of his favourite pilot and hurried off to call Margaret.

Meanwhile, back on Floonay, plans were well underway for the wedding and reception, which were set for the following Saturday. They had almost a week to prepare – plenty of time. Well, at least longer than Norrie's Mama and sisters had. Samantha's mum and her seven sisters became a veritable force of nature. They mustered the troops and got down to the serious business of prepping Castlebay hall. Norrie had thought they'd naturally use the hall in Northbay, as both sides of the family were from the north end of Floonay, but the invitation list was growing and they needed the additional room which was available at the Castlebay venue. That suited Norrie fine. Samantha would decide. The wedding itself, though, would be at the church in Northbay, as that was the church her family attended and that his family used to attend.

And in usual Floonish tradition, both Father John and Reverend Cullen would be presiding over the service. That, too, suited Norrie just fine. They hadn't quite got around to discussing religion and he certainly hadn't shared with Samantha the serious doubts he had at one time about the whole thing. But none of that mattered now. He would marry Samantha anywhere she wanted to get married. Thank goodness the best two pipers in the Western Isles were available, DP & Duncan, and also one of the top dance bands from Vatersay, The Vatersay Boys, were available for the reception and ceilidh. They decided not to bother with traditional invitations as it would simply be a colossal waste of time and paper. The invitations would go out by word of mouth. They would have to put a limit as the church could only hold so many and the hall kitchen couldn't handle more than 200. Anything more than that and things would get tricky; half the food would be hot, the other half cold. As for the ceilidh afterwards, however – well, it was understood that the door would be open to the whole island once the formalities were out of the way. One important thing that Norrie had to decide: who would be his best man and his groomsmen. To be made clear it was not custom on Floonay for the groom to have the equal number of groomsmen as the bride has bridesmaids, but in Samantha's travels she had attended a few weddings that this was custom. She liked the idea and since Samantha really wanted all seven sisters to be in her wedding party, she hoped Norrie could come up with seven men he thought befitting the role of groomsmen. 'If you can't, I understand, and we'll just go with one best man.' She'd replied, anxiously nibbling a lip. 'I'll see what I can do, honey.' He assured her.

Norrie went for a walk on the big beach to contemplate this. Looking out to Hellisay and north to Gighay and then towards the foreboding island of Stack, he reflected on his brothers and Papa. Doing so, a dark empty void conspired and teased him, daring at any moment to suck all the joy out of the world. That would always be there, somewhere, but that was okay. He immediately knew who three of his groomsmen would be. Mwaka, Akili, and Darweshi. He just had to come up with four more. Norrie's best old pal, Malcolm, was still roaming the world after all these years and so he was out of the question. And seeing as Norrie himself had spent so many years in his own version of exile, he had not forged deep friendships again. But he knew most of the local fishermen well enough. His mind scrolled to the night before the meeting in the ditch – it had started at The Heathbank. Ronnie and Eddie had been there first, then his cousin, Colin, had showed up with another fisherman everyone knew simply as Irish. Irish had shown up on Floonay via a trawler a few years before, and had decided to stay, much to the annoyance of his skipper at the time. He didn't sound Irish, but that was his name. And he didn't speak of his past, so no one asked. But he worked hard, got along with most everyone, and preferred to be paid in cash. He became accepted. Became one of the lads. The four of them had contributed to him winding up in the ditch. And if it wasn't for the ditch? *I'll ask the boys, I'm sure they won't mind.* That's it, sorted. As for who would play the role of best man, he'd let them decide.

Ch 32

The Big Day

Hank Stetson's jet landing on the Traigh Mhor was a sight to behold. And the view from the cockpit was just as impressive. 'You were right Hank, this is one helluva big beach. We've got plenty of room to land,' a voice came from the pilot's seat. 'Told you so,' Hank replied from the co-pilot's seat. The real co-pilot had, sadly, been stuck in the cabin for the whole journey playing with Hank and Margaret's children. On board, too, were a few folk from Stetson Industries research lab. Hank knew he'd never replicate Floonay's tayters, but he was going to see what his scientists could do to get as close as possible.

Hank Stetson's sleek bird landed without incident and with plenty of runway to spare, and before he knew it, Hank was breathing fresh Hebridean air for the first time in quite a while.

Unsurprisingly, and if one did not possess a keen eye for the order emerging amongst the chaos, the activity of the following few days could best be described as 'higgledy-piggledy'. To be sure some of it was, but in actuality most of it was not.

There were children running around, after all. How could you not have at least some higgledy-piggledyness trying to contain the excitement of youth. It was manageable at first with just Hank, Margaret, and their three children arriving, but two days later when Norrie's three sisters arrived with Akili, Darweshi, and Mwaka, and their broods, the wheels came off, or just about. Amongst all the joy and excitement, and the meeting of so many for the first time, a wedding was neatly coming together, one that would go down in Floonay's record book as one to remember.

Margaret Stetson was greeted with open arms and warm wishes by just about everyone. There were always ones who would sneer from a distance – and from an even greater distance, gossip, judge, jump to a conclusion or two as to why she remarried. It didn't really matter though, who thought what, for she could walk past them no longer in shame. Even when she crossed paths with the fearsome headmistress at the Top Shop, there was not a flutter of displeasure. Mizz Fizzlezwit didn't dare say a word. She glanced once and went on her horrible way.

With two days to go, Thursday evening, Norrie and Samantha found the time to sneak away for a little quiet time alone. It was a lovely, sunny evening so they decided to go for a walk along the long beach behind the dunes. Apart from a herd of cows milling about at the north end of the beach, and a small flock of sheep wobbling along the top of the dunes, they had the place to themselves. The mighty Atlantic rolled in gently, the water lapping at their toes as they strolled, arm in arm. They spoke of their families and were glad that everyone got along so well. Samantha asked Norrie how many children he would like and after a moment's thought replied, 'However many you would like.' She smiled, and they walked on. Further ahead the herd of cows seemed to be deciding whether or not to go for a swim. The sheep high atop the giant dunes looked on, seemingly interested in what was happening at the beach.

They walked in silence for a while, relaxed in each other's company, and then there was an 'ummm?' from Samantha.

'There's something on your mind?' Norrie asked.

Samantha looked up and they came to a stop. She nibbled a lip.

'What is it? Are you all right?'

Samantha nibbled a bit more, unusually uncertain.

'It's okay, Samantha – honey, what is it?'

After a moment she finally spoke. 'I was wondering...'

'Samantha, wonder away, it's okay.'

'Well, it's about the – the wedding.'

For a cruel millionth of a second Norrie felt as though the universe might cave in on itself – *it's about the wedding?* – she – no, it couldn't be – what about the wedding?!

Samantha saw what had flashed through his mind.

'Oh, honey, no – no,' she hugged him. 'I'm sorry.'

'What is it – whatever it is, it's okay, I promise you,' Norrie assured her.

It was Samantha's turn to be anxious and uncertain again. 'Oh – are you sure, Norrie?'

'Of course I'm sure. Whatever it is, it's okay with me.'

Samantha hugged him tight, 'Oh, Norrie. I do love you, you know that, a thousand times over. A million times. Even more than a million.'

'I know you do, and I love you.'

They just held one another as the tide lapped at their feet, and then Samantha looked up and spoke, 'Oh, I hope you don't think I'm, you know, strange or anything for asking this – because, after all – they've been worn by so many – through the centuries – even nowadays people wear them, even superheroes, and, well, there are caped crusaders, and funny thing is, they don't seem to wear out, get old or go out of fashion, you know.' Samantha was on a roll, albeit a slightly nervous one. 'And, well, the Count of Monte Cristo had one – have you ever heard of the Count of Monte Cristo, Norrie?'

Norrie shook his head, a little mystified as to what she was talking about.

'And even many of our own clan chiefs wore them. I think they did anyway. I know Zoro definitely did, and then there are all the knights who did, and kings, and princes – and well, Norrie, you are my knight, my prince, my everything...'

It flashed through Norrie's mind as to who found whom first. It was he who had been lying in the ditch and so he was of the mind that Samantha was the female version of a knight who had rescued him. Or an angel was fine, too, because that is what she was.

'Samantha, what on earth are you on about?'

She looked across the ocean and back up into Norrie's eyes. 'I had a dream one night, before I came home. It was about my future wedding and about the man I would one day marry – funny enough he looked a lot like you. I had been in the south of Spain and was ready to travel straight back but decided to head north and ended up walking the Camino de Santiago – have you heard of it?'

Norrie hadn't heard of it.

'It's an old pilgrim route – doesn't matter. But when I arrived in Santiago - - - Norrie, what is it?'

Norrie sat down, looked out to sea and for a moment didn't say a word.

'Norrie, are you okay?'

He finally spoke, and his voice was quiet. 'Santiago...' The name just hung in the air.

'Norrie?'

'It was my brother's favourite place. Duncan's. Santiago. Santiago, Chile, that is. I never really knew why, but he brought me my very own pipe from there. He even had Chile tattooed on his arm – there was a star representing

Santiago...' After a moment he told her what they had found along the beach following the first tragedy. He fell silent as she cried in his arms. Although Samantha could recall that something was found all those years ago she'd been just eleven, and all the adults had been evasive about the details with the island's youth. *Just a few remains is all. You know how quickly those crabs can nibble.* Norrie just sat there, silent, holding Samantha.

'I'm sorry Norrie.'

'It's okay.'

'I'm so sorry.'

'There's nothing to be sorry about.'

The weight of the moment kept Samantha from saying more.

They just sat in silence for a while before Norrie spoke.

'Whatever it is you dreamt about in Santiago must be important and so whatever it is that you want, whatever it is you wish for, it is yours.'

*

The day of the big wedding.

Father John and the good Reverend Cullen were looking holy and happy. Holy because they were men of God. And happy because although Mwaka, Akili, and Darweshi had shown up with their families in tow, they'd somehow managed to find the time, during the week, to give them a hand with all sorts of little jobs, not least their gardens which were needing sprucing up.

So there they all were, in Northbay Church, under the watchful eye of St. Barr. Norrie wearing the crimson cape Samantha had brought back from Santiago. Mwaka, Akili, Darweshi, alongside the four fishermen, Ronnie, Eddie, Colin, and Irish, and they were all wearing kilts. The whole congregation had taken a few curious glances when Norrie appeared. But the cape had been in Samantha's dream – and she had gone the extra mile to find the perfect one before travelling through France, crossing the English Channel, and heading home – and anyway, as he'd reflected, they weren't *that* unusual. On the right side were Samantha's seven sisters, all looking beautiful in light blue bridesmaid dresses. They were all waiting for Mr MacKenzie to march Samantha down the aisle. The wee church was packed to the gills. There wasn't even standing room left for a cartoon stick figure. Every square inch was filled, and the place was stifling as it was a moderately warm and sunny Saturday afternoon. Even the choir balcony up top was filled, with a line of children sitting between the railings, legs swinging fearlessly. Hank, Margaret, her three grown daughters and a few squirming children, sat in the front left pew, whilst the front right pew was crammed full of MacKenzies.

Norrie waited, a little nervously, at the centre with Colin at his side performing the role of best man.

The previous evening at The Heathbank, the four fishermen and three brothers, amongst others, had deliberated as to who should fill the role. They were all happy to. Looking to the brothers at one point, Ronnie said, 'Gentlemen, you're his brothers-in-law, you're family. I think it should be one of you.' To which Akili replied, 'But you have all known him for a very long time, you might as well be family. You *are* family.' Hank chipped in, 'Well, why don't y'all draw lots or put names in a hat, or some dang thing.' Then Irish looked to the barman, 'Joe, any ideas?' Joe was cleaning the perpetual glass, looking thoughtful, 'Aye.' Everyone waited. 'Flip coins, get it over with.' The rest, looking amongst themselves, all thought the same thing – *why didn't I think of that?* And so it would be through a process of elimination, Colin was made the best man.

Without warning there was a clatter at the back as the door opened and the day's light shone in. The big moment had arrived. On cue, from the golden pipes of the church's ancient organ, a well-known sound emerged and resonated throughout the packed church. In marched a proud father with his daughter. The congregation gasped as Samantha turned the corner, and at the altar Norrie had to pinch himself to make sure he wasn't dreaming. She was wearing a simple silk ivory wedding dress, the train being held up by two nieces. Her golden locks flowed halfway down her back and her emerald eyes and beautiful smile captivated the crowd causing more than a few wives to nudge their husbands back to reality.

Norrie had to pinch himself once again.

After a pause, Mr MacKenzie smiled, taking in the moment, then escorted his fourth daughter towards the altar. He shook hands with Norrie and kissed Samantha on the cheek, all smiles and emotion, then took his place in the front pew. Norrie and Samantha were lost in the moment together, then, arm in arm, turned to the altar. The music had stopped and the crowd, silent and waiting. Father John looked to Reverend Cullen, who nodded his assent – *you go first.* He cleared his throat, 'We are gathered here today, in the presence of Almighty God, to witness the marriage of Samantha Kathleen MacKenzie and Norrie Alistair MacKinnon....'

BANG! THUD!! CRASH!!!

Thump, thump, thump, thump!!

Huff puff, huff puff, huff puff....

The congregation, Norrie, Samantha, the whole wedding party, Father John, Reverend Cullen, all looked on – a mix of interest, disbelief, curiosity, shock, at the scene unfolding in front of their eyes.

It was wee Jack Mcphail, son of Ronnie – who was wondering what in heaven's name his son was doing, here, in the church – *with Peggy?*

Huff! Puff! Huff! Puff! Hands on knees.

Jack's sheep dog, Peggy, was also huffing and puffing.

Huff puff, huff puff...finally, a word.... 'The byre...' Huff puff. 'The byre – the big byre!' Huff puff. 'It's...' Huff. And one more puff. 'It's – on fire!'

For a split second there was nothing but a perfectly stunned silence. Then – a gasp, and then another. Everyone looked around. A buzz rose from the crowd.

'Hurry!' Jack yelled, with unusual authority. 'He's trapped!'

Ch 33

There's a Fire in the Byre!

'Donald Angus Campbell! He's stuck in the byre! He's yelling, he can't get out!! Hurrrrreeeeee!!! *The byre is on fire!!!!'* And as fast as Jack and Peggy ran down the aisle, they spun around 180 degrees and shot out of the church like two bolts of lightning.

Northbay church emptied quicker than a prison with its guards snoozing and doors wide open, and there was Norrie MacKinnon off like a rocket, his crimson cape blowing in the wind.

Ronnie was flabbergasted as he watched his son, who was barely eleven years old, go rocketing down the road in his beat up old van – *I didn't even think it ran anymore?!*, and there was Peggy's head sticking out the window. *He didn't even wait for me?!*

The township of Cleit was on the west side of Floonay, not that far from Northbay. By road it was a couple of miles. If one drove fast enough and knew the corners it wouldn't take very long – under 90 seconds. Problem was, the island's only fire engine was six miles south, in Castlebay, then it was another four miles north along the west side. Unfortunately for Donald Angus Campbell, most of the island's volunteer firemen were at the wedding. They had to move fast. Eddie, and four others who constituted most of the squad, hopped into the fastest four wheels in the parking lot and were off for a wild ride to Castlebay.

Everyone else headed for Cleit. But Norrie was ahead of them all – for a few hundred yards anyway. Colin pulled over in a packed van and said, 'Norrie, I know you've a cape, but I think we've got room. You ought to hop in.'

Puzzled, Norrie replied, 'Aye, I think you're right,'

It wouldn't take long for the byre to be razed to the ground. Every second counted. Norrie had never fought a fire before and didn't have a clue what to expect. He didn't actually know Donald Angus Campbell either. It didn't matter, for when he heard the man was trapped and yelling for help, well, something propelled him – inexplicably – to run faster than he'd ever run in his life. On reflection, a speeding van was definitely more practical. By the time they started arriving, each screeching to a halt, a few of Donald Angus's distant neighbours were doing what they could with a couple of pails of water and a hose that couldn't reach the byre. The roof was thatched and smoke was seeping through. Cruel, wicked flames were licking up and around its edges. Smoke billowed out of two small windows. The heavy front door was still in place though flames could be seen licking around its edges, eager to devour it. It appeared as though the fire was near the front of the byre. The buckets of water being splashed through the smashed windows and up onto the roof was better than nothing but it was not enough. *What could they do?* More vehicles arrived, people and buckets spilling out of them, and quickly, human chains were linked to the one garden hose that was 30 feet away. Donald Angus could be heard, though his yells were becoming less frequent and not nearly as vocal. Time was of the essence. Everyone had one eye on the byre and one eye on the twisty road leading to Castlebay – how long would it take for the fire engine to arrive? A few more minutes might be a few too many. The scene was becoming frantic. The seconds ticked away, the fire grew stronger, and still the fire engine was nowhere to be seen. People looked at each other, worried and alarmed that Donald Angus was not going to make it. Donald Angus was going to be roasted alive. Prayers were being muttered. *Please, God, save Donald Angus, oh, let him live!* A few were also whispering in their prayers if God would please make sure Donald Angus passes out from the smoke before he has to feel the horror of a flame. Hank had stumbled out of one of the cars and for all the resources at his disposal and the power he wielded in the world, he felt just as helpless as everyone else. He did his level best to pass the buckets as quickly as possible. He even whipped off his fancy cowboy hat and added it to the line of buckets going back and forth. Those women who weren't needed in the bucket chain stood back, keeping worried hands on their children.

Norrie was there throwing bucket after bucket onto the smoking front door and through the little smashed window. He knew their efforts were close to fruitless, and, unless a helicopter appeared in the next ten seconds with a belly-full of water, he knew that Donald Angus Campbell would die – if he hadn't already succumbed – for his voice had not been heard in over a minute. Norrie had known enough tragedies, as had his Mama and his sisters, and Hank, and countless others, too. He glanced over at Samantha and her seven sisters all looking on – there was nothing more they could do. This was her special day, Norrie thought. Their special day. It was *not* going to end in tragedy – for anyone – and out of the blue the thought struck him. Maybe, there was a purpose, a reason – maybe there was more to Samantha's dream than she realised at the time. The fabric was heavy and the hood deep. Samantha's dream might just save a life! He would never forgive himself if he didn't try.

'Norrie! What are you doing?!' It was Samantha. Startled, others looked on.

There was no time to waste. Norrie had run to the garden hose and doused himself with water. He made sure to soak the cape well and good. A few hands reached for him but he shrugged them off, and though more hands tried to stop him, not least of all Samantha's, Norrie passed them in one fluid motion flicking the hood over his head just as he kicked in the door of the byre and entered the inferno.

The screaming and yelling from outside was drowned out by the tremendous noise of the crackling fire. For a moment the heat knocked him back and he almost lost his nerve, his consciousness, too. *Just move! It can't be far!* His movements were fast and furious, but also deliberate and careful. He felt the body, limp on the floor. In one swift move he had Donald Angus Campbell over his shoulder and a few steps later he burst out of the smoking entrance, took a few more steps and tumbled to the ground, hitting his head on a rock and blacking out.

*

The next thing Norrie saw was Samantha's beautiful, worried face. Beyond that, more anxious faces, and beyond all of them a little bit of blue high in the sky.

Samantha's worried look turned into a smile. 'Norrie, you're okay?!' she leaned down and gave him a hug. Doctor Bartlett inspected the lump on Norrie's forehead, and with expert fingers stretched open each eye as he inspected the patient's pupils. Back and forth two or three times. Satisfied, he declared, 'You'll be fine, son.' And at those words the whole crowd cheered.

By the time Norrie came around Eddie and the rest of the fire crew had arrived. The byre, by that point, was engulfed in flames and there was nothing more they could do with their limited supply of water but watch it burn and ensure the fire didn't spread. Dr Bartlett and a few of the local nurses had gone to work on Donald Angus, and within minutes he was coughing and spluttering back to life. Dr Bartlett insisted that it would probably be best to keep him in the hospital for observation for a night or two, but Donald Angus Campbell was firm that what he needed more right then and there was a healthy dram, and from somewhere in the crowd a bottle appeared. It took him a few minutes to come around properly, and when he did the sight of his beloved byre up in flames brought tears to his eyes.

Mwaka, Akili, and Darweshi had hoisted Norrie up and were doing their best to dust him off. Norrie was half expecting to find what he was wearing to be a charred burnt mess. But as he inspected himself, to his – and the brothers', and eventually everyone's amazement – the cape he was wearing was unscathed.

Norrie looked to Samantha, puzzled, in wonder.... 'This cape? It saved my life, it saved Donald Angus's life. Your dream saved our lives.'

Samantha didn't know what to say, or, for a moment, do. But then she did, and wrapped her arms around him, and whispered that she never wanted to let go.

The crowd watched Donald Angus Campbell's beloved byre burn to the ground. The mood of the crowd was a curious mix: of joy – that Donald Angus had survived, and of relief – that Norrie was okay, and of empathy – Donald Angus was relieved to be alive but he could not help but despair at the loss of his byre. It was everything to the man. It contained decades of his life. But these things would be replaced, he knew that. The last element of the crowd's mood was something along the lines of: 'err, what do we do now?'

Samantha didn't waste any time. She whispered in Norrie's ear what she thought ought to happen next, and he shrugged and said, 'Why not?' They sought out Father John and Reverend Cullen and after a moment they looked to one another, shrugged and both agreed, 'Aye, why not. Why not indeed?'

When it became apparent what was happening next the wedding party took their positions, as they dusted themselves off.

And so it would come to be that Samantha Kathleen MacKenzie and Norrie Alistair MacKinnon tied the knot beside Donald Angus Campbell's smouldering byre. The sight of the caped man who had saved his life getting married on his croft – well, it brought joy back to Donald Angus faster than it otherwise would have. Father John and Reverend Cullen presented the married couple to the growing crowd and DP & Duncan fired up their pipes and marched them – they didn't know where to march them exactly, so they just marched them around for a while, and with a few bottles appearing out of nowhere, it could be fairly stated that the reception started earlier than planned, and not quite where it was intended.

The gathering did – eventually – make its way to the hall in Castlebay, and the evening would go down in Floonay's official record books as, I) One of the most entertaining, but also as, II) The most memorable wedding in the island's history. One of the photos an older Norrie and Samantha MacKinnon would have on their mantelpiece above the fire, amongst all the other wedding photos, would be of themselves on either side of a smiling Donald Angus Campbell, arms around one another, with the byre smouldering in the background.

Eventually it all came to an end early the following morning.

Chores called, children needed feeding, Father John’s and Reverend Cullen's flocks were waiting, and – for Norrie, the low tide beckoned. When he'd asked Samantha a few days before the wedding if she would mind at all if he spent a few hours of their first day married doing a little cockle raking: ‘...it won't be for long. I just thought it would be a good thing to...’, she hadn't let him finish. ‘Aye, Norrie, of course you can. Of course, *we* can.’ She'd smiled and hugged him tight. ‘I know I'm no good at raking. You rake and I'll pick them up and put them in the bucket. I can't think of a better way to spend our first day married than on the most beautiful beach in the whole wide world.’ Deep in Norrie's heart, and even deeper in his soul, he felt the warmth, the peace, the presence, of eternal love.

Ch 34

Out of the Blue

The Kenyan and Idahoan contingents wanted to stay 'just a little bit longer', but none more than Hank Stetson. He'd already pushed back their departure date three times and it was over a fortnight before he reluctantly clambered aboard *Flyin' Tayters!* for the long journey west. It had been the height of summer and the kids were loving every minute of their Hebridean adventure. The grownups, too, loved every minute of their little holiday, but eventually Akili, Darweshi, and Mwaka felt the pull to head back – there were so many needing their help. Norrie's sisters and Mama were getting a little drained by all the activity and were looking forward to heading back to their adopted homes and the comfort of their routines. Only Hank was still 100% in 'Dang Id'a love to stay here forever' mode. But, alas, he knew he couldn't. His people in Boise had been calling more and more, looking for answers and advice, and even his Argentinian compadres had rung him a time or two wondering if the party was over and would he be available for a meeting in Buenos Aires or Bogota? 'Dang, I guess ah better be goin' soon here, Norrie,' he'd lamented, whilst sipping a brew in the Nissen hut after Norrie and Samantha had returned from their honeymoon in Vatersay.

They were lucky there was a causeway to Vatersay, otherwise they wouldn't have been going anywhere. Norrie might have mostly sorted himself out over the years, but he still feared the sea, and would he ever step foot on a machine that flies through the air? Not a chance.

Hank's small squad from Stetson Industries' research lab had gathered as many samples as they possibly could, ready for more analysis and further review back at the main lab, but deep down Hank knew it wouldn't do any good. 'I don't know boys and girls,' Hank lamented to his research crew one sunny afternoon, as they were collecting samples at a tayter patch near the airport, 'ah gotta feelin' this ain't gonna do any good. Just look around this place – how can we possibly replicate all this? And that beautiful ocean breeze? Well, maybe, just maybe, it just ain't meant to be, you know. Hell, Idaho tayters are still pretty dang good. 'Specially our Stetson tayters – ah, whatever, hell, it's been a fun coupla' weeks though, ain't it?'
'It sure has, Hank.'

It sure had been. But the time had come for everyone to get back to work properly. The farewells and goodbyes went on for a couple of days, but eventually a full sixteen days after arriving, the Kenyan and Idahoan clans were ready to clamber aboard Hank's shiny jet. Next stop: London. Hank had insisted to Darwehsi, Akili, and Mwaka that they catch a ride with him for part of the way. 'That's very kind of you Hank,' Akili had replied after trying to refuse the offer. They'd been by the Nissen hut one evening flipping burgers on the bbq. 'That's no probs, my brother. You guys got all them kids runnin' around. Take a little stress out of the travelling, you know – and anyway, hey, I gotta little business meetin' I can tend to down in The City, with some big shot financiers,' he said with a wink. 'Will be able to write the trip off as a business expense, you know what I'ma sayin'? You pick up what ahm' a layin' down?'

Akili laughed, 'Ah ha, ha...yes, yes, I know what you are saying. You are a wise man, Hank, a wise man indeed.'

And so there they all were on a sunny afternoon. A procession of hugs and promises to visit. 'You better get your backside on over to Idaho one of these days, Norrie. I can't wait to take you to a good ol' ball game...maybe even a hockey game if you come in the winter – we'll shoot on up to Calgary or Edmonton...' 'And don't forget about us in Kenya...trust us, Norrie, cricket is much more exciting, if you don't mind me saying,' 'Aye, aye, of course, of course.' Norrie made evasive promises and before they knew it, *Flyin' Tayters!* was roaring along the beautiful beach, a large crowd present to witness the spectacle. She soared into the sky high above the westerly dunes that guarded the airport from the might of the Atlantic. She banked left and continued to rise and within a few minutes was only a dot high in the sunny southern sky.

*

Norrie and Samantha settled into their new life together and were as happy as newlyweds should be. Their love life wasn't lacking either. It took Norrie a little while to get up to speed, but Samantha was an eager instructor. With some careful guidance and a little patience, she eventually had them synchronised.

The weeks turned into months, and the months, a year. They had their first child, a beautiful girl whom they named Sofia (it was Samantha's favourite name in all the world). Time marched on, visitors came and left over the summer holidays and two years later they announced the arrival of another beautiful girl whom they christened Violet (it was Samantha's favourite flower in all the world).

One spring day Samantha approached Norrie while he was busting the rust on his favourite rake at the workbench in the

Nissen hut. She looked apprehensive and it showed. 'What's wrong, sweetheart?' Norrie stole a quick glance, keeping focused on the task at hand. It took a bit of humming and hawing – because she knew *he* was important to him, but the girls were growing, and – well...she just didn't feel entirely comfortable with... 'Oh, Honey, I hope you don't think I'm – I don't know, being picky or anything.' She looked at *him,* all quiet and faithful, and then back to her husband. 'It's Bonzo. I just don't know...with the girls sprouting like they are, and *he's* right there.' Norrie stopped what he was doing and, surprised, turned to face his wife. 'You want to get rid of Bonzo?' 'Oh, no, honey – I don't know, it's not that – it's...well, he's always right – there.' 'He's always been there. I don't understand,' Norrie replied. Samantha wore a look of worry you couldn't replicate if you tried. 'Oh, God, honey, I know...I just think, with the girls growing up and they're as curious as anything and forever touching and grabbing and sticking things in their mouth – and, well...it's not like he's *not* real...he's a *real* stuffed animal, he used to be real and alive and...I don't know, maybe I'm being too picky. I'm just worried.' It was something Norrie had never thought much about, apart from when he'd poked him out of sight way back, Bonzo had always been there propped up beside the old iron stove. Norrie, at first, had been uncomprehending as to what his wife was considering, then a little shocked, a little miffed, hurt – perhaps, but after he thought about it properly, he said, 'Why don't we put him up there on the shelf, out of the way of grabbing hands, but he'll still be in view, like he's watching over us.' Norrie smiled and Samantha hugged him, elated that he was so understanding. It went better than she had hoped. It was not long after that, that Norrie decided to cut back on his pipe smoking and stowed it away in a special drawer only for special occasions. It had surprised him, but it had not been too difficult to do. And he also gave up the one thing he thought he never would

– participating in the annual cockle raking competition. He had a family now, and so he raked for only one professional reason. This too surprised him, as he thought he would miss the competing more than he did. That's okay, he'd surmised, he'd had a good run. People change, everything changes.

Time did its thing, marching life into the future. Two, three, four, and so the years went. Norrie stuck faithfully to his routine of following the tides day in and day out. When Sofia was four years old he took up the offer of a wee pup and named him Patches, after its father. It had been long enough since Bonzo's passing. The time had long been right for another four-legged friend. A year later the time was, again, right for another four-legged friend to join the family, a Labrador that they named Sailor. Patches and Sailor would follow Norrie down to the beach every day and chase all the seabirds they could. Patches, being a lean Collie, had oodles of energy and never stopped running. Sailor, being a bit heavier, would tire quicker and often found his way to a dry patch of earth for a little snooze. Samantha, from the kitchen window, would look across the expanse of the Traigh and see her Norrie raking, and it always brought an immense feeling of joy, satisfaction, contentment – and pleasure. *I love you so much Norrie MacKinnon,* Samantha would whisper time after time.

Norrie got a heck of a surprise at the end of one fine autumn day. He, Patches and Sailor had made their way off the beach and up to the croft when he spied the postie driving off. Waiting for Norrie on the kitchen table was a postcard – out of the blue, from his old pal Malcolm MacLeary.

This is what was written on the back:

Dear Norrie, New Zealand didn't work out too good for me. The sheep shearing was going fine, but as for the horse doping and bootlegging – how should I put this? I had to make a run for it pronto! I'm now in Vancouver. Got some forged documents that say I'm some sort of marine engineer. Can you believe it?! I'm working in a shipyard and am helping to build this giant ship – it's colossal – that's what I hear people calling it. They say 'eh' a lot here. It's colder than New Zealand, but luckily not as cold as the Yukon, from what some people say. That's all for now. I'll let you know how things go. MM

Norrie had just about forgotten about Malcolm. It had been – how many years was it? At least five, six years since he had last heard from him. No one on Floonay had heard a word or knew anything. Like he'd dropped off the face of the earth. *Well, go figure. Perhaps we'll see you someday.* He put the postcard up in the Nissen hut alongside all the others he'd accumulated over the years.

The summers were filled with streams of visitors from Idaho and Kenya. Often, their trips would overlap and life would become quite chaotic for a while, but that was all right. Hank always made a point of swinging by during those trips, even if he'd have to reschedule a few business appointments. And every time it was harder for him to leave. But leave he had to. Of course, what was also inevitable, at least two or three times a year was this: 'Dang Norrie, I'da really love to see you come on over to good ol' Idaho...love to show you around, catch a ball game or somethin'...or 'Norrie, my brother, Kenya in April is most beautiful, I would love to show you a real live giraffe, and maybe even a hippo – but we better be careful – they can be so scary...and then we'll take in a cricket match....' But always Norrie would have an excuse. That bit was easy. Things were really busy with shellfish orders, 'a backlog of orders' was the go to excuse. That didn't preclude Samantha and their daughters from travelling to the mainland or further afield, and that they did. Their visits to Idaho and Kenya took the heat off Norrie. Samantha questioned him, just a little, every now and again. Instinct told her not to push, to leave him be, give him space. For better or worse, that was the one teeny (huge) thing in all the world that Norrie kept to himself. He shared with Samantha, gave her everything in his life he could think of, every ounce of love, every penny she needed. Whatever she wanted was hers to have, except for that one little secret. Samantha, of course, wouldn't press him too much (she understood more than she let on, perhaps more than she realised), and always would wave and blow a kiss from the deck of the big ferry, and promise to bring him back something nice from Oban, Nairobi, Boise, or wherever else it was she was travelling to from time to time. That is the way those years flowed. The tides of life.

Part Two

Ch 35

Lord of the Isles

'Papa! Papa! Who was the Lord of the Isles? Who was he?!' Puffing and panting, Sofia MacKinnon came running along the shoreline. She wrapped her wee arms around her father's leg. 'Papa, do you know? Was he scary like Jimmy McAndrew!?'

'Whoa, there, there, Sofia – what's the matter here?'

'Oh Papa! Jimmy McAndrew – he was so scary at school today! He had a big stick that he swung around and – and he said it was his sword and – and....'

'Whoa, hey there, calm down a little, and take a breath.'

Patches and Sailor had trotted over, keen to suss out the commotion.

'I'm sorry, Papa.'

'That's it, just calm down a little. You're safe here with me and Patches and Sailor. Look at how concerned you've got them.'

She reached out a hand and gave them a little pet which they enjoyed enormously.

Norrie MacKinnon let his rake drop to the sand and hefted his daughter into his arms, tousling her blonde locks and making her giggle with a little tickle. 'Now, what's all the fuss about?'

Calmer now, but still worried, little Sofia explained. 'Jimmy McAndrew in the schoolyard today, he said that he was the Lord of the Isles and that he was going to make us all do what he commanded. And then he pointed his sword at me and said, 'You! Sofia MacKinnon, you will be one of my servants! To the galley with you!' and then he laughed a terrible laugh and off he ran waving his scary sword.' 'Well, well, that Jimmy McAndrew is quite a little tyrant, isn't he?'

'He's not just a little tyrant, Papa, have you seen his belly, it's so big.'

'Well, that's true. But I wouldn't worry about him commanding anyone to do anything. He's just playing around, that's all. As your granny would say, 'Boys will be boys.''

'Are you sure?'

'Of course I'm sure. And even if he tried, Patches and Sailor here would make certain to send him running for the hills. Look at how much they love you. You've got them more concerned than I've seen them since, well, when was that? A month ago was it, when you skinned this wee little knee on the rocks over there...they were pretty concerned then, too.'

'Hmm. I guess...' she looked to her two four-legged friends.

'You think they would let anything bad happen to you?'

'Hm. Probably not.'

'That's right, young lady. There's nothing to be afraid of, all right?'

'Hm. Okay - but, Papa, who was the Lord of the Isles? Was he real? Was he scary like Jimmy McAndrew?'

'Number one, don't let Jimmy McAndrew scare you anymore. Okay....and number two, yes, the Lord of the Isles was a real person.'

Sofia's eyes widened. *Really?!*

'And he was quite the, well, what should we call him – perhaps a 'tyrant' will do for now.'

'Papa?'

'But there's nothing to worry about anymore.'

'Will you tell me about him? Papa, will you?'

'Are you sure you want to know? It doesn't look to me that you really, truly want to know.'

'Hm. Oh, I do Papa. I'll be brave. I promise.'

'All right, young lady, I'll tell you the story of the Lord of the Isles, after dinner. It's some tale. You see Hellisay over there, and Gighay, and up there Eriskay and the Uists and beyond?'

Sofia nodded. 'Yes, Papa. Of course!'

'Well, things weren't always quite as they are today.'

'What do you mean, Papa?'

Norrie thought for a moment, 'Let me just tell you this, you know your friend, Heather McGregor?'

Sofia nodded.

'Where is Heather from?'

'Hm. Oh! Castlebay.'

'I mean before she lived here, where was she born?'

Sofia frowned. This was getting complicated. 'Oh – I know Papa – Skye! The Isle of Skye.'

'That's right, sweetheart. Do you want to know a wee something about the past, the not-too-distant past?'

'Hm, okay Papa.' Not really sure if she wanted to know.

'Let's put it this way, for now – there was a time of fierce rivalry, clan against clan, island against island, tribe against tribe, shire against shire – hmm? I'm not sure if you're old enough for this story – what do you think?'

Sofia frowned deeper and considered saying 'no' but instead nodded, ever so slowly.

'All right then,' Norrie tickled Sofia's tummy.

'Papa!! Stop! *Please!*'

'Why don't you run along and find your sister and see how many winkles you can gather. But you better hurry before the tide rises too much. And take Patches and Sailor with you. They're good at sniffing out the winkles.'

Sofia giggled. 'They can't smell the winkles.'

'How do you know?'

'Papa – that's just silly.'

'I don't think it's silly. Look at those noses. They can smell everything. A thousand times better than we can smell. A million times even.'

'Hm,' Sofia bent down and petted her grateful friends.

'I'll see you in a wee while, honey.'

Sofia ran off along the shore with Patches and Sailor in tow, and Norrie's thoughts went to the Coquilleuous Rakkeronuous Almenikhiaka, where he'd first read about the Lord of the Isles.

*

'There was a time in history when all the islands in the Hebrides had their very own tyrant. Some were teeny tiny, some were regular sized tiny, some were in between sizes and others were as gigantic as you could ever imagine. But they were all tyrants nonetheless. A few were reluctant tyrants, many were eager tyrants, others were clueless tyrants, one or two were even loving tyrants, and others were...'

'Papa?'

'Yes, honey?'

'Is this a true story?'

'Of course it is. If it was written in the Coquilleuous Rakkeronuous Almenikhiaka it must be true. Of course, when it comes to history there's always going to be slants, variations, good is bad in one version, and "voila" fliparoo, bad is good in yet another.'

'Hm?'

Norrie was sitting in his favourite chair by the fireplace in the living room. Sofia and Violet were sitting across from him, their backs against the sofa. Violet's six-year-old mind was focused on the toy in her hands. Sofia's slightly more inquisitive eight-year-old mind was trying to stay focused on her Papa.

'Would you like me to continue?'

'Okay, go on, Papa.'

Norrie had the Coquilleuous Rakkeronuous Almenikhiaka closed on his lap. He knew the story back to front, inside out and even upside down.

'Ah, yes, the tyrants. There they all were, big, small, short, tall, angry, happy, and a few places in between, and they all ruled their little and not so little islands with iron fists. They couldn't agree on anything, all these tyrants, they....'

'Papa?'

'Yes?'

'How many years ago did you say this was?'

'Quite a long time ago. Centuries.'

'How many centuries, Papa?'

'How many do you think?'

'Hm. A million?'

Norrie smiled. 'Not quite a million, sweetie. Just a few.'

'Hm. Okay, Papa.'

'I'll continue then.' Norrie started, with Sofia's nod of approval. 'As I was saying, they couldn't agree on one teeny tiny thing except for one very big thing – which I will come to in a minute. They would shout grumpy things from island to island. Not everyone did, of course. Just a vocal portion of each island did. This went on and on, year after year, decade after decade, century after century. When each tyrant thought the time was right he would march his people to the shore and order them to shout – some liked shouting louder than others, of course – and then when each tyrant had thought all the shouting was sufficient he would order his people back to work. As I said a moment ago, there was one big thing that they all agreed on, and it was this – they all agreed that it would be a good thing to wage war on one another just for the fun of it. You see that Sound out there – the Sound of Floonay? Well, that's where many a sea battle took place over the years. The Hellisians would send a few ships out, then the Gighayolians. Inevitably a flotilla would descend from the Uists, and of course from our trusty shore, ships filled with brave Floons would all set sail and meet in the middle and have a good honest battle. This happened all over the Hebrides, from Mingulay to Mull, from Lewis and Harris to Tiree. Everyone got in on it. And then when the battling was done everyone would sail back to their respective islands, a little bruised and nicked up, and the awaiting nurses would patch them up and everyone would go back to work. On and on this went. And...'

'Papa?'

'Are you sure this is the story of the Lord of the Isles?'

'Of course. It's a little background of what is to come next. Is that okay?'

Sofia nodded.

'On and on this went. Eventually some people started getting tired of all this, and then so did a few more, and a few more after that. Not too many at first, mind you, but their numbers did grow. Put it this way, some people in some places started scratching their heads and wondering. The people going through this transformation, this change, came from all walks of life – some were a part of all the tyrants' high commands, some from the ranks of the merchant classes and some from the poorest of the dirt poor peasants, even a few of the mucky bog dwellers. What happened next was this – from each of all the islands these people started to send out little search parties. And what happened was that amidst the foggy clouds of the dark nights, when they would paddle quietly across the sea, they started bumping into one another. Boats clanging into boats, people tripping over people wading ashore. An oar would clunk another oar through the mist. That sort of thing.'

'Papa?'

'Yes, honey?'

'Look, Violet's fallen asleep. And you know what else, Papa, I can tell, this is going to be one of those super-long stories that no one really understands. So, I think I am going to put an end to it,' Sofia said, with unusual authority. Then added, 'I'm glad I didn't live way back then.'

'I'm glad you didn't, too.'

'And I'm glad you didn't either, Papa. Because if you had then I would have.' Sofia sprang up and hopped onto her father's lap. 'And Mama, and Violet too, and I wouldn't have been allowed to play with Heather because she's from Skye, or Morag from Uist or even Maithi whose people are from Mingulay.'

'That's right, my little buttercup, but thankfully things are a little different nowadays.'

Ch 36

Wheels in Motion

As Norrie MacKinnon walked along the shores of the Traigh Mhor, the tide rising and nudging him home, his two daughters running towards him in the distance, both desperate to jump into their Papa's safe arms, Alan Trout, for the first time in his life, was thinking deeply about the Isle of Floonay. *My goodness me, this shouldn't be too difficult to pull off.* He had visited the Hebrides only once, as far as he could recall. And once was enough. A 45-minute ferry journey to the Isle of Mull and its tiny (but hugely influential) neighbour, Iona, from Oban when he was a young lad of ten or eleven, along with his parents, two older brothers and twin sisters. First up was an overnight stay in colourful Tobermory. The following day a ten minute ferry ride took them to Iona for a two-night stay at a self-catering facility called Erraid House, situated under the shadow of the famous Abbey. On Iona he learned all about the importance of its Abbey, St Columba, the spread of Christianity in Scotland, and its part in a Gaelic kingdom called Dal Riata. Then he was told about the Viking raids, and he recalls finding that quite exciting. Other than that, his memory of the trip was distant – except, of course, for the memories that surfaced every now and again in the form of a nightmare. It was his fault. He had been warned, but he hadn't listened. You see, Alan and his brothers were told by the caretaker of Erraid House, Becca Knight, that the place was named after a real tidal island situated nearby, which just happened to be featured in Robert Louis Stevenson's novel, *Kidnapped.* That had got Alan's attention. *Wow! Exciting.* Ms Knight also happened to mention that the sailors who perished aboard the doomed brig ship *Covenant* haunt the local area from time to time. 'So don't go out at night, boys. Their souls are not at rest. *Kidnapped* is a work of fiction, but Erraid is real, as was the wrecked ship...as are the ghosts. They're always looking to kidnap young boys to take to sea, never to be seen or heard from again. It's said that they sometimes congregate just up the way there, near the ancient nunnery. Heaven only knows – or perhaps it's the devil that knows, what they get up to.' Well, Alan had been both equally fascinated and frightened. One can only guess what Alan did that first night in Erraid House as the rest of his family was sound asleep. He went out looking for the devilish ghosts, creeping silently through the nighttime shadows, and – by heavens, *he found them!* Right where Miss Knight said they might be, near the ruins of the old nunnery. He got the fright of his life and barely made it back under the covers. How many were there? There were a few, young Alan was sure, and they were up to no good, and – *and* they almost got a hold of him! He didn't tell a soul what had happened, except for his two brothers, who didn't believe a word of what he said. 'Ach, away. You've an overactive imagination, Alan. And besides, you should have listened to Miss Knight,' his elder brother had chided him.

Under normal circumstances there was little reason for Alan to remember the caretaker's name. But he had one good and lasting reason to remember it. Inexplicably, just as they were leaving Erraid House young Alan had put out his hand

and taken a small object off a side table. Into his pocket it went. It was such a fast manoeuvre that no one noticed. He had barely noticed himself. Why had he done it? Who knew...as a way of remembering? Later, when he dared to peek at the object he had stolen, he discovered that it was a tiny framed black & white photograph of a couple. And on its back there was a marking stamped with the name Ms Becca Knight. It was impossible to tell who the couple was. Was it a family heirloom? Through the years he could never bring himself to throw it away, instead kept it tucked away in a safe place.

Alan shuddered at the memory of the ghosts but as for Ms Knight – she had been really nice to them – and because of that he had felt a little guilty. Many years back it had crossed his mind to anonymously return the heirloom in the post, but he never got around to it, and time moved on. And who knew, perhaps Ms Knight had moved on, too. It stayed tucked away in a safe place.

Mull and Iona were not far from the mainland. If you tried hard, you could probably swim to them in half a day – something like that, anyway. But the Outer Hebrides? That was in another league altogether. When Remy, Dr Foo, and Achmed, had started explaining what their grand plans were, Alan couldn't help but think at one point, *My goodness, people still live out there? What on earth do they all do?*

Moses (or Remy) had done most of the talking, with Dr Foo and Achmed chipping in every now and again. Nigel had stayed quiet and let his bosses do their thing.

'...Alan, there is sixteen square miles of – a mix of land and sea – that we need control of. Total control. It is this area here.' Remy drew an imaginary box from the eastern shores of Floonay up towards Eriskay but not quite reaching it, then east and down the Minch side of the islands of Gighay, Hellisay, Flodday, Fuay, then back west again and closed the box. 'This is where we plan on building everything. First will be the resort, right there where the airport is, but that is just for starters, Alan. This is about more than that. What we plan to do with these islands is to create a research facility, the likes of which – not to get too ambitious, ah, who am I kidding, that is what we are in the business of – to out-ambition our competition. These islands are going to be linked by tunnels, both underwater and above water, and there will be "bubbles of protection" – and....I can see you're looking a bit confused. We'll explain more about these later, Alan. Now, you might be thinking, "This shouldn't be a problem, big business wants to roll in and invest billions, etc, should breeze through parliament," but there is one small snag here. I should add, this snag is almost, well, it is, a blessing in disguise. Alan, this is where you come in. This area has been designated as a "special area of conservation", an SAC. This is good and also bad. It is bad because it restricts what types of activity can take place in the region. More importantly, however, it is good, it is great, because it puts more power in the hands of very few people. By being designated an SAC – as everyone knows – central government controls it. Here's the deal, Alan, this is what we need to make happen. The area is used, is fished, by local fishermen. Simply put, we need all fishing activity in that area to cease. There will be too much activity with our planned future operations to worry about a fleet of fishing boats getting in the way, and we need the airport designation changed – there's been talk of this over the years, anyway. We will fully fund a new airport on the island's west side. Look – Foo, Achmed and I, we care deeply about our own communities. And we care about what seems to be a lovely little island in the Outer Hebrides. We don't want to take anyone's livelihood away – we just need those boats out of that area, and we need that beach under our control. Hell, look at that map, Alan, there's the rest of the Minch to fish in, it's a doggone big place. And over there on the west side, there's the entire Atlantic Ocean, it's gargantuan. But we need that Sound and we need that beach, and the SAC status, ironically, is going to help us get it. We're counting on you, Alan, to make this happen.'

Achmed had chipped in at that point. 'Alan, Remy is right – what he said earlier, that I am, humbly, one of the world's greatest salesmen. I can sell sand to a beachcomber and fire to the devil, but you, Alan, we think – and don't take this the wrong way – we think you are simply the master, the king, the sultan, of bullshit. This is not just good, it is tremendously fantastic. Of course, it would appear that you were a bit too good for your own party. You started to worry them and so they felt they had to contain you, to get you out of the spotlight. You had too many plans, were too ambitious for their liking. Too bad for them...but we understand you, Alan. We appreciate you. We respect you for who you are – a kindred spirit, perhaps. But back to all that yapping and bullshitting that you are so good at...we need that bullshit to make something happen.'

Alan had returned home that evening knowing that his wife would have raised an eyebrow at his being gone two nights in a row. He had a lot to think about, but then again, it wasn't *that* big a deal in terms of what he had to make happen. And – the money? £90,000,000? Now, that *was* a big deal. A tremendously big deal. So much to think about. But in the meantime, appearances had to be maintained.

'Everything okay, dear?' Nancy Trout asked as she applied tartar sauce to the fillet of sturgeon on her dinner plate.

'Aye, aye, my lovely, just another crazy day at the office, that's all. And with "you know who" banging about the place,' he sighed. 'I just have a lot on my mind right now.'

Alan had spent the better part of the day at The Canons' Gait pub, listening to the three wise men and it had to be said that the scale and scope of their plans was staggering. It went beyond bricks and mortar, and quarterly or annual reports. As Remy had said through his itchy beard, 'Alan, we are locked in a severe contest. In a struggle between moving forward and going back. It can be, it is, a struggle at times. But optimistically, old boy, forward progress will keep finding a way. But it is never easy. Alan, this is not just about sixteen square miles in the Sound of Floonay. It is about so much more. Son of a dog-gone-gun, though, things have got to start somewhere.'

*

'Oh Papa, Papa, can I come with you, can I?'

'Of course you can sweetheart, you know that.'

'And me too, Papa, can I come too, please Papa?'

'Violet, my favourite little flower, you know you can, too – see you honey...wave bye to your Mama, girls.' Norrie MacKinnon flashed a smile to Samantha who was standing at the front door.

Saturdays were Sofia and Violet MacKinnon's favourite days in all the world and had been for as long as their young minds could remember. Not just because it was the weekend, but because it was the day of the big adventure. The big adventure was landing day for Norrie MacKinnon. The day he took all the cockles he'd raked through the week to Nelson, the local shellfish buyer. It was only a two-mile trek to Nelson's big shed just down the road from The Heathbank in Northbay, but to Sofia and Violet, it might as well have been a thousand miles that traversed continents, and it was as exciting an adventure for them as one could imagine, with the mooing cows and the bahahaing sheep and the funny lambs gambolling all along the way. The road twisted and turned, and around every corner was something delightful that never failed to excite them.

As was his weekly routine, Norrie loaded up the trusty green wheelbarrow with the bags of cockles, and off he marched. Sometimes both girls would hop on top right away, and other times would follow alongside, darting off here and there, investigating and adventuring. Patches and Sailor were never far off either, forever running and sniffing and looking for anything to pee on. Norrie would chat for a few minutes with Nelson, Eddie and the others who were landing their weekly catches, and then, as was routine, would stop into The Heathbank for a pint of beer before heading home. This, also, was a fantastically exciting event for Sofia and Violet, for it meant they got to choose which bag of crisps they wanted. They would give the coins to Joe the bartender and hurry outside to sit with Patches and Sailor and wait for their Papa to finish his pint. Norrie would never stay long and it was always just the one pint on a Saturday afternoon. It was part of the routine. A swapping of the week's news.

'How's things, Norrie?'

'Aye, all right Joe, and yourself?'

'All right.'

'Busy week?'

'Och, not too bad. Picking up though. Quite a few meals.'

'Aye, aye.'

'How's the landing this week?'

'Aye, all right. Bit better than last week.'

'Aye, aye.'

The vast majority of all their conversations started with something like this, before transitioning to new news. Some weeks there wasn't much doing, and other weeks there'd be a little excitement or intrigue. Over the past few years there had been quite the fuss over the Sound of Floonay being designated a Special Area of Conservation. The locals had voiced their opposition to the government's sneaky plans, and what basically amounted to Edinburgh bowing to their masters (so long as it brought them a little more power as well). It had been a farce, and anyone with any sense knew it. There was not one sensible reason for it to happen, but it happened anyway. The truth of the matter was, once a plot is hatched deep in the bowels of government, it usually comes to fruition. This was about two things: A numbers game and control. Period. The numbers game side of it was just this: a squad of technocrats cracked knuckles, drummed fingers, put on their thinking caps – *hmm, excellent, perfect...* - and got down to the business of conjuring numbers and issuing directives. Each country was given a number, a target, to reach. In regard to Special Areas of Conservation (SACs) they were told to find 'x' number of places to 'protect' regardless of whether they actually needed protecting.

The part of it that did make sense to the ranks in Edinburgh was this: power. More power. Sure, half was appeasing their bosses. But in doing so, they were also creating a new law that gave themselves more power. And the whole world knows that governments crave power.

The designation of the SAC status for the Sound of Floonay was to protect the reefs, the underwater flora, and the slippery seals. This meant that all fishing operations in the area had to be static, which was precisely what the vast majority of the fishing in that area was. Fleets of creels were shot from the various fishing boats and would lie on the seabed not moving, waiting for the snippy crustaceans to enter. No problems there for the local fishermen, life would go on. And on it did. But the one potential problem was this: if a case of potential 'abuse' in a region holding SAC status was observed and reported by any Tom, Dick or Harry, to the appropriate authorities, the laws on the books allowed for an immediate cessation of all activities until an investigation was performed.

The way the law was written gave the government in Edinburgh enormous discretion.

It was all old news though and life had moved on.

On that Saturday afternoon that is just what it did. It moved along with nothing much to report.

'Ach, well, I better get these two back home.'

'Aye, aye, very good then Norrie, cheers for now.'

The wheelbarrow now empty of the bags of cockles, Sofia and Violet found it quite exciting to ride in it as Papa pushed them home, Patches and Sailor trotting happily alongside.

'Papa, can we go to tri-e-ash after lunch?'

'Aye, that sounds like a great idea.'

'I can go, too, right?'

'You're my favourite flower ever, Violet, of course you can.'

'How come I can't be your favourite flower ever?' Sofia protested

'Because you are my favourite cupcake in the whole wide world.'

'I'm not a cupcake, Papa!'

'You're not? Hmm – I thought you were.'

'I'm your favourite little strawberry.'

'Oh, ok. Little Miss Strawberry it is. With a dollop of cream on top.'

'You are silly, Papa.'

'I better learn to be more serious. Much serious, what do you think – do you want your Papa to, hm, to be the most serious person in the whole wide world? No more joking and, hm, no more crisps either.'

'No! Papa!'

Sofia and Violet meant the world to Norrie. From the time he held each babe in his arms on the day they were born, defenceless, vulnerable, crying, beautiful, his life took on a new and incredible meaning. Their lives were in his hands.

Their happiness, their safety, their everything, was his number one priority.

'And also, Papa, after tri-e-ash can we go up Heavel?'

'My goodness, you want to go up Heavel again? Have you forgotten about last weekend already?'

'No, Papa. I haven't forgotten.'

'Hm. Okay. Will you make it all the way on your own or will I have to carry you again?'

'I'll try as hard as I can, Papa. I promise.'

'All right, you have me convinced. To Heavel it is.'

'Oh, and can we stop in and see the nice ice cream lady on the way?'

'We'll have to see about that.'

'Oh, pleeeaassseee, Papa!'

'Okay, okay, but only if you promise to watch out for your sister going up Heavel. It can be a bit tricky in spots.'

'I will, I promise, Papa.'

'Are you going to read to us later?' Violet looked suddenly concerned.

'Of course, baby – that's what we do every Saturday night. Did you think this Saturday would be any different?'

'Hmm. No, Papa, I'm just checking, that's all.'

From before Sofia could remember, her Papa would sit with her in his arms and tell her a tale from the Coquilleuous Rakkeronuous Almenikhiaka every Saturday evening, as his Papa had done with him, and his father before him. He had not given it much thought, that he was carrying on a tradition. It had just happened naturally. Of course, the tales were edited and altered a little, to make them suitable for a growing wee girl. When Violet came into their lives it was the same with her. As they grew more and more, they would sit, either at his feet, or across from him on, or against the sofa. But when they felt the need – like when their Papa started telling a scary story – they would hop onto his lap and hide under his arms, to shield themselves from the scary sea monsters, and the like.

'Oh, and maybe, too, after we come down from Heavel can we stop in and see Geraldine and Elanor?'

'Woah, how many hours are there in a day? Our list of things to do is growing quite long. Maybe we'll have to leave out visiting the ice cream lady – what do you think?'

'No!!! Papa!' Sofia and Violet replied in unison, hopping a bit in the wheelbarrow.

'Steady, girls. I was just joking.'

The look on his daughters' faces said it all: there was no kidding about ice cream.

'Oh, look Papa! That sheep has his head stuck in the fence – those sheep are so funny, and look at the little lamb...it's so scared, it doesn't know what to do. Sailor! Come here! That's it, you better leave the poor sheep alone. Look how good Patches is – oh, Papa, Papa, look, it's the plane! The plane is coming!'

'Aye, aye. Look at that, there it is.'

'I love the plane. It was a bit bumpy last time though. But the big plane to Idaho was fun. Papa?'

'Yes honey?'

'Have you ever been on the plane before?'

'Hmm, let me think here. No, I don't think I have.'

'I wish you had gone to Idaho with us last year. It was so much fun.'

'Well, I just had so many cockles to rake. All those hungry mainlanders, they keep wanting more and more cockles, and over there on the continent, especially Spain, well, they keep sending orders to Nelson. It's hard to keep up sometimes.'

'Hm. Well, Papa, I think you should be able to take a little break sometimes, so you can visit Grandpa Hank – he says he wants to take you to a baseball and a hockey game. And uncle

Akili said when we were in Kenya that he wants to take you to a cricket match.'

'Well, we'll just have to see about that, eh girls. We'll just have to see – oh, look, your Mama's waving from the window...can you see her? Lunch must be ready. I hope those bags of crisps didn't fill your bellies too much.'

Sofia and Violet hopped out of the wheelbarrow and ran the last hundred yards home with Patches and Sailor in tow. And just as they did, Alan Trout was picking up the phone in Edinburgh to make a call that would alter the future of Floonay.

Ch 37

We Get the Big Picture

It was that easy to get the ball rolling. My goodness me, their lawyers were right, Alan mused as he pulled the cork out of the wine bottle, a succulent red. It was Colette's favourite. All they had needed was someone on the inside to *pull the trigger*, start the process, and ensure that things did not fizzle and die out. Brilliant. Alan could handle that easily enough. The trickier part would be conjuring up the 'alleged' violations, but, son of a bitch, Alan thought, even that didn't have to be a complete lie. One could interpret a kayak bumping into a reef, or an oar scraping along its side, as damage to the environment. The more he contemplated that side of things, the more he realised how simple it would be. Of course, the confidential and anonymous 'sightings' would be a total fabrication, but that didn't matter. They merely reflected what was probably going on anyway, Alan concluded. When the MEO (Ministry of Environmental Oversight) begins their investigation, Alan knew with certainty that they would throw all their efforts and influence into ensuring that the ban on all activities in the area would be enforced. The most awkward bit, however, would be the moment that control of the area is handed over to Remy and company. No doubt there will be a few well-intentioned souls in the MEO up in arms about that, but by that point it will not matter, and this is the key to it all. The way that the new legislation was written when a region receives 'special' status, the central government is afforded more control in what happens both in and to the area in question, taking out the need to appease local authorities or convince them to support the central government's decrees. What the locals thought mattered not one iota. Of course, they would perhaps stage a public consultation, but that would be *all it would be,* a staged event to make some people think they had any say in the matter. Remy's voice floated through Alan's mind, *Don't forget, Alan, this is for the benefit of everyone. This will bring money and jobs and opportunities, and, son of a gun, more prosperity than the island has seen in a very long time. We simply need total control, Alan.*

'Alan, honey, you've barely touched your plate. I thought you loved my cooking?' His mistress, Colette, was wearing a sexy red dress with a plunging neckline that left little to the imagination.

'Yes, yes. Sorry, you know I love your cooking, my sweet little thing. I just have a lot on my mind – you know how work can be...oh, hmm, this is scrumptious, wonderful, that sauce is marvellous. Where did you find this?'

'It's a new recipe, sweetie, I just discovered it today,' Colette replied, beaming at her lover's approval.

Alan's mind drifted from the sauce to Colette's neckline and back to Remy, Dr Foo, and Achmed. He wished he'd recorded their conversation. Their plans were staggering in scale and scope, and their accolades for him, their belief in him was – well, it was fair to say Alan was quite chuffed. *Alan, we've been watching you for a very long time. As we've said already, we know everything about you and that is precisely the reason we know you are the man for the job. Sure, we could have chosen someone else who would perhaps, maybe, with a little luck and a lot of guidance, see the job through, but none, as far as we could estimate could – will – pull it off quite like you. Things might, after all, get a little tricky, a hiccup here or there, and that's where your worth comes in Alan, your talent. Doggone it, Alan, we weren't kidding when we said we believe you are the king of bullshit. Hell, your party doesn't quite know the talent they have in you. And all those grand plans you had, well, I guess it was all just a little too much for your party. Too bad for them, but, hey, them side-lining you to the periphery, well, it's good for us, and ultimately, for you, too.*

'Sweetie, you're looking rather pleased, I'm glad you like this dish.'

'Marvellous, my dear, just lovely. Scrumptious. Can't wait to see what you have in store for dessert.'

What Remy had said next truly astonished Alan. How on earth could they have figured that out? My God, they are good. *And, Alan, we have to say, that was truly remarkable that you managed to make that happen – or should I say 'not happen' on the pitch. Unbelievable. Of course it's impossible for us to have seen footage of every tilt you ever played in – obviously – but from the footage we did manage to get our hands on, well, we are just assuming that you acquired that ability at a young age. Are we right – ah ha! Son of a doggone gun! That is fantastic – I mean, you never even got hit once! You danced your way out of every moment of danger – my God, Alan, the fear you must have felt in order to go to those lengths, it must have been tremendous – hell, that's okay, Alan, that's okay. We've all felt fear of some sort or another. Way back when I used to play college ball, well, shoot, I was getting hit all the doggone time...but, Alan, that footage? We saw there were a few 'almosts', them couple a fellas just about got their hands on you, but, shoot, either they would trip up or you would wiggle away...a little combination of both I reckon. Remarkable, Alan. Quite remarkable.*

'Alan, darling, you're looking a little worried. Is the souffle not to your liking?'

Alan, we get it. We get the big picture. That's what we are paid to do. But as much as we do and can influence, there are enormous obstacles obstructing our progress. This world is stuffed full of politicians who divide and divide and do all they can to make sure individuals think of themselves first and foremost, at the expense of others...not all, we know that, Alan, but a whole heck of a lot irresponsibly do, all to ensure that their constituents vote for their egos. Well, we've got plans for our political friends, Alan, big plans. And funnily enough, they've got a fair bit to learn from the corporate world. Let's just say, they better start learning how to pack their bags. There is no doubting, though, that we've a fair bit of convincing on our hands....

My goodness me, these people are a curious, serious, lot.

'Alan, darling, if you don't mind me being completely honest, you look like you are lost in space.'

*

'Papa! Look! I made it all the way on my own! I made it all the way up and you didn't have to lift me once.'

'My, my, look at you. That ice cream cone must have done the trick. You look like you've enough energy to climb even higher.'

'But there's no more mountain, we're all the way to the top,' Sofia replied and suddenly flopped over. 'Oh, I am so tired now, Papa. I don't think I could go one more step.'

'Papa, you can let me down now. I'm not tired.' Violet hopped out of her father's arms 'Look, I can see so far away – and look, how did those sheep get all the way up here?! This is our mountain, Mr Sheep...Mr Sheep!? Look! He's running away...Papa, sheep are so funny.'

'Can I have some juice, Papa?' the suddenly exhausted Sofia pleaded. 'I'm so thirsty.'

'Of course you can, sweetheart...let me just rummage around here – ah, there you are.'

'And can I have some, too, can I?'

'Papa carried you almost all the way, why are you so thirsty?'

'It's okay. There's enough here for both of you, and look – a little surprise,' Norrie said, revealing a few chocolate biscuits. This made Sofia forget her sudden tiredness and interest in her sister's desire for a drink. 'This will give you both lots of energy for the walk back down.'

'We're not going yet, are we?'

'Of course not, sweetie. We just arrived.'

'Oh, look, over there, there's more people coming up. Papa, oh, they look so very tired. And they're not as fast as we are.'

Norrie smiled. 'That's right, pet. You and I, and even Violet here, well, we're a pretty fast little family, aren't we?'

'Of course, Papa. Except, hmm, Mama's not here.'

'Well, someone has to get the dinner ready.'

'I guess.'

'She was pretty fast last weekend, though, and she even carried Violet halfway up. If I remember correctly your Mama and Violet beat you and me.'

'That's right, Papa!' The memory quite excited Violet.

'Well, not by much. Maybe just two or three steps. We weren't very far behind. And I did have to stop a few times because there were little pebbles in my Wellies. They were really bothering me.'

'Aye, aye, that's all right. We weren't really racing, anyway. It's just nice to make it all the way up – oh, look – what do you see – way out there. Can you see it?'

'What Papa? – oh, I see it now! The ferry!'

'Aye, aye. And what does the ferry carry?'

'People, Papa.'

'And what else?'

'Hm. Cars, Papa. Lots of cars...'

'And?'

'Hmm?' Sofia frowned. 'Is this a trick question?'

'No, no tricks...promise.'

'Oh! Lorries, giant lorries!' Violet squealed excitedly.

'That's what I meant, too! And Hector's bread van, and other vans, too!'

'Aye, well you're both right. And what is in all those big lorries and vans?'

'You don't know, Papa?!'

'I'm just asking to see if you know, that's all.'

'Well, Papa – they carry...hmm...lots of things.'

'Like your biscuits?'

'I think so. No! I mean, of course they do, Papa.' Sofia frowned a little. 'Is this some trick question again?'

'No honey, I was just wondering, that's all.'

'Oh, and the big white lorry that takes all your cockles far away,' Violet added, very excited.

'That's pretty good, pet'

'Oh, I knew that, too.'

Norrie smiled. 'Anything and everything you can think of is carried on that big old boat.'

'It is a giant boat. I love going on it – Papa?' Sofia looked to her father. 'Have you ever been on the ferry?'

'Well, of course I have.'

'Hm. I don't ever remember you coming with us – Papa, how come you've never gone to Oban with us?'

'Well, sweetheart, I was working, remember? There's always so many cockle orders to fill.'

'And you haven't been on the plane with us either?'

Norrie smiled and tickled Sofia's tummy. 'Well, young lady, someone has to work very hard, so we can buy sweets for this belly and bicycles and ice cream cones.'

'Please! Stop Papa!! That's way, way too tickly!'

'Ah, there's my next victim, here comes the big monster.' He turned his attention to his next squealing victim, who was both 'trying' to escape but was also delightfully ecstatic. 'Papa! *Pleeeeeassee!* Not too tickly!'

Ch 38

A Truly True Story?

'What about this story here, Papa?' Sofia was sitting on her father's lap jostling for space with Violet, pointing at an open page.

'Ah, this one, eh? I think this one might be okay for you two. I have to warn you, it is a very sad tale.'

'Is that a tree?'

'Aye, honey.'

'Look how sad it looks. Why is the tree so sad, Papa?'

'Well, once you've heard the story you will understand.'

'Does it get better, Papa, does the tree ever smile again?'

'That tree does look so sad...poor tree,' Violet said quietly.

'Well, I don't want to give anything away too early on. But, honey, you know, some things in life...hmm...maybe I should keep this one for another time...it might make you cry a little...it made me cry once.'

'Papa! It did not!' both girls said together, astonished, 'Did it really?'

'Well, maybe just a little, or maybe it was because a big rock landed on my foot as I was reading it. That made me cry.'

'Papa! You're silly.'

'Is it a true story, Papa?'

‘Well, if it was written in this big old book, I think it most probably, terribly likely and absolutely certain that it could very well have been...’

‘I mean a truly true story, Papa?’

‘What do you mean, honey? Don't you believe me?’

Sofia, a little inquisitive and a little confused, continued, ‘Hmm? Sometimes it's hard to tell which are true and which are truly true, Papa, that's all.’

‘Well, I think maybe we'll keep this one for another time, eh? It's a good story, but for this Saturday let's see if I can't find one that's a little more exciting.’

The big Saturday adventure-day always ended the same way, with Norrie reading to his two daughters. It wasn't quite the same as it had been when he was young. Back then it was just him and his father. His brothers and sisters had no real interest in the big book and so they always just did their own thing. The odd time they would sit in for a while, but it wasn't often. And his Mama was always doing her thing either pottering about in the kitchen or enjoying her own quiet time. It would only be on an extra special occasion that she would sit in with them. Michael MacKinnon would not have minded who or how many had sat in with them, as he himself was a little ahead of his time and wasn't of the mind that all mothers should just potter about doing housework. But he encouraged his Margaret do what she was comfortable with, as with his children, and so it would be that it was most often just him and Norrie. But now, in the present-day, Samantha would quite often sit in with her family. It hadn't been some seismic generational shift. Rather, a natural transition. Samantha's family had not had a big Almenikhiaka handed down from generation to generation, but she had travelled the world and occasionally told her own adventurous tales. Before the girls visited Kenya and took a Safari with their cousins and saw for themselves what a real live giraffe looked like, they couldn't believe that their Mama had seen one, too, years ago. And some wild hippos. And also, a giant snake in South America, and some creepy-crawly tarantulas in a desert in the southwestern United States. *They were hairy and scary and when they crawled up your arms this is how they did it!* And she'd run her fingers frantically up their wee arms That had made them squeal with horror and they'd run out of the living room as fast as they could. 'Do you think I overdid it, honey?' she'd asked Norrie, to which he'd replied, 'Aye, maybe just a bit.' Story-time had ended early that particular Saturday. But that had been all right as another kind of 'time' started a little earlier than usual, and that suited Norrie and Samantha just fine.

Sundays also had a similar cadence week after week. Samantha would take the girls to church and Norrie would go cockle raking if the tide was right. If the tide was too high for raking he would find something else to do: tinker in the Nissen hut, go for a stroll with Patches and Sailor, collect buoys washed up along the shores – anything to pass the time. Norrie didn't completely disbelieve – it's best to put it this way: the tragedies affected Norrie enormously – why did he grieve more than some, less that others? Who knew really? And after the tragedies, were the letters to God that went unanswered. As a grown man he'd gradually transitioned from that dark, doubting place to a place where he simply existed. It had been an enormous relief to finally make that shift away from where he'd found himself, and a fair part of what nudged and cajoled him along that rotten path, had begun with all those questions and doubts and his own version of unanswered prayers. It was too dark and too horrible, and so to protect himself, he would never go back to that 'place' of thinking and questioning and wondering again. And now, with a wife and children, he lived for them, and he could not jeopardise their needs, their happiness. That is the way things were now. When the girls asked why their Papa never went to church with them, Samantha would simply reply that he was busy working and that was that. Samantha didn't pry. If Norrie didn't want to attend service that was fine with her.

A regular part of the Sunday routine, also, was a barbecue when the weather allowed. They occasionally would have a traditional Sunday roast, but Norrie had taken to barbecuing more than most other islanders, and Samantha, being a woman of the world, was happy with the arrangement, especially because Norrie would take care of all the cooking and she could enjoy a little break. The girls loved it, too, as they got to munch on hamburgers, hotdogs, and sausages with lots of ketchup and mustard. Not infrequently, guests would drop in. It was fun and informal. The kids would all have a great time, and the men would all stand around looking at the smoking barbeque and have a chat and a beer, and the women could talk about things women liked to talk about over a glass of wine or a G&T.

'Papa, look – it's brand new from the Butcher's. I'll just put it here,' Sofia said as she placed a container of ketchup on the kitchen countertop.

'And look, Papa, look what I got. Mama said it was okay because I was so good in church.' Violet was holding an orange juice box.

'You're supposed to be good in church – Mama let you have it because you're a baby,'

'I'm not a baby. I'm this many years old.' Violet showed her sister a handful of fingers plus one extra finger.

'Woah, hey there, it's okay girls. It's just a little juice box. Here, let's see what else is in this bag, eh?' Norrie, the diplomat, took control of the groceries. 'Was it busy at the Butcher's?'

'Hm, pretty busy, Papa.'

'Aye, aye, and who did you see?'

'Oh, Papa, Heather was there. I invited her to the barbecue tonight. Mama said it was okay. Her parents are coming, too. We had to get some extra hamburgers and buns.'

'Oh, well, well, and that's, let me see, hmm, I think six others already, plus us four, plus Heather and her parents, hmm? How many does that make?'

Violet started counting fingers, but Sofia beat her to it. 'That's thirteen, Papa!'

'My, my, thirteen, I do hope we have enough to go around.'

'Look, the ketchup is brand new, Papa. There's lots of ketchup. It's okay.'

Norrie smiled. 'That's right, sweetheart.'

'You forgot three others, girls – don't you remember?'

Sofia and Violet gave their mother quick, confused, competitive glances. Who was going to remember first?

'Oh yeah...'

'Oh, uh...'

Their mother started. 'Father John – and?'

'Oh, and Reverend Cullen!' Sofia replied as quick as she could.

Another pause.

Samantha, again, 'And – who else?'

This time Violet. 'Glo! Glo too, Papa!'

Norrie chuckled. 'My, my indeed, this is going to be quite a little gathering. This time I really do mean that I hope there's enough of everything.'

'I made sure of that, honey,' Samantha said, giving Norrie a peck on the cheek. 'I was chatting with Glo after the service. He's on his own for the weekend. Morag and the kids are shopping in Glasgow. Said he should nip around, if he liked.'

'Aye, aye.'

'And Father John and Reverend Cullen were right there – they were looking hungry,' she smiled, 'so I said they were more than welcome.'

'Aye, aye, of course. I'll have to get the good Scotch out, then.'

'Oh, by the way, there's something afoot.'

'Oh?'

'Just murmurings.'

'About what?'

'Queuing at the Butcher's I caught a few words – did you hear this and that, and "they're at it again." The council and Edinburgh were mentioned,' Samantha shrugged. 'There's always something.'

'Aye, aye, of course, there certainly is.'

Indeed, there was always something to report on. To talk about. Gossip can take any teeny scrape of a snippet of information and make it into a beast of its own. And on an island like Floonay, Norrie knew full well how fast word could spread. It was probably nothing, Norrie thought, but as much as he tried to ignore it, it lingered in his mind.

'All right, who wants to go hunting for buoys on the beach?'

Sofia and Violet squealed their delight.

'We'll pack a little lunch, eh, what do you think? It's such a lovely day. What do you think, sweetheart, you want to come, too?' Norrie looked at Samantha.

Samantha did a split-second mental check of what she had in mind for the afternoon. 'Aye, that sounds wonderful. Girls, why don't we take our swimsuits? I haven't been in this year yet.'

Sofia and Violet screamed their delight again and rushed off to their rooms to find their swimsuits.

'And what about you, honey – you want to take a wee nip into the water?' Samantha pinched Norrie on the bum.

'I am quite happy watching from the shoreline, and you be careful with Violet – those tides can be lethal, and you know I'll be of no use if something happens.'

'Don't worry about that, and besides, I just want to take a wee dip. You really should take a few lessons. You don't have to learn in the freezing Minch anymore. The pool is fantastic. Marion and Geraldine give lessons, in case you didn't know.'

'I'm a grown man, honey, there are some things grown men don't do, and one of them is learn how to swim.'

Samantha shrugged. 'Oh well. It's fun, you'd like it.'

*

'Are you serious?'

Norrie listened quietly as the others talked. This *was* serious. Even Patches and Sailor detected something serious and lay quietly at their master's feet, heads down. For once, they had refused to run off and play with the girls and their friends when they came calling.

Glo, who lived three crofts down the road, took a sip of his dram. 'Aye, that's what she said, anyway.'

'Ach, it can't mean much – surely?' Ronnie played the optimist.

'Those bastards.' Eddie spat in disgust. 'I knew it. I knew something would bloody well happen one day.'

'But it doesn't necessarily mean they have to, that they'd take action?'

'I don't know. The whole thing might amount to nothing.'

The seven were huddled by the barbecue, riveted to the same topic the women were most likely discussing around the kitchen table. It had become the topic of the day all around the island. Word had come from several different sources so there was no way there wasn't at least some truth to the story. And the word that had leaked from the deep bowels of Edinburgh was that a handful of 'sightings' and 'complaints' were being reviewed by government officials regarding the Sound of Floonay.

‘Any word on who?’

‘Not a clue.’

‘Probably bloody tourists.’

‘What did they see?’

‘No clue again. The only word I've heard is just that sightings of something or other led to complaints, and that they're being reviewed.’

‘If worst comes to worst, they could suspend all activity right throughout the Sound, and you know, bloody hell, everyone knows what the boundaries are. It includes that bloody beach out there, too! You know what that means Norrie? It would be a blanket ban on all shellfish harvesting activities...no more cockle raking,’ Eddie said.

‘Aye, aye, what happened to that one place down south, how long did that ban last?’

‘It was close to a year.’

‘A third of my creels are in the Sound. Those bastards. I'll have to shift the lot.’

‘Bastards. Bloody flipping bastards.’

The words that sailed through Norrie’s mind were not as tame as ‘bloody flipping bastards.’

Ch 39

We Believe In You

'If, and let's just hope it's a big "if", this does lead to a ban, I'm not sure how long I could go, how long we could go, without me working. There's not that much in the bank.' And it wasn't only that.

Norrie and Samantha were lying in bed.

'Oh sweetheart, let's just hope it all comes to nothing.'

'I know, I do, but what if?'

'Put your mind to rest, honey, right now there's nothing we, or anyone, can do about it.'

'Aye, aye.'

'In the meantime, baby.' Samantha wiggled closer to her husband. 'Hmm, I think there's something I can think of to take your mind off things.' A hand sliding under the covers. 'What do you think?'

*

'That was a good job, Alan. Very impressed. Doggone impressed.'

Alan shrugged. 'It didn't take much. I lifted the phone – two calls later, poof, that was it.' He was starting to get used to

Moses, Confucius, and the Sufi Mystic. Somewhat anyway. It was early the following week and the scheming ensemble were meeting for lunch at the top of the Royal Mile, in a wee ancient pub called The Ensign Ewart. Quarters were cramped but it was cosy. They were hunched over and huddled around a table from the Middle Ages.

'Key here is to see things through, to be the advocate – as quietly as possible. Make sure no one forgets about the SAC and, of course, the powers the government can exercise.' Moses winked.

'Aye, aye, of course.'

Moses continued, 'We've got the four "witnesses" – don't worry about that side of things. They are reliable and loyal. And we also have a team of scientists running their own analysis on the effects of the damage to the environment. They're working in parallel with the Ministry of Environmental Oversight. It's insurance. A "just in case" our Ministry – our MEO "friends" findings aren't quite what we are expecting.'

'MEO? *Meow.* That funny acronym for government body,' Confucius accurately observed. 'In China, we have Ministry of Ecology and Environment The People's Republic of China. Boring. No good acronym.'

'Same with Zanzibar – or Tanzania I should say – we have the National Environment Management Council. NEMC not very catchy,' one extraordinarily rich Sufi Mystic commented.

'Meow. I think name-maker here is cat lover,' Confucius thought out loud.

'Yeah, yeah, and we got the EPA, the good ol' Environmental Protection Agency. E-P-A, or "EPA" sounds boring, too. Whipty-diddly-do. Let's get back to business here boys. Where was I? That's right – so, we don't think there should be a problem though, considering the lengths they went to have the Sound designated an SAC. They'll be eager to defend their designation. They'll assess that the seal population will drop by 50%, and the reefs are a wreck, and on and on. But, you never know, there's no doubt a few sensible souls employed in their ranks.'

'Alan?' Confucius spoke again. 'When we first hatched this plot, this grand scheme, a long time ago, there was but one goal. One point. One direction. Make no mistake. And we have stayed true, stayed focused on our purpose, *the* purpose. We're not going to get all metaphysical on you now. We're going to keep this grounded. We live in the real world, after all. Our business planners have been planning, our researchers, researching. We've had architects doing their part and development teams ready to begin the implementation process. We will, of course, use as much local skill and labour as possible but assets from around the world will need to roll in. But this last crucial bit, the seizing control and dealing with the government, we knew full well that it would be the trickiest bit, the hardest part, and so we knew we would have to wait till the last moment and then, *voila!* make things happen extremely fast, like a lightning strike, in order to confuse, confound, trip up opposition, and then seize control before anyone really knows what's happening. It is a little like warfare, Alan – have you ever read Sun Tzu, The Art of War? No – Hm. Too bad. I recommend you do.'

'My friend,' said the Sufi Mystic, 'You are beginning to look confused. Don't. Relax, have another drink. We'll try not to overwhelm you with too much information all at once. Remy mentioned the "bubbles of protection" the other day – you recall?'

'Aye?' Alan responded with a curious nod.

'Let me explain. Have you ever been to the Middle East? – No?' Achmed chuckled. 'Of course, we knew that – just testing your honesty. That's good, Alan. Very good. You passed another test. Do you think you could go skiing in the Middle East? No? Well think again,' he sighed. 'Of course, I mean apart from the established resorts like they have in Iran – there is some wonderful skiing there – I recommend you go sometime. Start with Dizin. It is amazing. I am trying to convince a few of our global ad giants to mount a massive "Ski Iran" campaign – flood the worlds' billboards and news organisations – with one goal, to put more of a human face on the country. There are people there and they love to ski – some of them anyway, and they smile and laugh and do everything you and I like to do. I digress about the skiing, Alan, what I meant was, do you think you could go skiing in the middle of a roasting desert? Do you? No? Well, think again, my friend. Think again. To say they are simply "indoor" ski slopes is a bit of an understatement. They are enormous temperature-controlled domes – gargantuan, and in them, mountains have been built – well, pretty big hills anyway. What we have planned as the "bubbles of protection" is a little different to just building a dome for skiing. And is on a much larger scale – not quite on the Lost City of Atlantis scale big, but big enough.'

'My, my, indeed, I see, I – see?'

'Alan, it's all right to be a little uncertain right now,' Moses drawled. 'It's early days. We've just hit you with quite a bit. But, shoot, you got the ball rolling. You just stay cool, make certain to act like nothing funny is going on in the office and all, and around your ladies – and important, very important, when you are applying pressure, advocating that action be taken on the SAC in the Sound of Floonay, well, make sure not to come across as too zealous, too unreasonable, you cannot for a moment allow anyone, and that means anyone, to start sniffing that something is up, is not what it seems, you know what I am saying? Good, good. Real good, Alan. You'll do all right. We're counting on you. We believe in you.'

*

As Alan, Nigel the tourist, Moses, Confucius, and a Sufi Mystic exited The Ensign Ewart pub, Norrie MacKinnon was doing what he had been doing for as long as he could hold a rake. It was a pleasant enough day and he'd managed to push thoughts of what might happen into a mostly quiet cupboard in his brain. Nothing more had been heard in the past couple of days. Who knew, maybe everything would blow over? Maybe it was all one big mistake? Maybe they'd got the SAC wrong? There were enough of them scattered up and down the country after all. Perhaps that was it? No news – or in this case, no more news would be good news. Looking out across the Sound he spied a fishing vessel passing Greanamul, north to south. Further east was another, along the western shores of Hellisay. In all, about a dozen fishing boats worked out of Northbay. Norrie knew that the boys made their money, the real money, on the west side and along the eastern shores of Gighay, Hellisay and on down, either on the lobsters or the big brown crabs. And for boats that ventured further out, there were other tasty creepy crawlies, like prawns and langoustines. Within the Sound itself, one would find the odd brown crab and a few lobbies here and there, but nothing you could rely on for a decent wage. What snippy inhabitants the Sound was filled with were velvet crabs and green crabs. The greens were always a miserable price but if caught in enough quantity one could make something resembling a wage. There was a fair wage in velvets though, and especially so at the right time of year. More than a wage, what the Sound did provide was a little shelter, depending on the direction of the weather, and so lowered the ever-present danger of toiling on the rough, high seas. In the exposed parts of the Sound it could be fierce, but the benefit of it was this: there were numerous wee islands, which allowed for tactical fishing – if the weather was coming from the northeast, you put your fleets along the southwest of the various islands, and so on. This allowed for a little dependability, as there were many seasons when the area would get hammered with bad weather day after day, week after week, from one direction. If the boats were forced only to work out along the east or west sides of Floonay, they would be exposed to more danger, pushing the fishermen to take risks they should not be taking. All the boys could manage, though. It might be an enormous inconvenience and sometimes quite dangerous, but they could, and would, carry on. It was different along the shore. The only beach on Floonay chockfull of cockles was the Traigh Mhor, and it lay within the boundaries of the SAC zone. Therefore, only one harvester of shellfish would be mortally wounded by a ban, and it was...the cockle raker.

What would his father think of this, and all the way back to great times eight Grandpa Cloon? A travesty, an injustice, shameful, just plain wrong. That some far-flung entity was dictating how they led their lives, what they could, and could not, do? They simply would not understand. But also, Norrie could not help but think of the crime committed by the inaction of the government beginning in the early decades of the 20th century. The insatiable demand for herring had sent ships, hundreds of them, to fish the waters of the Minch. Every square inch of it. Castlebay was a processing centre. It was a period of plenty. At that time, one could walk from Floonay to Vatersay stepping from boat to boat, right across the expanse of bay when a catch was brought in for processing. Certainly, this provided jobs for a time and a few local boats benefited as well, but the Minch wasn't simply overfished, it was filleted and then filleted again, until there was almost nothing left but a translucent skeleton. To be fair to all fishermen, whether he was sailing out of Mallaig, Stornoway, Uig, or from wherever, how could you sit there and watch the fleets pass you by? You had a family to feed, a community to support. There was money to be made and there was endless demand. How could you not lift your anchor and cast your nets?

This didn't just happen to the herring, this happened to species after species, and then the bigger boats came from ports even further away. Decade after decade. The Minch did not stand a chance. No one would listen. And the government sat back and watched it all happen. Or sat back and didn't have a clue what was happening. And now the pendulum had swung from inaction and had smashed out of its casing and flown so far in the other direction that it beggared belief.

But the consequences were even more dire for Norrie MacKinnon. The others could shift their gear. Norrie had nowhere else to go. *I don't know anything else. I can't go anywhere. I can't quit. And I can't lose my routine.*

Norrie walked home after his shift was done, leaving his catch for the day securely tied up for the tide to wash over. Patches and Sailor followed along, and further along the beach his two daughters were running eagerly towards him. He smiled and opened his arms 'Papa! Oh Papa, at school today, it was so much fun...'

Ch 40

Aye, Right?

The mood on Floonay that week was mixed. The SAC/MEO was all the talk. Rumours flew regarding who had witnessed what, and what complaints had actually been lodged. Islanders, especially, could be quite imaginative, and though there was an overarching solidarity, there were still rivalries and suspicions. Finger pointing and gossip made its usual rounds.

But the days went by and life carried on. People went about their business. Norrie found himself working longer and harder than usual. The minute the tide ebbed the tiniest fraction to the point the first cockle could be harvested, he was out there, and stayed out there until the tide nudged him, inch by inch, all the way back. His tea breaks barely existed leaving Patches and Sailor whining a little. They were used to him giving them a little attention but this had disappeared. Not even one quick pet. He even turned away his precious daughters telling them it was important that he kept working. He normally spent some time playing with them, even if it was a cursory fifteen minutes, before sending them off with Patches and Sailor to pick winkles, but not for the last few days. He had changed. They weren't used to this new version of Papa and it upset them. They'd turned away, sulking. Norrie was focused only on raking. He swore that he would not, could not, quit, and raked as much as possible. He had a family that depended on him. He didn't want to think of it as landing as much as possible, to make as much as possible, before being told he couldn't cockle rake anymore, but reality whispered to him, *get a move on, pal*. The ban might, or might not come, but the bills always would. And from the deepest, primal recesses of his brain, the region concerned with instinct and survival, an unsettled thought began to take shape – *what if they try and take away your routine?*

There had been no news for days and people were starting to think that that was an encouraging sign. But Norrie had spent the majority of his life standing out of doors, in the midst of the elements, where land meets water. It was a special place to be, by the tide, always, as it ebbed and flowed. It was as though one became a little more connected to the forces of nature. And, being in that special place, Norrie had become like a super-tuned weathervane. He sensed a wicked storm, hissing venom, in some faraway place. Its course was set.

*

Moses picked up the tab, again. They were at Deacon Brodie's Tavern. 'Keep the change, ma'am.'

'He does this wherever and whenever he can, Alan. You would not believe the lengths he goes to, in order to pay a tab. But when he is in Zanzibar, he cannot. Everyone knows me, and they know to put it on Achmed's account, and never take even so much as a shilling from any guest of mine.'

'Same in Shanghai. Everyone know. Send Foo bill. But when we travel, what can we do? He beats us to it every time.' Confucius shook his head in disapproval.

'Settle down boys, settle down. I can't help it, that's all. One of you all can get the next bill.'

'That what you said last time,' Confucius responded.

'And the time before, Remy,' Achmed added

Alan was confused. *He hadn't noticed this exchange the last few meetings he'd had with them.*

Achmed, being the super-aware salesman, could read a face before the nerves twitched and moved the muscles into position. He explained, 'That's because Nigel was with us. When Nigel is on duty it's his job. But when it's just us? You didn't see, but at The Canons' Gait he got the note to the barman first.' Achmed shook his head.

'Aye, aye – right?'

'All right boys, all right, that's enough. Next time. I'm sorry, I truly am – where were we, anyway?'

'You were saying "the time" something or other?' Alan reminded him.

'Oh yeah,' Moses leaned over the table, his voice dropped. 'Alan, we do believe the time is right for the next step. As they say back over yonder. It is time to – *click click,* pull the trigger.'

'Alan, you look worried,' Achmed the Consoler, started. 'Is there something wrong?'

'No, no, of course not. I just didn't think we'd be, err, "pulling the trigger" this quickly.'

'Hmm, I see, I see,' Confucius, the thoughtful, spoke gravely. 'Perhaps we misread your abilities, hmm.'

'No, no, ha!' replied Alan, suddenly a little nervous.

'Come on, Foo, you got it right. I ain't known you to get a calculation wrong.' Moses turned to Alan. 'You should peek inside his brain. He makes quantum physics look like basket weaving, no offence to basket weavers, of course. Hell, we all got it right. And I ain't ever known Achmed to be wrong about no deal, ever. Ain't that right Achmed?'

Achmed nodded. 'Humbly, I would say that's accurate.'

'I, of course, I ain't quite got Foo's brain, nor Achmed's mind-reading powers, but I got instinct, and my instinct says we are right about you.'

Alan found his voice. 'Gentlemen, it shouldn't be a problem, it's barely been a week. I just thought when you said soon, well, soon would be – I don't know, a few weeks, a month, maybe two. You know how slowly the wheels of government turn sometimes. It can be painfully slow to get some things done. And getting the MEO to make that call to suspend all activity, theoretically, it can happen pretty fast, but under normal circumstances it usually takes a bit more time, sometimes a really long time.'

Achmed smiled. Reassured, he said, 'I am certain now more than ever before, Alan, that is why we picked you.'

'Hmm,' Confucius added. 'Yes, I agree, now that I reconsider my analysis. My calculation was accurate.'

'You see, Alan, Foo, Achmed, me, we believe in you. You can make it happen. And don't forget, these sure ain't 'normal' circumstances.'

'How soon is "pull the trigger" soon?' Alan asked.

'Well, as soon as possible.'

'A couple of days, perhaps? I'll need to speak to a few people. Can't appear too pushy and all.'

Moses winked. 'You got that right, Alan. And that's where all your skills are going to come in handy. All the slick talking and darting around that you learned on the rugby pitch – well, this is where it's your time to shine. And don't forget, The Art of War? Speed, lightning speed, is an asset. You will outmanoeuvre and confuse, well, not that I should call them our enemy, but you get the idea. The ball is rolling. You made the first couple of calls. People are already aware that the complaints by our four "witnesses" were handed to you. So, hey, you are already one step ahead of the MEO. You, Alan, are at the heart of this now. You are the pivot man between the four concerned souls and the MEO. So, it's up to you, to use those complaints, read through them and get on the MEO's tail – ha! No pun intended – to make their decision pronto. After that, of course, thanks to the little clause in the legal rights to an SAC, well, that part is tricky, too, but it shouldn't be difficult once the area is in legal limbo land. Hey, don't worry about it, Alan, you'll do just fine. And don't forget, you are on the good side.'

As Alan descended the Royal Mile on his way back to work, he put aside thoughts of how exactly he was going to make things happen as soon as possible. They could wait, for a little while anyway. What was on his mind, once again, was Remy, Foo, and Achmed's grand plans. The resort was one thing. Great. That's doable. The "bubbles of protection" – or biospheres? Again, a large capital investment, but they had the capital. The science laboratory was routine – they would be analysing and evaluating the potential for wind and wave power in the area. Fair enough. The plans for the underwater tunnel network seemed a bit of a stretch, but he reminded himself that he had read some no-nonsense literature that these things were being built in a few places – or had that been in his sci-fi comic collection? He often got the two mixed up. There was definitely a Chunnel under The Channel, that was for sure. They would be using them as research for high-speed underwater cargo carrying "subtrains", as they called them. With many islands close to one another it would be an ideal location to prototype what a larger network would look like. Basically, it would be like an enormous train, or subtrain, set. Err, okay? Alan knew his limits. He was no engineering or technology aficionado.

That was all fine, as far as Alan was concerned, but it was the Think Tank that they planned to build on the small island of Greanamul that had him thinking most of all. *My my, they are ambitious, but goodness me, when they explain things as they do, they have a point – I must give them that, what do I know about these matters? Indeed, indeed, the pace of change is increasing. Most people would get that. But to try and convince people how divisive politics is? How it slows down the march of progress, and that it pits one against another? Gentlemen, you have your work cut out for you. Fair enough, Remy, you make a good point. Remy's voice scrolled through Alan's memory. 'How often have you seen a debate live on stage or broadcast on TV, or listened to it on the radio, and two seemingly intelligent rational decent individuals take polar-opposite positions on every doggone thing under the sun. Monetary policy, fiscal policy, when to borrow, when to take a risk, when to extend a hand in need? And this ain't just every now and again, this is over and over and over again, Alan. It is nonsense. It is a shame. No, it's worse than a shame, it is a disgrace. And the tragic part is you can't fault them. They are products of a lifetime of being influenced to think in – you could argue "brainwashed" to think in only one way. They have been tricked and deceived, or a part of their brains have anyway. Even if they did see the wisdom of a different idea than the one they were promoting and even if a ray of light did shine through, that bastard thing called pride often slams the door shut. Thank goodness, Alan, there are those willing to listen, to learn, and to accept the fact that perhaps there is a new way, a better way, a more efficient way. You see, the reality is, circumstances are always changing. Always, Alan. And life sure ain't black and white. It is complicated – and tough, bold decisions constantly need to be made. And I will tell you Alan, this is where many of your folk, I mean your fellow politicians, across the global spectrum – my beloved republic is crammed full of 'em, Alan – that divide and divide. They dumb down life to a few one-liners and they make statements that ought to be banned for their irresponsible nature. Half of these bastards, these so-called advocates of democracy are too deluded to see reality and the other half just don't care. And year after year, they are influencing people and people are voting for them. Let me be clear here, Alan, life is beautiful and tragic. It is full of optimism and hope. It is also full of despair and hostility and you can fill in the rest. It needs our help. It demands our help. Divided we are conquered. Only united do we flourish. Ain't that right, Foo? You see, Foo gets the long view. The most important thing is unity, stability, and awareness – awareness of what, you might ask? Awareness of everything. This is a loaded statement, Alan. Think deeply about it. At the same time think deeply of how to inspire more, motivate more, help more. Sometimes how to do these things requires sacrifice from others and this is where those divisive politicians get it wrong, and they trick people into not voting for the progress of man. Alan, life ain't about me looking out just for me and maybe those closest to me. Do you understand what I am saying? You've got a wife and two other ladies in your life. And, of course, you got your little constituency. That's a good start. But, hell, this ain't just about you and them, Alan, I'm just pointing that out. Now, understand this, and listen to me very carefully, this is where our friends in the political world have a lot to learn from the world of business. Mark my words, Alan. And don't forget that the wise business gets it. That success comes from improving the whole. Alan, I'm a businessman through and through, an oilman. Me, Foo here, and Achmed – we are all advocates for one thing and that is the progress and advancement of man, which means most importantly – the rise of our youth, all our youth. Let me stress this point – out there amongst the rubble of humanity, amongst the dispossessed and the hungry, and I don't just mean way over yonder on some distant continent. I mean right in our local neighbourhoods, too, near and far, where there are people quietly suffering in one way or another, amongst all those masses, lie a million undiscovered gems; talent and strength untapped, unseen. The next miracle is waiting to be found. Do you see what I am saying? It is our job, our mission, to discover those gems and to turn to the world and say, "Here, this is your next doctor, your next scientist, your next engineer" I think you get what I am saying, what we are about. Lastly, Alan – back to stability and unity, amongst which we thrive. The world, me, you, everything, is more interconnected than we could ever imagine – this is a tricky matter here, Alan – what I am trying to tell you is a force, a stable entity, that is above the division and chaos of politics, a light that shines over, across the world, that people from near and far, of different races and languages, can look to, and see goodness, charity, strength, virtue, well, that can only be a good thing...' My goodness me, these fellows are making me dizzy.*

Ch 41

Charlie and Chester

As Moses, Confucius, and a Sufi Mystic took an open deck bus tour of Edinburgh, after leaving Deacon Brodie's Tavern and saying cheerio to Alan, Norrie MacKinnon was sitting on his own in the Nissen hut. He'd creaked open the Coquilleuous Rakkeronuous Almenikhiaka and was flipping crusty page after dusty page, looking for any entry with a title something along the lines of 'What to do in the event you can't cockle rake anymore' or 'The beach has run out of cockles, what next?' Patches and Sailor were lying faithfully at his feet. He even looked in the secret compartments that held the extra special secret tales (not that he believed in them – Norrie knew fine that the big, old book was a fair mix of fantasy and reality. Sorting what was what was another matter), but he found nothing.

'Hm, didn't think so,' he muttered under his breath. He knew the big, old book inside and out, or mostly anyway. He thought he'd check just in case he'd missed two pages stuck together, or an article that actually was meant to be read back to front to understand its proper meaning. Nothing about what to do in the event one can no longer cockle rake though....however....*hmm, what's this?* He read on. He was astonished. *I never knew.* Two small articles, off to the side of a larger lesson on 'tides' that dominated the page. It wasn't much, just two paragraphs. Of great x four grandpa Angus and x six Ruithie. Angus had had a nerve-wracking fear of hot air balloons, and Ruithie a morbid fear of speaking in public. *My my, interesting....*

'Everything okay in here, honey?'

'Oh, hey there, didn't hear you come in.'

Samantha smiled. 'Here, I brought you a cup of tea.' She gave Patches and Sailor a wee pet.

'Thanks.' Norrie took a sip and placed the cup on the workbench.

'The girls have been asking me what's the matter with Papa.'

'Aye?'

'Aye, really.'

'What did you tell them?'

Samantha shrugged. 'Just that you have a lot of work to do. Lots of orders to be filled. And that you're a little, well, I had to keep things quite simple you know, just that you've a lot on your mind and you don't have as much time to play with them, that's all. And – Norrie, that it would pass?'

'It'll pass.'

'I know it will, sweetheart.'

'It's just, well, I'm not sure what I would do if – I don't even like to think about it – I can't help it.'

'Any answers in there?'

'No.' Norrie closed the big book and placed it on the work bench.

'Well, you know what I think?' Samantha sat on her husband's lap. 'I think everything will be just fine. Don't go worrying about it too much, okay?'

'I'm trying. But we have bills to pay. We couldn't go more than, well, not very long – and, it's – it's my life, it's all I know.'

‘Oh honey, please, don't worry too much. Everything will be all right. After all, there's been no more about the whole thing. It will probably all just blow over.’

Norrie wasn't so certain. But he had two daughters who were missing their Papa. He smiled. ‘Maybe you're right.’

‘You'll see, sweetheart. I'm sure of it,’ Samantha replied, with a hug.

‘The girls will be home shortly. Maybe I'll take them on a scavenger hunt. What do you think?’

‘I think that's a great idea. It's almost the holidays, you know. This Friday is their last day.’

‘Right. I forgot. The year has whizzed along.’

‘And you know what that means – they'll have their little rakes out and you're going to have some company for the next wee while.’

Norrie laughed. ‘Aye, aye, of course.’

Patches and Sailor were wagging their tails. They sensed the excitement.

‘And we've got your sisters arriving in three weeks, I think it is, and your Mama and Hank and their brood. It's going to be a pretty hectic house for a few weeks.’

‘Aye, you're right about that. It's going to be chaos. I think I'm going to move out here for a while.’

Samantha hugged Norrie tightly. ‘I think I'll move out here with you, sweetheart.’

‘Mama, why are you sitting on Papa's lap? That's our spot – Mama? Papa?’

‘Oh, hello there young ladies, you sneaked up on us. I was just testing to see how much your Mama weighed.’

‘And how much does Mama weigh?’

‘Well, let's see here, about, hmm, I think about maybe as much as 500...’

Don't you dare.

‘...Marshmallows.’

That's better.

'Papa, come on, be serious!'

'I'll tell you what I will be serious about – who wants to head to the west side?'

Sofia and Violet hopped up and down excitedly.

'We'll start way up high at the golf course and go all the way along to Bagh Halaman.'

'That far!?'

'What, you don't think we can make it?'

'Hm, no – Mama, do you think we'll make it back in time for dinner?' Sofia asked.

'Well, I'll just make sure to keep things warm for you.'

Violet hugged her Mama's legs. 'Can't you come, too?'

'But who will have dinner ready for you when you get back with empty tummies?'

'Hm, oh I know, Mama, I know.' Sofia, suddenly inspired, suggested, 'Maybe we can eat in Castlebay. We haven't eaten in Castlebay in such a long time. I like Kisimul Café. It's my favourite place. We can sit outside, and that way Patches and Sailor can come too.'

'And it's my favourite also,' Violet came to the aid of her sister.

Samantha looked to Norrie. *What do you think?*

'All right girls, why not. Let's go and pack a wee snack bag.'

This sent the girls into a tizzy. Samantha ushered the two balls of energy out of the Nissen hut. Norrie placed the big, old book back on the shelf and finished the rest of his tea. 'What do you guys think, eh? Is that a good idea?' he said, giving his four-legged friends a pet.

Tails wagged and tongues flopped about. It was definitely a good idea.

*

Alan Trout replaced the receiver and looked to his number one confidante. 'It's set. They'll be over in two hours.'

'You think you can pull it off?'

'I'm going to give it my best shot.' He shrugged and added, 'We'll see.'

Infinitely curious, James asked, 'How on earth did you come up with that idea?'

Another shrug. 'I don't know. It just fell into my head, and I thought, no, I knew, I was like "aha", perfect. If I make it personal then, well, let's hope whomever they are sending over aren't robots, you know.'

'Aye, aye, indeed Alan. All I can say is good luck with it. I truly hope that it works.'

'If it doesn't, well, I just don't know. I can't get too pushy with the whole thing. The way I see it, if I manage to make an impression and if they care about the environment as much as I am about to, they'll either agree right away and they will – as our friend Remy says "pull the trigger" – and all activity will be immediately suspended. Either that or they're going to feel really sorry for me but our four complaints are just entering the bureaucratic mill and won't be seen or heard from again for quite some time. Who knows? But you know something James, I've got a feeling.'

'Aye, aye. By the by, do you want me to stick around for the meeting? Just an idea – not sure if it'll help things or not.'

'Hm – I wonder, I wonder if that would help?' Alan mused, fingers drumming on the desk. 'If you're here then you'll be my support, they'll see you as someone for me to lean on and all that, whereas if it's just me and them, I'll be totally alone, vulnerable, with only them to console me. No, I think it's best that I do this on my own.'

'Very well, then. Just curious, Alan – have you ever done any acting before? I mean, like proper acting?'

'James, my friend, you ought to be able to answer that.' *I've been acting my whole life.*

Two hours later the lovely Harriet Joyce was ushering in two suits from the MEO. A man and a woman. Dr Jennifer Paterson and Dr Horatio Goodfellow. Dr Paterson looked to be in her thirties, auburn hair tied in a ponytail. Behind a pair of glasses was a pair of beautiful brown eyes. They were wide and clear. She had a few freckles on her cheeks and everything about her was delightfully pleasant. Dr Goodfellow was somewhat older, perhaps early fifties. He had a full head of greying black hair which was unkempt. His beard was also greying and frizzly. Alan thought it could do with a trim. *My goodness, a small bird could live in there.* He looked the part of a stereotypical scientist – like he was constantly thinking through some complicated equations.

Time to put on the show.

'Thank you for coming so soon. Please, please, do sit. I'm so sorry about all this – it's, just, it's so terrible. I can't believe this.' A distraught Alan took his seat. First, he ran his hands through his hair, then he placed them on the desk, making them shake a little, then he rose from his chair and took a step away. 'I'm sorry.'

'Mr Trout, are you okay?' a concerned Dr Paterson asked, looking to her colleague.

He turned. 'I'm sorry, yes, yes. Please, call me Alan.'

'Of course, Alan,' she responded with a caring smile that seemed to say, 'You'll be okay'.

Excellent, that's a start.

'God, these last few days, I've been going through these statements, and it's just, it's just appalling. It brought back some dark and distressing memories – I haven't been able to sleep, to think people would do that, keep doing that, to – to our oceans. Thank goodness for those four divers.'

'We agree, Alan, of course. That's what we are here for, to protect our land and sea. Our precious natural environment.'

Alan was staring into space. 'If I had done something sooner – they – it was so, so horrible.' The first sniffle. 'But I didn't, I – waited – I didn't know, I was so young...oh, the guilt that came later.' The second sniffle. 'Those poor dolphins, those poor, poor baby dolphins, they looked like twins.' He was staring off into his made-up memory. 'They looked so happy together, playing and splashing, and the water was so pristine – at first – and then, and then it came – I could see it in the distance. It was horrible. I could have warned someone so they could have rescued them before it was too late.'

Dr Paterson leaned forward inquisitively. 'Alan, what are you talking about?'

A dramatic pause, and then Alan continued, 'We were on holiday, I was about twelve. It was the second day and I was playing in the sea, and there was an estuary that ran off it. There I met my two friends, I even gave them names, Charlie and Chester. They looked so happy, and they would come near me by the rocks and we bonded instantly. The chirpy noises, it was their way of laughing.' The third sniffle. 'I promised them I would visit them every day, and I did, days three, four, five – it was a lovely holiday, out on the beach, building sandcastles, running in the dunes, and always, faithfully, I would visit Charlie and Chester and they would be waiting for me – and I would splash around with my two friends and they splashed around with me – I'm sorry, I'm going to get too emotional, if I go into this too much.'

Dr Goodfellow circumspectly asked, 'What happened next, Alan?'

'On day six is when I first saw them, further up the estuary, five of them, five horribly rusted contaminated barrels.' More sniffles. 'I could see the black sludge seeping out of them and it was trickling into the estuary.' Alan looked mournfully between his guests. 'The barrels, they looked ready to, I don't know, break apart completely. They were all rusty, and, well, I didn't think.' The first tear ran down a cheek. 'I said to Charlie and Chester, "Make sure you stay away from that spot over there, okay? Good little dolphins." The next day I visited my new friends and the next, and I was so pleased they were being good dolphins and they were staying away from the bad area.' Another tear. A sniffle. 'It was the following day – oh my God, I'm sorry – I, I couldn't believe what my eyes saw.' A few more tears rolled down his cheeks. More sniffling. 'There was Charlie and Chester, they were covered in oil – the barrels had bu-bu-broken open.' And at that point Alan burst into an uncontrollable, inconsolable, sob. 'I'm su-so su-su-sorry t-to bu-bu bother you with this.' His words were swallowed by more tears and he cried like a child who'd just dropped his favourite coloured lollipop down a drain.

'There, there, Alan, it's all right, please,' Dr Paterson had risen from her chair and placed a comforting arm around him.

'Th-thank you, du-du-doctor.'

'Alan, please, call me Jennifer. There, there, you'll be okay. It wasn't your fault.'

Dr Horatio Goodfellow just looked on, totally lost, and for the first time in his adult life was not thinking about one single equation. *What a curious, sad man.*

'Th-they died, they cu-couldn't be su-saved.' The tears flowed and the sobbing continued, until finally, Alan, hugging the arm of this caring human being, calmed down.

*

'It was easy after that,' Alan said with a shrug.

'We are doggone proud of you.' Moses was the first to congratulate him.

Next was Confucius, 'Good thinking, Alan. Ingenious. We knew you'd come up with something, shall we say, "appropriate."'

'Top job, Alan,' Nigel the tourist, complimented.

And finally, Achmed the Sufi Mystic, added, 'My, my, that must have been some performance.'

'Funny thing this, but it was as if at that point those complaint reports could have been blank, or not exist at all. Poof. Gone. When I proposed we speed things up a little to avoid any future regret, it was like *voila* they went into "Let's get this place shut down as soon as possible" mode. Well, the one doctor did, the woman. I think the fellow was rather dubious, a little anyway.' Alan shrugged. 'But he went along with things. That was that. The order was signed.' He took a sip of his drink, sat back, relaxed. He was getting used to his new friends.

It was a sunny afternoon and so they'd chosen a place with outdoor seating for this rendezvous. They were sitting around a patio table outside the imposing Bank Hotel halfway up the Royal Mile. People were streaming up and down the street.

'You know, Alan, if your peers, or your constituents for that matter, spot you sitting here with men of faith, they're going to think you've finally found God, not that that would be a bad thing,' Moses remarked.

'Indeed, Remy, it would not be a bad thing. I recall my days wandering the deserts of North Africa, a young boy, then as a young man, with my adopted family. It was out there, way way out there, was where I came to understand my faith,' Achmed the Sincere, added.

'And I, Foo, I too found my faith – my philosophy – in a special place. I began to understand the wisdom of Master Kong.'

Alan fidgeted with his drink, not totally uncomfortable, but not entirely comfortable with the subject. He wasn't a man who gave faith or God or religion too much thought. Didn't quite get the whole thing. Like there was some place you went to after you died. Some poofy cloud city where everyone has wings and everything is free and you are always happy, and all that. Another version has a few dozen virgins waiting to satisfy you – if that were the case that's the version Alan might go for first – but, Alan dismissed the whole lot. He lived in the real world and it was a tricky enough place to negotiate, to navigate, without thinking about what happens once the lights go out.

Achmed could read his mind. 'Sorry, Alan, we should not have mentioned our faiths – our philosophy. We do not want to make you feel uncomfortable.' He smiled a broad smile. 'What is most important, after all, is how we live in the here and now.'

Ch 42

No Cockle Raking

Norrie didn't notice the signs going up along the edge of the beach. They just appeared. No one came down to say anything to him, nor to the part timers who were there raking. If Patches and Sailor hadn't used the one sign to pee on he would have walked right past. It was a simple sign and not big at all, just a foot in height, it was almost lost amongst the windswept marram grass lining the dunes. But it was there all right, and on it was a freshly painted notice: No Cockle Raking. That was it. For a moment it did not compute, but when it did Norrie chuckled. *Some prankster no doubt, one of the local children having a bit of fun.* He thought no more of it and walked home. There hadn't been any more news over the last few days, and though it hadn't made him feel better about the whole thing, he had adapted somewhat, learned to live with the uncertainty. He had Sofia and Violet to think of, after all.

He was going to be thinking about it a whole lot more now, however.

Eddie, Colin, Ronnie, and Irish were waiting for him at the Nissen hut. They didn't have to say a word, either someone had died or it had happened.

It had happened.

Ronnie offered a few encouraging words – about the first time ever that both the harvesting and selling of cockles was temporarily banned. "...They even discussed it in Parliament. And it didn't last long, it was just a few weeks. Three maybe.'

'Aye, that was different altogether,' Irish said, 'That was due to the algal bloom, the DSP or whatever it's called. The toxin.'

Norrie was in a measured state of shock. How could it have come to this? Eight generations of MacKinnons have made their living on the Traigh Mhor. And just like that they are being told no more. A bottle emerged from somewhere and drams were poured. Norrie's didn't last long. His countenance spoke volumes. The others knew this had knocked him for six.

'Norrie, hey – if you need to, when you're ready, you can crew with me,' Eddie offered.

The others, likewise, said they'd make space aboard their boats – just say the word, Norrie. This time it was different, being offered work on the boats. He'd been offered the opportunity years ago. The cheque Hank had given him in case he wanted to get in on the game himself was still tacked up in the Nissen hut, lost amongst the lines of old, dusty postcards. As a young lad he'd thoroughly enjoyed his experiences on Eddie's old boat. But cockle raking had always been his favourite. There was no doubting that. When he'd been offered the opportunity, it was easy to turn it down. He could make a living cockle raking. But it was more than just a living, it was his way of life, that which had been passed down from generation to generation. It was in his blood. Most importantly, it was the routine of toiling alongside the shores that provided peace, perspective, balance. There was nothing quite like it. He had a family now, a wife and two daughters who relied on him. Before, he hadn't needed to explain why he could not go to sea with them because he had the beach to protect him and to provide for him and his family. How could he turn them down now? How could anyone understand? The story of great-times-four grandpa Angus flashed through his mind – he was afraid of hot air balloons. And then there was great-times-six grandpa Ruithie who was frightened to death of speaking in public. He had concluded when he'd first read these stories that he must be predisposed to whatever it is you called that condition. It had just taken until the age he had been when he jumped off the ferry, for it to manifest itself within him. Oh well. You deal with it, you protect yourself, and you carry on. No different to anyone else who carries an affliction. There are plenty to go around. No need to see his as any different. In fact, his was just fine, thank you very much. He didn't like thinking about it a lot.

'Thanks lads, I'll let you know. Maybe you're right, maybe it will blow over shortly, and we'll all be back to business as usual.' He forced a smile.

'Aye, Norrie, that would be grand.'

News had spread round the island earlier that day in record time. It had started with a secret telegram from Edinburgh to the local council office. The MEO was taking the necessary action to ensure the Sound of Floonay was protected from any further damage. And it was with the legally binding authority that comes with a region being declared a Special Area of Conservation that they decreed all commercial activity cease within its boundaries. The right of through passage was still allowed. Any fishermen with fleets of creels in the area had forty-eight hours to remove them. There would be a thorough investigation into the atrocities committed, then some more investigating, analysing, and further review, and even deeper analysis. And then we'll decide what the future holds for the Sound. Thank you, and that is all from us for a very long time, or until we decide to get in touch, whatever suits our fancy. Please make the local constabulary aware of the ban. No commercial activity means just that, no commercial activity.

Period. Full stop. The constabulary will be receiving, in due course, a list of the penalties for any infractions. Additionally, harvesting for cockles on the beach for personal consumption is also banned. (It would be too difficult to differentiate who was raking for what purpose) Signed: the powers that be deep in the bowels of the MEO. That was, more or less, the contents of the secret message.

'Papa, Mizz Fizzlezwit looked happy today. She normally never looks happy. She is the grumpiest and meanest person I have ever known. Why would she be so happy today?' Sofia asked, while drawing train tracks with a fork in her mashed potatoes at dinner.

Samantha and Norrie shared a look. Norrie and Mizz Fizzlezwit had an unwritten, unspoken, and most of the time unthought of, cast iron rule: they stayed well clear of one another.

'Well, sweetheart, maybe someone told her a funny joke and it made her happy.'

'Papa, have you ever seen Mizz Fizzlezwit before? I bet you she's never laughed at a joke in her life.'

'Well, you never know, maybe she has once or twice.' *But probably not.*

Sofia shook her head. 'I don't think so, Papa.'

Norrie just smiled.

'Papa?'

'Yes, honey?'

'I don't think she likes me very much.'

'That...' On second thought, 'Honey, Mizz Fizzlezwit doesn't like anyone.'

'Hmm, yeah, but she looks at me – and sometimes Violet, too, a little differently from the others. She gives me the shivers.'

Samantha piped up, 'Now, let's not go worrying about Mizz Fizzlezwit too much. Make sure you eat those potatoes before they get cold. That's an awful lot of train tracks there.'

'I will Mama, I promise. I don't mind them cold, though.' Sofia forgot about the headmistress for a moment. 'They're still as tasty as ever.'

'Yeah, tasty,' Violet chirped.

'That's because they are Floonay potatoes, honey, the best ever.'

Sofia, with *her* riding on a broomstick back into her mind's eye, looked to Mama and then Papa, 'How come Mizz Fizzlezwit is the headmistress? She is so so frightening – I think even all the teachers are scared of her.'

'Well, honey, that's just one of those funny things,' Samantha tried to explain.

'Mama, there's nothing funny about Mizz Fizzlezwit.'

'Not funny at all,' Violet added.

'Hmm, I wish Mrs MacLean was the headmistress. She's so nice. She's my favourite teacher.' Sofia was lost in thought and still laying train tracks.

'Oh, Mama, you know what?'

'What's that darling?'

'I love the summer but I'm also looking a little forward to going back to school.' Sofia looking expectantly, eagerly awaited the question.

Samantha cracked a smile. 'And why would that be, young lady?'

'Because Mrs MacLean said we're going to keep making our Barrahead board game next term and she said my pictures were very good. I've been practising some more.' Sofia puffed out her little chest and was as proud as a peacock.

'I wish I could make a board game.' A grey cloud crept over Violet.

'Don't worry, another couple of years, Violet. You'll have to wait till you grow up a little,' her older sister explained.

'Hmm,' Violet thought, not without impatience.

Sofia's thoughts, like most children's, flew inexplicably and without warning in another trajectory. 'Oh, Papa, can we go to Tri-e-ash after dinner? Can we?'

'Your father has important business to see to this evening, but I will take you, if you want.'

Sofia and Violet looked at one another – confused. Mama was serious. The only time their Papa was referred to as 'father' was when they were in trouble. Well, they weren't in trouble but they knew there would be no exception.

'Okay Mama,' Sofia said, a little sad.

'You don't like going to the beach with Mama? Your Mama knows how to have fun.' Norrie winked.

'Yes, Papa, Hmm, I don't know. Sorry Mama, it's okay.'

'That's all right, sweetheart,' Samantha replied, smiling. 'I know your Papa is the best at the beach. I think he is, too. He just has something very important to do tonight, that's all. There will be plenty more days and evenings and mornings and everythings this coming summer for Papa to take you, don't worry. And only a few more days and school will be out. You will have all the time in the world to go with Papa to the beach.'

'Okay, Mama,' Sofia replied, a little happier. 'But you have to help us build a sandcastle. A big one.'

'Yeah! A giant one,' Violet added.

'Of course, I can do that. You don't think I know how to build giant sandcastles? I once built one so big that you could walk right through the giant front door. It even had a – err – drawbridge!'

Two pairs of eyes widened. 'Really, Mama?'

'Really.' Norrie winked at his wife. 'I saw it. It was on our honeymoon. Over on the big beach on Vatersay. I was gone for a while looking for something. I can't remember what now exactly, but when I came back – there it was. A giant sandcastle! I don't know how Mama could build one so big, and so fast. And she wouldn't even tell me.'

Sofia and Violet looked at one another and then to their Mama, and it was as if she had just stepped out of the red phone booth at the end of the road dressed as Wonder Woman.

Norrie smiled. *Good luck sweetheart.*

*

The Heathbank was busier than usual that evening and Joe had the MEO to thank. Every fisherman from the north half of Floonay had shown up, and most of those who sailed out of Castlebay had, for that evening, switched allegiances. The chatter was much as it had been all day, but it was such a significant event that talking about it at length was permitted. What was known about the reported 'sightings'? Only that four visitors – *Blasted visitors! It was always an outsider that caused trouble!* - had been diving in the area and witnessed contamination amongst a few reefs. What contamination? No one really knew. What information had been gleaned was patchy and vague. It didn't matter much at this point. The focus was the designation. From the time the area received its special 'status' it was a metaphorical time bomb. Any say, any rights, the local community once had in the governance of their own affairs, on their local land and sea, was coldly, clinically, methodically wrested away. This had been happening for a long time, the SAC designation was just another domino to fall.

But life would go on, and the ninety nine percent of those in the pub that evening with a job, would be going back to their jobs the next morning. Eddie, Colin and the other fishermen, would be shifting the gear they had in the Sound to the west or to the east, and they would keep fishing. Only one man in the room no longer had a job to go to and gradually everyone got a stronger sense of this as they thought about things properly. But he did have the offers to join a few of the boats, and that evening was told a spot would be found for him at the fish factory, if he wanted it. His main buyer, too, said he could find work for him for a few days out of the week. There was no shortage of work about, for one willing to make an effort. There was grass to cut, windows to wash, fences to mend. That was all well and good, but everyone was keenly aware it was not just about making a wage. Most people remembered his father, and the older ones, his father's father before. And most of them knew that the MacKinnons had been cockle raking for a very long time. The memories were still there of Norrie winning the old annual cockle raking competitions, how he beat the socks off his own category and that of the grownups. It was all he knew. But, hey, one can't always do what one wants to in life. Sometimes one had to adjust, make a change, and move on.

Norrie had other plans.

He nudged his main buyer. *A quiet word,* 'Nelson?'

'Aye, Norrie?'

'You're not banned from landing cockles, are you?'

Nelson frowned. 'No – I've still got the landings that come in from Uist. Why?'

'Aye, of course, of course. I was wondering what to do with what I've raked so far this week – whether I can land it?'

'Aye, aye, of course you can land it.'

'I should have known.'

It was evident to Nelson that there was more to come.

'And what about next week – what if I were to bring you a landing, would you take it?'

Nelson hesitated, frowning some more. He leaned in. 'Norrie – what are you talking about?'

'Just that.'

'You'll get caught. You can't.'

'But you would – accept the landing?'

'Well – aye, but, Norrie, think about what you're saying. That's a big beach and there's nowhere to hide. You'll get caught eventually. It might not be tomorrow or the next day or even the next. It'll happen at some point though.'

This, of course, was an obvious point to Norrie. What was he thinking? How long could he keep it up? How long did he need to keep it up? It was a tremendously uncertain proposition.

It was instinct. It was his routine. Nothing more.

'Look, Nelson, this is what I'm thinking – there's a suspension of activity in the area, Aye?'

'Aye.'

'Their focus is on the reefs out there – whatever whoever observed, well, it has nothing to do with the Traigh – aye?'

Nelson responded with a dubious, 'Aye.'

'Hear me out – so their focus is out there somewhere in the Sound. They're planning on doing a survey to assess the damage, if there is any, and let's say the worst case scenario – if we take that case down south as a benchmark, well, it was for about a year that all activity was suspended. Best case – who knows – how fast can they work – let's just say two or three months. Optimistically, let's hope it's closer to the best case than the worst case. Point is Nelson, at some time the ban will be lifted. Look out there for heaven's sake, it's not like an oil tanker has foundered and is spilling its contents. Whatever it is, is fairly minor – but has to be investigated nonetheless, right?'

'Aye.'

By this time, it was no longer 'a quiet word'. Eddie, Colin, Ronnie, Irish, and a few of the other fishermen were listening in.

'This is the way I see it – we're a long way from the mainland, number one. The focus is on the reefs, number two. Finally, number three, who the hell is going to look out there onto the beach, see a tiny figure in the distance *and* report that figure for maybe, just maybe, harvesting cockles?'

The look shared across the panorama of faces around him answered that question: Norrie, our community has its share of busybodies. Don't underestimate the lengths they'll go to.

'Okay, look – all I'm saying is, there's a good chance that if I keep on doing what I'm doing, nothing will come of anything, and the weeks will go by, and at some point they'll do their survey thing, and hopefully will pay no attention to a lonely figure on the beach, and time will march along, and the ban will be lifted, and I'll keep on doing what I've always done. No problems'

'Norrie, someone from the council put those signs up, you know?'

'Aye, aye,' Norrie shrugged casually. 'They had to. They're half hidden in the grass, anyway. You can barely see them. Maybe they don't care much, you know?'

The panorama of doubting expressions answered that question.

'Look lads, all I'm saying is, I just have to get through a tough patch. It's not forever. I'll make sure I'm well up by Orosay, you'll barely be able to see me from the south side, there's some decent spots on the other side, too. I'll be well out of view. I just have to get through whatever length of time it is. Who the hell is going to care about one man on the beach with a bucket and a rake?'

'Aye, aye, I see your point Norrie,' Ronnie said. 'Us fishing out there whilst they're surveying is one thing – maybe you will be "off their radar."'

Norrie continued, 'I mean, it's one thing if this was an SAC on the mainland somewhere, some higher visibility spot. We're almost to St. Kilda for God's sake. Who the hell is going to go to that much bother?'

'You're really not going to quit, eh?' Colin said as he sipped his beer thoughtfully.

Norrie shook his head. 'I can't – it's, it's not just about earning a wage. I appreciate the offers of work, you know. It's just, all I know is that beach, that beach and following that tide. If I don't have that, well, I just wouldn't know what to do. It's that simple.'

'Aye, aye....well, well....the bloody MEO.'

The consensus seemed to be: keep at it? Why not. Why not, indeed.

'Excuse me, gentlemen, pardon our intrusion, we couldn't help but listen in.'

'Oh, Father John...'

'Reverend Cullen...'

'Our apologies, please do forgive us, we were just enjoying our drams here and honest to the Good Lord, were trying to mind our own, but we caught a few words there quite by accident, and, well, we couldn't help not listen in to the rest. We just wanted to let you know,' the good Reverend leaned in, doing his best to not act as though he were involved in some surreptitious activity, but was not doing a very good job. 'Well, it is our opinion that – why don't you tell them Father?'

Father John joined in. He looked at Norrie and around the huddled gathering. 'We know what the Good Lord would advise on a matter as important as this.' Eyebrows raised, he let the answer speak for itself.

Ch 43

The Good Side of Life

'Psst, Alan, we're over here.'

Confused, Alan spun around and was staring at a talking hedge.

'Have they gone?'

Alan looked around. It was just him standing in a *close* off the low end of the Royal Mile. There were residential flats, a few parked cars, a few garden plots, and one talking hedge, but there were no other people in sight.

'Uh – there's no one else here.'

'That's good, that's real good,' came Remy's voice, as Moses, Confucius, and a Sufi Mystic emerged from behind the greenery.

'We came within an inch of our lives, Alan,' Achmed the sincere, explained.

'It was not good. We lucky. Even my kung-fu skills would have been put to the test,' Dr Foo said, shaking his head,

'And my six-shooter wasn't doing me no good locked in a desk drawer in Austin.'

'What on earth happened?'

Earlier in the day Alan had received a call from Nigel with instructions regarding where to meet later that evening. *Aye,*

aye, that's fine. I know the place. See you then. Oh, you won't be there? Just the others? Very good then. Talk to you later. Cheers now. It was a little eatery just up and around the corner from where he was now standing. He'd arrived on time but there had been no sign of Remy, Foo, or Achmed. He'd waited around for a bit, still nothing. He asked the staff if they'd seen three curiously dressed men. No, no one had, not recently anyway. They had always been prompt before. It had crossed his mind to give one of them a ring but held off. He had decided to do a wander, just in case he had got the name wrong – there were countless bars, restaurants, cafes, eateries of all sorts up and down the Royal Mile, and poked into nooks, crannies, and closes all along the way. If there was a few square feet of commercial real estate, someone was selling something. He'd wandered into the close where he was now standing. No little shops or eateries here, but he had found the talking bush.

Remy explained, 'We were just coming up along the street there, just down yonder and over a bit. We turned a corner and happened upon a, well, we weren't sure what they were doing, but they didn't like the fact that we'd spied them. There was half a dozen of them at least, rough, tough looking fellas. Scars and muscles and angry scowls, and just like that, blades appeared and a baton or two. They jumped and we spun around and ran as fast as our legs could carry us. Luckily, we ran in the right direction. These robes sure were slowing us down. Doggone that was close.'

'Come gentlemen, let us go and have that drink,' Foo added, dusting himself off, 'and let us hope we don't bump into those rogues again. For a moment, I thought I back in Shanghai. Thankfully, Edinburgh's version of rogues do not run as fast as the ones I have witnessed, and on occasion, crossed paths with, in my many years of experience. Yes, Shanghai rogues fast, but Foo just little bit faster.'

'And let us walk a little further up the road, it's getting late in the evening. I think we shall be safer with more people around,' Achmed the Concerned, added.

'Too right, my friend,' Moses replied.

'Aye, aye, of course,' Alan said, still befuddled. 'I know a good spot. It's called The Piper's Rest. I think you'll like it. There'll be plenty of people about.'

*

Remy did it again. As they'd passed into the bar, he made sure he was the last to enter and as he did so, pressed two £100 notes into a waitress's palm, and whispered, 'Bring us four drams, single malts, you choose. Please, and much obliged. The change is yours.'

Before the others had finished adjusting their seats a beaming waitress was handing them each a Speyside malt. Achmed and Dr Foo could do nothing but thank the nice young lady for the proffered libation. *One of these days Remy.*

Moses, giving a little chuckle and a wink, quipped, 'I'm too fast for 'em, Alan – ahh, now this is what I call a dram.'

'At least you chose well,' Achmed commented.

'Hmm, yes, I think this might be a Macallan. I agree Achmed, at least he's got good taste,' Dr Foo added as he savoured his drink.

'Aye, quite smooth, this.'

'All right, Alan, let's get down to business here.' Remy leaned forward, voice lowered. 'So far, so good. The region has been successfully sealed off and control, total control, has shifted into the hands of the government. That's good, real good. From what our intelligence people are telling us, everything is a-okay, smooth sailing. Doesn't seem to be any red flags popping up anywhere. The investigation into the matter would normally commence sometime in the next three to four months, as I am sure you're aware, and it is in this time that we must – you know what I'm gonna say Alan, that's right, click-click, *pull the trigger* on the next bit – that is, the government handing the reins of the region over to us.'

Foo took over. 'Our lawyers are certain, Alan, that the way the law is written, that part of things should not be a problem. It is ironic really, but the "Special Area of Conservation" designation actually makes it easier for the government to do what it likes – it's the "asterisk" bits at the end of the law, they are legal loopholes so big you could steer an oil tanker through them while passed out at the helm.'

They all had a chuckle at that.

Achmed followed up with, 'Obviously, Alan, the locals are more than likely up in arms right now about the whole thing, but that will soon die down. We think a month will be sufficient distance from the original ban to pull the trigger. In doing so, we will be well ahead of the investigation the MEO will probably barely have planned, and once they're made aware of the letter of the law and the little asterisks, well, we are betting – they can't do anything else – they will shrug and move on to the next assignment, of which they have many.'

'One question.'

'Fire away Alan.'

'What about the airport?'

'Alan, we, of course, have thought about that,' Remy answered. 'Part of the agreement that we will be signing with the government will stipulate that commercial flight operations can continue on the beach until a new airport is built, most likely somewhere on the west side. The east side is too hilly but from what we have been told there are a few top spots along the west side. This won't need to be rushed too much. Most importantly, we will have the control that we need.'

'Another thing?'

'Fire on, Alan, what is it?'

'If this all becomes public knowledge too soon, don't you think, well, someone, or a lot of people, will smell a rat?'

At those words Remy, Foo, and Achmed, chuckled.

'Of course, Alan, of course,' Foo started. 'You should know, that is the easiest potential obstacle to deal with. It is called spin, an enormous twisting of the facts. By the time our spin-meisters are done, anyone curious about anything will be left feeling like they in the middle of kaleidoscope.'

Alan frowned.

Remy resumed, 'Don't worry about it. Might there be the need for a public consultation? Sure, we'll have one. It will be a lot of nonsense – a public consult-nonsense-tation...'

Chuckles all around.

'...and at the end of it all we will still have control and everyone will quickly forget everything once the money and jobs start rolling in – it is as simple as that, my friend, and Alan,' Remy winked, 'Don't forget, we are on the good side of life.'

*

'Sweetheart, do you think that's wise, I mean, you could get into trouble?'

'I really don't think it will be that big a deal. As I've said, it's just a temporary ban until they do their investigation – and the beach is on the edge of the designated zone – I don't know why the hell they had to include it in the SAC zone, ach, whatever.'

'If it is just a temporary ban, why not just take a break from it. God knows you've spent enough of your life out there.'

With the girls tucked away and dreaming of the upcoming summer holidays, Samantha and Norrie were chatting quietly in the living room.

'You've had enough offers for other jobs – why not try something else for a while. Who knows, honey, you might end up liking it.'

'All I know is that beach. It is not about the money, honey – well, it's partly the money – I've got to do something to make a living – but it's also my routine, it's my life. I can't stress enough how important it is for me to keep that going. I was knocked out of my rhythm once, and for a very long time, and you know what it almost did, (Samantha didn't know what Hank knew, just that he'd become a wreck for a while) I cannot let that happen again. You're lucky you didn't know me a little while before you found me – you would have left me in that ditch to rot.'

'I never would have left you, no matter what.'

Norrie half smiled. 'Well, I'm glad you didn't know me then. It was ugly and messy and not a very fun place to be.'

'Honey, you made it, that's the important thing.'

'I know. God, I don't know how. Something kept me going, if barely.'

'Never mind all that now, it's in the past and you and I are here. We've two daughters who love you more than anything, as do I – more than I ever thought possible.' She smiled, resting her head on his shoulder. 'I fell in love with you before I found you. I knew you were waiting for me. I don't know how, I just did. And you made what I thought was impossible love, possible.'

Norrie, his arm around his wife, replied, 'I think it was the other way around. It was you who did that to me. I didn't even know what love was until you found me.'

They sat quietly, content not to say a word for a little while.

Norrie's mind was back to the tides of the planet. 'I really don't think it will be a problem. It'll just be for a few months and things will be back to normal. But in the meantime, honey, one thing is for certain – even if a bag of gold or cold hard cash was to drop into our laps right now – I cannot quit.'

It was business as usual for the next few days. Norrie made sure to stay well at the north end of the beach, tucked in close to the wee isle of Orosay. From the road wrapped around the sweeping beach, it was about a mile to where he was. For one to notice him, one would have to be looking for him. And it would appear that no one was. *Good.* He ordered Patches and Sailor to go run around in the grassy dunes lest they attracted attention darting all over the beach. They were happy enough to comply and so it was just him and the beach. On the first day after the ban was imposed, he watched *Odyssey II* and a few of the other boats lift their gear and depart for the east and west coasts. The week ended without incident and for the girls the holidays had begun – they were over the moon with excitement. They joined their Papa for the big adventure on Saturday afternoon, landing his week's take with Nelson at the big shed. Nelson and the boys all had one question for him – 'How're things out there?' Fine, so far. Not a peep from anyone. None of them had heard a word, either. It was the same chatting with Joe at The Heathbank. He hadn't heard a thing. That was good news. Only a small group of people knew what Norrie had decided, a loyal band of individuals who would not say a peep. But, at some point, word could very well dribble out. Someone was bound to spy him on the beach, a question would be asked, and who knew what would happen next. But so far, so good. That evening the girls enjoyed the fantastic tale of the greatest cockle raker who ever lived, Tumsch Galbraith, and, as his Papa had done with him, he even managed to avoid seriously disappointing his daughters when they looked at him and said in unison, 'Papa, we thought you were the greatest cockle raker ever?' He used the same technique his Papa had used and thus Violet and Sofia seemed quite pleased that their Papa wasn't even as low as the second greatest cockle raker in history, but 'first and a third'. Sunday turned out to be a difficult day for Samantha and Norrie as they had an enormous hurdle to clear trying to explain to two tremendously disappointed and tearful young girls why they wouldn't be able to cockle rake with their Papa. After arriving back from church they had hurried in and excitedly rushed out of the Nissen hut, with their little pails and rakes in hand, asking Papa how soon would they be leaving for the beach. Well, the whole episode almost brought Samantha and Norrie to tears. Sofia and Violet could not understand, and only after a six-hour adventure along the west side to look for buoys, did the wound start to heal. Norrie and Samantha knew that they had their work cut out for them keeping the girls occupied for the next few months.

The first sign of trouble came strolling along the beach the following Monday morning. It was Constable Currie.

'Hiya Norrie.'

'Morning Callie.'

'How're things?'

'All right, you?'

'Aye, just fine Norrie, just fine.'

'Lovely morning, eh?'

'Aye, that it is, Norrie, that it is.'

Norrie kept on raking.

'Norrie, perhaps you haven't heard?' By this time Patches and Sailor had spied the Constable. They came trotting over and he gave them a pet.

'Heard – what's that?'

'Norrie, the SAC ban. It includes the Traigh. There's not supposed to be any activity in the area. That includes the harvesting of cockles.'

Norrie stopped raking, propping an elbow on the top of the rake. He was almost done for the day anyway. He liked Constable Currie. He had been good to him many years ago.

Norrie didn't want to put him in an awkward position. Yet, he was not going to quit altogether. But for that day he would. He was curious as to who had nudged the Constable along the beach to have a word with him. Norrie knew well that Callie would not have come of his own volition for what he considered to be a petty affair. But when asked, he would do his duty.

Norrie hesitated, then enquired, 'Who was it?'

'Norrie, you know I can't tell you.'

'Aye, I understand.' He was quite certain Mizz Fizzlezwit or one of her acolytes was responsible. *I should have known!*

'It's just a warning this time, Norrie.'

'Aye, all right.'

'Good day, then,' Constable Currie replied and petted Patches and Sailor before turning and walking away.

Norrie had hoped for a longer stretch of time without something like this happening. It hadn't even been a week. He cursed Mz. Fizzlezwit and her lot. Not a word was mentioned that evening to Samantha as he knew it would upset her. The next day he would rake on the other side of Orosay. It was completely out of view from the road that wrapped around the Traigh Mhor. For someone to see him they would have to go all the way to the north end to do so. Someone would have to go out of their way and be actively searching for him, to do so. He would find out soon enough what the story was.

Tuesday passed without incident, as did Wednesday and Thursday. Early afternoon on the Friday, as Norrie was finishing up for the day and the tide was nudging him home, the second sign of trouble came strolling along the beach. It was Constable Currie again.

'Norrie, how's things?'

'Aye, all right, and you?'

'Aye, just fine Norrie, just fine.'

'Not a bad day eh?'

'Aye, it's grand.'

Patches and Sailor came trotting over and received the obligatory petting.

'Norrie.' Constable Currie looked over Norrie's shoulder to the line of mesh bags, the tops of which were just visible in the rising tide. 'Those wouldn't happen to be cockles, would they?'

It was five days' worth of raking. Norrie had no excuse planned or elaborate lie ready on the tip of his tongue. The truth was, he was simply going out and doing what he was meant to be doing – toiling by the tides. He was not about to deceive Constable Currie. And for a moment he felt sick about what might come of his week's catch.

'Aye.'

Constable Currie had a manila envelope in a hand. 'I've been receiving one of these every day this week, Norrie. Do you want to know what's in it?'

Norrie didn't have to think too hard to venture a guess.

'They're photos of you, Norrie, out here, raking. Every day.'

'Aye?'

'Aye, that's right, Norrie.'

He had made it through another week. He had a decent landing to take to Nelson the following day. All he cared about at that point was the landing and his routine. He dared not think of what might happen, or how he might react.

'You've gotta stop, Norrie. I can't keep these people at bay forever. If I don't do something, they will go up the chain – and, Norrie, let me be clear here, I don't want to see anyone from Lewis or Skye or Inverness, coming here to deal with you. Do you understand?'

Norrie nodded. 'Aye.'

Constable Currie pulled a black leather notebook from a pocket. He flipped a few pages, scribbled for a minute, then handed Norrie his copy.

'It's a £100 fine for the first offence. In breach of the SAC ban. I'm sorry, I have to give you this.' He glanced one more time at the row of bags in the tide. 'Good day, Norrie.' Patches and Sailor were demanding one more pet before he turned and walked away.

*

He couldn't not tell Samantha that evening. At least he now knew what the consequences were.

'It's just a £100.'

'A £100 is a lot of money.'

'I know it is. I'll just have to rake even more.'

'Aye, Norrie, and that £100 is for the first offence. What do you think the penalty is for the second or third offence?'

'I don't know.' Norrie didn't want to think about it.

'It's probably at least double, if not triple. You could end up in jail.'

Again, Norrie did not like to think too much about these things – he had simply resolved to keep doing what his family had been doing since great x eight grandpa Cloon had made the great discovery.

'He had photos?'

'Aye.'

'Would Mz Fizzlezwit go to that length?'

Norrie shrugged. Mz Fizzlezwit was capable of anything. 'Who knows? Perhaps the MEO have their own people lurking about. This time of year, with all the visitors, it's easy to blend in.'

'Speaking of visitors, Norrie. We've got your sisters coming in a week's time. This place is going to be absolutely heaving with bodies, and your Mum and company. Why don't you just – I don't know, pretend like it's an extended holiday. Take the next four weeks off and then we'll see. You've made it through almost two full weeks with the ban imposed. You landed last Saturday, and thank God, it seems as though Callie doesn't mind you landing this week's catch tomorrow. And, hey, maybe whoever was taking the photos, well, they'll see that you're nowhere to be seen for the next few weeks and they'll stop their spying. And in four weeks you can head back out and see how things go – and that way, too, you'll take the heat off Callie. He'll appreciate you doing your part, you know, if he doesn't have to write you another ticket for a little while, well, I am sure he will do all he can to treat you favourably...but Norrie, if you keep flouting the law? I don't know, I don't like to think about it.'

Norrie didn't either and that's precisely why he chose not to think about it.

'Come here, honey, I've got something in mind for you.'

Ch 44

Operation Greanamul

'Gentlemen, gentlemen, good to see you again.'

'Sit, sit, Alan, no reason to be so formal. We're all friends here.'

Seeing as it was a pleasant afternoon Remy proposed they meet on the welcoming patio of Logie Baird's Bar, in the old Bank Hotel halfway up the Royal Mile (Remy had also called in advance and their drinks order had been waiting for them).

'Alan, did you know, the man this bar is named after – well, it says here he invented the TV?' Moses had a guidebook in his hand. 'Well, well, I'll be damned...and look, it says here a man named Dunlop invented the tyre....and this one fella came up with penicillin, and another one, the bolt-action rifle. Doggone it, even the founder of the US Navy came from over here, and that's just for starters...'

'You will have to forgive our friend here,' Foo said, shaking his head. 'He has been going on and on all day about what ideas, inventions, movements, milestones, etcetera have poured out into the world from these shores. I wish I had never bought him that book.'

'Hey, come on now.' Remy put the book down.

'Remy thought everything worthwhile was invented in Austin,' Achmed explained. 'And that Adam Smith was born in a barn in Amarillo.'

'Now, now, that ain't true. And I do know about Adam Smith, and his pin factory or whatever it was. I am a businessman after all. Not that I've read A Wealth of Nations from cover to cover...'

'If I may, Remy?' Foo interrupted.

'Why of course, Foo, anytime old friend,' Remy replied.

'Alan, history lesson aside, the important thing is that we trust one another. You understand trust, Alan? Proper one hundred percent trust?'

'Uh – aye.' Alan, curiously, felt like he was being tested again.

'That is good, Alan. Very good.'

'Hey, Foo, why don't you do the honours?' Remy said, leaving talk of history behind them.

'Alan, we brought you something,' Foo announced formally whilst reaching under his robe. 'Here, this for you.'

'Well, well, thank you – I don't know what to say...' his voice trailed off as his brain began computing what exactly he was being handed. *My goodness me, what is this?*

'Alan, that there is a book,' Remy said in a dead serious tone. 'It ain't just any book, though.'

Aye, I can see that.

He automatically opened it and a – *my goodness me? What on earth?* – it actually was The Earth. A sphere of the world rose from inside the covers.

Again, quite involuntarily, a hand went to a small lever along the side of the page. He gave it a little pull and the world turned.

'Alan, it's a pop-up picture book.'

'I – I don't know what to say.'

'You don't have to say anything. Just read.'

He flipped one colourful page after another. On one page he pulled a lever and a suited man rose from the flat pack position, slid to the right, his left arm rising, holding what looked like a...

'That is a financial analyst reviewing data concerning "asset backed securities" and CDSs...that's "credit default swaps."'

Alan tried to hide his befuddlement.

'Alan, what do you know about the world's capital and bond markets? It's derivative markets? Currency exchange markets?'

'Aye, well, I do have a few investments,' Alan started, nervously.

'Relax, Alan,' Achmed reassured him. 'We are not testing you. We know what you know, and we know it is not very much. Do not forget we know everything about you and one of those things is how you struggled with that course in university. Praise be to Allah, but only he knows how you managed to get through it. But that is all right. What is explained in that book – in simple terms – is everything you need to know about these matters.'

'Alan, hey,' Moses added. 'Don't be insulted or nothing. Hell, only one person at this table knows – as in properly understands – the big, bad, world of international finance, and that man is Foo.'

'Alan, let me tell you first rule when analysing all that data out there,' Foo began. 'It is, obviously, all human made. Human derived. Human concocted. Human influenced. But, Alan, do not forget, *ever forget*, it is also often driven, motivated, by greed and sometimes fear. It is human distorted.'

Remy piped up, 'Don't look so confused, Alan. All he's saying is when you tread into these markets you better be careful.'

'Sorry, but I'm not quite sure...'

'Alan, this is what we are all about – well, partially about – and this is what we seek to influence, just a little bit more. Specifically, how to correct the quote unquote "in-corrections". This is what our Think Tank on Greanamul is going to be thinking a whole lot deeper about...'

'May I ask?'

'Shoot Alan.'

'Why build a Think Tank out on a small island? Wouldn't you rather it be in – well, who knows, Frankfurt? Singapore?' Alan shrugged. 'Back home in Austin?'

The question made Remy, Foo, and Achmed chuckle.

'Let me explain, Alan,' Achmed said, leaning forward. 'It is simple. Out there on Greanamul they will be more focused. In big fancy cosmopolitan cities, everyone gets lured into the nightlife and that's all they end up thinking about – having a good time. On Greanamul, they will be as focused as a man or woman can get.'

'I see, I see.'

'There's more to it though, Alan. Here, flip a few pages.'

Alan did as he was told. *My goodness, what's all this?*

'That, Alan, is where your lot, your lot meaning "politicians", get entangled in the whole affair.'

Alan moved a lever and three smiling paper people moved their arms towards a ballot box.

'That other lever there, Alan, you can make them slide back and forth. Pretty neat, huh? But that's not the important bit, what you need to pay attention to are the depictions behind the people.'

What on earth?

'Alan, I have told you before, this half mad, half beautiful, half unstable, half crazy, half optimistic world, needs more stability, more continuity, more synchronicity. You lot have an enormous responsibility, and funnily enough, for all the "in-corrections" in the world of finance, there are enormous lessons for politicians to start learning from the business world. This is a sensitive one, so let's just leave it all alone for now. We just wanted to give you that there book so you don't have to sit here and listen to us explain it all the time. It's there for you to read at your leisure. And in giving you a copy of that most treasured asset, we are saying, Alan,' Remy winked and continued, 'Hey, we trust you. We believe in you. We are sharing with you what lies behind the front, the façade. The resort on the beach is one thing, and it will provide a lot of jobs and bring in visitors, but that's just the fun, entertaining part of our businesses. What will go down on Greanamul is the serious stuff.'

Foo added, 'It is about what I learned from my old master, my teacher, the man who rescued me from the streets, my adoptive father – who raised me as if I were his own blood. May his soul rest in peace, for he is no longer with us on this earth. It is about, Alan, the *long view* and the improvement of the whole world.'

Ch 45

Covert Cockle Raking

'Have you ever cockle raked at night before, Papa?'

'Hm, let me think here, it's been a few years.'

'How come you are now, Papa?'

'Well, hmm, that will give me lots of time during the day to go on some big adventures with you. Isn't that a good idea?'

'I guess, Papa.' Sofia inquisitively continued. 'But I don't know why we can't go cockle raking with you during the day. We promise to be good and not bother you too much. We've got Patches and Sailor here to play with.'

'I know, honey, I know. It's just not a good time right now. The council are doing some tests and they're looking at moving the runway a little bit and there's supposed to be a big monster hiding in the dunes looking for little girls...'

'Papa!'

'Okay, sorry. There's no big monster. I promise you, it won't be too long 'til things are back to normal.'

'I hope so, Papa.'

'So do I sweetheart.' *So do I.*

'I can't go the whole summer without going cockle raking with you, Papa, I really can't.'

'For now, let's just think of all the fun things we'll be doing this week, eh? We've got – how many beaches do we have here? We've got so many beaches in every direction, and the weather is supposed to be lovely this week and we can go up Heavel as many times as you like, and then even stop in at the nice ice cream lady's place on the way up, and maybe we'll even go across to Vatersay and say hi to the Vatersay cows – I think they moo a little bit differently from Floonay cows, what do you think?'

'Papa, the cows don't moo any different!'

'No? What about the sheep – they definitely bahaha differently, don't they?'

Sofia and Violet looked at one another. *Did they?*

'You know when you hear a Mama sheep bahahaing and then you hear her little lamb bahahaing?'

The girls nodded.

'They all sound just the same, don't they? To us, that is. All those Mama sheep all looking the same, white and woolly – or like Mr Magee's black sheep, black and woolly and they all sound the same, bahahaing away, but all those little lambs can tell the difference in their Mamas' bahahaing and the Mamas can tell the difference in the little lambs' bahahaing, so I think it stands to reason that Vatersay sheep sound different to Floonay's sheep – and the same probably is true with all the mooing cows.' Norrie shrugged. 'Next time you're visiting Idaho, you ask Grandpa Hank to take you to see some sheep and cows and listen very carefully to what they sound like – I bet you they'll be totally different.'

'Oh! Grandpa Hank will be here soon! I'll ask him then what they sound like. He'll know.'

'I'm sure he will. In the meantime, why don't you go and scrub those hands before dinner. You two look like you haven't bathed in a week.'

‘It was Patches’ and Sailor’s fault. We had to follow them. We ended up in that boggy bit over behind the big rock.’

‘You just be careful of all those boggy bits, okay? Little girls can get into trouble if they're not careful. I'm serious. If Patches and Sailor run into any more bogs, you are not to follow them. You wait for them to come back. Or you call to them, you know they'll come to you when you tell them to.’

‘Sorry, Papa.’

‘That's okay sweetheart. Go on now, I'll be in in a second. Your Mama's probably wondering where you both are.’

It was a pleasant Sunday evening, and under normal circumstances they would be having a barbecue and the occasional visitor would be stopping by, but circumstances were no longer normal. Norrie would be heading to work late that evening, which did not lend itself to entertaining beforehand. With the tide shifting approximately an hour every day, Norrie reckoned he could take advantage of all the hours of darkness the forthcoming week had to offer. Not that there were that many 'hours of darkness' at such a northern latitude. It did not get dark until midnight, and even then, it was more of a dark dusk, and by 4 am it might as well be midday. He had to take advantage of the few hours available. He would continue to earn a wage, but most importantly, he was not quitting. He was staying in rhythm, keeping in sync with the tides of the Earth.

A cool north breeze was Norrie's only night-time companion. Patches and Sailor had been left in the Nissen hut to rest, very much against their wishes. He'd taken a small risk and struck out across the beach in the dying light of dusk. If he'd waited until it was the darkest time of the night, then no sooner would he be planting his rake, than the sun would be rising. It was quiet and peaceful, and he quickly settled into his nighttime routine. It just didn't last long enough. As he caught the first sign of the glow preceding the rising sun he raked a little faster and had to draw on all his skills to ensure a decent night's take. Even the tide seemed to beckon to him, 'Don't leave just yet, there's more right here. And here. And over there, too.' But, alas, with the sun impatiently rising to its full glory, Norrie was forced to make a quick exit from the beach. Safely back on the croft, he put his rake away in the Nissen hut, said a quick hello to two excited canines and made for his bed where his wife waited, not without a little uneasiness.

The following night was much the same; quiet, peaceful, a light breeze, the tide lapping at his feet. A decent catch, considering the time spent raking. Again, dawn came far too soon and he was forced to make a hasty retreat. The following night he received a surprise visit. No sooner had the light of the torches caught his eye did he hear the hushed guilty voices.

'What on earth are you two doing out here?'

'I'm sorry Papa, we wanted to cockle rake with you.'

Sofia and Violet had their little rakes and buckets in hand.

Norrie whispered in a quiet version of furious, 'Girls, you shouldn't have come down. That was extremely dangerous. Anything could have happened!'

'Sorry, Papa.'

'I'm sorry, too.'

Norrie was of two minds. It was either take them straight up to the house and put them back to bed or let them stay.

'Okay girls, you can stay here with me, but this is my only warning, you will never come out at night again. Do you understand?'

They nodded – slowly, deliberately.

'If you ever do this again, I am warning you, there will be no more cockle raking, period – during the day or anytime. Understand? You do not leave your rooms in the middle of the night like that, unless to use the bathroom – that's the only time. Okay?'

More nods.

And before they started to cry, he said, 'All right, let's get to work then – that's a good spot right there, and just a little over there, too. That's it, go on.'

Once again, the night lasted not nearly long enough. Before he knew where he was Norrie was beating a hasty retreat with two unwitting co-conspirators in tow.

After quietly tucking in the two excited cockle rakers and warning them not to get out of bed until the small hand was at least at the nine, Norrie brewed a cup of tea before finally making his way to bed. Samantha stirred as he slipped under the covers and sleepily asked how his night was. 'Fine, sweetheart, just fine.'

The fourth night of starlit cockle raking brought an even bigger surprise.

'I caught them trying to sneak out.'

'Aye?'

'They were on the verge of tears. I was furious – at first. Then I thought, "why not?" I'll bring them out myself.' Samantha shrugged in the shadows. 'It's the summer and this is Floonay after all, not Sao Paulo's city centre.'

And so it would be that all four MacKinnons spent the remaining hours of the night on the Traigh Mhor. Samantha, wrapped in a blanket, was in charge of the torch and thermos of tea. Patches and Sailor were there too, perpetually excited, as Sofia and Violet tried their best to emulate their Papa and make him proud.

They beat a hasty retreat as the sun broke across the horizon.

Before setting out on the fifth night Norrie implored Samantha, 'Please, try and keep them in tonight. We've made it through the week, but the tides are turning quickly. I've got to make tonight count and squeeze out as much as I can for the landing tomorrow. Ah, I know – if they start to kick up a fuss tell them that there is no way they will be awake and in shape for the big adventure to Nelson's shed tomorrow, okay? There's no way they'll risk missing that.'

The final night of starlit cockling brought the biggest – and oddest – surprise of them all. And it was a good thing that Samantha had managed to keep their daughters focused on Saturday's big adventure, because if they had been out with their Papa and witnessed what he had, they would have jumped with terror and might have been too frightened to ever venture back again on to the big beach, whether the sun was up or down. They knew the story. They'd seen the picture – the pictures – they'd heeded the warnings: don't ever, ever, ever, cockle rake like that man in the picture, lest you go 'you know what'. 'You see all those frantic, squiggly lines, that tangly mess there? That's not the work of a normal brain.' The story had half frightened the girls, and Norrie had even sanitised and glossed over things, as well as tried to make some bits humorous, but even through all that, Sofia and Violet keenly sensed something ominous in the terrible tale. They could not wait to move on to the next story. 'Make it a funny one, Papa, a really funny one. No more with that man in it.'

It was Walter Wellington.

And there he was, cockle raking in the shadows of the night, on the Traigh Mhor.

Norrie was sure of it.

Who else would be out in the middle of the night moving the way that man was moving, shuffling one moment, then darting the next, in and out of the shadows cast by the light of the moon? Norrie had never met the man. Not many had. When it was said he was a recluse, it was a fact. When it was said he was half-mad, well, Norrie only had the stories in the Coquilleuous Rakkeronuous Almenikhiaka to go by. It was written that the man ventured down onto the beach only when he thought he was alone, late at night, or went to some secret spot, and did so only to try to tame his brain. Well, as Norrie spied the man in the distance, darting and hopping and zig-zagging all about, raking for a second here, or ten seconds there, doing acrobatics – and – heaven's sake, *cartwheels,* in the air – *what is that man doing?* He didn't look like he was doing a very good job of taming anything. Norrie frowned, and was a little unnerved being so close to such an anomaly of nature. Norrie was certainly no fan of linear cockle raking, having a great appreciation for the interconnecting ovals and the sweep and even the wiggle, but what that shadowy character was doing in the distance was in a category all its own. The man was like a fizz-bomb spinning out of control.

I've only got a few hours left till sun up. Get back to work here. Never mind him. If he cartwheels his way over here, I've got this trusty rake to fend him off.

Norrie put his head down and tried to ignore the figure flitting about on the moonlit beach. It was difficult at first to get his mind off that most curious man, but eventually, *mostly,* he did. One stroke of the rake after another turned into a dozen strokes, which soon turned into a dozen dozen and the night fairly moved along. Before he knew it, Norrie was staring at the tip of the rising sun. Dawn was spilling out over the island, his cover evaporating. It was time to make his last hasty retreat of the week. He'd made it another week. *Excellent.* Norrie took a last glance around. *Hmm?* Walter Wellington seemed to have cartwheeled himself off the face of the map for he was no longer anywhere to be seen.

Norrie moved swiftly along the shoreline, trying his best not to look conspicuous, though that was proving difficult on a wide-open beach. He was soon climbing the rocky embankment that bordered his croft when he was taken completely by surprise. The figure, sitting amongst the rocks, had blended in with the long, charcoal grey coat he was wearing.

The man was sipping from a cup, a thermos at his side.

Who is that?

'Care for a cuppa?' The man smiled.

'That's – all right.'

'You look confused.'

'Sorry, no.'

'I'm not sitting on your rock, am I? My apologies if I am, I can move over here a bit.'

'No, no. That's okay, that's not my rock.'

The man settled back down. 'Ah, well, that's good. Lovely morning, eh?'

'Aye, yes. Yes it is.'

'We've had quite a few this year.'

'Aye, aye, it has been. Some year.' *Could it be?*

The accent was unmistakeably from somewhere beyond the shores of Floonay, but where exactly? Norrie hadn't a clue. Could be a tourist out for an early morning walk. Could be anyone. But, there was something about the man – something strikingly familiar.

'I'm sorry, terribly rude of me. I should have introduced myself. I'm Walter, Walter Wellington.' A hand went out.

Indeed, indeed you – are?

'You seem a little surprised.' His hand was still extended.

'Aye, no, sorry. Norrie MacKinnon.' He shook the man's hand. He didn't look quite as asymmetrical as the man pictured in the Coquilleuous Rakkeronuous Almenikhiaka, but there were similarities. A little eccentric? Maybe. And there was – whatever it was he had witnessed under the light of the moon just a few short hours ago?

'You still look puzzled.'

'You'll have to excuse me.'

'You're probably wondering if that was me out there on the beach.'

Norrie, at a loss, tried not to show his bewilderment. 'Aye?'

The man, Walter, sipped his tea, as calm and content as could be. He said, 'I must admit, that was me.' He didn't elaborate.

Norrie, cautiously, not sure what to say, but feeling obligated to ask. 'What – exactly...'

Walter Wellington saved him the discomfort. He laughed. 'It's my most recent works, they're driving me round the bend. I come down here to let off some steam, relax, reconnect with the world around me – or, put it this way, just to get out of the house, you know?'

Norrie hesitated. 'Aye?' *I guess.*

'I take it you *might* know of me?'

A pause, 'Aye. I think.'

Walter smiled. 'I thought so.'

Norrie was at a loss for words.

Walter smiled. 'I've seen the picture – in that big almanac of yours. Your grandfather, Hector, showed it to me. He was the one who drew it, you know. I thought it was a little unfair and told him as much. But that's all right, we had a good laugh about the whole thing.'

Norrie was thrown.

'I met him down here, Norrie, about five years after I had started coming here – though he'd already spied me doing my thing. He offered to change the picture a bit, but I told him to leave it the way it was...you sure you don't want a cuppa, there's a spare cup here?'

'Aye, all right.'

'I knew your father, too.'

Norrie shot him a look that had a physical impact.

'Sorry, I should say I met your father, it was just a few times – down here. I take it he never told you – judging by the way you're looking at me now. Perhaps I should not have mentioned that. My apologies.' He paused before continuing, 'They were good men. They left this place too young – and your brothers – or, rather, this "place" let them go too soon. Sorry, you don't need me to tell you that. Perhaps I am speaking out of turn.'

'Perhaps you are.'

'You'll have to forgive me. I don't get out much. Conversing with other humans is not my forte.'

'That's all right.' Reconciling fizz-bomb Walter with measured talking Walter was proving difficult for Norrie.

'I'm, as you can tell, Norrie, on the older side of life. I've been coming to Floonay for sixty-odd years. Stumbled across the place really. After I'd sold my first painting, I decided to go on a sort of treasure hunt for a nice remote spot, some place that would afford me the solitude and inspiration I needed – I still need – to ply my trade, and as luck would have it, I ended up on a ferry that brought me here, and a chance meeting in Castlebay guided me past Grean and Cleit, and the rest is history.'

He continued, 'You might be wondering why I'm telling you this. To tell you the truth, I'm not really sure. But to tell you even more of a truth, I think I really do. I might be a recluse, but I do keep a finger on the pulse of the world. I keep up with what's going on. I know, Norrie, your people, specifically your father's line of MacKinnons, have been working these shores for generations. Archie, all those years ago. He discovered something quite remarkable along this shore. It's a shame what has happened recently. It's more than a shame. It must be very difficult to have that taken from you. But you are out here, so you don't lack a defiant spirit. That is a good thing. Well, well, would you look at that sun...it's well on its way up. I should probably get moving here. By the way, I've seen you over there on the west side, with your family – walking along the beaches – you'll have to pardon me, I've a big telescope – you know my house – I've quite a vantage point from there. Any time you're in the neighbourhood do feel free to stop in for a visit.'

Ch 46

Just a Small Matter

They liked the patio at Logie Baird's Bar, so that was the rendezvous point once again. Achmed thought he'd finally beaten Remy to paying for a round but as he tried handing over a few notes to the smiling waitress she politely declined, noting that their bill had been prepaid.

'I called in again. Sorry, boys,' Remy explained with a chuckle.

'That breaking rules,' Foo chided his friend.

'What rules?'

Foo and Achmed shared a disappointed look.

'One of these days, Remy.'

'Don't worry about it, boys – hmm, my, this is a doggone tasty pint. Perfect for a sunny, summer afternoon.'

'I must say, this beer does complement the day well, hmm, very well,' Foo remarked. 'I will have to see if this brand is available in Shanghai.'

Achmed the Thoughtful, sipped his beer and directed his attention to MSP Trout. 'Alan, if what we have planned weren't so evolutionary, some might call it revolutionary. But it is not. Or,' he looked around the table and smiled – Moses and Confucius smiled, too. Alan looked bewildered. 'Or, perhaps it is? Call it what you like. The one thing we know, what we have planned – it is the way of the future. But there is much work to be done, many details to sort out – that is, as they say, where the devil resides.'

'Indeed it is, Achmed, indeed it is,' Foo agreed. 'Alan, do not look so lost, and if you have read the bits in the book about what we have planned for your lot, do not worry too much – by the time that all of that is happening, I am sure you will be well out of politics. What we have planned will take some convincing, but, my friend, it will happen, it is just a matter of time. More urgently is how we might influence, shift, alter, the state of the world's finances. This is no easy feat, trust us. It is a wicked, wild, messy place – the global markets. Understanding it, controlling it, influencing it, taming it where necessary...this is no small matter. It is a bit like trying to control a typhoon, or as you call here, a force 10, 11, 12, off the charts, gale.'

'Or like lassoing a Texas twister tearing through a trailer park,' Remy added. 'Not easy at all.'

'My friends, some things in life are not meant to be easy, but are necessary,' Achmed the Thoughtful, reminded them.

'Too true, Achmed, too true.' Dr Foo turned his attention back to the befuddled politician, 'Alan, let me explain something here – what we are up against, it is not a matter of the size of the mess, but it is its tricky nature. Alan, in case you didn't know, the world of accountancy and high finance? To put it plainly, it contains more supernatural phenomena than a Star Wars movie. Contains more creativity than Peter Pan and Alice in Wonderland combined. The hidden places and murky spaces. This means that, and that is not what it seeMs The literary world and the arts? They have nothing on the creative magic acts that occur in finance and accountancy. Black and white and neat little boxes no longer exist. Perhaps they never did.'

Alan's mind drifted to his university courses. *Of course, of course, just like in economics, not to mention politics. There's sorcery there, too. And so there is in the financial and accounting worlds? It's the perfect place to operate, but, aye, it is all a little confusing, no doubting that. Confusing, but perfect. Perfectly confusing. One must be careful.* As for the philosophy part of his university courses, the meaning of it all, he steered well clear of thinking about all that. That was dangerous territory. The world was tricky enough as it is.

'He ain't fibbing, Alan,' Remy felt the need to add.

Foo continued, 'Make no mistake, there is a good side to all that creativity, but there is also a messy dark side to it all. So sad. And when it leads to human suffering, it becomes *our* problem. It is our moral duty to address these matters – urgently. And with a clarity of vision.'

'A clarity of vision, Alan,' Achmed repeated.

'A clarity of vision, Alan,' Remy echoed. There was a twinkle in his eyes as blue as a Texas sky. 'Like the crystal-clear vision that I saw when I found the Prince of Peace in an old, rotting mineshaft, me lying there half-dead – I've not told you that story, Alan – some other time. He lifted me out of that place and said, "Remy, I have work for you. It will not be easy, but you must fight hard and not give up" – well, it was along those lines anyway.'

'And it is the same vision that the Prophet bestowed upon me, Alan. Many years ago, as I wandered the desert – he guided me and he said, "Achmed, prepare yourself. I am giving you a great gift. Nurture that gift. You learn how to use it and make something useful happen with the days that you walk this earth" – those were, more or less, the words he whispered to me.'

'We know you don't believe, Alan, we understand.' Dr Foo sipped his beer. 'Perhaps you will come to understand this 'struggle' in your own way...Alan, you still look confused, but you also look like you've something to say? Please – feel free to speak, any time you like.'

Alan hesitated. 'It's nothing really, just a small matter.'

'Oh ho. Back in Shanghai, when someone says, "just a small matter", it usually means something different.'

'Ach, it's nothing, shouldn't be anyway.'

'Alan?'

Curiosity all around.

'I shouldn't have said a word – sorry...'

'Do tell, old boy, do tell.'

'Let me assure you gentlemen, that it should not – it will not be a problem. Ridiculous to even think it could pose a problem.'

Achmed leaned forward, 'Are you going to tell us what *this* is all about?'

'Aye, aye – sorry. It's not a surprise really. When you think about it.'

The three wise men were waiting, a little impatiently.

'My sources are telling me that there is one individual who has been defying the ban.'

Remy, Foo, and Achmed exchanged looks.

'Please, do go on, Alan.'

'After the ban was activated there was, naturally, a fair bit of grumbling. To be expected.' Nods all around. *Of course, of course.* 'But the fishermen who had gear in the Sound did dutifully shift everything, either east into the Minch or out to the west side. However – there was, there is, one man who has refused to quit.'

The three amigos collectively thought, *And?*

Alan, a little embarrassed, continued, 'It's nothing. The laws in place will take care of this.'

Achmed the Interested, queried, 'Refused to quit? Quit what exactly?' *You just said all the fishermen shifted their gear.*

Alan found the whole thing a bit ridiculous. He'd never heard of such an occupation before. He shrugged. 'It's just this fellow on the beach. He's a harvester of shellfish. One type in particular. Cockles, apparently. He's a, er, cockle raker.' *Er, that's it – really.*

'Ah, coquilles! Cockles – hmm. My goodness, they are so scrumptious!'

'Too true, Achmed, too true. The mention of cockles has me all excited.'

Remy, not to be left out, declared, 'Cockles, huh? Don't think I've ever had me any before, but if they're at all like my favourite shellfish, that bein' oysters, well, I bet you they're pretty doggone good.'

Alan, the Befuddled, looked around the table: Moses, Confucius, and one happy Sufi Mystic, did not seem concerned in the least. *Of course it was nothing. Ridiculous. Shouldn't have said a word. But there was just one thing.*

'As I said, gentlemen, the laws on the books will take care of this. He's already been fined for his first offence, for not quitting, and he doesn't know it yet, but will be receiving a second fine tomorrow, for breaking the law again this past week. The fines will only increase, and of course, there will be the threat – and eventually, if he doesn't quit – a custodial sentence. My one concern is just this – that if too much of a fuss is kicked up and the community rallies around him and they demand a public consultation on the whole matter...well, with the evidence and all, we don't want it scrutinised too much.'

'Alan, Alan, it is good to be wary, but I think you are worrying a little too much. The data our scientists have conjured up, and the MEO have on hand, is perfectly inauthentically, authentic,' Remy said with a wink.

'Aye, of course, of course. It's just, in my political calculation, it would be best if this would go away as soon as possible. The less news about it the better. Everyone will forget and we – you – can proceed without further disturbance.'

'That would be ideal, Alan, old boy. But this ain't an ideal world. Beautiful? A lot of the time. Tragic, at other times. Of course, there's hope. Plenty of hope. But as for ideal? Well, that's one thing that we can't always count on, Alan. Son of a doggone gun, you're a politician, you ought to know that. We plan for these things, though – you pick up what I'm layin' down? Our people, and, naturally, the MEO – the government – can handle a public consultation. Certainly, it would be best if that didn't happen and this fellow found himself another occupation.'

Achmed the Illuminated, added, 'I am sure that beach is not the only one in the world suitable for cockle raking. He will just have to find another beach.'

Nods of assent all around.

*

Sofia and Violet were oblivious to the serious nature of Papa's and Constable Currie's conversation at Northbay bridge.

'Norrie, I'm sorry, I have to fine you. There is nothing I can do about it.'

Norrie felt sick. The fine was £300. £100 he could handle. £300 was a different matter, and especially when the week's take wasn't quite what he'd earn had he been raking full shifts every day. It made a considerable dent in his wages.

'For God's sake, Callie, who the hell would go to that length, taking photos at night?'

Callie sighed. 'I don't know. What I know is simply that I am receiving them. "On high" is involved. It is out of my hands. I'm sorry.'

Norrie didn't know what else to say. The knot tightened. *300 quid?! This isn't right.* He looked at the bags of cockles piled high in the wheelbarrow.

'How long did you think you could keep this up?'

'Until the ban is lifted.'

'That could be a very long time.'

'Maybe not.'

'Aye, maybe not. But it just might, Norrie, and in the meantime you are breaking the law.'

'This whole thing is a bloody farce.'

'It might be, but rules are rules, the law is the law...'

'To hell with the law.'

'Norrie, you've got to stop. There must be something else you can do until things are resolved with the MEO. People everywhere are forced to make changes. Circumstances dictate.'

Norrie had nothing else to say. He took the proffered ticket and bid Callie a good day.

'Why don't you two run ahead to the shed. Take Patches and Sailor with you. And watch the traffic.'

Norrie pushed the cockle laden wheelbarrow along. The weight of his thoughts slowed his pace. *What am I to do? I cannot quit. This is all I know. But it is not just that...* Looking east across the bay, most of the moorings were empty. Two of the larger trawling boats were tied up at the pier behind the fish factory, and by the slip he spied two boats he knew well: Shamrock and Odyssey II. They were tied up, also landing their catch for the week. *If only I could do that. Perhaps, perhaps I could make a change. I cannot! And anyway, my people have been cockle raking for eight, now nine, generations. This is what I was destined to do. And that's all there is to it. With any luck the ban will be lifted sooner rather than later. In the meantime – I will do what I have to do to carry on.*

News spread around Nelson's shed about what had happened, and it was like a punch in the collective gut. Every man there, at one time or another, had lost a portion of his landing, due to either a breach in a storage cage caused by wear and tear, or by the crustaceans sawing and nibbling their way to freedom.

Nelson, Norrie and a half dozen fishermen were gathered by the entrance to the big shed. If the landing was being confiscated and disposed of – in short, wasted – any one of the men would tell Norrie that his actions were a crime against the sea. But Nelson could sell the lot, as he did with the weekly shipment of cockles from the Uists. Instead, what Norrie was doing now was just plain stupid, not to mention irresponsible. He had a family to provide for.

'To be fair to Callie, he said he could have confiscated the lot.'

'Jesus, Norrie, why don't you head to Uist? The boys wouldn't charge you for the ferry fare.'

'Aye, Norrie?'

'They obviously mean business, Norrie. Leave 'em to their bloody investigation and join my crew for a while!'

He couldn't explain to anyone why he could not quit. And besides, it wasn't only because of his fear of the sea. Half was his aversion to the sea, and half was simply that toiling regularly by the tides was the only thing that kept him in rhythm with something beyond his comprehension. He didn't dwell on that for long, but he knew with a certainty that he was a part of something bigger than any one person could begin to understand. In Norrie's estimation, he was being more responsible keeping in time with the tides of Floonay, but he also understood that he had to make all the money that he could. *Whatever the fine is next, I will rake even more. And if it rises after that, I will rake that much more. I will keep raking more and more until the ban is lifted and then go back to regular raking.* Fear and rhythm. It was, for better or worse, a fifty-fifty partnership.

Ch 47

I See...the Future?

Sofia and Violet were told that it was too late to go to tri-e-ash. Mama had dinner to prepare – and no, Papa couldn't take them as Mama and Papa had something important to discuss. When Sofia heard this her eyes widened. 'Is it to do with my birthday?' she asked. 'It's only two weeks away.'

'Maybe so,' Samantha fibbed. And no, they couldn't bake a cake instead. They were to go out and play with Patches and Sailor and if they wanted, to make a little sandcastle down by the shore, but not to go too far. They departed with a chocolate biscuit in each hand.

Norrie and Samantha were alone in the kitchen. Samantha left her tea untouched. Norrie sipped a dram as he recounted the events of the day.

'Three hundred, Norrie?'

'Aye, three hundred.' Norrie handed Samantha the ticket.

'This can't continue.' It was as simple as that.

'It won't last forever.'

'What – the ban?'

'Aye.'

'Norrie, it's only been a few short weeks and you've already been fined four hundred pounds. And there's no news about the investigation even *starting.* This could – will – go on for months. Maybe longer.'

'I'll just have to rake even more.'

'And what will the next fine be?'

Norrie shrugged.

'Jesus, Norrie. It'll be at least two hundred more. Probably double again, even triple, as you are flagrantly defying the law.'

'I guess it means I better rake my socks off.'

'Norrie, this is not a joke.'

'Do I look like I'm joking.'

'Please, Norrie, you have got to be reasonable now. You, we – have bills to pay. Food to put on the table. And Sofia's birthday is just a few weeks away and I haven't bought her anything yet.'

'I'll find a way.'

'Find a way? To do what?'

'To rake as much as I can.'

'Just to give – what? Fifty, seventy, ninety percent away as a fine? It's not right, Norrie. Please.'

They had been married for almost ten years. There was now an urgency – a desperation – in Samantha's tone that Norrie had never heard before.

'Your Mum and Hank are coming in less than a week, and your sisters as well. This house is going to be teeming with people. We've got enough to see us through the month – that I am sure. Please, try taking the time off. Just give it a few days and let's see how things go. But, Norrie, my God, it's just not right for you to go down there and spend eight, ten, twelve hours raking just to give it all away. And you would have to pay tax on top of that – we would owe tax on an income you earned but had to give away. Please, Norrie, think about this – properly.'

'I have.'

'No – you haven't!'

'It's not about the money, it's...'

'Norrie, it will quickly become about the money! For God's sake, don't you see – can't you see that – *get that!*' came the exasperated reply.

Norrie sipped his dram and didn't say a word.

Samantha softened her tone. 'Norrie, I know, everyone knows, your line has been cockle raking here for eight generations. Now you are the ninth generation of cockle raking MacKinnons. That is something to be immensely proud of. And, you know, the thing is, your story, your predicament – *our* predicament, Norrie – it's a story that's been told, it *has* happened, countless times the world over, through the ages. Time marches on, things change, and people have to change. There's many a farmer's son, who, perhaps, wished he could have carried on, but the modern world pushed him into the city. There's many a stonemason's son who was forced to do the same. There were – are, countless endeavours, pursuits, careers, whatever, that people have had to give up to make ends meet, to carry on – they change with the times – because at the end of the day, they, we, all need to make a living....and the thing is, Norrie, your way of life is not even being taken from you completely – it's a temporary ban. If you want to keep raking you could head up to Uist daily – it's nice up there. I don't know why you've never been. Or *please,* just take a little time off and think about it all with a clear head.'

Apart from what he concluded was a mostly minor fear of the sea, (His fear of the sea was an inconvenience at best. Who cares? There's probably not much to see on the mainland, anyway, or in Hank's Idaho, or his brothers in law's Kenya, or any of the exotic places Samantha spoke about) there was the one other aspect, or event, that Norrie had never shared with Samantha. As much as she meant the world to him, that other event belonged in another galaxy, and to get to that memory he would have to travel into and out of a black hole (which was inconceivable). It had remained between him and Hank. The inconvenience of being confined to a beautiful island was easy to deal with. And anyway, there were lots of people in lots of places who never left clearly defined areas. Whatever. It was not that unusual. But what was not easy to deal with and quickly becomes a tricky, twisted, rubble strewn journey, is when one loses one's rhythm. When that happens things start disconnecting, fragmenting. The prism through which life is viewed, felt, experienced...becomes a distorted, curious thing. Communicating through it is close to impossible – nothing comes out right. Losing his rhythm had led Norrie to choose between one of those three things: the gun, the rope, the pills. If he hadn't swigged down that last mug of whisky, he might not have passed out before reaching out his hand...but he did, and down he went. And then Hank arrived. And now he was here with Samantha.

He could compromise, somewhat. There had been times, after all, that weather conditions were so stormy on the Traigh that no one ventured out to do anything. 'I'll take a couple of days off.' *But that's it.*

Samantha smiled. She gave Norrie a hug. 'Thanks sweetheart. Things will work out, one way or the other, I know they will.'

*

Meanwhile, way over yonder in Edinburgh, a casual walker descending along the steep trail that leads to the clifftop summit overlooking the city might take a second glance at the quartet ascending and passing by. The quartet: three robed men, (a quiet jingle coming from somewhere) and one man kitted out in adventure gear from a bygone era. *What an interesting foursome.*

‘Looks like we've gone about halfway. Doggone, this is some good exercise.’

‘Indeed, it is, Remy, but as Confucius say sometime, 'don't be fooled by winding road. It is illusion. Further to top than you think.'’

‘I do not know why, but this reminds me of my ascent to the summit of Kilimanjaro,’ Achmed observed through huffs and puffs. ‘I think I know why... (huff puff) ....as I look around....it is the view, spectacular. Different, but spectacular...come let us stop and rest...look how far Alan is falling behind.’

Alan caught up with the three and was handed a cup of orange squash.

‘Many, many thanks.’ Alan, out of breath and perspiring heavily, accepted the offering. He collapsed in a heap.

‘Are you all right, Alan?’

Through laboured breaths, Alan replied, ‘Who me – yes, yes, just fine. Think I'm dehydrated. That sun is hot. This kit is heavier than it looks. And I was out at the show with the wife last night – after party and all that...should have known better.’ After more deep breathing he held out the empty cup. ‘Is there more of that squash, by chance?’

‘Of course, Alan, of course.’ Achmed the Generous, refilled the cup and he frowned. ‘Those bottles – on your kit?’ He counted three military grade canteens.

‘I forgot to empty them.’

‘Forgot to empty them?’

‘They're full of pebbles...don't ask.’

‘I see, I see.’

‘You should have worn shorts and a t-shirt, Alan. You would have been much more comfortable.’

‘Aye, aye,’ said Alan as he huffed and puffed and began to come around. ‘How are you gentlemen faring? In all those robes, I mean.' He started emptying the canteens of their rocky contents.

'We're getting used to it, Alan,' came Remy's no-nonsense reply. 'Like the cowboys of the old days, crossing the panhandle, driving cattle under a devil-hot cloudless Texas sky, wearing leather boots and denim. Reckon they got used to it, you know, just like we are.'

Alan frowned. 'The costumes – are they really necessary, all the time? I mean, even up here?'

Dr Foo smiled. A bit out of sympathy. 'Alan, Alan. If you knew, truly knew, the ways of the world. Look around – it is even easier to spy on us up here. We have told you before. We operate in a league of hyper-competition. To be sure, more are collaborating, but the ocean, if you like, is a big place. Does that make sense? We are strong and we have allies who are also strong, but there are sharks out there waiting, and watching, and sniffing, and searching – do you understand? We must take unusual security precautions sometimes, and as this project is the most ambitious of our lives, it demands the greatest efforts to ensure things stay secret for as long as it takes. We have competitors who try to emulate us, steal our ideas. And then there are those who want only to crush us, seize power and wealth for no other reason than to seize it.'

'And it is for your benefit, Alan,' Achmed reminded him.

'Aye, Aye – I see, I see.'

'I hope you do, Alan – we – hope you do.' Confucius held out a hand to help him up. 'Come, I think we rest long enough, let us see if we can make it to the top without another break.'

A short time later the four men were standing high atop Arthur's Seat as the sun shone through the lightly scattered clouds to the east, casting its light on the city down below.

'Not a bad effort, eh boys?' Remy remarked, as proud as a boy scout after his first ascent.

'Not bad indeed, Remy, not bad at all.' Foo scanned the horizon with the keen eye of a ship's captain. 'My mentor, my father, was right, this is a special place. Alan, do you feel *elevated?*'

'Ooh, Aye, aye,' he replied through sips of squash.

'And if I had not adopted Zanzibar as my home, perhaps I would have chosen this place. I have not told you the story, Alan, of the parents I never knew. You might know, if you have done any research – it is, after all, published in my holding company's historical section, that I was raised by desert-wandering-nomads, but here, look at this.' Achmed pulled a photograph out from under his robe. 'You see this man?'

Alan looked at the picture. It was a grainy black and white photo, but the sandy uniform was unmistakable, as was the location, and the jeep he was standing beside. They were like the pictures he'd seen in many an adventure story.

'Aye?'

'I believe this is my father. This photo was found tucked in my rags...for many years I have thought of researching who he is – was...but I am not sure. There is no doubt that he came from these shores. I do not know my date or place of birth, but from what I can guess I was not born until more than a dozen years after the war.' Achmed shrugged. 'Who knows, maybe he travelled back to his love, my mother, maybe he never came back to these shores, your shores, and stayed in North Africa...it is a mystery that I am not sure I want to unravel.'

Remy interrupted with, 'But we didn't bring you up here, Alan, for a little family history, y'understand?'

Then Foo put an arm around Alan's shoulder, as a Zen master would his pupil and asked, 'Alan, look there, what you see?'

Alan sipped his orange squash, squinted, and tried to feel *elevated.* He was staring at the panorama that was Edinburgh and the communities nestled close to her. If he tried to follow a direct line, a laser, projecting from the end of Foo's finger, what was he looking at? He squinted some more – it was hard to say – he could see the Castle and the rooftops of a lot of buildings beyond. He could see Waverley Station and the rooftops of the buildings lining Princes Street. He could see the Spaghetti Bowl, also known as Holyrood. He understood enough that Foo was not merely pointing out some tourist attraction, so he ruled out naming any of the landmarks. *What is Dr Foo wanting me to see? I must try to make an impression here.*

Alan frowned, hesitated. Then he spoke. 'I see the future.' He hoped that didn't sound too ridiculous. The three wise men were poker faced.

'That a good try, Alan,' Foo said encouragingly. 'What you are seeing, as a matter of fact, is old town *and* new town. Do you see?'

Of course! You idiot!

'That okay, Alan,' Foo patted his shoulder. 'What else you *see*?'

Alan's frown deepened and he searched harder.

Foo continued, 'There, in same place.' He didn't need Alan's focus wandering off and looking for some mysterious thing on the horizon.

It could be any one of a hundred or more different things? What could he be directing my attention to?

Alan did not want to look the fool, but also felt the need to impress. *Dr Foo emphasised the old town – and – the new town. What could he have meant by that? Aha!* Alan, of course, was not without grandiosity when it came to his visions, not that any of his parliamentary peers ever paid him much attention. But these men were fellow visionaries, they would understand. He took a big leap. 'I see the old teaching the new (*like Yoda teaching Skywalker,* flashed through his mind, but he decided not to make words out of that image), and, er, vice versa...the new teaching, um, and improving – the old.' *God, that sounds utterly ridiculous.*

A few nods.

'That not too bad, Alan,' Foo replied encouragingly.

'Let's cut to the chase here, old boy,' Remy said. 'We ain't got all day to hang around up here and play guessing games. What you see in the old town is history, and a lot of it. And what you, we, see in the new town is also history. A little of it. Alan, take any subject, idea, concept, discovery...*entire* nations, in the past, have benefited from time, a lot of it. Centuries of forming, of....'

Achmed the Wise, interrupted, 'Remy, my friend, I think maybe this is much too big a subject to get into right now.'

'Yeah, you know what, I think you are right.'

'We plant the seed in your brain, Alan,' Foo added, 'the world very complex. It need more order, stability, or chaos take over. Chaos bad. Rule of law good. But for now, just enjoy the view.'

Ch 48

A Funny Odd Thing

Norrie kept his word and took a little break from cockle raking. He reflected on the longest spells he'd gone without picking up the rake. There'd probably been a dozen or fifteen times over the years that stretched a week or more. Weather conditions could deteriorate and stay deteriorated for weeks in the Outer Hebrides. It was just one of the realities of the wild Atlantic. He considered himself fortunate though, as there had been countless times when the weather had been abominable but he had been able to plant his rake, and back turned to the howling wind, make a full day's shift of it, in conditions that no sane fisherman could venture out into.

So, all the guests would be arriving in a week's time. He decided he would take five days off. There were things to do about the croft anyway, and he could tinker in the Nissen hut, but he was determined he'd be back into his regular routine before everyone arrived. With any luck, the heat would be off Constable Currie. He also decided that perhaps once the guests arrived, he would rake on alternate days. He'd rather not, as going too long with an interrupted rhythm does not feel good, but he'd give it a shot.

One day at a time right now.

He filled the days with plenty. Mending and repainting the fences, building a few new shelves in the Nissen hut, and most exciting of all – for Sofia, Violet, Patches, and Sailor, building two brand new doghouses together. There was, of course, a mandatory excursion to the beach every day. It was best to take advantage of the sun peeking through scattered clouds that seemed to be carried by gentle but steadily rising winds. Samantha was busy getting the house ready for the guests and so it fell upon Norrie to entertain the girls. Everyone was happy with the arrangement, and Samantha was especially happy to see Norrie steering clear of the Traigh. As he no longer had to follow the tide tables for work, there were a few pleasant strolls down to The Heathbank. Patches and Sailor excitedly followed, and once at the pub they'd sit outside and swap dog-gossip with whichever other canines came cruising through the neighbourhood. Inside the bar it was business as usual. Although modern technology was great, it was still better to interact person to person.

With the regulars gathered round one evening, Eddie asked Norrie a direct question that was quite unexpected. 'You ever thought of emigrating?'

'Emigrating?' *What was that?*

'Aye.'

'No. Can't say I have.'

'I've thought about it a time or two over the years.'

'Aye?'

'Aye. And with this MEO shite, well, you never know what's going to happen. Be a tough decision now, though. Too young to put my feet up and too old to start afresh doing God knows what. All I know is the sea.'

'I'd head for Canada,' Colin said, his pint halfway down his throat.

'Aye?'

'Aye. Maybe Newfoundland or Nova Scotia. A lot of our kind there.' The pint was now gone.

'There's a lot of our kind *everywhere.*'

'Aye, aye, but there's just something about Canada...and the Gaelic is spoken in a few places.'

Ronnie asked Joe across the bar, 'Where would you head, Joe?'

Joe frowned. You could see in his eyes he was travelling a long way. Finally, the thought returned, 'Australia.'

'Aye? Why's that?'

'I'd like to learn how to ride a kangaroo.'

'I don't think kangaroos can be – how're you going to get the saddle on it?' Colin looked at the barman a little sideways.

Joe smiled. A wee chuckle.

Eddie continued, 'In all seriousness though, some of us here are not of the emigrating age. What would you do if you were forced away from all you've known? We've still got our boats – for now. But Norrie here, well, it had just crossed my mind and I thought about it some more, that if this ban stays in place for who knows how long, he might be wiser not to join any of our crews. Thing is, he's still young enough to start anew, if he really wanted to...'

'I wouldn't go anywhere,' Norrie interrupted. 'Ever.'

'Like, ever?'

'Even if you had to, as in there was no choice?'

'There is no "no" choice.'

The others shared a look. It wasn't lost on Norrie.

Ronnie responded encouragingly, 'Well, let's just hope everything works out, eh, and this bloody investigation doesn't last forever, repeal the ban, and they can *you-know-what* back off to wherever they come from.'

'Aye, you are being far too polite, Ronnie.'

The five days were over in no time, which suited Norrie just fine as he'd done all he could around the croft. He'd been finding himself holding up the bar too often, and he was really beginning to feel out of touch, though he tried hard not to show it. The shore was calling him, so on that sixth day before the crack of dawn he was off to the beach. Sailor and Patches were elated. They, too, had been missing their routine. He stuck closer to the north end, and as was the new routine, when the plane landed and departed, he'd nip over and hide in the rocky shore of Orosay. Keeping a wary eye on the shoreline and looking for any spies amongst the dunes, he risked working a full shift. It felt good to be back in sync.

He arrived home to a not completely displeased wife, but not a pleased one either.

'I said I'd take a break for a while, not quit altogether.'

'I know, Norrie. I just didn't realise it would be today, that's all. I got a wee fright when I woke up. You'd sneaked off.'

'Sorry. I was careful. I don't think anyone saw me.'

'I hope not.'

'It was a pretty good catch. Almost a hundred kilos.'

'I hope we get to keep it.' Samantha's voice was measured but there was worry in her eyes.

'We will, honey. I promise.' He gave her a hug.

'Now, go on, the girls have been dying to get to the beach. I've a lunch packed, and feel free to keep them away for as long as possible. Everyone's arriving tomorrow. I've a few last things to get ready.'

'You don't have to worry too much.'

'Norrie, your sisters have eleven children between them. I can't even keep track of all their names. And Hank and your Mama have three.'

'They're not all staying here.'

'Norrie. I know. But the house will still be full to the brim. Now go on and let me do what I have to do.'

Before setting off for the beach Norrie did something he had never done before – he loaded the Coquilleuous

Rakkeronuous Almenikhiaka into the wheelbarrow, along with their lunch supplies, a few towels, and a blanket.

The Big Book had never left the croft.

They made their way past the docile cows perpetually grazing on the machair behind the airport, and all the way up to where the big grassy dunes began. Norrie left the wheelbarrow behind, and between the three of them they carried their supplies up and over the big dunes. This was the girls least favourite part because sometimes the grass was prickly. They couldn't wait to get to the other side, but it was worth it because it was the second most beautiful beach in the world, the Traigh Mhor being the most beautiful. Not far from where they had spread out their MacKinnon tartan blanket was another family with a handful of children running around, and so it didn't take long for Sofia, Violet, Patches and Sailor to make new friends.

'Perfect,' Norrie thought. He could sit back in peace. It had been Eddie and his talk of emigration that had steered Norrie's thoughts back to the Big Book and his 'aversion' to the sea. It wasn't his fault. The sea had taken from him his Papa and brothers. Every single one. How anyone managed to spend a whole day at sea was beyond him, never mind cross an ocean to another continent. He creaked open the centuries old book and leafed through to the page containing the brief articles about great x four grandpa Angus and great x six grandpa Ruithie, and their dislike of hot air balloons and speaking in public. The stories were written a long time ago – there wasn't much to them, just a couple of paragraphs. There was no word about what had occurred (had they lost someone close in a hot air balloon or in some public setting?), or – unfortunately – of a remedy. *It seems incomplete. Whoever added this, perhaps, didn't have time to explain further what might have happened – or, or, didn't want to...what might have been....but.....I....*

I lost four brothers and a father to the sea. I have a reason.

And yet, as he looked at Sofia and Violet splashing along the shoreline with their new friends, Patches and Sailor doing their best to stay in the thick of the action, he knew he loved just that: the shore. It provided for him, it brought him peace, it gave him his rhythm. Without it he would most probably be dead.

What a curious thing.

He looked beyond the waves lapping up and down the shore, and way out to the horizon – it was nothing but a giant blue blanket. There was not a break in it anywhere. It was all connected. Moving together. *That thing that I dread the most is connected, is a part of that which I love the most, that which I cannot do without. What a strange, odd, thing.*

And now there was someone, some force, who wanted to take it all away from him. An action that would disconnect him from his rhythm with the tides, with the world around him.

Casting a glance again, well out to sea, Norrie thought, *I don't know why you do what you do to me. My Papa and brothers were not enough for you and your monster, but instead of taking me you confine me. That is fine.* And then he looked along the shoreline and thought. *You are another matter. I cannot do without you. I love you. They, whoever they are, and for whatever reason, they can throw the weight of the world at me – I will not budge from your side.*

'Papa? *Papa?!* You look like you're thinking deeply.' It was Sofia, soaked and half-covered in sand.

'What does that mean?' added Violet, also soaked and completely covered in sand.

'My goodness, where did you two come from?' *I better start paying attention.*

'Look what I found, Papa, look!' Violet had a big broken shell in her hand.

'Well, well, look at that.'

'Here, Papa, you can have it.'

'Well, thank you, my little scavenger.'

'You're welcome.'

'Papa, will you help us build a sandcastle? It's always so much better when you help.'

That's probably a good idea. 'What a great idea. Come on, let's see how big we can make it.' Norrie sprang up, causing Sofia and Violet to hop around with joy, which in turn caused Patches and Sailor to reappear from amongst the grass and join the building party.

Norrie kept them at the beach until well past seven o'clock. They were shattered by the time they left the colossal castle for the long walk home and barely managed to walk through the prickly dune grass to the wheelbarrow where they collapsed in a heap.

But before making it through the sandy maze, Norrie stopped at the top of the first dune and looked back at the castle they'd built. It was impressive. A moat system, draw bridges, an innumerable number of turrets, flags made from flotsam, the lot. He also glanced one last time out to the blue horizon, the sun still high in the sky, arcing west, its incandescent light shimmering off the ocean's surface. As he turned back to his weary princesses a glint caught his eye. It prompted him to look again and scrutinise the distant seas. But it was gone.

He turned and made his way through the prickly maze to the other side.

'Oh, Papa, you're going to have to wheel me home, I am so tired,' moaned one.

'Me, too, Papa,' said the other.

'That's all right, just hold on here. It's a little bumpy through this first bit.'

As they made their way home a dangerously shallow memory surfaced in the ocean of Norrie's mind – the glint on the horizon.

Ch 49

From Nairobi to Nantucket

It was a sight to behold. Word had spread that it was on its way so there were more than the usual number of spectators down at the sandy airport. The daily arrival from Glasgow of the trusty prop driven twin-otter was a fan favourite of both visitors and locals, but to witness the sleek American jet come scorching down was in a class of its own. To use a sporting analogy, you love to see your home team play well, but if Messi is visiting you enter a special category of awe and wonder.

After circling once, *Flyin' Tayters* came roaring in east to west, touching down just past the middle marker and came to a halt with plenty of beach to spare. The whine of the engines increased as she taxied up. As she pivoted and approached the terminal, hands could be seen waving through the oval windows. Sofia and Violet were jumping up and down unable to contain their excitement. The door opened, steps folded out and down, and a few moments later twenty-two bodies, the whole of the Kenyan and Idahoan contingent, emerged.

'Dang, Norrie, it is good to see you! It is good to be back on Floonay.' Hank gave Norrie a hearty hug and sniffed the fresh Hebridean air. 'Man, I was a missing this place somethin' fierce.'

'Aye, good to see you too, Hank.'

'Oh, Norrie, come here, give me a hug,' said Catherine as she reached for her brother, with Morag and Maggie not far behind.

There were hugs and handshakes and screaming children, and for a while everything was a little chaotic. When Mwaka, Akili, and Darweshi greeted Father John and Reverend Cullen they asked about the state of their gardens. Their sheepish looks caused the three brothers to laugh. 'We will come and see what we can do to help,' Akili said much to the delight of the two local men of God.

The mob eventually made it back to the family home where tea, scones, sandwiches, biscuits, and juices were waiting. Sailor and Patches were going bonkers with so many children around. It was a dog's paradise. There was no shortage of bodies to throw a ball, a bone, or an old piece of wood. Perfect.

The five men, naturally, made their way to the Nissen hut leaving the women to chatter in the kitchen as the sixteen children rampaged around the croft and down along the shoreline and out on to the beach. The older children had strict orders to keep an eye on the younger ones.

'Lookin' pretty good in here,' observed Hank. 'Funny thing, you know, my replica back in Boise, I got it about as eye-dentical to yours as I could, even got me some creels an' fishin' rope from See-attle. Little stove like you got, an old radio almost like yours – for listenin' to the ball games.' He looked all around. 'Hell, the shelvin' and everythin' is just about mirror image i-dent-ical, but, man,' he was nodding, (It was an 'I'm impressed' nod) '...it just ain't the same. Guess it's a bit like the tayters, you know. Ah, that's all right, I don't mind havin' second or third place. But, man, it is good to be back in the numero uno of Nissen huts.'

'You are right, Hank, this Nissen hut is very special,' Mwaka remarked. His brothers were in complete agreement.

'Hey, I tell you boys what, I know we all got kids an' all now, but we gotta see if we can't get the ladies to let us have a night in here on our own, you know. Like we did before. Tell a few tales, have a little nip, maybe two.'

'Ooo, well, I would like to say that is possible. We will have to see. We will have to see,' Darweshi cautioned.

'Oh, hey, I got somethin' for you boys,' Hank said and disappeared out of the Nissen hut only to return a moment later carrying a big box. A cooler actually. He put it down, opened it, and handed out a few bottles. 'Got a few microbrews here – Idahoan, of course, and some Blue, too, from north of the border. That's what I drink when I head up to Alberta to catch a hockey game. I think they put something in it to make you like hockey more. Here, go ahead, there's plenty. More stored on the plane, too. Hell, there's probably enough to see us through the whole trip if need be.'

As bottles were opened, the conversation turned to what the brothers and Hank had already heard through the family grapevine.

'Fill us in, my man, what in theeee hell is goin' down here?' Hank took a big swig of beer. They knew only what their wives had mentioned. That there'd been a temporary ban on cockle raking and all fishing activity in the Sound of Floonay. They didn't know about the fines or that Norrie had been sneaking out to the beach to keep raking.

Norrie filled them in on everything, including the fines, keeping out only the private parts: his aversion to the sea and his need to keep in snyc with the tides in order to keep his rhythm.

The men were shaking their heads.

'Gosh-danged governments. I'll tell you boys somethin'. Them people get into them offices and they turn into little dictators, cloaked as self-appointed guardians of democracy, thinkin' they can tell everyone what to and what not to do. Some bullshit I tell ya.'

'You are right, Hank, it is a travesty. The power they wield over people,' Akili remarked. 'They think not of anything but their agendas and party loyalty. Shameful.'

'This gettin' the whole dang area declared a special area of conservation. When did that bullshit happen?'

'Ach, the initial SAC declaration – it was years ago. It didn't make a difference at first. Life carried on. But it did give them the power to do what they want, when they want. And, as you know, they've just exercised that power.'

'Norrie, my brother, what will happen next?' Darweshi asked.

Norrie hesitated. He shook his head. *How much to explain to them?* 'The ban? It can't last forever. With any luck the investigation will happen sooner rather than a long time from now. And things will get back to normal. That's it.'

'But – Norrie, what about *until* then?' Akili asked.

There was a pause in which Hank and the brothers detected something significant. What – they were not sure.

'I'm going to keep on raking.' There was no avoiding explaining that.

'But Norrie, what if you get fined again?' Mwaka queried.

'It won't be forever. I'll just rake a little more to make up for it.'

'The penalty, Norrie, it's going to go up and up. What if you get to the point that you can't cover it?'

Norrie just shrugged. 'It shouldn't get that bad. Let's just see, eh?'

'Dang, Norrie, givin' all your earnings to the government. It just ain't right, you know? You ever, you know – I see you still got that cheque pinned up on the board there from years ago – that's pretty cool – you ever think maybe it's time to get that boat? Wouldn't take you long to get up to speed. I remember what Eddie said...'

'Aye, that he was a bit of a natural is what he was...what he is,' came a voice from behind them.

'Oh, hey boys, how you all doin'?' Hank shook hands with Eddie, Colin, Irish, and Ronnie.

'Aye, aye, all right. Just wanted to stop in and say a quick hello.'

'Here, boys, grab a brew.' Hank reached in and passed a couple of bottles over. 'All the way from Idaho – and Alberta.'

Beers were sipped and Hank spoke. 'Yeah, Norrie's just been bringin' us up to speed. As they say back home "what a crock of shit", you know.'

'Aye, you can say that again, Hank. It's a bloody crime is what it is.'

'Dang right, Eddie. I'll tell you boys somethin', and this is the plain truth, government bodies from Boise to Birmingham, Nairobi to Nantucket, you gotta watch 'em. They get an inch of power and they stretch that inch into a million miles and more.'

'Aye, aye.'

'Too bloody right.'

Hank's mind went back to the big 'what if' – as he cared enormously for Norrie's wellbeing – and he had a family now. Looking at Norrie he said. 'But, hey, what if the ban does continue, you reckon you might decide then to head to sea?'

Norrie had no desire to discuss that issue. 'Ach, things'll work out. It won't be necessary.'

'Well, I sure hope so, Norrie. Man, I feel bad. I'd a hate it if I weren't allowed to plant any more tayters, you know.' Hank looked all around. 'I think I'd a go crazy or somethin'. Imagine, if you boys weren't allowed to do the good work that you do.' He looked to Mwaka, Akili, and Darweshi, and then to the others, 'Or you boys weren't allowed to fish – at all, anymore. How to put it eloquently? It would suck somethin' fierce, you know?'

'Aye, aye, that it would, Hank. Let's just hope Norrie's right and that the ban is eventually lifted,' Ronnie said, trying to sound encouraging. But everyone knew that it would take a miracle for the wheels of government to move with any semblance of speed – and for the outcome to be a favourable one.

Colin looked to the man from Idaho and said, 'You're staring into some far-off place, Hank, and looking quite thoughtful. What's on your mind?'

'I'm glad you asked, Colin, I'm glad you asked. You know, just to add to the whole "not bein' able to do your thing" thing.' He looked at Mwaka and his brothers. 'I take it you boys do what you do because you felt "called". Like it's what you were put on this earth to do. You could do no other. It wouldn't feel right.'

Mwaka, Darweshi, and Akili nodded.

'Of course, Hank. The Lord beckoned and we could not refuse.'

'You know, that's a little how I feel 'bout my tayters. I found those mushy tayters, or somethin' guided me to 'em. And somewhere along the way I knew this was what I was meant to be, to do.' Hank looked all around, serious and sombre. 'If it weren't for them tayters, boys, there's no doubting, I'd a be a dead man.' He took a swig of beer. 'Shoot, sorry, don't mean to get so dark an' all...I'm just a realising, you know, Norrie here, his people have been cockle raking for hundreds of years – don't know if you feel, felt, quite called to it, but it's all you know, it's in your blood.....I'm just thinkin', just sayin', I hope it's all sorted out real soon, that's all, and Norrie can rake without worry of all those dang fines...'

They were interrupted by six screaming children and four dogs who blew into the Nissen hut and blew out just as quickly, which was enough to allow the conversation to change tack, much to the appreciation of Norrie. A few more beers were passed around and soon enough Samantha was poking her head in to remind Norrie it was time to get the barbecue on.

'The children didn't sleep much on the plane. It's probably best to get them fed early and off to bed. They might not look it now, but they're going to be shattered in a few hours.'

That is precisely how all the travellers felt by the time they had had their fill of burgers, sausages, crab claws, and scallops. With full bellies, they found their way to bed for an early night. By the following day their body clocks would be in the right time zone and considering there were sixteen children to entertain, it would be non-stop for the rest of the trip. Every adult was enormously grateful to be on Floonay, as all they had to do was open the door and let the children loose.

*

'It looks like he's at it again, gentlemen, and it's not just that,' Alan said, sliding a manila envelope across the table. 'Here, take a look.'

Moses picked up the envelope and out slid half a dozen 8x11 photographs.

Curious, Achmed and Dr Foo leaned forward. They were huddled around a table in a shadowy corner of The Ensign Ewart, high atop the Royal Mile. Remy had, again, rung ahead and placed an order. This was really starting to piss the others off.

'Interesting, very interesting,' Foo mused.

‘My, my, look at this one,’ Achmed the Inquisitive, pointed to one in particular.

‘Doggone, who's that?’

‘And – these?’

‘It would appear as though things are getting a little, shall we say, out of control,’ Foo, ever the calculating one, said. ‘This truly is a fascinating development.’

The six photographs included two of Norrie raking by himself, but the other four included one of a man in cowboy boots and hat, one with three well-built black men, one with two little girls, and the last one had all of them together, along with at least a dozen other figures.

Satisfied they'd seen enough the three wise men sat back.

‘Alan, old boy, what on earth is going on out there?’ Remy asked without hesitation.

‘He won't quit.’

‘I can see that.’

‘And the fines?’

‘They've been doubling every day this week.’

‘How many times has he been fined?’

‘I think it's six, no seven now, and he'll be getting another one today.’

‘And – these people?’

Alan shrugged. ‘It's his help. From what my source tells me, it’s his extended family.’

‘And the local authorities?’

‘There's just the one policeman, a Constable Currie. He's doing his duty, issuing the tickets when he receives word. I get the sense, though, he's doing the absolute minimum in terms of enforcement. He's a local from what I can gather. You know how some of these small rural communities can be like?’

‘Hmm. Hmm. Interesting.’ Foo's brain was processing data four times as fast as anyone else at the table.

Alan continued, 'The next logical step is to have him jailed for a day or two. If the local constable is unwilling to exercise the law to the max, we will bring in reinforcements from Eriskay and Vatersay....perhaps beyond.'

'I see, I see. And what of the others?' Foo was thinking very carefully.

Alan shrugged. 'Whatever. Let them off, for now. Make an example of the main culprit and the rest should slink away quietly.'

'And what if they don't?'

Another shrug. 'We'll start fining them.'

'And?'

More shrugs. 'More fines.'

'And?'

'Eventually stick them all in jail if we have to.'

'How big is the jail on Floonay?'

'Not very big, enough for four or five. Tops.'

'What will you do with the rest?'

More shrugging. 'Have them shipped to the other islands, or the mainland if need be. Was thinking maybe even a prison ship – ha – that's just a joke – er, gentlemen.'

'Or what about airstrike? Take out whole lot in oner? Ha ha – that joke, too...this no time for joke, Trout,' Foo, the Incredibly Serious, warned.

'Sorry, of course, gentlemen, of course,' Alan mumbled, a little nervous. *You stupid fool, Alan!*

The three wise men sat back, deep in thought. This was a serious development and they could not have anything standing in the way of their grand plans. The three huddled together and conferred quietly, leaving Alan, for the first time, out of the loop. He felt foolish and his thoughts turned dark and uncertain.

'Alan, it okay. Relax,' Foo said.

The huddle was over.

'This is what we're thinking, old boy,' Remy started. 'You, I, we, all realise this is a significant development. We can't have the whole population rising up in arms and making a big, old scene, y'understand?'

Alan responded with an obedient nod.

'That's good, Alan, real good. The project will get bogged down and news'll spread and, well, we would eventually get the go ahead – of that we are supremely confident, you dig?'

'Aye, aye.'

'Good. Real good. But it would take a lot longer than we'd envisioned. We need control of that area asap. You've done a real good job so far Alan. Real good. We're proud of you. Don't forget that, my man.'

'Uh, aye.' Alan felt a little better.

'So, this is what we're thinking...we're thinking we gotta head out there and do a little investigating of our own. Check things out with our own eyes and ears. See what we're dealing with.'

Alan was taken a little aback. 'Are you – sure?' *That's necessary? Bite your tongue!*

'Of course, we're sure, Alan.' Remy leaned forward. 'Aren't you full of curiosity? I – we, find it fascinating that there's someone out there who is, against the odds – not willing to make a change, is refusing to quit.'

'But...'

'We gotta see this up close and personal. So that we know what we're really dealing with. The better informed we are, the better we'll be prepared to make our next move.'

'But – the...law?'

'Alan, Alan,' Achmed the Practical, chimed in. 'Think about everything we have just discussed. Quick, do a little rewind in your brain. It's not difficult. You're not an idiot. We wouldn't have chosen you otherwise. We have to contain this situation as soon as possible. You understand. Everything hinges on expediency.'

'Uh, of course, of course.' *We can just stick him in jail! That's what the rule of law is for. It's easy! Ahh! There'll be no delay.*

'We can see you have your doubts. That's all right, Alan. A little bit of doubt is a good thing.'

'Uh, aye.' *I think. I don't know. Why can't we just stick him in jail!? And whoever else breaks the law??!! Ahhh!*

'Alan, Alan. Relax. We know what we're doing. Do you think we got to where we are without knowing? Do you?'

'Uh, no – no, of course. Pardon me, gentlemen. My apologies.'

Achmed the Consoler, continued. 'No apologies needed, Alan. You know, when I was lost in the desert all those years ago, I had doubt hammering me from every angle.'

'And me, too, in some tricky situations, many years ago,' Foo revealed.

'And, hell, Trout, doubt once had me wrapped in a nasty, rotten prickly blanket. And it wrapped tighter and tighter. It tried to squeeze, to suffocate, the life out of me. But through that – well, that's another story – let's just say, we understand you, Alan. It's a-okay if you have a little doubt.'

'Aye, aye, of course. Sorry.'

Moses added, 'No worries, Alan. Just take her easy, old boy. It'll be fine. We just got a little extra investigating to do, that's all. And this has to happen – well, we'll have to take a look at flights and all.'

'Well, I guess I'll just be seeing you when you get back then – of course you can call me anytime...'

'Alan?' Remy looked to Foo and Achmed and back to their main man. 'You're coming, too.'

Who? Me?

'What's up, old boy, you look a little surprised?'

'No, me? – it's just that...not really sure what...'

'Alan, my good man, you are now in our inner circle – have you been reviewing the book we gave you? A little, eh?' Remy, Foo and Achmed looked at each other again and smiled. 'Alan, we have so much to discuss.'

*

For all the adventuring Alan did in his mind he rarely left Edinburgh. When meetings arose outwith the city limits he delegated travel as much as possible. He had no phobia about travel, he just felt most comfortable walking the streets of home. But if Remy and company wanted him to travel to Floonay with them, he would, obviously, agree. He was, however, disappointed that they wouldn't be travelling in one of their sleek private jets or helicopters. 'Alan, we have to stay undercover to keep our competitors off our tail. And we can't arrive conspicuously in some grand fashion. We have to travel incognito and with the masses, you understand? Good. We'll be leaving as soon as possible from Glasgow on the commercial puddle jumper.' That particular day, however, the plane had been cancelled due to mechanical trouble and wouldn't be serviceable again for at least a full day. As a result, the plane was fully booked the following day, and because of the backlog from the cancelled flights it would be fully booked for a few days to come. So, the Caledonian MacBrayne ferry from Oban would be their mode of transportation. They would leave Edinburgh late in the afternoon and be in Oban by eight o'clock. Alan, again, was disappointed that there would be no limos or private cars. 'Alan, we are travelling with the masses. We will catch the next train from Waverley. Oh, and Alan, since you are, let's say, not quite famous, but you are a politician, people know who you are. We can't have anyone recognising you on this clandestine trip, so you're going to have to go in disguise as well, and that kit you wore the other day up to the top of Arthur's Seat won't quite do...you were still recognisable. You need to be under some deep cover – you dig? Good. You look worried, Alan, don't be. Everything will be okay. Nigel, as we speak, is leaving your disguise in the closet of a hotel room nearby. When we're done here, you do what you have to do to tell your office you'll be gone for a few days, then grab a few things, pop on over to the hotel room, change – don't worry about checking out – obviously – that's all sorted – and meet us at the platform fifteen minutes prior to departure – you got it Alan? That's good, real good. Oh, and don't forget, don't let your – our – little spy on Floonay know we are coming. No one can be made aware of more than necessary. It's called "compartmentalising". This project has to stay top secret – well, this part of it anyway, you understand what I'm sayin'? That's good, Alan. Real good. Oh yeah, and make sure to tell your MEO friends to be ready for a snap, impromptu, consultation, just in case it's required. Gotta be prepared Alan. All right, see you later, old boy.'

Alan showed up at Waverley station feeling utterly ridiculous. During the whole walk from the hotel he felt ridiculous. Putting on the disguise he'd felt ridiculous. The whole thing was just that – ridiculous! Preposterous! Absurd! But it seemed to be working. He'd even walked past a few fellow MSPs near the station and they were none the wiser, and a few people even nodded out of respect along the way. When he arrived at the platform the three wise men were waiting. 'Looks like we're now a quartet of faith, eh, Alan?' Remy chuckled and grinned through his beard. 'You're looking pretty good there, don't you boys think?' Foo and Achmed agreed enthusiastically. 'You look good in disguise, Alan. Very good. Don't forget, if you meet a fellow Rabbi, pretend you are temporarily mute. We don't need you blowing our cover because you don't know shit about any religion. We're booked into a Bed and Breakfast in Oban. Greencourt something or other. And on Floonay, a nice little B&B called Orosay. Ferry leaves early afternoon tomorrow. Gentlemen, it looks like the train is ready to leave. Tally-ho, or some doggone thing like that.'

*

The following day brought some bad news – the main ferry, the Clansman, was also cancelled due to a major engine problem, but the smaller relief ferry, Lord of the Isles, was available. There would be a few hours' delay for the company to re-arrange the various ferries' scheduled routes and the crossing would take a little bit longer, but at least a ferry would be going that day. *Thank goodness boys.*

Despite the delay, before they knew where they were, the 'quartet of faith' were stepping aboard with the hordes of travellers, handing their tickets to the ticket collector at the top of the gangway, and making their way into the belly of the ship.

'Been a while, boys, since I've been on a proper ship – that palace I got floating in the Gulf of ol' Mexico aside, you know – this is pretty doggone cool. Why don't we make our way to the bar and get ourselves a drink? I might even let one of you all buy the round to mark this special occasion. Next stop, Floonay.'

Ch 50

The Convalescing Quartet

Hank Stetson was no good at raking cockles but he was determined to do his best. On the first day after everyone arrived Norrie headed to the beach on his own to work a full shift, keeping an eye out for cameras lurking along the shore. All seemed okay. On the second day he did the same again. There was plenty to keep the Idahoan and Kenyan contingents busy those first few days; beaches to explore, people to visit, dogs to run ragged, hills to climb. Once again, all was okay. No sign of Constable Currie and no telltale signs of anyone lurking in the grass, snapping photos. Good. Samantha had her doubts and wished that Norrie would take a few days off in between, but he assured her that he was being careful. 'Norrie, let's see what happens Saturday. If Constable Currie stops you on the way to Nelson's shed, you are going to receive a really big fine.' That was no matter as Norrie was determined to keep in sync with the tides. Every day that passed was a day closer to the investigation starting, and with any luck a day closer to the ban being lifted. In the meantime, he had to keep on raking. People stopped by and the evenings were filled with barbecues and visits and impromptu ceilidhs.

Hank had designated himself the Nissen hut barman and all in all everyone was having a good time.

Well, it didn't take until the following Saturday for Constable Currie to appear. Hank witnessed his appearance through a pair of binoculars from the edge of the croft. 'Dang. That don't look too good.' Norrie and Constable Currie were at the far end of the Traigh, near Orosay, but Hank could see a hand extending and then another – Norrie was obviously accepting something. But he wasn't being arrested. At least that was a plus. They seemed to part amicably. That, too, was good. And it didn't look like he was being made to dump what he'd raked. Good again. Hank struck out across the beach to meet him halfway.

'Norrie, my man, don't tell me it was another fine.'

'Aye.'

'How much?'

'Five hundred.'

Hank cringed. 'Eww, Norrie. Shit. That hurts. That is not good.'

'Aye, I know.'

'I feel sick hearin' that.'

'Aye, so do I.'

They walked slowly south as the tide lapped at their feet nudging them along.

'Norrie, my man, let me help you out here.'

'Thanks, Hank, but that's all right.'

'Norrie, be sensible. You barely raked that much in the last couple of days. This can't go on.'

'I am not quitting.'

'Shit, Norrie, you don't need to quit – unless they end up sealing off the beach. Then you'll be forced to. But at least let me help you out a little. Let me pay that fine for you.'

'I'll manage, Hank.'

‘Be reasonable. Shoot, Samantha is going to go bonkers when she hears the news.’

‘Don't tell her.’

‘It's too late...the others saw, too, when I spied you through the binos.’

‘I mean the fine amount. I'll just say it was the same as the last one.’

‘Come on now, you are starting to tread down a dangerous path.’

‘Just this once. We'll see what happens the next few days, okay?’

Hank reluctantly agreed, but he felt a little guilty when the story was recounted back at the house. Norrie played it down as much as he could and did everything possible to make light of things. Samantha wasn't impressed, but they had visitors and as Norrie said, ‘It's not the end of the world, and in the meantime, I've got to get this barbecue going.’

The following day Hank decided to pick up a rake to give Norrie a hand. When he'd followed along Norrie had objected at first, but eventually relented. Hank was good company to have around. Next it was Mwaka, Akili, and Darweshi. They were all terrible cockle rakers, but Norrie, in a way, appreciated the effort, the willingness to help. And as they confided, 'Norrie, please, let us stay, it gives us a break.' 'Aye, aye, of course.' You could never keep Violet and Sofia away from the big beach for long, and then their Idahoan and Kenyan cousins joined in. Hank observed, ‘Norrie, this is a big beach. A giant beach. There's no hiding from whomever is taking the pictures of you – probably of all of us now. They could be taking the photos from way up there by the big rock, or way, way over there from the top of Picnic Hill...anywhere. So, hell, we might as well just rake as much as we can and to hang with the consequences.’ It turned into a bit of a circus for a few days, but Constable Currie had yet to return. Samantha, her sisters-in-law and Norrie's Mama were the only sensible ones left. 'You know, what you're doing isn't going to do any good. You are all going to be fined now. Not just Norrie.'

That statement was prescient.

The following evening as Norrie, Hank, and the brothers were prepping the barbecue and sipping beer, Constable Currie came knocking.

'Evening gentlemen.'

'Constable.'

'Evening.'

'Evening.'

'Can I get you a beer, Callie?' Hank said, reaching into the cooler.

Constable Currie hesitated. 'Aye, why not.'

The women were watching from the kitchen window, and the other children who'd been running circles around the croft had all stopped and watched warily from a distance. Patches and Sailor hid under the picnic table.

'Norrie. Gentlemen. I've been handed more evidence.'

'Evidence?' Hank tried to play dumb.

'This can't continue and there is nothing I can do about it. Norrie, your new fine is £750. Gentlemen, yours are £100 each. All the wee ones out there – they're getting verbal warnings.'

'Dang. You serious?'

'I'm sorry, the law is the law. There is a ban in place and there's nothing any of us can do about it.'

All Norrie could think was, *I'm not giving up.*

'Can you do me a favour and round up all your wee helpers so I can issue them their verbal warning and tell them they're not to cockle rake on the Traigh anymore – or until the ban is lifted, anyway.'

'You can't be serious?'

Mwaka, Akili, Darweshi and Hank looked to one another. *Uh oh.*

'Aye, Norrie, I am serious.'

'They're just children.'

'I know, I know...but...'

'And it's Sofia's birthday tomorrow. You'll make her cry if you tell her she can't cockle rake anymore. I'll tell them. I promise. I'll make sure they don't set another foot on the beach, well, with a rake anyway.'

There was a pause that hung in the fresh sea air for longer than the brothers or Hank would have liked, but eventually Constable Currie spoke.

'All right, Norrie, you tell them.'

'I will, promise. No more help.'

'Norrie, that means you, too.'

'Oh aye, aye, of course.' *I will never quit.*

'By the by, I've received word that reinforcements might be sent from Eriskay, Vatersay, and maybe even from Coll and Tiree. Gentlemen, Norrie, if they do that, they'll be setting up a round the clock watch on the beach. If that happens, it will be completely out of my hands. I even heard a rumour that they might try and fence it off, but that most likely won't happen – it's just too big an area. But, Norrie, if officers come from across the way, they'll be more inclined to, well, I don't think I have to finish that sentence. I'm sorry, but you have to find something else to do.'

Hank, Mwaka, Akili, and Darweshi were deflated.

Constable Currie finished his beer, but before he left, he said, 'Tomorrow's Saturday.' *Landing day.* 'I've got something important to see to out in Cleit. Will be quite busy. I'll be up there most of the afternoon, if you understand, Norrie...'

Dang, he's an all right fella. 'Hey Constable?'

'Aye?'

'Is it all right to ask, you know – who seems to be so keen on takin' all these pics?'

'We've got our share of busybodies. But truthfully, it doesn't matter. The law is being broken.' Constable Currie wrote out the five tickets and handed them over. 'Good evening, gentlemen.'

As Constable Currie departed, Hank turned to his compadres. 'It's all my fault boys, well, partly anyway. Shoulda maybe kept away, maybe Norrie woulda' evaded this one, who knows – come on and give me them tickets.' This met resistance. 'Boys, come on now, and even you, Norrie. Look at *Flyin' Tayters* way over yonder, I ain't no braggin' man, but let me just say I know one hundred pounds is a lot to you boys, and as for you Norrie, if you don't let me pay that ticket, well, I ain't no fightin' man, ain't been in one since I was in the army, and that was a long time ago, but I might just be inclined to kick your bee-hind. Well, maybe I wouldn't really, just let me take care of these, boys, and you got Sofia's birthday tomorrow. I ain't lettin' you part with seven hundred and fifty pounds the day before such an occasion, and you already got that ticket from a few days ago to take care of.'

Mwaka, Akili, and Darweshi relented and handed their tickets over – and, amazingly, so did Norrie.

Hank cracked open a new brew and stretched his back. 'I gotta say boys, those few days rakin', well, they nearly done me in, you know what I'm sayin'.'

Akili answered for him and his brothers, 'I know what you are saying, Hank. I am sore all over.'

'Hell, at least we tried, we gave it a good go, you know.'

'Of course, we tried, but – sorry, Norrie, we weren't very much help.'

'Aye, that's all right, lads.'

Hank was shaking his head. 'Norrie, this whole deal, this just ain't no good, you know. There ain't even been any word of the MEO startin' their little investigation. Let's just say, and this is a big and optimistic "let's just say" it starts here in the next few weeks – well, I'll tell ya, if these types of thinly disguised arm's-length government agencies are anything like they are in Idaho, it's gonna be quite some time before they make a final ruling. I hate to say it, Norrie, but you are a little backed into a corner.'

Norrie didn't see it that way – didn't feel it that way. All he knew was that he belonged by the tides. If he couldn't keep in rhythm with the earth as he felt and he knew he should, there would be no more Norrie. The tides had flowed through generations, centuries, of his blood. Some people make changes, but not everyone was meant to. *I am never, ever quitting the shore of the Traigh Mhor.* Call it stubborn, single-minded obsession, stupidity even. It was none of these things to Norrie. And besides, there was no mention of quitting in the Coquilleuous Rakkeronuous Almenikhiaka, therefore, he would not. A few days off here and there, fine, but to give up completely was to open the door to giving up on life. He lost his rhythm once, and for a very long time, had become disconnected and disillusioned. He vowed – and especially now he had Samantha, Sofia, and Violet in his life – that he would never dare let himself get close to that again. And that was all there was to it. Simple really.

*

Remy didn't have to decide whether to let Foo or Achmed buy the first round as one was bought for them as soon as they'd made their way into the ship's bar. Another man of faith was ordering a couple of drams when the quartet approached. Reverend Cullen insisted, Remy tried to insist otherwise, Reverend Cullen insisted some more, and that was it.

‘Gentlemen, please, sit with us. It is wonderful to meet fellow men of faith,’ announced Reverend Cullen, and looking at Foo, added, ‘Well, faith and philosophy, of course.’ He gestured over to a waving Father John, who was seated at a table ringed by a semi-circle couch and a few poofy stools.

‘I am much obliged and would be honoured to sit in your company. I'll have whatever you are having. My, my, those are some measures. Let me give you a hand with those.’

The quartet and Reverend Cullen made their way over and introductions were made all around. They used their real names, sticking to 'Remy', 'Doctor Foo', 'Achmed', and 'Alan'. There was no blowing their covers by doing so. As they were seating themselves Remy whispered to Alan, ‘Go into “bad throat” mode. No speaky for you. These gentlemen probably know more about your religion than you do.’

Achmed, being the number one salesman on the planet, seized the initiative as soon as the initial pleasantries were out of the way. This conversation needed some serious steering, and he needed to do his best to steer the conversation away from religion. Certainly, he, Remy, and Foo had a certain level of knowledge of their faiths and their philosophies, but they were not 'classically' trained, as ordained men of the cloth would be. They would be expected to have knowledge of subjects about which they were clueless. And as for Alan, he had no faith at all. If he opened his mouth even an imbecile could smell that something wasn't right. Deep cover was essential. He smiled broadly, making a show of looking all around – the place was filling up quickly, and in a corner a couple were lifting an accordion and a fiddle out of their cases. Then he spoke. ‘We are so excited about this trip. None of us has ever been to the Outer Hebrides before. We are looking forward to seeing all the sights. Beautiful beaches, stunning scenery, hills to climb, oodles and oodles to see and do.’

‘Oh, aye, aye, we have it all. Especially Floonay. A lovely island from end to end,’ Father John replied.

Before Achmed had a chance to continue Reverend Cullen asked, his eyes flitting from robe to robe, ‘Are you travelling in some – *official* capacity?’

Achmed, after a small chuckle and thinking extremely fast, and realising that they hadn't a chance of avoiding the inevitable question, dressed the way they were, answered, ‘No, no, of course not. Quite the contrary. We are on a sabbatical of sorts. A break, really.’ He lowered his voice and leaned in, altering his countenance to suit what he was about to say, ‘Actually, I must confide in you, to be completely honest. We're, the four of us, we're burned out...that smile I just made, that little laugh, it took much effort...’

‘Oh, my...’

‘It's not a big deal – really. Well, actually, I guess it is. Our “Orders” advised us to take some time off...a bit like sick leave, convalescing. We'd been working, preaching, practising, too hard. Our Superiors told us, “Go, take a break, gentlemen. See the sights, relax, and take it easy. And don't do *anything* remotely related to work. Don't even think about work, let alone talk or even discuss privately. Nothing. Zilcho.”’

‘My, my...’

‘Alan here, he's been working so hard, thinking too much, preaching like he'd been sent straight from the other side. Well, he's not from the quote-unquote other side, he's just a mere mortal, and now, he can barely speak anymore,’ Achmed said with a tired sigh.

Remy and Dr Foo had no clue where Achmed planned to take the conversation but quickly realised they must act the part. They immediately ‘slumped’ a little. Remy nudged Alan, who did the same.

‘My goodness...’

Achmed could see that there was some confusion being shared between their new friends. He continued and explained a little more, looking exhausted, but contented and safe in such well-known company. 'We're old childhood friends. We grew up in a small village that embraced all our different faiths – and philosophies – a bit like Jerusalem, but on a smaller scale. But then, Remy's parents, missionaries themselves, took Remy back to Texas, Alan back here, me, to Zanzibar, and Foo was whisked back to China. But we kept in touch through the years...remarkable really...'

'I see, er, remarkable indeed...' there was still a little confusion.

No matter. It was time to move on.

'We thought maybe a nice island in the South Pacific or a quiet retreat in the Andes, but the good doctor here had read about these mystical islands we are sailing into, Floonay in particular, and it dawned on us, like a revelation. The shores and hills and lush green fields of Floonay would be where we will rest and mend our tired souls, recharge our spirits...'

Son of a gun, Achmed, let's not go too far with this. I ain't as good of a bullshitter as you. Remy interrupted, 'I'm just a lookin' forward to a little rest, relaxation and seein' the sights. Maybe read a little, take a few nice leisurely walks along the beaches, that kind a thing.' *Finito, Achmed.*

Father John and Reverend Cullen assured them that they'd chosen a fine place to do just that.

'Whether you've excitement and adventure in mind, or peace and relaxation, gentlemen, you will find on Floonay just what you are looking for.'

'Well, that's good. Real good. As a matter of fact, I'm feelin' a little better already. Another round?'

Ch 51

Striking at the Heart

The faithful quartet managed to pry themselves away from what was turning into quite a seafaring ceilidh and make their way to the mess deck for a little nourishment. Their two new friends of faith were happy to stay and enjoy the singsong.

'Whew, I'll tell y'all, there ain't nothin' like a good ol' Texas barn dance, but that lot in there are makin' a barn dance seem a little tame. And we're only two hours into our journey.'

'Well, it is the holidays, Remy,' Achmed reasoned. 'It's the Hebridean version of setting sail for Ibiza.'

'Nice fellas them, Father John and Reverend Cullen, but I'm a glad they stayed behind. Alan, we got a lot to talk about – bring you a little more up to speed with things. You got the book we gave you?'

'Oh, aye, it's right here.' Alan pulled it out from under his robe.

'Ah, that's good, real good. How's the reading comin' along? You properly wrap your head around chapter nine yet?'

'Well, I, hmm...'

'Doggone, Alan, you really don't like reading nothin' but those adventure yarns, huh?'

'Oh, no, no – I've, well, just been quite busy.'

'Alan, this is important stuff here. And we even made it as reader friendly as possible. It's a pop-up book, for heaven's sake. Here, open that thing up to chapter nine.'

Alan did as he was told.

'Alan, pull that lever – that's good. You see that – what do you think? Interesting huh?'

'Oh, aye, aye.' *What on earth is this?*

'Alan, that there is the future of politics. We figured that section at least, would interest you.'

'Oh, aye, aye, of course.' Out of the corner of his eye he could see a pretty blonde in tight jeans walking past carrying a tray. Half his mind followed along.

'Alan, old boy, look at me and focus. This is serious business and we've a lot to think about. That's why the sooner we get that Think Tank built on Greanamul the better. Check this out. You see, this isn't just about the reconstruction, the continuous improvement of the global political mechanisms, the levers of government, but beyond the levers and switches and coordinating apparatus. This asks some pretty big questions of you, and me, and everyone. It is a very sensitive, touchy area – you remember when I made the comment about politicians learning how to pack their bags, remember that? That's good. Well, think of this like "new politics" one-o-one. And this is one of the things they are gonna have to learn from the corporate world. What they – our political *friends,* are going to have to learn is how to serve others. Period. Others outside of their constituency, as it is presently known. Can you take a mental leap and see where we are going with this? Simply put, you want into office, you want to "serve the people", how willing are you to serve another group? Another region? What they can learn from the corporate world is the not-so-radical concept of working, collaborating, with people from different regions and nations, to solve a problem, create a better product....'

'Remy?' Foo interrupted. 'I think you try and explain too much, too soon. Look at Alan, he already totally confuse. He drop roll in soup and not even notice.'

Alan blinked. He was indeed confused and – yet, 'Gentlemen...forgive me, but if I have the vaguest notion, outline, of where you are going with this...you're striking at the heart of democracy...I think you are...'

Achmed the Simplifier smiled. 'We never said that what we were planning was, is, easy to comprehend. But regarding what you just said, it is and it isn't. Basically, it's improving it – you will understand one day...I hope.'

Remy added, 'Put it another way, how much do you care about improving the lives, the predicaments, of others? And how fast do you want that improvement to happen?'

After fishing his roll out of the bowl of soup, Alan countered, 'Being in the position I am in, I know one thing for certain regarding politics in general, people vote – primarily with...' *how to sum this up? All politics is local.*

'Please, Alan, old boy, I know where you're going with this,' Remy continued. 'Let me ask you, you've a sister in Dundee, right? Of course, of course...hey, her local council? Who votes them in? Whose responsibility is it? The locals, of course...it's their neighbourhood, their city, their say, right?'

Foo interrupted once again, 'Remy, forget it right now. It too much to take in, to digest right now....it way too big a subject...Alan, only know this...the progress of man is real, walls are coming down, environments are changing – fast. Understanding, too...the world is not what it was many years ago...we must adapt. Everything must adapt.'

*

'Papa, look – it's the ferry, I can see the ferry!'

'I can, too, Papa.'

'I saw it first.'

That pleasant Friday evening, after the barbeque, there were hours of daylight left, so Norrie, Hank, and the brothers, decided to climb Ben Heavel. They took all the children with them to give the ladies a few hours of peace. The view from the top was spectacular once again. And the sight of the ferry sailing into harbour – lumbering past the rocky islet of Muldonach, swinging hard to starboard for the final leg, gliding gracefully past the timeless castle in the middle of the bay – only added to the magnificence.

'She's a bit late, girls. Should have been in at the back of seven – oh, and look, can you tell which one it is?'

Sofia and Violet were stumped.

'The Clansman must be broken down again – look, it's the Lord of the Isles.'

'Oh yeah, I knew that.'

'Me too, Papa, me too!'

'How's the leg?' Norrie looked to Hank who seemed to be struggling as they reached the summit.

'Ah, it ain't too bad. More my age, Norrie. I ain't twen'y anymore, you know. Dang, that is some view – whew...I am outta breath.'

'Hank, here, have a beer,' Akili passed a can out of the small cooler they'd carried up.

Hank cracked the can and took a drink. 'Thanks...Ah, that's better.'

Akili, Mwaka, Darweshi, and Hank, watched the ferry as it slowly cut across the bay, past the castle and towards the pier, and for a moment all thought of the incident they'd been told about, all those years ago. Of Norrie falling – or jumping, overboard, and having to be plucked out of the water by the lifeboat crew. They, of course, did not say a word at that moment. It just happened to cross their minds. It crossed Norrie's mind, too. He ignored it. He had more important things to occupy his thoughts, primarily how he was going to keep raking without being spotted. It was virtually impossible at this time of year. There were simply too many hours of light in the day, and the Traigh Mhor was just too big and too exposed. What he wouldn't give for the dark dead of winter to envelop his movements. Then he would be free.

But here he was, only a few weeks past the summer Solstice, the light shining well into the late evening, and starting to shine again not long after it had slipped away. Constable Currie was right – Floonay did have its share of busybodies who loved nothing more than gossiping and spying through binoculars. There was nothing he could do about that. And, of course, there was the MEO itself – they could easily have assets observing the area. Either way, it was what it was. All Norrie could do was keep on doing the only thing he knew, and as long as Nelson continued accepting his landings, he would find a way to get by, to make it until (with any luck) the lifting of the ban, and life on Floonay was back to normal.

Norrie hadn’t planned to work a shift on the Saturday morning before landing, but upon waking early decided otherwise. A few hours at the crack of dawn while the house was still sleeping wouldn't do any harm. So off he went with Patches and Sailor in tow. They seemed happy that they weren't being run ragged by all the children and that it was back to just them, Norrie, and their usual routine. The sun was peeking out, rising through a thin band of hazy clouds on the horizon. It was Norrie's favourite time of day on the beach. Calm and peaceful. Just him and the tide – and his two four-legged pals. It was also Sofia's birthday. Norrie had left the present buying to Samantha, but he had yet to pick an extra special story from the Big Book. As he raked, he did a mental scan through it. There were countless to choose from. But there was many a tale too alarming for some of the children in attendance. Notably of the sea monster – the whale. It was all a long time ago, but it also seemed like only yesterday. Time was a peculiar thing.

Unconsciously, he glanced up and looked north and east towards the passage between Stack and Eriskay. The sea and that bastard. *You took them...you robbed me...us.* Enough! Norrie forced the thoughts to the edges of his mind. *On to other matters! What story to tell for Sofia's birthday?* With a larger audience than usual, it was an easy choice. Sofia and Viloet knew the story – as did all of her cousins, but they wouldn't mind hearing it again, and if they were at all like himself, wouldn't mind hearing it again, and again. (Are you kidding?! They absolutely love the story!) *The story of the greatest cockle raker ever.*

The sun continued to rise. It had just gone seven and Norrie decided that was enough. He didn't need the children waking and running down to the beach to try and join in. He carried the bags of cockles along the shoreline and staged them with the rest of the week's catch, ready for the big trip to Nelson's shed at noon. Norrie looked around – the island seemed to still be asleep. Norrie didn't know it, but from a hired Range Rover in the wee parking lot beside the airport, he was being watched by the quartet of faith. Well, more specifically, by the three wise men and one hugely doubting Thomas.

*

'Interesting, very interesting,' Foo remarked, peering through a fancy pair of binoculars.

'It's a good thing we got up when we did. Looks like he's finished, for now anyway.' Remy, too, was peering through an even fancier set of binos. 'Here, take a look.' He handed the binos back to Achmed.

Alan had to be careful, but he couldn't help himself. 'Gentlemen, with respect. We've caught him red-handed, again...if we just call the authorities...isn't it time he spent a day or two behind bars?'

'Alan, Alan, don't get too impatient here. Yes, we need this problem solved asap, but don't forget, we also need this problem to disappear quietly and with no fuss, you dig?'

'Aye, aye,' Alan nodded, trying not to show his frustration.

They'd been sitting there for an hour so the sight of *Flyin' Tayters* parked a hundred yards away was becoming normal, but when they first arrived it had taken them by surprise.

'That is one impressive bird. I've got one just like it in my fleet,' Remy observed.

'I know I do. Mine in Hong Kong, I think.'

'I've got two just like that. I have no clue where mine are,' Achmed added.

My goodness. These men are in a league of their own.

'You ever travelled in a corporate jet, Alan?' Remy asked.

'Uh, no...'

'Would you like to, one day?'

'Uh, aye.'

'Well, don't you worry, old boy. I'll get you a ride in one of RIG's birds sometime.'

They watched the solitary figure with two dogs running circles around him, walk back up the rocky shore and disappear into a house. They stepped out, stretched their legs, and walked around admiring the view.

Remy wandered along to the small airport building and called back to the others, 'Hey, it says here the cafe opens at 8am. Not long now. I don't know about y'all but that bowl of cereal and banana didn't exactly fill me up. I could do with a proper feed. Some sausages and fried eggs an' all.'

‘Ah, excellent, I am starving, Remy. Good idea.’ Achmed the Excited, replied.

‘Me, too. That little muffin, it “poof” and disappear. My belly so empty,’ Foo remarked.

Alan, too, was feeling peckish. A proper breakfast did sound like a grand idea.

A short time later the door opened and a nice lady who introduced herself as Gillian was taking their orders. Full Scottish breakfasts all around. Dr Foo had been keen on placing the order in Gaelic, but they'd decided it best he didn't. There would be too many questions, and they needed to stay incognito, which was especially important in a small community where word travelled fast.

When the plates arrived, Achmed the Inquisitive asked, ‘That big plane over there, it seems a bit out of place here?’

‘Aye, yes, it is. It's a visitor’s – he's here with his family. He's from Idaho. Big businessman.’

‘Well, well, isn't that interesting.’

Gillian enquired where they were all from.

Remy answered for them, ‘From the four corners you could say. We're here for some R&R. A little time off.’ He stuck with the story Achmed had told Father John and Reverend Cullen.

‘Well, you've picked the right place for that,’ she replied and tried hard not to stare too much at the four curious guests. ‘Enjoy your breakfast, gentlemen.’

And enjoy it they did, especially the Stornoway black pudding.

‘Hmm, hmm, this is some tasty stuff.’ Remy ran the last piece of black pudding around the plate with his fork, soaking up the remaining egg yoke, and popped it in his mouth. ‘I ain't never had nothin' quite like it. I sure hope I can get some of this exported back to Austin. Better late than never in discovering somethin' so good, eh gentlemen?’

Dr Foo and Achmed heartily agreed.

'You are a lucky man, Alan, to have this right on your doorstep.'

It was nearing nine o'clock and the airport was quickly filling up, not that it took much to fill the compact terminal. The first flight of the day was due in at nine-thirty, so Remy and company decided to stick around and watch it land. They made their way back outside where others were milling about also waiting to watch the plane come in.

'This is some place,' Remy said, looking all around. 'Perfect for the hotel.'

'Indeed, Remy, it is indeed,' Achmed replied. 'Just there, you have the Atlantic, and this way, the Sound of Floonay and the Minch – you see over that way, Alan....just past that island, further out is Greanamul. You couldn't conjure up a better spot for our Think Tank.'

They made casual conversation with those standing nearby and it became clear that a few people already knew of them. Father John and Reverend Cullen had apparently already been talking. Remy reminded Alan quietly, 'Don't forget, Alan, you're not to do too much talking.' That was fine with Alan, as, to be honest, he didn't really know what he would say anyway.

'Oh, look, there it is,' came an excited voice from somewhere.

And sure enough, off in the distance, a teeny little dot grew in size. As it came closer and started to descend, its wings could be seen wobbling from side to side. It came directly towards them, descending, and eventually touching down a few hundred yards out, creating a big plume of sea spray. A few moments later it was taxiing up to the terminal. People clapped and others took photographs. Then a little tractor made its way out to transport the luggage and daily papers. A door opened, a set of steps dropped down, and 30 seconds later the passengers were being greeted by family and friends.

'Much quicker than airport in Shanghai,' Foo commented.

'You got that right, Foo. And Austin on a busy day is a right pain in the backside.'

'Thank goodness we now have our own planes,' Achmed reminded them.

They chuckled. 'Of course, of course.'

It wasn't long before a line of fifteen or so passengers emerged from the terminal and made their way out to the plane. People waved and blew kisses while others shouted a final goodbye. A short few minutes later the turboprop engines were winding back up and the trusty twin-otter taxied east, turned, and a moment later was airborne.

'This has got to be the most scenic airport in the world, wouldn't y'all think?' Remy instinctively waved as the plane passed overhead.

Achmed and Foo were also waving. Only Alan didn't wave as he felt a bit awkward about the whole thing, but Remy gave him a nudge, 'Go on, give a little wave. Look, everyone else is.' Alan did as he was told.

'It is a good thing that we will keep sightseeing flights from here, and with the hotel right in front – it will be spectacular,' Foo commented.

'Hey, why don't we take a walk up there to that big rock on top of that hill,' suggested Remy, pointing south. 'I could do with a little exercise after that big breakfast....and we can discuss, without anyone overhearing, what we should do to make this little problem go away without too much fuss.'

Ch 52

Let's See What's Left

Remy, Foo, Achmed, and Alan, huffed and puffed their way up to the top of the hill where the big rock protruded from the earth like a sore thumb.

Breathing heavily, Foo recounted. 'There some story of this rock. Tall tale, of course – I think. How it got here. Can't remember exactly. A giant man throw all the way from Eriskay. My adoptive mother told me tale many year ago in Hong Kong, when I was a young lad. Forgot story, and she gone now...I wish I remember.'

They all took a breather and sipped some orange squash that Achmed had smartly remembered to bring along.

'Pretty doggone amazing though, you know. You look all around here, this rugged beautiful place carved out way back when....and then splat! – right here, like it dropped from on high is a big ol' rock, all on its own.'

'You are right Remy, very amazing, very interesting.' Achmed the Inquisitive patted the giant rock, as though communing with it. 'When I was in the desert all those years ago, I saw many amazing things that made me wonder....' He squinted thoughtfully and seemed ready to tell some mystical tale of old. 'But that is for another time,' he said, snapping back to the present.

'You got that right, Achmed, we got a little here and now situation to sort out.'

'Too true, Remy, too true,' Foo added, finishing off his squash.

Remy continued, 'The way I see things, we got two options. One – as Alan here has suggested, let the law run its course. This poor fella will spend a day or two in jail. If he still doesn't quit after release, it'll be a few more days and a few more after that, and hopefully, with any luck, this will wear him down and eventually defeat him. The others who were giving him a hand, well, they won't be back – let's just assume that...after all, who was out there this morning? It was just him. Looks like the tickets and verbal warnings scared the others off, but not him. But he will not last, he can't. There is too much stacked against him...but the key thing here, gentlemen, is how long that all takes....and – and, this is hugely important, we do not want news to spread. The less anyone knows about it the better...right?...and so we take a chance that he will eventually wear down, who knows how long that might take, a few weeks, a month, maybe more....and word doesn't get out and all will be fine.....or, option two: we do what works ninety-nine percent of the time.' Foo and Achmed understood, but Alan didn't get it right away.

Foo nodded and finished Remy's thought, 'We throw money at the problem.'

'Exactly, my good man, exactly. Only problem with that is there is also the chance of news leaking and potentially creating an even bigger problem....'

Achmed picked up on his thought. 'Of course, of course. Obviously, we can buy him off, we can buy anyone off. Praise be to Allah, gentlemen, we can buy off entire countries. But there is the massive chance that someone will, at some point, smell a rat. Let's say he's no longer cockle raking, maybe he decides not to do anything else because we've given him enough money to see him through all his years. Of course, our project gets underway and, well, a snoopy someone might start to wonder a few things...hmmm...hmmm...this is a little tricky, my friends, could be tricky indeed.'

Remy added, 'And let's not forget, if we do try and throw money at it, there is the one-percent chance that he can't be bought, and if the alarm is raised it could become very problematic. To sum up, whatever we do, we need to keep a tight lid on this.'

'For what it's worth, gentlemen,' Alan felt the need to chip in his tuppence worth, 'I think we let the law run its course. Option one sounds better, the least problematic route.'

'Come on now, don't be so quick to choose. You ain't being stingy, are you? Think of that big ol' number, Alan,' Remy replied, and Alan flushed.

'Oh, sorry, no – no. It's just, as Achmed pointed out....as we all agree – I think,' Alan stammered, 'it could make things worse.'

'Alan, relax. It okay.'

'Sorry, of course...'

Remy gazed across the vast expanse of beach and out towards Greanamul, Hellisay and Gighay. 'Gentlemen, all I am one-hundred percent certain about is that this project is going to get off the ground and we have to make sure nothing stands in its way. Once we've solved this little problem, people will quickly forget, and, Alan, once you ensure the government exercises its legal right and sells the area to us, well, life will move on. The money and jobs will pour in and what happened in the past will be a distant memory.'

The quartet made their way back to the parking lot and decided to tour the island. They drove along the west side and descended into the main town, Castlebay. Parking at the top of the street, they got out and had a little walk up and down. Along the way they received a few hellos, nods, and curious stares. They stopped in at the main shop, the Butcher's, and picked up a few snacks, papers, and postcards. While checking out at the till, Remy asked for a dinner recommendation.

Barry was working the till and replied, 'Well, you've Cafe Kisimul just down the road here, Rachel's curry is the best this side of Mumbai. You've the Craigard just up the way, Francis and Della's fish and chips are superb. You can't go wrong with Chef Paul at the Castlebay Hotel, or the Halaman Bar of course, and, if you like scallops, I'd say Joe's at The Heathbank are about the best you'll find. Hand dived.'

'Well, well, I guess we're not short of options.'

Achmed leaned in, adding, 'Excuse me, but is there any chance of hiring bicycles here?'

'What a great idea, Achmed!' Remy enthusiastically chipped in.

'Aye, aye, just up the road there, go right at the top of the street and about a hundred yards along, past the Craigard, there's a wee bike shed. John should be about. If he's not, call the number on the door.' By this time Dr Foo had crowded in leaving Alan staring at the shelves of odds and ends, wondering what on earth they were doing. 'That great. Good call, Achmed. Such nice day...come on, Alan, we're going for bike ride.'

Barry bid them a good day, and the four robed men bundled their way out.

'Perhaps I'll drive the car and...' Alan attempted.

'Come on Alan, it'll be fun. Where's your sense of adventure?'

But...this – these – robes? How the hell... He daren't share his thoughts.

A few minutes later they were striding up to the wee brown shed where a middle-aged gentleman was just locking up.

'Ah, good day sir, good day,' Remy called. 'Looks like we got here just in time.'

The man appraised the trio walking towards him, and the one straggling behind – and the look spoke, err, volumes. 'Gentlemen?'

'We were hoping to hire a few bikes.'

'Well,' It came out slow and measured as if the brain transmitting the message was calculating what to say to such company.

'I assure you, we can all cycle, no need for trainer wheels,' Achmed chuckled. Remy and Foo followed suit. Alan half-chuckled praying the man wouldn't hire them any bikes.

'I am Achmed, this is Remy, and Doctor Foo, and – *our* good friend, Alan. We are here visiting your beautiful island. Convalescing. A little R&R.'

'Oh, aye...I might have heard of you.' The man, who introduced himself as John, turned and unlocked the door. 'Let's see what's left that are of any use...most went out this morning.'

A few minutes later, and to Alan's chagrin, the four of them were astride bicycles.

'I'd recommend you gents go the west side...that hill to the east is steep.' John gestured towards Heavel.

'What d'you boys, think? I'm feelin' a little ambitious, though it does look, dare I say – foreboding? That ain't no supermarket speed bump, that's for sure.'

Achmed the Certain, replied, 'Lead the way, Remy, I will follow.'

'Me, too! Come, Alan....are you ready?' said Foo.

No, not really. 'Oh, aye. Of course.'

John shrugged and smiled, 'Suit yourselves. Have a good day, gentlemen.'

*

It took an incredible amount of spin and effort, but Samantha, Norrie's sisters and his Mama, managed to keep Sofia, Violet, and the cousins, from trailing after Norrie on his trip to Nelson's shed. Hank and the brothers steered clear as they knew they would have caved in and let them go. Sofia had been particularly upset seeing as it was her birthday, but it also worked to the ladies' advantage. 'It's because it's your birthday, Sofia. Something's being planned. You don't like to ruin surprises, do you?' Samantha hoped, no. 1 – Sofia would forget what she'd said in a few hours. Unlikely. Or no. 2 – Norrie would come up with something good to surprise her with. In any case, Norrie made it to Nelson's shed with only Patches and Sailor in tow.

The scene at the shed was much the same as it had been for the last few weeks. The other fishermen were landing their catches and wondering what on earth Norrie was thinking. Something would have to give at some point. Each man wished, hoped that the MEO would pack up and take their SAC status with them. Wishful thinking. They just cared about their friend who was standing in its shadow, not willing to budge. It was not much fun watching a solitary individual battle the inevitable.

'No crisps?' Joe asked as he poured Norrie's pint.

'No. Left the girls at home with the others. Considering the circumstances.'

'Aye, aye.'

'Anything new?'

'Much the same, you know. Been quite busy.'

'Aye, well, that's good.' Norrie sipped his beer.

It was becoming difficult for anyone to converse with Norrie without wondering what he was going to do next. He had to do something, bar a miracle. He had a wife and children to support. And that meant being somewhat sensible.

‘I see Celtic and Rangers are playing friendlies in the States this evening,’ Joe said. Neither he nor Norrie bothered much with the game, or any sports for that matter, but it was better than talking about what hadn't changed regarding the special area of conservation and the MEO.

‘Aye, aye.’

Norrie, too, was finding it difficult to have any genuine interest in anything except not quitting.

‘Vatersay Boys will be in tonight.’

‘Oh, aye?’

‘You should bring Hank and the others, ought to be a good evening.’

‘Aye, might just do that...’

The door opened and Eddie, Colin, Ronnie, and Irish walked in, their week's landings safely in storage in the back of Nelson's big refrigerated lorry – and....just behind them, exhausted and almost tripping over one another – *who in heaven's name are they?*

Ch 53

I Will Never Leave You

The quartet nearly collapsed into one giant heap of living, breathing, and perspiring colourful robes. Alan would have if it were not for the quick hands of the others.

'Come on there, old boy, you'll be fine.' Remy huffed and puffed as he placed a steadying hand on the bar counter. 'My god, that was some struggle.'

'Struggle is not the right word,' Achmed the Weary said, wiping sweat from his brow.

'Confucius never mention road *that* up and down. Maybe it my age.'

Alan had nothing to offer as his lungs begged for more oxygen.

Joe, Norrie, and the rest in the bar could do little at that moment but – observe.

Joe finally enquired, 'Gentlemen, are you all right?'

Remy, after more huffing and puffing replied, 'Yes, yes, thank you – and no...just need a little break, my goodness....we should have taken John's advice and gone the west side.'

'You lead, we follow....it all right. We made it.' Foo steadied himself and was coming around.

'I thought we'd lost Alan up that last bit there before the sign for – what was it again? Bogach?' Achmed panted, hands on his knees, looking up at Joe. 'My friend, I hope you have something refreshing on tap.'

Joe adjusted his glasses – curious about what was unfolding in front of him, as though it was a product of his imagination – no, they were still there, 'Aye, we've lager, ale, Guinness, Irn Bru perhaps, Strongbow?'

'Ah, Strongbow, perfect!' Remy slapped a fifty-pound note on the counter. 'And a round for these men here, and for yourself.'

'I Foo, nice to meet you.' He extended a hand to Eddie.

'And I am Achmed.'

'I'm Remy. And this here's our good friend, Alan. He's still a little out of breath.'

Eddie, Colin, and company introduced themselves, appropriately intrigued...but even more intrigued were Remy, Achmed and Foo – when Norrie introduced himself.

'Ah, nice to meet you, Norrie.'

*

'You don't say? Doggone governments, you can't trust 'em.'

The conversation had meandered through pleasantries, the quartet's concocted tale of why they were visiting, their folly at choosing the east versus the west side to get to Northbay, and then without warning Dr Foo had asked, 'On ferry we hear something up with some MEO? Who *meow?* This not cat problem?' Polite chat aside, they were there to investigate and suss out their opponent. And they heard what they had expected to hear. The story told the other way around, from the other side.

Remy, Foo, and Achmed were tremendously careful, tiptoeing their way around the conversation. They had an advantage in that they appeared to be men of religion – and philosophy, and thus, people would expect them to be naturally curious and concerned about the wellbeing of others, but still, they couldn't push and prod too much.

But they had to take a chance. Remy started, saying, 'Shoot, I ain't no fan of governments meddlin' and all that, but...' he had to hear and to see for himself who they were dealing with. He looked at Norrie and added, 'You ever thought about making a change?'

The reaction of the others spoke volumes. Been there, done that. Nice try.

As Alan's inner voice screamed, *'Call the constable and stick him in jail! He'll soon learn!'* Remy and company had one thing on their minds: snap consultation, Alan. We gotta make sure the MEO makes clear how serious this is. You'll have plenty of time, make it happen. They could now comfortably shift gears. There was no reason dwelling on the subject and the conversation moved along, winding up on the tasty choices of where to go for dinner. When they heard that they were in the company of the man who dives for Joe's scallops, there was no further debating the matter and a booking was made for 7pm.

'And we've live music this evening, gentlemen, if you're interested.'

'Well, well, that sounds like a grand idea.' Remy looked at his compadres who thought it grand, too. 'We might be here convalescing, but it don't mean we can't have a little fun.'

*

And fun that evening they had, everyone but Alan that is, who had a persistent feeling of discomfort trying to relax in disguise, not to mention had a body full of aches and pains from cycling round the island. They received plenty of second glances, and even a few third and fourth ones, but after that they were just accepted for, er, whoever they were.

The quartet was sitting around a table in a back corner, opposite to where the band had the place thumping.

Remy nudged Alan, 'Relax, old boy, have one of these drams, I doubled them up. Don't be so self-conscious, you don't look *that* out of place, you are human after all. Ah, hey, look who's coming in...'

A big mob squeezed their way through the crowd, led by Eddie, Norrie, and the others they'd met earlier – along with a few they hadn't.

*

It had been next to impossible for Norrie to escape story time that Saturday evening, with Sofia, Violet, and all their cousins, begging him to tell the story of the greatest cockle raker in the world just one more time. But manage he did, with the help of Samantha and his sisters. Hank and the brothers looked on, unsure as to which way things would go.

Finally, they were free, and the five men made their way to The Heathbank as the sun set across the Atlantic.

They crossed paths with Eddie and company as they made their way up the steps, and a few moments later were jostling their way into an already heaving venue.

'Those must be the fellas you was talking about?' Hank leaned towards Norrie, pointing to the quartet waving from the corner. *Dang, they are a curious lot.*

When the Vatersay Boys were playing things always got a little rowdy – and that Saturday was no exception. Drinks were passed around and Mwaka, Darweshi, and Akili were especially happy to meet – these *entirely* interesting fellow men of faith. Foo was desperate to speak in Gaelic with Norrie, Eddie, and the other fishermen, but alas, it had been decided it wouldn't fit their disguises. That was all right though, because many spoke the Gaelic around him, switching easily between English and Gaelic depending on who's talking to whom, and the nature of the conversation. No one would have guessed that Foo spoke Gaelic, so he managed to eavesdrop – *so far so good* – no one appeared to suspect that they were anything other than who they presented themselves to be, and nothing suspicious was said about them. Rather, to his delight, he found everyone friendly and accommodating.

When speaking with whomever, Remy, Foo, and Achmed, stuck to their standard line: they were convalescing, under strict instructions by their Orders to get away for a while and just take it easy. Alan kept up the sore throat routine and did his best not to say a word.

'You look like you are convalescing pretty well here, gentlemen,' Darweshi half shouted into Remy's ear, trying to be heard over the noise of the thumping band.

Remy smiled, nodding, 'Oh yes, of course, of course – this island, the fresh air, walks on the beach, it's so relaxing, beautiful...rejuvenating...'

'You are right, Remy, rejuvenating and beautiful, they are good words for Floonay....I love Kenya, but yet, I do not like to leave here....it is very tough. My god, those drums are going to have my ears ringing!'

To the relief of every pair of eardrums in the place, even the drummer's, there were a few tunes that did not call for full-on banging. For every dram poured, another tale was told. Remy, Foo, and Achmed, tucked into a cosy corner bench, were told in confidence the story of the terrible tragedy from years before. (It was never talked about around Norrie). Such stories have a way of cropping up, as it did that night, but it wasn't before the group had accepted Eddie's offer to take them for a sail out of Northbay the following day – actually, it would be later that same day.

Foo reflected on his wife's words before he'd kissed her goodbye at the airport in Hong Kong, *Be careful, darling*.

He leaned in and asked, 'Eddie, are you sure the weather will be okay?'

'Ach, aye, forecast is fine, honestly.'

Next it was Remy, who glanced from Eddie to Colin. 'And what about – that whale?'

'It hasn't been seen in forever...they swim the seven seas, with any luck it got stuck among some icebergs and is long gone.'

A few nervous chuckles followed.

'There'll be no surprises tomorrow, you'll be fine.'

Hank was having such a fine time that he suggested to Norrie they have a little ceilidh back at the house. 'The girls'll be wanting a little singsong, I'm sure.' A grand idea. And so that's what they wound up doing, a half dozen others in tow along with the convalescing quartet. By the time they left The Heathbank Alan had loosened up, and it had taken a few sharp jabs from Achmed to remind him of his deep cover, as he'd started chatting up the bar staff, who had taken his advances a little by surprise.

There were a lot of children sleeping in the house, so Samantha wisely said to Norrie, 'We've got the barbecue tomorrow night, sorry, tonight, and your sisters and I are taking the children to the beach after church. I don't want them waking up, I'll never get them back to sleep. Let's go to the Nissen hut for a few tunes.' And so that is what they did. As it happens though, the hours fairly slip along at that sort of time and when people are in that sort of joyful mood. It was four am before anyone knew it. Samantha, Norrie's Mama, and sisters wisely decided it was time for bed.

But not so wisely, Hank said, 'Boys, come on, I wanna show you the inside of *Flyin' Tayters*. You ever seen the inside of a big ol' bird like that before?' The question was directed at the now slightly tired, sweaty, and drunk men of faith. Remy, Foo, and Achmed looked at one another, and simultaneously thought the same thing, *yes, lots of times,* but, hell, they were up for a little wander over.

'Aye, why not,' Eddie said, looking at Ronnie and the others. They'd never seen inside *Flyin' Tayters* or any other fancy jet, for that matter. 'We're in.'

By this point Alan could hardly stand and it was Akili who said, 'Should we carry him over or leave him here?'

'I've a camp bed here, we can unfold it for him,' Norrie offered.

'Yeah, that's a good idea,' Remy replied, 'he had a tough go of it cycling round the island. He needs his rest.'

'No need to refill your drinks, boys. The bar is fully stocked on board,' Hank announced and headed across the beach, which had started to brighten as the sun began peeking over the Minch.

It had been quite refreshing for Norrie to have spent the entire evening and night, and now early morning, not talking, or thinking, or answering repetitive questions reworded one way or another about the 'inevitable' topic.

A few tales were told, Hank poured sloppy measures of some expensive single malt, and without a ceilidh band energising everyone it was peaceful aboard Hank's plush ride. It didn't take long for everyone, comfy and reclining in large leather seats, to start dropping off into the land of nod.

Norrie had pressed a button and his seat went back a little further. He was drifting off and could hear Hank talking, perhaps with a bit of a slur, and could hear Mwaka – saying? – it was unintelligible. He glanced to his left and out the porthole the last thing he saw before falling asleep was the gentle, ebbing tide half a mile away, and the last thought that ebbed, then flowed, through his mind was, *I will never leave you.*

Ch 54

If I Could Freeze Time?

'Dang, I am all screwed up. This ain't no good, no good at all. I think your Mama's a little mad at me. Come on, Norrie, I say you and me get on outta here while the gettins' good. Fresh air and a walk'll do us good.'

'Aye, great idea Hank.'

The wounded soldiers had woken up ever so groggily at nine o'clock, to the sound of two barking dogs outside the aeroplane. Mwaka, Darweshi, and Akili were particularly concerned as they'd promised to give Father John and Reverend Cullen a hand with the services that day. *Oh, my brothers, we are in trouble today.* When they arrived back at the croft they were met by three impatient wives who whisked them off to get them ready for the first service. Remy called the proprietor of the B&B they were staying at for a lift. Norrie's Mama said little to Hank as she prepared to take the children to church – as for Samantha's part – well, Norrie steered completely clear, choosing to find things to do in the Nissen hut until they had all left.

They were now gone, thank goodness.

'It's a halfway decent day, what'd you say we head on out to the west side?' Hank suggested after making his way out to the Nissen hut.

'Aye, that sounds good. Don't think I'm up for cockle raking today anyway.'

Patches and Sailor barked their approval – they thought it a great idea.

'I've packed us a few snacks and got a thermos brimming,' Hank chuckled, 'Those were some interesting fellas, Remy and them.'

'Aye, you could say that.'

'That one fella, Alan, he was a bit of a strange cat.'

'Probably just feeling a little out of place.'

'Well, he wasn't feeling too outta place when he was hitting on Maggie Anne and Karen, that's for sure.'

'Aye, aye...I wonder how they're going to get on today.'

Hank whistled, 'Shoot, who knows. I'll tell ya, I wouldn't be heading anywhere near the sea today.'

Join the club.

'Eddie and the boys weren't in much better shape than the rest of us, you reckon they'll cancel?'

Norrie shook his head, 'They were born on the sea, they'll be there.'

Hank chuckled, 'Well, I wish 'em luck, or smooth sailing...something like that.'

'Aye, aye – not too sure how much convalescing they got done last night – or this morning.'

'No doubt, my man, no doubt. And they're comin' on over for the barbecue tonight...there's gonna be quite a crowd.'

'Let's see if they make it through the day first. Dillon might be tucking them into bed early.'

'Or bypassing home and whisking 'em straight to the hospital.'

Norrie smiled, 'Aye, give it a few days and they might be cursing Floonay.'

*

'Thank you, kind sir, thank you.' Remy accepted the proffered tray of tea and scones from Dillon, the B&B proprietor, in the wee living room. Foo, Achmed, and Alan, were all seated – sort of – a little worse for wear.

'And here's some porridge, it should help. The scones are from Elma down the road. The best.' Dillon's wife, Elspeth, laid another tray on the table.

'Ma'am, you are too kind.'

'We'll just close this door, gentlemen, and leave you....'

'Oh, and if you could, in case we oversleep, give us a knock on our doors at noon. We're heading out with Eddie and a few of his pals.'

Dillon and Elspeth looked at one another. *Really? Well, good luck. We're impressed, sort of.*

Alan looked at Remy – *horrified. What?!*

'Noon it is.' Dillon and Elspeth retreated closing the door behind them.

'Let's just get a little chow in us here, a few hours to snooze and....'

'Remy, if I may say.' Alan roused himself, 'Are you sure it's a wise idea to, you know....is it even safe to...'

'Relax, old boy, you ain't never had a hangover before? You'll be fine.'

I'm not sure if 'hangover' is the right word for this. Something a little more serious perhaps.

'I not feeling best myself. But I go.' Foo sipped his tea. 'It will be fun. We make it fun.'

Alan lifted a shaking spoon of porridge to his lips. *Ouch.* It burned his lips.

'There's milk there, Alan,' said Achmed the Advisor, pointing.

Alan was not a religious man, but running through his head was: *Oh, please God, what have I done?* What he wouldn't give to be back in the safe bosom of Edinburgh, curled up with Colette, or Jessica, or even his wife.

Remy, as though he had read Alan's thoughts, said, 'Alan, think of *you know what.* Persevere, old boy. We didn't choose you accidentally.'

Yes, but – why a boat ride?! Oh, dear God.

To focus Alan's mind somewhat, Remy told him their plan: snap consultation tomorrow evening in Castlebay's community hall. The MEO would be presenting all the facts as a way of reminding the community how serious the matter was. 'Talk to your man, James, and get the wheels turning.'

Alan replied, forgetting his hangover for a moment, 'Aye, aye, that's not a problem. We'll say the memo must have been lost. Thirty-six hours is not unreasonable. Heaven knows how many meetings of much more importance – no disrespect, gentlemen – have been convened on much shorter notice. Happens all the time.'

The others smiled. *That's our man, Alan.*

*

'I gotta question for you Norrie,' Hank just managed, as he gasped and panted, as the pair ascended the north side of Grean point near the golf course. A stunning panorama of sea and sky to their right and splayed out down below was a seemingly endless stretch of sand and dunes interspersed with timeworn crags. If they could only speak, what a tale they would tell.

'Aye?'

'If you could freeze time, when would you?'

'If I could freeze time?'

'Yeah – I know, I know, might seem a dumbass question an' all. I was just a wonderin', that's all.'

Norrie reflected a moment and was uncertain, and yet...

'I mean, puttin' aside freezin' time to avoid past tragedies, well – what I'm meanin' is like what moment in time, place, would you like things to stay for-ever the same? Subtracting being able to go way way – ah, this question kinda sucks...'

Norrie interrupted, 'Not sure, Hank, to be honest.'

'Yeah, I guess it's a toughy....it just got me thinkin' you know, with this whole MEO fiasco and them a bannin' fishin' and cockle rakin' – well, I just remember talkin' a while back there, I was up in Alberta and havin' a good ol' chin wag with a few ranchers I know and they were just a reminiscin' about the good ol' days – hey, me and them, we're a few years older than you – we tend to do that from time to time....they was goin' on about new rules and regs and not just to do with their cattle, you know.'

Norrie's mind scrolled through all the tales, tips, techniques, and warnings he'd read in the Coquilleuous Rakkeronuous Almenikhiaka and couldn't think of any that addressed freezing time.

'I can say that there's plenty of fond memories,' and plenty of not so fond ones.

'Yeah, yeah, hey, I guess I'm just bein' a little nostalgic – pretty stupid question, I guess. But if I could, I'd freeze it the day before they put that dang ban in place. I guess I'm just a little concerned, you know what I'm sayin'?'

Yes, Norrie got what he was saying.

'Hell, Norrie, now you know I ain't braggin' but you know I've got all the money I'll ever need, and that is puttin' it lightly. I can set you up with whatever it is you might want to do next – if things don't work out.'

'I appreciate that Hank, but...' *it's not about the money.* 'I don't know.'

'Don't forget, my man, you can always head up to Uist, or further afield, to rake. Hell, I'll even buy you a house up there, or you can commute.'

'It wouldn't feel right.'

'But you gotta do something, Norrie.'

Hank had kept his word over the years. He was the only one who knew about what almost happened in the Nissen hut. He knew, too well, what could happen if he fell out, or was forced out, of his routine – his rhythm. It was not pretty.

'You've got a family now, my man, you know?'

Hank suspected, as did others – that there was more, there was always more – to it, *to everything.*

Norrie replied optimistically, 'They haven't concluded their investigation, the ban can still be lifted – it was with that one place down south. The damage they'd said was caused by whatever, it was minimal. They're a bunch of interfering bastards, but there must be a few reasonable souls in the organisation. Surely.'

'I gotcha, I gotcha, but, man, I guess this comes down to, you know, in the here and now – you really, truly, could wind up in jail. What if they shipped you off to the mainland for a spell with the real baddies?'

Ship was not a pleasant thought. *They would never catch me.*

'Let's take a little break. That thermos handy?' Norrie decided it was time to change the subject.

'That's a good idea, I'm already worn out – whew. What a mighty view that is – *hmm* – seems like the wind's up a bit, I wonder how the boys are gettin' on?'

*

'Welcome aboard, gentlemen, how are the heads today?'

'Ain't too bad, Eddie, ain't too bad,' Remy replied as he steadied himself, stepping from the pier to the gunnel and hopping down onto the deck.

Sadly for Alan, Dillon had remembered to knock on the doors at noon. There was no avoiding what was to come. Elspeth had prepared sandwiches, snacks, and flasks of tea and coffee for them, and off they went for the three-mile drive to Northbay pier.

'This is some boat. Impressive.' Achmed surveyed the deck and poked his head in the wheelhouse checking out all the electronic gear. He wanted dearly to tell Eddie about a few of the boats he had in harbours around the world but – obviously – could not.

'This is kind of you to take us out, we are very grateful.' Foo wished to say it in Gaelic, but – again – deep cover was essential.

'No worries, gents, we'll have a pleasant trip.' Eddie glanced at his watch then continued, 'Shouldn't be too far off now...Ronnie's on his way, he's picking up Colin and Irish – he's always running late. Alan, you're looking a little pale, are you all right?'

No, I'm not. 'Oh, aye, aye. Just fine.'

Fifteen minutes later, Odyssey II, with eight souls aboard, was steaming east out of Northbay for a three-hour tour. Turning to the northeast, Eddie navigated the boat through the 'orchard' scattered with tricky reefs and wee islands, now populated only by sheep. Ronnie, Colin and Irish – happy to be out on a relaxing day off – pointed out landmarks to their guests and told tales passed down through the years.

'Thought we'd head out the back of Hellisay, nip into the lagoon – a lovely wee spot,' said Eddie, as she sipped from a can of lager. 'That's Flodday...'

Ah, yes, of course, of course. Remy surveyed the area. He knew most of the names from the charts they'd studied – and further to the north and west was Greanamul, the future home of their Think Tank.

'And this whole area, this where the fishing ban is in place?' Foo sipped his tea, already knowing the answer.

Eddie replied in the expected rueful manner, but they were out for a pleasant day (even if it was choppier than he was expecting) so he wasn't going to dwell on it, though it pissed him off mightily.

As they passed the imposing cliffs on the southeast corner of Hellisay, the motion of the ocean increased substantially. They were now fully exposed to the swells of the Minch pushing in relentlessly from the east. It was by no means dangerous sailing for a boat as reliable as Odyssey II, but it was not the most relaxing conditions for a pleasant day out.

Remy, Achmed, and Foo didn't seem to mind – rather, they found the rocking back and forth all quite exhilarating. It was just poor Alan who was having a tough time coping.

'Alan, try focusing on the horizon,' Colin called out, 'It'll help stabilise your equilibrium.'

No, that didn't seem to work. He held his head in his hands and tried to take deep non-vomit inducing breaths. It seemed to help a teeny, tiny bit. He was struggling but – Remy's words floated through his topsy-turvy mind – 'think of you know what. Persevere, old boy. We didn't choose you accidentally'. Yes, but – *why the hell did I come? We don't have to do everything together. Ah! I feel like Dante has made a circle of Hell just for me....*

'Try a hefty dram, that might help.' Ronnie had a bottle of Famous Grouse in hand.

Alan did not want to even think about that, and it was to his great pleasure a few minutes later that they were turning west and heading into a narrow passage between Hellisay and

Gighay, which took them into a secluded lagoon – it was flat calm and absolutely wonderful.

Alan, feeling somewhat better, but embarrassed, spoke up, 'Pardon me, men, I'm not normally like this on boats – last night and all.' *Last night? This morning for goodness sake! What are any of us doing out here?*

'You'll be all right there, Alan, old boy,' Remy said, slapping him on the back. 'Irish was just saying there's some old ruins here on Hellisay, we're gonna go check 'em out, you'll be on dry land in no time.'

But they also had to make it back to Floonay. The thought of doing so lingered with Alan as they trekked around the rugged island. And little white caps seemed to be multiplying in numbers as he looked out over the Sound, making the thought even less pleasant. The others appeared to be having a fine time and there was much being said to which Alan wasn't paying attention. He followed along and tried focusing on Remy's words of advice. *I'm trying Remy, I'm trying.*

Ch 55

Do I Even Have to Say?

Sightseeing aside, Remy, Foo and Achmed's business minds were hard at work as they crossed the Sound back to Floonay. Their investment, they were certain, would be welcomed by an overwhelming majority of the locals. There would always be a minority opposed to any decision. That was life. There was no pleasing one hundred percent. Their new island friends were still fishing, albeit not in the Sound. They were certain that even they, eventually, would recognise the benefits of what had been planned. It was a shame that there was this one man who stubbornly refused to give in, but who knew, perhaps even he would eventually come to his senses and make a change. Sooner rather than later.

'Hang in there, Alan, it's not far now,' Ronnie said encouragingly. 'Colin, can you pass me a beer?'

Alan was curled up in a foetal position on the deck, moaning.

'Do you see that boat coming in over there?' Colin directed the group's attention east across the swells, as he passed Ronnie a can. 'That's the biggest boat in the Northbay fleet. She's called "Spray". Her skipper takes her miles out for prawns. You gentlemen like prawns?'

They nodded. Absolutely.

'We'll get some for the barbecue this evening.'

Remy and company were immeasurably grateful for the welcome and hospitality they were receiving. Remy loved his native republic, and Achmed's adopted home of Zanzibar held a special place in his heart. Foo, too, always felt a comforting warmth when arriving back in Shanghai or Hong Kong. They were all special places, but to be sure, they felt something particularly special – unique – about this small island community. And it was because of that *uniqueness* that they knew deep in their hearts they had chosen the perfect location for their newest, and most ambitious, investment.

The acute distress Alan was experiencing finally faded away when they arrived back at Northbay pier. Terra Firma. Stability. *Much better.*

Remy and company conveyed their many thanks, to which Eddie and company replied that it had been their pleasure.

'It's not very often that we get the opportunity to help gentlemen like yourselves convalesce...you're looking much better, Alan...we'll see yous at the barbecue, then.'

By the time they arrived back at their Bed and Breakfast, Alan was feeling even better. They had a few hours to rest before the barbecue – ought to be a relaxing time, though Alan would feel more comfortable *sans* the disguise. He doubted that many people would recognise him, and certainly not in the Outer Hebrides. He wasn't on the front bench. Quite the opposite. His party had tried its level best to keep him well out of the public eye – but, ah, you never knew. It would only take one keen eye and questions would be raised. So, alas, the disguise it had to be.

The only thing left was the public consultation, and then he'd be hotfooting it back to Edinburgh the following day. *Thank goodness!* Alan had phoned his chief confidante before the "boat ride through Hell" asking him to get the ball rolling, contact the MEO. 'If you encounter any resistance, James...' James had interrupted him, 'Alan, I'll take care of it. Thirty-six hours is not unreasonable. The memo must have got lost, remember?'

*

'Papa, Papa, where have you been! You weren't at the beach and we were missing Patches and Sailor – Papa!?' Sofia ran to her father as he and Hank made their way towards the house. Violet was right behind.

'Come here – my, my, ohh, you are getting so, so heavy.'

'I'm not that heavy, Papa. I'm only this many years old,' she replied, spreading her little hands, blossoming fingers.

'Well, maybe it's me, then, maybe I'm getting too old to swing little girls around, what do you think?'

'No!!' both girls protested in unison.

'Pick me up, Papa – Papa – pllleease!!' Violet cried out desperately.

'Maybe Grandpa Hank can – ah, look at that, there you go.'

Preparations were well underway for the barbecue by the time they arrived home. The brothers' predicaments seemed to have improved and Norrie's sisters appeared to have forgiven them for their tardy and groggy start to the day. Norrie's Mama and Samantha, also, had too much preparing to do to bother being upset with their men any longer.

Norrie and Hank made themselves useful by staying out of the way – in the Nissen hut. They'd be taking care of barbecuing duties when the time came for it.

'Here you go, Norrie.' Hank tossed him a bottle from his seemingly bottomless beer cooler. 'That's a good hoppy one. It's an IPA. Careful opening it.'

Mwaka, Akili, and Darweshi appeared looking for a refreshment from Hank's cooler, and it wasn't long before others started arriving. The wind had picked up, but it was a fair enough day with plenty of sun peeking in and out of swiftly moving clouds. It was certainly not barbecue-cancelling weather. Eddie and the boys arrived with their families. Their children ran off to play with the other children. Wives and girlfriends migrated to the house and the men congregated by the Nissen hut door. It didn't take long to hear some out of the blue news: 'Did you hear? There's a public consultation tomorrow evening.' 'Aye?' 'Aye. Well, well. A little short on the notice.' The news did not dominate the evening, however, as it had been hashed through already. Consultation or no consultation, they were there to enjoy themselves and that is what they intended to do.

The faithful quartet finally arrived and by that point Alan was feeling much better. He was ready for the drink that Hank was offering.

'I hear you gentlemen had a good time today.'

'Oh, aye, aye.' Alan was pressing a mental 'delete' button on the memory. No reason to dwell.

'It was very good of Eddie to take us out. Odyssey II a fine boat,' Foo commented.

'You got that right, Foo,' Remy chuckled. 'Were some pretty good waves, but it was all a lot of fun. Interesting, too. We took a walk around Hellisay. You know people used to live out there...makes Floonay seem pretty doggone big.'

The tricky bit for Remy, Foo, and Achmed, at this point, was how to ensure their host's stubbornness did not magnify any light being shed on the ban. In this day and age, it didn't take much for a story to go viral. No one seemed too up in arms on the island – that was a big plus. But if this man kept raking, if he refused to quit, things could change. They hadn't told Alan yet, but they believed that nudging things along the appropriate legal path – eventually jail – was not the best option. That was the most sure-fire way to incite protests from the locals – and news spreading would follow. It had happened before – a small band of protestors, or raiders, end up creating an incident that was heard about round the world. Foo had related the story he had been told by his adopted mother, the story of the Vatersay and Ardmhor Raiders. That was the last thing they needed. So, it came down to: 1 – buying him off (surely everyone has his or her price) or, 2 – having someone convince him to choose another profession (surely someone could knock some sense into him). The whole evening, as stories were told, laughs were had, and bellies were filled, Remy, Foo, and Achmed, watched and calculated.

They needed Norrie MacKinnon out of the picture.

After the last belly was satisfied and settled, the gathering morphed into a ceilidh. Accordions, fiddles, and a set of pipes emerged from boxes, and the first series of tunes had half of those in attendance lined up for dances.

Remy, Foo, and Achmed stayed as close as possible to wherever Norrie was conversing. It wasn't difficult to do as everyone was so friendly. The ban, the MEO, the SAC, and Norrie's 'situation' surfaced every now and again, and they listened intently searching for any sign of – weakness, doubt, uncertainty, something – anything they could exploit, use against him. There was nothing. They shuffled around, following. There was one point where Foo wisely halted his two partners in crime and whispered, 'Stop! He only go for pee.'

Alan had loosened up after a few stiff drinks and found himself trending towards what he liked to do naturally: check out the ladies. Fortunately, Achmed had spotted Alan, and sensing he was about to make his move, intercepted him, 'Don't blow our cover, Alan. Why don't you try a little dancing? Keep your mind somewhat *elevated*. You're supposed to be a convalescing man of God. You are not supposed to be out looking to hook-up.'

'Of course, of course, pardon me, was just going to have a chat – I'll just make my way this way....'

'And don't forget, talk as little as possible – keep your thoughts on "you know what."'

The evening fairly moved along. Young danced with old, and old with young, and it was at one point wee Sofia MacKinnon grabbed the hand of the funny looking man standing a little by himself and staring into space (relaxed but uncertain of what he was supposed to be doing). He was tapping his toes to the music so he must be having a good time, Sofia thought.

Alan Trout was being dragged out for a dance.

The sudden tugging on his hand took Alan by surprise and he lurched forward, half tripping on his robe....and as he did...

It....

Dropped....

The Nissen hut was full of music and dance, chatter and laughter. Not a soul noticed – except for Alan, a surprised young girl, and the three men of faith standing not far away, ears on the story Ronnie and Irish were recounting in tandem, but eyes flitting over to the stumbling politician.

What on earth??

*

Sofia's eyes widened at what tumbled to her feet. She picked it up.

It was too late by the time Alan regained his balance. Sofia had it firmly in her grip and was already opening it – and my, oh my – but the look of joy that spread across her lovely wee face.

'You got this for – *me?!*' It was ninety five percent statement, only five percent question. She was beaming. 'You knew yesterday was my birthday??!' Ninety eight percent statement, two percent question. He *must* have.

Sofia pulled a lever – and, oh my goodness – look, it's spinning – and look at all the colours – and there are more levers to pull on!.....she hadn't read a word but it had already become her favourite book in all the world!

She turned a page and a man rose up from it....another lever pulled, and....*the man was moving!!*

And Sofia's smile spread even wider.

Alan stammered and reached down....and for the briefest of moments.....it crossed Sofia's mind.....was he?? No! Of course he wasn't!

Sofia snapped the book shut. 'Oh, Thank you mister! I'm just going to go and put this in my room,' and with that she spun around and was out of the Nissen hut in a flash.

Amidst the revelry only the three wise men had noticed the exchange. A moment later Sofia came running back in and tugged on her Papa's sleeve. He was in conversation with his brothers in law and Hank, not far from where the trio of faith were still half following Ronnie and Irish's tandem story....eyes flitting to their number four, who stood in a state of bewilderment....*have I done something wrong?* He couldn't tell what message Remy and company were trying to transmit. Foo gestured for him to come over. *Uh oh. I'm sorry.*

'Papa, Papa, that man over there, where is – oh there he is, that man got me a book for my birthday. It's a pop-up picture book! It's my favourite book ever! Well, your big book is still our favourite, but it's yours. This book is *my* favourite.'

'Well, wasn't that nice of him...I hope you said, thank you.'

'Of course, Papa!'

Alan was now standing with Remy and the others. He looked over and acknowledged Norrie and company, giving a weak smile and a little wave. *Aye, aye, no problem, no, er, problem.*

'Oh, that's right!' Sofia tugged on her Papa's hand and guided him a few feet over. 'Mister, this is my Papa....he has a super big book. It has a long, funny name and he tells us stories from it, but it doesn't have pop-up bits like the book you gave me. But it is old – it's ancient!'

As Remy, Foo, and Achmed looked on, their brains were calculating what could be the outcome of the book dropping out from under Alan's robe. What on earth was he doing with it here anyway? He should have left it in his room. Staying undercover was absolutely vital. They were grateful that the book was what it was: a colourful pop-up book. Its true message simplified and disguised. What they were immediately concerned about was that if an adult took a look inside – would they wonder what a grown man, a man of faith, ostensibly on the island convalescing, was doing giving a young girl such a curious book? In short: would it be out of place? Would it raise any questions whatsoever? Who were these men of faith? Would anyone even look at it? The wee girl had run off with it, and obviously put it in a place where treasured things go. That was good. It was, hopefully, well hidden.

As for Alan, his thoughts were more on how much he might have screwed up. *I should have left it back at the B&B! But it fit so perfectly in the pouch.*

By this point the musicians had put their instruments down, and those who'd been dancing were wiping their brows and refreshing themselves. The place buzzed with chatter and laughter....and Remy, Foo, and Achmed were intrigued by this young girl's enthusiasm.

'Well, well, young lady,' Remy began. 'I sure think big, old, ancient books are pretty interesting, don't you gentlemen agree?'

Achmed and Foo nodded enthusiastically. Alan followed along limply.

'Oh, Papa's big book is the most interesting ever....Papa? Can you show them your big book, can you?'

'Well, sweetheart, I don't think these men....'

'We are men of faith – and philosophy. Of course, we would be honoured, good sir,' Foo replied. Achmed and Remy nodded eagerly. Alan, again bewildered, followed along.

The Cockle Raker's Almanac was no giant MacKinnon family secret. Others were aware of its existence, and many were familiar with some of the stories contained within it. Quite a few of the stories were already in the public domain, they just happened to have been interpreted, in one way or another, by a long line of MacKinnons. The tips and techniques section was what it was, lessons about cockle raking, as explained by eight generations of Norrie's forefathers. It had never been some centuries long oath that the knowledge contained within the book be passed on only from MacKinnon to MacKinnon. It's just how it happened, son to son to son....and in Norrie's case, to his two daughters.

As Norrie thought a moment, Hank chipped in, 'Boys, it's some book, I've heard a few of the tales from it.'

Mwaka added, 'It is quite fascinating.'

Well, Norrie thought, I don't suppose it can hurt. Sofia seemed eager. Why not?

'Here, come on, then.' Norrie escorted the four convalescents into the house and showed them to the living room. He opened a cabinet, hefted it out, and placed it on a table, 'This is the *Coquilleuous Rakkeronuous Almenikhiaka*...'

Remy, Foo, and Achmed, nodded thoughtfully, thoroughly curious. Alan's brain went like this: *The what?!*

'It started way back with my great times eight grandfather Cloon. He's the man credited with discovering cockles here on Floonay, or according to his record book anyway. You know how these things can be. Something is discovered in one place

– or time – and it might take a little longer for it to be discovered in some other place.'

Nods all around. Well, three nods anyway and one confused politician in disguise.

Norrie began to give a little history of the Cockle Raker's Almanac. It was what it was: a book of tips and techniques, stern warnings, and marvellous adventures.

'Not all the tales took place out there – the beach, or here on Floonay, obviously...it would seem that along the way others in my line would add tales heard from places far and wide and undoubtedly added their own spin on things.'

Achmed ran a hand over the shells on the cover and said, 'I once met a man when I was lost in the desert, he had a book a little like this – I believe it was of similar importance.'

Remy added, 'I have to say, I ain't too much of a book man. But I find it fascinating that you have a book that stretches back eight generations of your people.'

'Aye, well, eight generations on my father's side, anyway.'

Foo said, 'That your great times eight grandfather decided to first put pen to paper, or maybe it was quill or pencil, at the time – you must be immeasurably grateful.'

Norrie thought for a moment. 'Aye. If it wasn't for him...well, who knows....'

'And... you have added – to it?' Remy wondered.

Norrie hesitated, thinking of the few lines he'd scribbled. 'I'm not much of a writing man, but I've added a few lines. I've put my mark in it, you could say.'

'And?' Achmed the Careful, asked, (They had only just heard the horrible story the previous evening) 'Your father?'

Norrie hesitated, 'Aye, he added a few tips. A few tales.'

Sofia had been quiet up to that point. She now spoke sadly, 'Papa, I wish I'd known my MacKinnon grandpapa.'

'That's all right, sweetheart.'

'I am sorry, I misspoke,' Achmed the Contrite apologised.

'No, no – that's okay.'

'Oh Papa, I know,' Sofia said more cheerfully, 'why don't you tell these men a story?'

'Ach, I don't think they really....'

Remy, Foo, and Achmed looked at one another, nodding eagerly. Alan just stared, clueless.

'Well, maybe just one then. Why don't we...'

'Oh, hold on.' And with that Sofia disappeared out of the living room and thirty seconds later was back, puffing and panting. 'Papa, everyone wants to hear the story.'

'What are you talking about?!'

'In the Nissen hut, Papa. Where else? I asked. It's okay, Papa,' she said, still out of breath.

'Sofia – there's thirty, forty, people out there.' This was unprecedented. This was never the way. Norrie was a little cross with his eldest daughter.

But the look in her eyes. The eagerness, the joy. Well, just this once.

And so, the quartet of faith, philosophy – and doubt – shuffled back outside, following behind Norrie and wee Sofia.

Norrie, resigned to his storytelling duties, asked Sofia, 'Which tale do you want me to tell?'

Sofia looked up at her Papa, her brow crumpled, 'Papa, do I even have to say?'

'I just told you that story – *again* – last night? Are you sure?'

Of course she's sure. Sorry for doubting.

Ch 56

This Can't Go Viral

When word spread of which story was about to be told, all the children dropped into position quickly and obediently.

By the time Norrie closed the big, crusty book, uttering the words, 'and that is the tale of the greatest cockle raker who ever lived,' the children's jaws were on the floor, as though they had never heard the story before, and the adults were looking similarly impressed, in a slightly more composed way. The few single women in attendance all had the same thought, *send me that cockle raker and I'll marry him right now.* Even Patches, Sailor, and the other canines in attendance had remained nearly motionless with only ears tweaking and tails wagging occasionally, thumping the floor. Brilliant! Fantastic!! Extraordinary!!! A few barks of approval. They loved the story as much as the humans.

'That's preposterous, ridiculous, one man couldn't do, couldn't be - all that!' was what Alan was thinking.

'Aye, I thought I'd heard about him. Something my father had said years ago,' Colin commented.

'You should ask Nugget about him. He has some unique insight,' Norrie said.

'Dang, I've heard some tales, tall and not so tall. But that's gotta be the best one ever. I love that story every time you tell it, Norrie,' Hank said and sipped his brew.

Sunday evening merged into night, and the following day was not a day of rest, and so, as the sun set across the western sky guests started heading home.

'I don't think we should head to *Flyin' Tayters* saloon tonight, eh, Norrie?'

'No, that's probably not a good idea.'

'Oh, my brothers,' Akili cautioned, 'It will be a long time before I spend a night – a morning was it not – in *Flyin' Tayters* saloon. Father John and Reverend Cullen were not very happy with us. I was not very happy with me.'

'To be sure, I do not know how we got through this day, but here we are,' Darweshi added encouragingly and with a smile.

Remy, Foo, and Achmed, offered their many thanks and bid their sincere adieus when Dillon came to collect them. Alan – part lost, part clueless – followed along. *What on earth are we doing here. This is absurd. Ohh, I shouldn't have lost that book. If we – if I, hadn't come...ahh, to be back in Edinburgh...to be away from here....I hope I'm not in trouble...*

'Stop by, anytime, gentlemen,' Norrie said.

'And make sure y'all get some good convalescin' rest, 'specially you, Alan.' He wasn't just looking a little tired, Hank reckoned, he was looking bewildered, lost...his Order definitely had him marked correctly for a little R&R. As for the others? Hank knew well enough that some people could hide the symptoms much better than others. Maybe their Orders did have them marked right, too.

*

As the MacKinnon household drifted off into the land of nod, Remy, Foo, Achmed, and a reluctant Alan, sat up in their B&B living room conferring, planning, conspiring, plotting what to do next to ensure news of the MEO's SAC ban did not, accidentally, go viral. They rehashed what they knew: 1 - This man, this Norrie MacKinnon, was a stubborn bastard – they liked the man, to be sure, but he was still a stubborn bastard. If they didn't play their cards right, his bullheadedness could cause serious delays if not potentially inflict mortal damage to their grand scheme. This was not an option. 2 - Buying him off seemed unlikely. His mother's new husband was a potato-millionaire. They assumed that if Norrie wanted to, Hank would and could set him up doing anything, even if it was just a lump sum to manage and invest for the rest of his life. No, they had sussed out that it was not about the money. That much had become clear. 3 - It frustrated them, and, it seemed, everyone, that the man was unwilling to head to Uist or further afield. If it was cockle raking that he loved so much then why not go somewhere else and rake to your heart's content? But he would not. That, too, had become clear. 4 - He had a family though, a good family. Two lovely daughters and a wonderful wife. He had to live for them. He could not continue down a path that would lead to...his downfall. That would affect them. He had to think of them. Surely? 5 - He had known tragedy. His whole family had. 6 - His attachment to the Traigh Mhor was obvious. He had a long family line of cockle raking MacKinnons, *and* that remarkable book (What a good idea his great times eight grandfather Cloon had come up with). 7- That was some story about the greatest cockle raker the world had ever known! (In Alan's brain: *Preposterous! Ridiculous!*) 8 - Alan losing the pop-up picture book shouldn't be a problem. Thank goodness they had simplified it so much for Alan that it did actually read like a proper children's story. (Alan's brain: *Whew!)* 9 - The three wise men reminded Alan that they had brought him into their inner-circle because he possessed a certain skill, a knack, of wiggling about when necessary, to make something happen (Alan's brain again: *ah, oh, thank you, thank you!)* And....finally, 10 - Nothing, absolutely nothing, was going to stand in the way of their plans. There was too much at stake, too much time, expense, and effort put into it to allow one man to ruin things (Alan's brain, once again: *ah ha! that's more like it! That's confidence! Send in the law if he kicks up a fuss. Lock him up!*)

That night, half the MacKinnon clan's children dreamt of adventuring with the greatest cockle raker in the world and the other half dreamt of playing on the Traigh with Patches and Sailor, while Norrie dreamt of what had caught his eye on the Atlantic horizon two days before. This dream plumbed the depths of his subconscious, swallowing him into such a bottomless abyss that he snapped awake in a cold sweat, dripping with panic. In their B&B, Remy, Foo, and Achmed drifted off to sleep, thinking deeply about the future of Floonay and the progress of humankind. For his part, not surprisingly, Alan Trout drifted off thinking only of his desires.

Ch 57

The Big Consultation

It was summer. It was the holidays. There were lots of children packed into the MacKinnon family home, and a few homes nearby, and Monday morning they all came to life as one would expect. Fast and furiously. With a bit of breakfast in the fizzing and buzzing little bellies all the adults had to do next was open the door and 'poof', the tiny tornadoes zigzagged their way out. Patches, Sailor, and the other neighbourhood canines took over responsibility for the youthful herd.

Peace for a little while.

Norrie had promised Samantha that he would not sneak out for a shift on the beach. Given the public consultation would be that evening, officials from the MEO most likely would be arriving on the early flight, if they were not already on the island. Simply, there would be too much attention that day on the Traigh and the Sound of Floonay. The public consultation did not evoke Norrie's interest because it did not sound as though there would be too much consulting going on, and it wasn't even clear if the MEO had started their investigation into the matter, let alone arrived at a conclusion. All that was clear was this: the MEO were to visit Floonay, carting with them heaps of scientific data to explain what was what. Undoubtedly, when a government body tried to explain something, 'obfuscate' more accurately came to mind.

And then they would leave, dragging their colour graphs, mighty formulas and cryptic spreadsheets with them, and Norrie would be back out doing what he'd always been doing, hoping that Constable Currie would be turning a blind eye.

Could it be there were a few sensible souls buried deep within the MEO? Perhaps. As such, Norrie held on to a fragment of hope that one day the ban would be lifted. But there was no stopping him until then.

'Hmm...hmm, this is good stuff...hmm..hmm,' Hank couldn't help reminding the others sitting around the breakfast table, 'Hmm.'

Stornoway black pudding held a special place in Hank's heart, and his belly. Had it not been for it, he and Margaret might never have met – two ships passing in the Butcher's. But there it was, his curiosity had been piqued, he asked a question, and love blossomed on the spot.

'I gotta get this stuff imported, I keep meanin' to...hmm, hmm.'

'Make sure you send some to us in Kenya, Hank.' Darweshi held up a fully- loaded fork he had just used to neatly bayonet four equal portions of black pudding, bacon, toast and egg.

'I'll see what I can do, my man, I'll see. I just hope the FDA don't have any probs with it. You know how those fellas can be.' From Nantucket to Nairobi, Leviathan wasn't much different.

The conversation turned to plans for the day. The sky was a mix of blue and cloud, and there was a fair breeze – a low pressure system was moving towards them, so the weather would worsen over the next few days. Could be the last chance to enjoy the beach.

'Why don't we head to Tri-e-ash, the kids love the dunes,' Catherine proposed, 'pack a big picnic.'

You couldn't taste Tri-e-ash like you could black pudding, but nevertheless, it held a special place in the hearts of Maggie, Catherine, and Morag, for it was there that they had met Mwaka, Akili, and Darweshi – where they had found love, or where love found them.

Nods of agreement all around. That was the day planned up until dinnertime. Then everyone would be trundling up to Castlebay community hall for the big meeting. Norrie wasn't keen on attending but Samantha had warned him – he better be there – he was the one most affected by the whole thing.

What Norrie felt about Tri-e-ash was in a league of its own at that moment. It had nothing to do with it being a 'special place'. For the last three days, something – the glimmer, the glint, he had spotted on the horizon when he'd looked back towards the Atlantic from the dunes – had unnerved him. And it had woken him in a panic. He was thinking deeply, beginning to realise...beginning to understand...

Norrie ate his breakfast, not saying very much.

*

The hall was packed to the gills and humming with conversation. Not a square inch was free of a chair or a person standing. There were even heads poking in through the windows. Up on the stage were two tables. Seated behind one was the local councillor, Harry Hammond, and his assistant, Febe Innes, and behind the other, four MEO officials, laptops open in front of them. To their right was a pulldown projector screen. The MacKinnon clan were all seated or standing near the back. Also tucked away in a back corner was the mostly faithful quartet. When Sofia spied Alan, she approached him and tugged on his robe and said, 'Excuse me, Mister, I read some of the book you gave me. It's funny. I don't know what some of it means...but when I pulled the levers it made Violet and all my cousins laugh.' Remy, Foo, and Achmed shared a satisfied look. *You're lucky, Alan.*

Way up in the front row sat Mizz Fizzlezwit and a few of her cronies (they were like mini-Fizzlezwits). She knew full well who this ban affected the most and was thoroughly, madly, and enormously delighted with the whole thing. There wasn't a chance she was going to miss out on this meeting. Confirmation, verification, that that horrible little – now big, monster's way of life was about to be stamped out, exterminated, crushed mercilessly, and with it – *him!* It made her salivate with glee. The Good Lord was finally answering her prayers! (Sometimes these things take a little longer than expected. That, she now fully understood. *Oh, the joy!*) She would then set her sights on what to do about his poisonous offspring. She could barely sit still, it was all such a delight!

Councillor Harry Hammond was tasked with kicking off the proceedings – and he, reluctantly, did his civic duty. He was no fan of the ban and wished dearly that this consultation was not taking place.

The MEO officials were introduced. Two fell into the management camp, Cicero and Anastasia, and two were scientists, Refugio and Yareli.

Cicero stood up and smugly thanked Harry, trying his best to hide his distaste for *these* islanders. He reminded himself of what his boss had told him before he left, 'I know, Cicero, it can be difficult dealing with these simple folk, but do try.'

For the first fifteen minutes, everything that came out of his mouth everyone was already painfully aware of. *Bloody well get on with it!* was on most people's minds.

To the relief of everyone, Cicero's presentation finally came to an end and he handed the proceedings over to Yareli, one of the scientists. She had a remote control in hand and seemed a little shy. Yareli directed the audience's attention to the first colour slide that illuminated the screen. For the next twenty minutes Yareli clicked through slide after slide of graphs about endangered seals, delicate reefs, and fragile underwater grass. There were percentages, ratios, numbers – tons of numbers, statistics, life expectancy projections. There were pie charts, column charts, bar charts, line charts, XY charts, bubble charts, half a dozen were both a line and a column chart. Then there were cylinders, cones, and pyramids representing more data, more analysis.

'And if I could just point to these figures here. We believe that if what happened before, happens again, it could, if our probability formulas are accurate, wipe out the seal population by almost half...possibly.'

At least Yareli was pleasant, clearly passionate, and sounded genuinely concerned. If Cicero had been doing this part of the presentation the men in the hall would have taken him out to the woodshed.

Remy, Achmed, and Foo, made furtive eye contact. The MEO were doing a spot-on job. Just what was expected of them. The numbers told the whole story and predicted the future so precisely that the future might as well never come, because it was already there, in numbers.

'If I could now please turn your attention to....'

At that point, the manager who was introduced as Anastasia, took control. 'Thank you.' She made a show of clearing her throat, and a drama out of adjusting herself. She started giving details of the crime perpetrated on the seabed. What the divers had come across?! It was shocking, appalling, an environmental catastrophe waiting to explode! She had been affected personally by the reports she had read, and the data reviewed. It was a terrible case, and they were lucky it had been discovered when it was. The MEO knows best about these things. They had already started a deeper investigation into the matter. More samples would be analysed, more data would feed into more formulas, and there would be more damning statistics. In summary: you are lucky the Sound is even open for *any* traffic. Anastasia went on and on, and there were more than a few in the audience who had a thought that her gruff personality did not fit her very lovely name.

In the audience, it was dawning on every man, woman, and child, what was being said. This was not simply a meeting to bring the locals up to speed with where things were, or what was about to happen next. This was a meeting to tell them what had already been decided! There was no turning back, *there would be no lifting of the ban!*

And it made many in attendance feel sick. Not for themselves, but for Norrie. Up until then there had been hope, a chance that at some point, the ban would be lifted. Surely? It had happened down south. Only Mizz Fizzlezwit and her cronies wiggled around in their chairs with barely contained excitement.

Constable Currie was standing off to the side and was greatly troubled. What would he have to do next? *My God, Norrie...why?*

Of course, the wider MacKinnon clan were all in particularly heightened states of discomfort. Akili, Darweshi, Mwaka, and Hank, exchanged greatly troubled looks. Maggie, Catherine, Morag, and their Mama, all nibbled their lips – what was going to happen to their brother, to her son?

Samantha was particularly nauseated and was not looking forward to the arguments that would undoubtedly follow.

Only Norrie felt none of this. Perhaps foolishly, he blocked it all out. The Traigh Mhor was where eight generations of his people had toiled, and it was where he would continue to do so. He was not going to quit.

Samantha looked at her husband, and she could see he was a million miles from that place, *Oh, Norrie, my darling, please....*

Apart from not quitting, there was one giant thing preoccupying Norrie's thoughts. One thing that made all of this meaningless.

*

Alan was satisfied with how the meeting was going. He was certain Remy, Foo, and Achmed would finally see the wisdom of letting the law run its course and take care of any transgressors, which amounted to one individual. And as they'd pointed out, once the money and jobs started rolling in, what had happened in the past wouldn't matter. As for news spreading about one newly enacted law being broken and enforcement duly administered? *Come on, we're on a small island halfway to Greenland, no one will care.* And anyway, Alan reasoned, surely this stubborn bastard's wife will finally knock him into line. And if not that, the look on his daughters' faces should do the trick.

The night before, Remy, Foo, and Achmed's deep thoughts had led them to the only conclusion possible. They were unwavering in their commitment to progress. When they woke up early that morning they conferred without Alan, who was still dozing and dreaming of Swiss chalets and yachts in Monaco. 'I am glad, gentlemen,' Remy had said, summing things up, 'that we are in agreement as to what we must do to ensure news does not spread, and I am glad we are as committed as we always have been. I pray that nothing is going to stand in the way of this now slightly altered plan. Once again, I think we have shown one another how well Shanghai Global, Zanzibar Holdings, and RIG work together.'

As Anastasia handed the proceedings back to Cicero, Remy looked at the others. He took a deep breath and asked, 'Are you gentlemen ready?'

Foo and Achmed nodded gravely.

Who? Ready – for what? Alan was confused.

'Come on.' And with that Remy shuffled forward, with Foo and Achmed (who was nudging Alan along) following.

What the hell are we doing? Alan almost tripped as he stumbled along sandwiched between Foo and Achmed.

Given how full the hall was, it wasn't exactly easy for Moses to part the sea of people. He managed but it was causing a commotion. People did their best to make room for – err, these four convalescing characters? More and more people were looking over to the right, where the quartet shuffled their way forward. *What on earth are they up to?*

Cicero was trying to explain something, but he was becoming more and more distracted by the commotion in the crowd. *Who were – what the hell – my God...my Gods...*

Remy finally reached the stage, 'Here can you give me a hand there, this robe is making it a little difficult...' Remy had a hand outstretched, 'Come on there.'

Cicero wasn't sure what to do. He was aghast.

Councillor Harry Hammond reached a hand down and helped Remy up. 'Can I, er, help you gentlemen?' Harry hadn't met them, but he had heard of the convalescing quartet. Most of the island had heard of them. Now most of the island was seeing them.

'Ah, just a sec there.' Remy reached a hand down and heaved Achmed up, then Foo, and Foo pulled up probably the most perplexed person in the whole hall. Alan Trout. *What am I doing, what are we doing up here?*

The hall had erupted into chatter. The baffled sea of faces said it all: *what is going on?*

'Can I borrow that?' Remy looked at Cicero's microphone.

'What? Uh...' he backed away, not arguing.

'It'll just take a moment, come on.' Remy managed to slip the microphone out of the back-peddling man's hand. 'Thank you.'

He turned and looked out at the crowd. There was a lot of shifting about going on and the noise level was rising. He recognised some of the faces, many he did not, but they all wore the same confused expression.

Remy tapped the mike. Yes, it was still working. 'Hello there, hello. Good evening everyone.' He started off as though everything was completely normal. The noise was still quite loud and people were looking noticeably uncertain. 'Good evening.....well, yes, could I please have your attention....'

The noise started dying down.

'Thank you, thanks a lot there....this won't take long.' Remy looked about the stage – everyone but Foo and Achmed, as anticipated, appeared befuddled.

At the rear of the hall, the thought that drifted through Hank's mind was this: *Dang, what in thee hell are those boys doin'?*

Remy raised a calming hand and waited a moment as the volume finally reached an acceptable murmur. 'Thank you, thanks a lot. We just wanted to let everyone know something important here – real important....'

Puzzled faces turned curious.

'It's actually, well, I'd say it's a little more than important. Well, I guess you could simply call it the 'truth'...yeah, I guess that's about right.'

Expressions seesawed between puzzlement and curiosity.

Achmed and Foo caught Remy's eye, *be brave.*

Alan: *what are you doing?!*

Remy looked out at the crowd and continued, 'This whole thing, this,' his hand gestured towards the projector. 'It's a sham, a deceit, a fabrication...it's all made up.'

It took a few seconds for what he said to sink in. Then someone in the crowd called out, irritated, 'Aye, we know that...' *But get off the stage!*

'No, I mean really. It's all just make-believe. None of this actually happened.'

The crowd was quickly losing its patience with these convalescing characters.

Hank wore a pained expression, feeling an enormous amount of embarrassment for them. *Dang, looks like they've a cracked up pretty bad. Not surprised about ol' Alan there, but the other three seemed in not too bad a shape.*

'Please, please, listen to me...we,' he looked to Foo and Achmed and back out across the crowd and tried again, 'We set this whole thing up. It was – is, all our fault.'

Alan's mind was a shambles and it showed.

What Remy just said silenced the crowd for a moment. The sheer incredulity and audacity of what this man was saying stunned them.

Remy managed to continue, 'It was all part of a grand plan we had. We're billionaires.....we have....'

The crowd didn't stay quiet after that delusional declaration. *These men were crazy!*

A few people began to confer with Constable Currie, and Dr Bartlett was talking to Miss Campbell. *I think it's time to get the sedatives out.*

Oh shit. Of course. Remy looked to the others. *Quickly!*

What happened next, once again, brought the crowd to near silence. Within a moment, Remy, Foo, and Achmed had whipped off their robes, pulled off beards and various other bits and pieces – and there, front and centre on stage, three of the four convalescing men of faith, and philosophy, crumpled to the floor in a heap of colourful robes. And in their place were three men dressed in dark slacks, crisp shirts and ties. Alan's lip was quivering, as profoundly lost as he'd ever been in his whole life. Even the terror he'd first felt on the rugby pitch wasn't as bad as what he now felt.

With the crowd still silent Remy began again, 'As I was saying, we are billionaires. We're really sorry, we had this elaborate plan, but....'

The crowd did not stay silent for long. *These men were not just a little bit crazy. They were way on the far side of actually insane!*

Constable Currie and a few men had begun moving in....and Dr Bartlett and Miss Campbell were on their way to the exit to nip over to the Doctor's surgery across the road. 'I think we should double the recommended doses,' Nurse Campbell said to which Dr Bartlett replied, 'I most heartily agree.'

This was not unfolding as Remy, Foo, and Achmed had planned. They knew it would be difficult.

'Remy, quick, give me the mic.' Foo snatched the mic and what happened next stunned the crowd into total silence....that..........was.......................lasting....

The MEO officials didn't have a clue what he was saying, nor did Alan Trout. Remy and Achmed understood a few words, just because they'd spent so much time in Foo's company and often heard him conversing in.....

Close to everyone in the crowd understood him. And they were all looking at one another, stunned. There were a few bursts of laughter at what Foo had just said. The crowd could not believe it.

This man from Shanghai was talking in Gaelic. And my God, it was good Gaelic!

Foo kept on talking.

The crowd heard about his adopted mother having Vatersay connections.

He asked a question.

A few people called out, 'Aye, aye, I know who you're talking about.'

The place remained hushed as Foo explained, still in Gaelic, how his own family had died in an avalanche, but eventually good fortune smiled on him and he was adopted by an east coast banker, east coast Scotland that is, who had worked between Hong Kong and Shanghai (who had married a Vatersay girl, whose family had moved to Glasgow because work had been scarce). He summarised things and introduced his two partners in, he joked*, in crime*....the crowd had a little laugh.

Remy motioned for the microphone. 'Can I?'

The place stayed quiet. Still intrigued.

'I hope you don't mind – I've gotta talk in English. Foo's taught us a few Gaelic words, me and Achmed here. But we're not quite at the conversing level.'

The crowd appeared receptive, but Foo's Gaelic could only carry them so far.

Remy spoke quickly of his and Achmed's background and then he turned to Alan, 'And this is Alan, but he is not the Alan you think he is. Alan, would you do the honours?'

Who me? He shook his head, frightened.

'Come on, Alan, it's alright, go on and take that robe off.'

'I – I, err.' He trembled with fear.

'You ain't naked under there, are you?'

'What – no – it's just,' *Oh shit. I should have said....ahhh...what am I doing here!?! This has to be a dream....oh please!*

'Well, go on there, Alan, old boy, don't be shy. We gotta lot of explaining to do. We've still got a plan. Come on there.'

He peeled off his false beard....and timidly, slowly...disrobed...

My goodness me. There was a collective furrowing of brows......*my, my indeed.*

‘Alan, good heavens,’ Remy looked on with sympathy. ‘Superman pyjamas?’

Alan hesitated. A nod. It was a weak, embarrassed nod.

Remy turned to the crowd. ‘Does anyone have a blazer?’

‘Here you go.’ Councillor Hammond slipped off his and handed it over. At least the top half was covered.

Remy introduced Alan as Alan Trout, MSP. A few gasps escaped from the crowd.

For the next fifteen minutes Remy broadly explained their grand plans. The crowd stayed silent but there was a mixed reception about the whole scheme. Remy continued on, explaining Alan's role in the whole affair and the duping of the MEO into banning all activity, and further went on to describe what was to happen next – the government would use its 'asterisk' clause in the law and sell them the land they needed. It was masterful, it was wonderful, it was going to bring an enormous amount of investment to the area...but......

All the while Mizz Fizzlezwit and her cronies were shifting uncomfortably in their seats. This was an outrage! This was not how things were supposed to go. *Who in God's name are these men!?* Fizzlezwit's 'security clearance' on the matter was compartmentalised, need to know only, strictly limited. She'd received a clandestine message from a government 'agent' (who happened to be James). *'To ensure the SAC ban is not ignored we'd like you to conduct a covert operation. A little spying is all.' When Fizzlezwit heard the word 'spying', well, she was all ears. She was all about keeping tabs on other peoples' affairs. But, still, she couldn't help wonder 'covert operation? Why me?' James had sensed the question and responded before she'd had time to question herself, 'Mizz Fizzlezwit, because we've heard of you, you come highly recommended.' Well, when Fizzlezwit heard the sincerity in this man's voice, a wee drop of warmth trickled into her cold, cruel heart. James wasn't Alan's number one by accident. He knew how to research and just what to do. 'You'll be receiving a package in the post, it's a special camera...just stay out of view and keep an eye on the area...' Truthfully, Fizzlezwit felt a little ridiculous on her first outing, crawling through the long grass, and wasn't sure anything would come of it, but – but, when she spied HIM! On the beach...breaking the law! She shivered with wicked glee and started snapping away.*

'...It dawned on us, that in spite of our good intentions, our sincere desire to build something good and lasting here...well, this is your home, homes that you have invited us into, and it has become clear to us that – simply put – it is not *quite* what you all would want to see happen.' He went on for a few more minutes and the mood became a curious mix of interest and growing outrage. 'We had so many regions, places, to choose from. It was Foo's Vatersay connection that made us finally decide. Vatersay wasn't quite right for the hotel, but the airport location was perfect, and of course, Greanamul for the Think Tank and the Sound for the rest,' Remy paused and looked to the back of the hall where Norrie was sitting, and then over to Foo and Achmed, and solemnly back to the audience, 'I'm going on a bit here. I guess more than anything, we realised, came to realise, what we were proposing would deny one person the one thing he loves doing more than anything,' *and I guess in the only place he feels is the right place. Search me, not everything can be explained. I reckon the Good Lord works in mysterious ways.*

Remy looked to Constable Currie and back out across the crowd. 'At this point we have one big situation and just one plan. Problem is, we, and especially Alan, have broken the law big time. To compound the problem is simply this – if news gets out, we, and especially our political friend here, to put it politely, are in deep do-do...but we also have what we think is a plan. A pretty good plan. Achmed, do you want to take over?'

'Thank you, Remy.' Achmed took the mic and surveyed the murmuring crowd. There were a variety of expressions out there. 'We are at your mercy, and if you do not agree, especially Constable Currie, well, none of this will matter. We want to make amends, make it up to you, set things right. But we also need, if you all agree, to keep quiet about the whole thing. Mum's the word. Now – obviously,' he glanced over at the MEO officials, 'we're probably not going to convince everyone here, but considering the data is mostly bogus, out of embarrassment, hopefully our MEO friends will keep quiet, but even then....with so many – even if you all agree to this plan, word could eventually seep out in dribs and drabs......'

The receptiveness of the crowd wavered.

A little arm was raised at the back.

'Yes?' Achmed called out.

It was Sofia MacKinnon. 'Does this mean my Papa can keep cockle raking?'

'Yes, yes – of course!'

The crowd was digesting an enormous amount of information that caused a roller coaster of emotions, but to hear *that* being said the murmurs in the hall intensified. Samantha was overcome and all she could do was hug Norrie and start to cry. Similarly, Hank, the brothers, Eddie, Colin, Ronnie and all the rest felt a wave of relief flood through them....*but* – what these men did, had done – to them, to Norrie, to the whole island?!

This wasn't right!!!!!

Only Norrie's mood had not changed in the slightest. He wasn't going to be quitting anyway. Legal or illegal, he was never going to abandon the tides of the Traigh Mhor. And his mind was firmly fixed on something more significant.

Sofia and Violet were jumping with joy, as were the cousins, and it took a fair amount of time for the crowd to quieten down, though the mood was hardening. Darkening.

They might be contrite billionaires who were ready to offer some sort of deal, but they had played with the emotions of an entire community, had manipulated and schemed. What they had done was not right! This was not going to be an easy sell, Achmed the wily salesman could read that much in the crowd.

'We have done a great wrong and we ask for your forgiveness. Truly, we had in mind the best of intentions for all of you. These times are tough economically, and the world is a competitive, sometimes too competitive, a place. What we humbly offer you is...well, anything you want.' He let the statement hang in the air. This was not going to be easy.

The murmurs increased and people were looking from one to the other.

'What do you mean, exactly?' someone called out.

'We will invest – in your island, whatever it is you might want, might need.'

Remy, Foo, and Achmed were prepared to pay cash handouts if need be. They could more than easily manage a significant chunk to the roughly one thousand islanders. But this was their community and they could see that the people cared deeply for it – and though Remy and company came to realise that the hotel would be a bit of a blemish on the Traigh Mhor, perhaps there were other investments they might consider appropriate.

'As Foo has talked about so often – he heard the story from his mother, of her family having to leave for the mainland because of the scarcity of jobs, they were so sad. I am certain you are all are aware that this has happened to many places over the years.'

Of course, of course – it was a common and perpetual problem for small rural communities.

The mood of the crowd seemed to shift, as though oscillating about in a mental blender. The chatter continued to grow, but Achmed had yet to receive a response.

'Let me offer you an idea,' he began. 'As we all know, with modern technology much more can be done from remote locations. We have plans for a few business centres, ones that will not only be productive, but will inspire. Our plan is to rotate various companies' people in and out for different lengths of time. Those who come will be inspired and rejuvenated. Imagine a glass domed structure along the west side, with views looking over the Atlantic, blending in nicely with the landscape, of course, with a world-class arboretum.' He went on to explain what already existed in many places around the world. It would give the local community a significant boost, open more doors for its younger people, and open up the place to more than just tourist travel. 'These business centres, we haven't yet decided on where to locate them, perhaps we could build one here?'

The mood seemed to settle. People were mulling this over. It was precarious.

'It can be anything, you name it.'

Finally, a hand went up.

'Yes sir.'

'What about a bowling alley. We've been trying for years to get the funding.'

Achmed looked to Remy and Foo. *A bowling alley?* A little unexpected, but of course, of course – that won't be a problem.

'Consider it done.'

The murmuring grew and another hand went up.

'Yes?'

'There's a few old buildings, if renovated, could...'

Achmed interrupted. 'Whatever it is, consider the renovation fees paid for.'

More murmuring.

Another hand went up.

'Yes sir.'

'I've a son in Glasgow, he'd like to set up an accounting firm out here. Says he has plenty of clients he can handle remotely, only it's....'

'Whatever it takes, it's done.'

Remy, Foo, and Achmed knew they had to be enormously mindful here. Guaranteeing significant sums to just a few right there in front of hundreds of individuals was not going to convince too many. What they needed was broad agreement on significant investments from which the whole island would benefit.

A little arm went up in the back. It was the same one from before.

'Yes, Sofia?'

'Um,' she started speaking but could not be heard. Samantha coaxed her up to the front. She was a brave little thing and after a moment's hesitation made her way up. Achmed leaned down. 'What would you like, Sofia?'

Sofia whispered in Achmed's ear for a minute and then ran back to her seat.

What a fantastic idea! Achmed thought. Another rather unexpected one. He addressed the crowd, smiling. 'Last term Sofia's class made a board game based on the Island of Berneray – Barrahead – and said they had so much fun with it. And she was wondering if we could build a board game making factory. Sofia is certain they would sell plenty. Sofia, consider it done!'

The crowd started buzzing even more.

A hand went up.

Remy had taken back the mic from Achmed.

'Yes ma'am.'

'A wind farm at sea sounds a fine idea – just make sure it's well out there, far away from the Sound.'

Remy, Achmed, and Foo had billions ready to go in their capital investment accounts. Shrugs all around. *Why not?*

'Ma'am, we think that's an excellent idea.'

Another hand. 'Yes sir?'

'Perhaps a wave-power farm? And you won't even need a research centre to test for potential wave power. We can attest there's lots of waves out there and they are powerful.'

Without hesitation, Remy replied. 'We'll certainly work on it. It is being researched further north, after all. Perhaps we'll skip the R&D bit and go straight to production. We promise, we'll do our best.'

Things were looking better, Remy, Foo, and Achmed thought – ever so delicately. More ideas for investments could come later, but they needed to know if everyone was onboard. If more than a few jumped ship and started singing? Remy looked at Constable Currie, who looked right back. The place could do with some serious investments and Currie was a man who'd sailed the seven seas and stepped foot on every continent. He wasn't naïve to the ways of the world. He shrugged. A subtle nod. *Why not?*

Remy breathed a sigh of relief! The biggest obstacle was onboard.

A little hand went up near the back – it was wee Sofia MacKinnon again.

Remy gestured for her to come forward. He leaned down and she whispered in his ear for thirty seconds – *hmm, well, this is an interesting one* – Remy involuntarily glanced to the front row. *Her? Uh oh.* Sofia then turned and hurried back to her seat.

Remy pondered this most recent request and called over Foo, Achmed, and a still embarrassed Alan.

'Relax, Alan,' Remy said.

'That what I say, too,' Foo chipped in. 'It okay, Alan. It only pyjamas – not end of world.'

'Boys, we got an interesting request here,' Remy began, 'real interesting. Complicating matters a bit. Alan, it's time for you to earn your money again. That's what I'm thinking, anyway...considering, well...this is gonna take some doing to convince a few people, I reckon.' Remy looked over to Councillor Harry Hammond – he seemed a reasonable, decent fellow. 'Harry? Can you come here?'

'Aye, aye.'

'What do you think so far?'

'We've needed some serious investments for a long time. You've got my support.'

'Great! That's excellent. Super-fantastic. But listen up boys, we've got an unusual request. One which I am not sure how we're going to make happen – but I sure don't want to disappoint that nice little girl.'

Foo, Achmed, Harry, and a relaxing Alan waited – *go on Remy...*

'Sofia would like a new headmistress, a Mrs MacLean. She says Mizz Fizzlezwit frightens her. Problem is, gents, we're in the business of capital investments and job growth, wealth creation, that sort of thing. We're not in the business of making people disappear and appointing new headmistresses. Alan, you gotta come up with something....by the by, Harry...*Fizzlezwit?* – it don't sound too Hebridean, you know? Is she originally from Floonay?'

Harry shook his head. 'No. I honestly don't know where she's from. She showed up one day a few decades ago and got the job, seized the job more like it. She "frightened" her way into the position. She is a formidable character and you won't convince her of very much.'

That Mizz Fizzlezwit was Alan's local spy was a fact they did not need to share with Harry.

'Alan – time to shine, old boy. What do you think?' Remy asked, and as he did so, his and his two business partners' brains were whirring away – what could possibly be done to uncomplicate this complication?

Feeling more confident, Alan thought, *she'll be perfect!* Alan turned to Harry and asked. 'Are you sure she really is that formidable – that frightening?'

'Ohh, aye, she's governed that school with fear for many a year. You don't get more frightening than her. If she were to leave Floonay, she would not be missed.'

'What you thinking, Alan?' Foo queried.

'She'll be bloody perfect!'

'For what?'

Alan, with his confidence back, had forgotten all about the pyjamas he was wearing. 'My party – we're looking for a new *Whip!*'

The others shared a look that was not without a heavy shade of doubt. But hope was there, too. 'Do you think you can make it happen? I mean, we spotted your talent, but, Alan, you're not exactly numero uno on your party's favourite MSPs list, and you'd have to convince her to go *and* keep her mouth shut?'

'No, no....Remy. I mean yes. No! Yes! I think I can make it happen. I really think I can!' and with that he climbed down off the stage, made his way over to Mizz Fizzlezwit, and politely beckoned her to follow him, with a wink and a natural politician's smooth style. Remarkably, she did. The crowd parted for them and they disappeared out of the hall.

Remy asked the crowd for a little quiet as he had a question. The chatter eventually subsided. 'Is there a Mrs MacLean present?'

One hand went up, then two more, then another – and two more....and, Remy was losing count...

Remy focused his attention towards the back and caught Sofia's eye. He gestured for her to come forward.

A moment later Sofia was whispering in his ear again, and quickly disappeared back into the crowd.

Remy stood back up. 'Is there an Anne Marie MacLean present?'

Near the back right, a hand went up.

'Ma'am, may I have a word with you?'

Anne Marie MacLean made her way to the front of the hall where Remy greeted her, introduced her to Achmed and Foo, and then asked her point-blank, 'Anne Marie, how would you like to be Floonay's new headmistress?'

Who, me? A tremor passed through Anne Marie and it showed. She glanced to where Mizz Fizzlezwit had been sitting.

'Mrs MacLean, it's alright. Mizz Fizzlezwit is going to be leaving Floonay.' *We have faith in you, Alan, you better convince her.*

Anne Marie blinked, shocked at what she was hearing. 'I, I'm not sure...I,'

Achmed the Consoler remarked kindly, 'Anne Marie, we know, much has happened here this evening. It is quite natural to be a little uncertain, a little in shock, surprised. But, there is a young girl who believes that you would make the best headmistress ever.'

Anne Marie looked at Harry. *Can this even happen? There's a process, applications...* Harry shrugged. *Who knows? Why not?*

Foo reassured her, 'Anne Marie, if you want the job, we have ways of making it happen, do not worry about that.'

'I...I – guess....sure....'

Remy was beaming. *Fantastic!!*

Still, the problem remained – did they have everyone on board? And it wasn't just those in attendance, which was about a third of the island's population. Even if that third were all in, they'd have to convince the remaining two-thirds. Could this possibly happen? Things were looking good though – they had the island's Constable, Councillor, soon to be new headmistress, young Sofia, and it certainly seemed that a fair number of the rest in attendance were showing interest – a growing enthusiasm....

A few people he recognised were making their way through the crowd, and then a few more. A moment later, Eddie, Ronnie, Colin, Irish, Nelson the shellfish buyer, Joe from The Heathbank, Dillon & Elspeth, and Barry from the Butcher's, approached the stage. Others crowded in. For a brief moment, just a flash, Remy thought the worst.

To be sure, everyone, at some point that evening, had felt a level of betrayal, of anger.....but, as the emotions churned and they thought matters through, and talked.....things changed.....there's always change....that's life after all.

Eddie spoke in Gaelic, and a moment later Foo, ever so relieved, bowed and replied in English, 'We so sorry for what we put your friend through. I would like to also call Norrie *our* friend. We are indebted. You have our backing, our full support, our full enthusiasm for this – for these – lovely islands.'

A moment later Remy, Foo, and Achmed were face to face with Samantha MacKinnon. She wanted to slap each and every one of them. But she did not. 'What you put my family through, my husband, me, my daughters...it is as close to unforgivable as you can get.'

Remy, Foo, and Achmed bowed their heads in shame.

'Perhaps, if it weren't for Sofia...I might tell you to...well....it doesn't matter now. Sofia is happy – and she likes that strange book your weird friend gave her. And she seems to like you lot. As for Norrie – he was never going to quit anyway. Curiously, he doesn't seem to care about the whole thing.

You've got my support, my word, I won't say a thing,' and with that she turned and went back to her family.

And so it would be, that every man, woman, and child in the audience all agreed to keep a lid on what had transpired that evening and promised to keep the whole thing as big a secret as they possibly could. Even Mizz Fizzlezwit's cronies crumbled and went along with it. She hadn't come back from wherever she had gone and thus they had been left vulnerable and uncertain. Frightened, they followed the will of the crowd. Surprisingly, but perhaps not completely so, even all four MEO officials had agreed. The two management types, Cicero and Anastasia, were a little reluctant, but eager to protect their reputations in the face of such a fraud, agreed.

Those in attendance were certain that they would be able to convince the others. They didn't need to tell them all the sordid details after all, and anyway, it was those who had attended the consultation who were the most interested and passionate about the whole affair. If they were in agreement and willing, then convincing the rest would be much easier. For his part, Alan, might have his hands full back in Edinburgh, as others in government were aware of the ban on the SAC. It wasn't a massive, priority number one, item on the agenda. It was actually fairly inconsequential as government *'things to do'* Inbox items go, but it had made the radar. It had been Alan who had placed it there, after all. A few inquisitive souls might be out there. Why was the ban being lifted and what had transpired at the consultation? Well, he would just have to get creative, do a lot of verbal wiggling about, but for MSP Alan Trout, when he was confident and feeling in control, that would be a piece of cake.

It was Monday and the evening was getting on, so many who had to work early the following morning started leaving. Mum's the word and all that. But it was still the summer holidays and the weather was turning – it was borderline whether the boys would be fishing the next day – and a few musical instruments were never far from reach. Neither were a few bottles, and so a spontaneous ceilidh ensued.

Sofia, Violet, and the cousins were all particularly excited. *Papa! – Uncle Norrie! Can cockle rake again! Hooray!!* They stayed on the dance floor the whole time. Sofia and Violet were the most excited of all the MacKinnons. *They* would be cockle raking again with their Papa – *anytime they wanted!* Norrie's Mama, sisters and wife were as relieved as divers whose tanks had run out of oxygen 100 feet down but had just managed to burst through the surface and take their first breaths in what seemed like ages. Once the anger and the shock had faded it turned into a simply joyous occasion. For their parts, Hank, Mwaka, Darweshi, and Akili were relieved, but in a manner more suited to men.

'Whew, boys, I tell ya, I've been around a while an' all, but nothin's had a sweeter taste than to know good ol' Norrie here can get on back out there and do what he loves doin' – and can stop payin' all them dang fines, you know.'

At some point in the evening, all of Norrie's fishing pals, and a whole lot of others, stopped by to express their relief, their joy, that the whole business was over. The beach was open to raking again!

'You haven't danced at all this evening, you alright sweetheart?' Samantha wrapped an arm around Norrie and squeezed.

'Aye, aye, of course.'

'I'm so happy, Norrie, it's over. It's all over....and you can go cockle raking tomorrow and....*oh, god!* It's just great. I was talking to your sisters. We might take a trip to Idaho together when school's out for the autumn break. It'll be so much fun! Oh, Norrie, I am – are you sure you're okay...you look like your mind is a million miles away?'

Norrie blinked the *glimmer* away, but it didn't go far. He smiled. He gave Samantha a kiss. ‘I'm just fine sweetheart. I can't wait for tomorrow.’

Epilogue I

Three questions spread like wildfire the following morning, and when they intersected, the magnitude of their potential significance stirred up a profusion of confusion. If they were linked – *my God?!*

'Has anyone seen my boat?' asked Eddie, skipper of *Odyssey II.*

'Has anyone seen mine?' asked Ronnie Mcphail, skipper of *The Provider.*

'Has anyone seen Norrie?' asked a concerned wife, after looking all around the house, the croft, in the Nissen hut, and out to the Traigh Mhor. No sign of him anywhere, and Patches and Sailor were present – they always followed him wherever he went.

The questions were all eventually answered when sightings to the northeast, then the north, then northwest, and further along the west side, started trickling in. They were spotted. And *He* was spotted, through a few pairs of powerful binos. They were certain it was Norrie MacKinnon. It appeared as though he was wearing a lifejacket. *What the hell was he doing? It,* too, was spotted?! And spotted again. *My God?* They and *it* were converging!

'Oh please, God, tell me he isn't...please.' Samantha half fainted and collapsed into the strong arms of Akili.

Norrie's mother sat before she had a chance to faint.

The MacKinnon household – and every house the news spread through, were...*stunned* was not a strong enough word. Gutted, incredulous, frightened, disbelieving, circle back to stunned....it can't be! No one felt the cruelty like Samantha and his Mama and sisters.

But – what....what on earth is he thinking??!!

Hank slipped out of the house and reappeared a moment later. He whispered to Mwaka whose eyes stretched wide like two full moons. 'The shotgun is gone.'

Hank had kept the one secret that he and Norrie shared as just that – a secret. Not his Mama, nor sisters, nor wife, knew what Hank knew. What had caused Hank to check? He didn't know. But he wasn't going to use it for that? He had a lifejacket on? He had his job back, his way of life....it had never left. He hadn't quit! And yet, he was towing Ronnie's boat with Eddie's, out to where *it* was spotted?

Dang!?

Son of a gun Norrie, why didn't you tell us! You are going to need a lot more than a shotgun to stand any chance!! We could have organised an armada – with harpoons, plenty of harpoons...

Every man and woman on Floonay was thinking, *Why?!* Of course, along with *why?!* There was also, *You stupid bastard!* There was only one person (not even her crumbling cronies found any joy in the news) who fizzed with glee as she packed her bags for her big trip to Edinburgh. *Excellent! My prayers are being answered – even better than I could have imagined his demise! His wife, mother and sisters will all go mad – they'll snap, crackle and pop! They'll never be the same again! His daughters will be institutionalised! My work is done here! Next stop: parliament...*

*

The glint he had spied on the horizon the previous Friday – *the glimmer* – deep down he had known, he knew, that reflection. The story had been with him since childhood. That horrible monster! It had brought tragedy, death, misery to the four corners. He had heard of bad things happening as a child but had never guessed in a million years how bad these could be. In a million years, he had never imagined that scale of tragedy, of cruelty, could swim into the Hebrides, into his family, his life. But it had. Of course, he had never heard back from God – all those letters...he was naïve and stupid. *He* never sent his Papa or his brothers back – because? It didn't matter now. In that dream – that nightmare – he had plumbed into the abyss....and in the abyss the Coquilleuous Rakkeronuous Almenikhiaka creaked open – and surrounded by his darkest fear, he finally understood...

All those years ago, Norrie MacKinnon, at the age of fourteen, had sworn if it took him a thousand years, he would hunt the monster down. Well, Norrie thanked the currents of the Seven Seas for bringing the monster back.

*

Apart from the crew of the RNLI lifeboat who were rushing to Castlebay pier to launch the only boat that had any chance of reaching Norrie in time, most of Floonay's population were congregating in spots along the west side, tracking the two boats, and the whale, which was surfacing and diving, and every now and again would explode through the unsettled surface and come crashing down on its back.

'Dang, that whale does not look happy.'

'Hank, my brother, I fear the worst. I am silently praying but doubt is everywhere,' Darweshi confided.

A large group was amassing near the top of Grean Point just past the golf course. It had been impossible to keep the wee ones away. Samantha and Norrie's Mama and sisters had wanted to keep them all at home – they were so torn. They could not stay away.

'Mama, is that really Papa out there? Mama, what's Papa doing?' Sofia asked.

Oh, my darling, I wish I could tell you. 'It's nothing baby, he's just – out on the boat.'

'Mama, then why is everyone here?' asked Violet.

'It's okay sweetheart. They're all just out for a walk.'

'This is a fast walk, Mama.'

Remy, Foo, and Achmed, dragging a reluctant Alan along, were there too. Alan had thought they'd be on their merry way, now that matters had been sorted out. At least they weren't in disguise and he'd had a chance to change out of his pyjamas into something appropriate, Alan mused, still a little embarrassed about the night before. But offsetting that embarrassment was the confidence gained from handling Mizz Fizzlezwit. *Brilliant! Quite a stroke of genius!! Just what the party needed!!!*

The growing consensus was that Norrie was going to try and lure the whale to smash into *The Provider,* affording him a chance to shoot at it as it passed. If he had the right shells loaded he might inflict a bit of damage. If he aimed well, that is. Otherwise, they would only bury harmlessly into the mounds of blubber.

'Maybe he's going to aim for its other eye,' Eddie considered as he spied through a pair of binos, 'then it'll be blind, and, well, that will be the end of it – might even beach itself or just swim in circles for the rest of its days.'

'That's a hell of a chance he'd be taking! It could come at him from the wrong direction...it might hit your boat first and then mine.'

Whatever he had planned, the odds did not appear to be in his favour.

'Holy mother of God! Look at that thing!' Remy watched in awe as the whale propelled into the sky like a giant bullet, and in slow motion came crashing down into the rough seas.

Achmed the Slightly Fearful commented, 'I have seen many things in my days, in my journey through life, but this is – I do not know where it ranks. What is that man doing?'

'It not good. I hope we not responsible at all. He now have assurance of job back?' Foo wondered. 'Why he take such terrible risk?'

The growing crowd watched as Odyssey II, with The Provider in tow, drew closer and closer to where the bastard of a monster was putting on quite a display. It wasn't more than half a mile in distance and closing fast.

'Oh my God, the lifeboat's not going to make it! Jesus, it's heading right at him!'

The mass of islanders watched in horror – and it wasn't without a curious and irresistible fascination – as the inevitable approached with the RNLI boat and her crew still three miles away.

The whale circled the two boats, and circled again, coming in ever closer. Circling and circling, closer and closer. It was seeking, sussing, considering, evaluating...for it had never forgotten...

*

'Come on in, you bastard, that's it,' Norrie whispered, as he raised the weapon, 'Just a little closer. This is going to hurt.'

Those in the crowd with binoculars could make out the action clearly. Word spread in seconds. *God's sake, he's about to fire!*

And fire he did.

A gasp went up in the crowd.

It disappeared down below.

There was no sign of the whale and for a moment more than a few thought – and then expressed those thoughts: He's scared it away!...That's it, that's all he wanted to do!...Like they say, if you punch a shark on the nose...Remarkable!

It did not last. There it was, surfacing from the deep a few hundred yards north of the two vulnerable boats. It started slowly, but the enormous mass quickly gained momentum – its speed increasing – it was a sight to see, and it was heading straight for Odyssey II.

'That's it, come on.' *I have one chance, one chance only. Do not miss, you bastard! Do not miss.*

Samantha put her hands over Sofia's and Violet's eyes. The crowd watched in horror as Odyssey II exploded into pieces, the enormous monster crashing right through her.

'Oh, Norrie, what have you done?' Samantha fell to her knees and sobbed.

She wasn't the only one.

*

As the whale slammed into the starboard side of Odyssey II, Norrie flung himself over the gunnel. He had one chance, if it could even be called a chance...most would call it madness. He had to try. There was no other option. *The dream, the nightmare, the vision...*

Arms stretched out, his entire body flying through space as one hundred tons of whale started passing underneath him, he – just managed...just barely...slipped for a moment...to...

Grab a hold!

With a millisecond to spare he lashed the length of rope round his right forearm, round and round. He would now not let go. Could not let go.

It was the rope trailing from the end of the harpoon.

A deep breath. Mouth shut.

They descended into the icy sea.

With two strong hands he held fast the harpoon. They dived deeper – eyes and mouth shut tight, Norrie felt the pressure tighten like a vice on his chest, his ears, his entire being. Squeezed and squeezed and squeezed. Further down they went, ever deeper and deeper...

And then she rolled over and shot straight up like a ballistic missile being fired from a submarine and a moment later they were breaking the surface and for a full second were suspended in space, before the beast started coming down....in that moment Norrie took a deep breath and adjusted himself, and in that very same moment those on land who caught a good glimpse – some murmured half in shock, some blinking, disbelieving what they were seeing, and some called out excitedly, 'It's Norrie! He's got a hold! He's trying to jam it all the way in!'

And then Norrie and the whale disappeared below the surface. They plunged even deeper than before, and Norrie thought he was going to implode from the pressure change. Moments later they shot back up again and broke through the surface. Along the shoreline, the half-horrified, half-fascinated spectators caught a glimpse. He was still holding on!?

'My God! What is he doing!?'

'Holy mother of the high seas, how on earth?!'

'Dang!'

'There's no way!'

'He's really going to jam it in further – get that bastard, Norrie!'

They disappeared below the surface once more and moments later were ascending above the sea only to come crashing back. Disappearing once again. Norrie, his arms wrapped firmly around the harpoon, started turning it, twisting, inch by inch, back and forth – the great beast writhed in agony and broke above the surface, all the while Norrie twisted and twisted and twisted what had been lodged in one position for who knew how many decades....it turned, inch by inch by inch....

Those on shore could not believe their own eyes – *he was still there!*

'My God! Look! He's – getting ready....'

They again plunged deep into the icy sea, the deepest dive yet. The great beast let out an agonising bellow. Norrie's resilience started fading to black. He almost let go. His chest burned. Then she twisted and once again shot straight up. And up. And up. Norrie kept twisting the harpoon back and forth, even as the mighty mammal writhed violently. Her powerful spasms projecting them ever faster to the surface...

This is my only chance, once we break the surface...

It would not be possible below – for the weight and the rush of the passing water would be too great. He had to be free to steady himself. To stand. It would only take a moment, a second, maybe two. The harpoon had been sufficiently loosened. It was now free to be...

*

'Holy mother of God! Look at him!!'

'He's standing straight up!'

'What's he doing?!'

'He's about to drive it all the way in!!!'

'End the bastard, Norrie!'

The MacKinnon women could not watch and though they tried, Sofia, Violet, and all their cousins managed to wiggle free of censoring hands – and watch – in awe – astonishment...disbelief...sheer fascination.

Hank, Mwaka, Darweshi, and Akili just watched – they were so dumbfounded that their emotions didn't know what to do.

Eddie, Colin, Ronnie, Irish, the rest of the fishermen, Remy, Achmed, Foo, and everyone else, to a man, woman, and child, were in much the same state...for his part, Alan couldn't help but wonder what it would be like to ride a bucking whale – was it like a bucking bronco?

*

In that moment – suspended in mid-air, in time, Norrie, standing atop the great beast.....

You killed my Papa and three of my brothers, you forced my other brother to leave...you indirectly killed him, too! You have brought misery into countless lives...

And with one of the greatest secrets in the world firmly on his mind – that which revealed itself once again in the abyss of that nightmare – the secret he'd sworn to never believe in...the power of it...

I....

for....

give....

you....

And with that, he pulled with all the strength his body, mind, and soul could muster.

The harpoon burst from the whale's eye....and with a mighty bellow the giant beast did a 180-degree flip in mid-air and came crashing down.

Go...you are free...

Norrie was flying through the air, his arms outstretched and a moment later crashed through the surface. Except, he kept descending and descending and descending.

He was not free.

With the rope lashed around his right arm, the weight of the heavy harpoon took Norrie further down. He struggled to unravel the rope, but it was proving impossible. He had exhaled just before plunging below the surface and therefore did not have two lungs full of oxygen, and so his chest burned in agony. Still he plunged deeper and deeper. Powerless against the weight pulling him down. He screamed silently. The pressure built. He tried to untangle himself. He could not. His mouth opened. A rush of water filled his lungs.

I'm sorry my little buttercups....my sweetheart. I'm sorry, please forgive me...

A moment of pain. Then nothing. Darkness. An explosion of light.

Epilogue II

One year on, Mizz Fizzlezwit would prove a most reliable and efficient party whip. As a matter of fact, she became the most feared whip her party had ever known. There wasn't a party member within or outwith Edinburgh's borders beyond her reach. The only person immune to her ferocity was Alan Trout, for it was he who had nominated her for the position and because of that he was the one person for whom she had a soft spot. But that was it. Not a single other soul! And the fantastic thing for Alan (as he had just managed to convince his party's leaders, elders, bigwigs) was this: he was brought out of the shadows, the embarrassing back bench of his party. Not too far, of course, but they allowed him a little more space to operate. But he eventually quit politics, along with his number one aide and confidante, James, because they now had plenty of loot (Remy, Achmed, and Dr Foo had made payment in full).

During this time little bits of news inevitably leaked out, through a variety of news outlets, of the strange goings-on on the Isle of Floonay the previous summer – too many people had heard too much – but Alan Trout, being Alan Trout, and importantly, being an integral part of the government mechanism, of Leviathan, managed to ensure the message was twisted, distorted, and befuddled. It would end up nothing more than a puddle. A splash for a moment and then gone. Like a weather report on the half hour. This made Remy, Dr Foo, and Achmed happy men, for they were free to operate without suspicion or worry of prosecution. It went without saying that they kept their promise to the people of Floonay, and invested everything that they desired, needed, to ensure a sustainable future. And, to a man, woman, and child on Floonay, they kept their lips sealed about the whole affair. Occasional visitors would inevitably ask about the rumours of the previous summer, but their queries were met with shrugs and 'I don't know' and 'Didn't hear or see a thing.' The rumours that had seeped – well, it didn't really matter – they hadn't come from Floonay, nor Remy, Foo, or Achmed, nor Mizz Fizzlezwit (she was wickedly happy with her new job and didn't want to risk losing it), nor Alan Trout, and not even from the four *Meow* officials present at the big consultation. Others within their organisation started sniffing...thankfully it didn't lead very far.

*

But one year before all that transpired, something quite remarkable occurred deep below the surface of the choppy Atlantic, off the west coast of Floonay. Perhaps it was not so remarkable – this is life after all. It is full of...

Tragedy....Grief.....and....

Wonder.

In that explosion of light as water rushed into his lungs, Norrie spoke to the sea, 'You took my brothers, my Papa. Now you have me. I hope you are happy. Though I am sad, not for me – I am gone, I no longer matter, I am sad for Sofia, Violet, their Mama, for others.'

'I am sorry you are sad,' the sea replied.

'No, you are not, you do not care one tiny bit.'

'That is not true.'

'You take, and you take, and you take.'

'And I give, and give, and give. Everything I have.'

'But you also take, cruelly. You destroy, you crush lives.'

The sea was also sad. 'But I also make life, create life, sustain life.'

'Then why do you also destroy life?'

'It is not just me – I am not in full control.'

'You let that whale swim within you...you could have conspired...'

'I do not have that power. That took you...'

Norrie laughed, 'It took me?! To what? You have the strength of the Seven Seas, of a million gales, and the same again in hurricanes, typhoons and floods! You do as you please.'

'I do not. I bend to another will. Look above. Look beyond. The sun. The moon. The wind and the stars all conspire.'

'It's a little difficult right now. I'm down here with you. And anyway, I don't care. You all conspire to create misery.'

The sea moaned, 'I do not. We do not. We bend, respond, to one universal will. It is difficult to see. I am just the sea.'

'And I am just Norrie.'

'And you forgave. You freed that whale. You didn't have to.'

'I know.'

'But you did.'

'And look at me now. I think a few crabs are starting to nibble my toes.'

'That's impossible. You still have your yellow wellies on.'

'Ah, whatever. It doesn't matter anymore.'

'Norrie, of course it matters. *You* matter.'

'No, I no longer do. I am gone.'

'You tried to make yourself gone once. The wind told me of that. Perhaps fate.'

'Perhaps dumb luck.'

'But you didn't try to make yourself gone today. You are wearing a lifejacket. You meant to survive. You meant to climb aboard *The Provider.*'

'This lifejacket isn't doing me much good now. I'm down at the bottom of you attached to this harpoon, and *The Provider* is a long way up.'

'Norrie, you have lived in fear of me for most of your life. But you came out here, in spite of that fear, because you finally understood the power of what you read in your father's book.'

'It wasn't just his. It goes back a long way.'

'I know, but you finally believed in the power of *it.*'

'Aye, and a fat lot of good it did me. Look at me, you ice-cold salty bastard. I am at the bottom of you and I am dead.'

'No, Norrie, you are not. And anyway, do you know what brought that whale back? You. She needed you. But she couldn't know for certain what you would do, how you would react and how she should in turn react. I couldn't know. No one could. You had to decide. Norrie, all those years ago, she had only been trying to help, despite the pain, the burden, she carried most of her life...she had tried to steer them to safety.'

*

'Dang, look at that thing, it's back.' Hank looked through misty eyes. It was the whale........*holy mother of – whatever.......and in its giant mouth was a...body?*

It surfaced beside the RNLI lifeboat to a surprised crew. Its mouth gently opened. *Go on, take him, and watch the harpoon, it's heavy....*

The crew reached over and lifted the limp body of Norrie MacKinnon onto the deck, along with the rusty old harpoon and the tangle of rope, and after sixty very focused and slightly frantic seconds, Norrie was vomiting sea water, vomiting back to life. Within another few seconds, word was transmitted to those ashore.

Back on board the RNLI boat, Norrie, his head rolled to the side, whispered to the sea and the whale something none of the crew heard.

Walter Wellington watched from a distance, through his telescope, and whispered something only the wind heard. *Fine job, son. Your father would be proud. Between the fear and the shame, you are learning a little bit more.*

Epilogue III

By the time the RNLI boat rounded the south of Vatersay, passed Muldonach, Kisimul Castle, and was coming alongside the main pier, the entire island was congregating in Castlebay to see *him* for themselves. Had it just been an apparition, some magic act, or would he, Norrie MacKinnon, actually walk on dry land again? Within moments Norrie was disembarking, wrapped in a big woolly blanket. He was no apparition. The pier and streets were quickly filling but space was made for Samantha, the girls, and the rest of the MacKinnon clan. Samantha was too stunned to do anything but wrap her arms around Norrie. Sofia and Violet each had hold of a leg.

In the future Sofia and Violet would often ask their Papa what it was like to ride atop a whale, and it would always go something like this: 'Is it like on TV where people get rides from dolphins?' 'A little, sweetheart.' 'Can I one day, Papa, can I?' 'Probably not the best idea.' 'Hmm? But maybe?' 'Why don't we take Patches and Sailor and head to the west side, see if we can find some washed-up buoys to hang on our shiny little memento here?' 'Okay, Papa, but that harpoon isn't so little. It's huge.' 'Papa, I bet that whale is the happiest whale in the ocean now.'

And Samantha MacKinnon felt so happy as well for she knew something special had happened, that was also a little secret. ‘Mama, Papa said he might come to Oban with us next month!’ ‘That’s wonderful, girls.’ *Give him time.*

In the meantime, on the crowded, noisy, jubilant pier everyone was still coming to terms with what they'd witnessed, and those who had not witnessed it (a great frustration for some) could not believe their ears. But so many gave the same account. *Trust me, it happened, and, my God Father, was it a sight to behold!*

Hank reminded Akili, Darweshi, and Mwaka more than once that day – and for days to come – that no one would believe a word of it if he were to tell this tale back in Idaho. 'They'll think I've gone way round the bend. You know what I'm a sayin', boys?' To which the brothers heartily agreed. The same reaction would, most likely, meet their story back in Kenya, if they tried to tell the tale. 'We would be accused of falling under the spell of some curious Hebridean magic. Voodoo, North Atlantic style, something like that.' 'I think we better just keep this story to ourselves, boys.' 'Wise words, Hank.'

‘My mother was right, as I have told you many times. These islands are special,’ Foo commented to Remy and Achmed. They were standing off to the side of the crowd. Remy and Achmed agreed and were relieved and overjoyed that things turned out as they did. They were also honoured beyond words that they would be able to invest in Floonay's future as the Floons wished.

With the blazer that he'd lent to Alan the night before back on, Councillor Harry Hammond approached Remy, Achmed, and Dr Foo and said, ‘I couldn't help but think, gentlemen, about this plan you had for Greanamul? It might be a bit too small out there and look a little out of place. But perhaps you would consider some spot right here on Floonay for your Think Tank?’

Remy, Foo, and Achmed looked around appraisingly, their view drawn to the top of Ben Heavel, as it timelessly watched over Castlebay, and then out to Kisimul Castle and Vatersay beyond. Three certain nods. All thinking the same thing.

THE END

ACKNOWLEDGMENTS

I would like to thank the fishermen of Barra for their guidance, patience and friendship. A very special thanks to Diane Cullen, a skilled crocheter, mother and teacher, and to Morag Ann MacNeil, author of *Granaidh Afraga* and *Artair sa Chaisteal*, for their invaluable advice. Thank you also to my parents and two sisters, Justine and Lorraine, for their editorial efforts. My brother, Alistair, provided moral support from the sidelines. There were others who also contributed in one way or another. Too many to mention. Thank you. One final huge thank you to Margaret Turner, who, during the final editing phase provided countless morale-boosting sausage rolls, chocolate cookies and cups of coffee. You are a star.

Printed in Great Britain
by Amazon

81073411R00315